THE JADE DRAGON

Garrett Hutson

Warfleigh Publishing first edition June 2017

Cover design by Steven Novak
Maps by Julie Bickel

For more information, or to book an event, please contact the author at www.garretthutson.com

ISBN 978-0-9982813-3-9 (paperback)
ISBN 978-0-9982813-2-2 (eBook)

For my mother, Patti Hutson, who loves mysteries

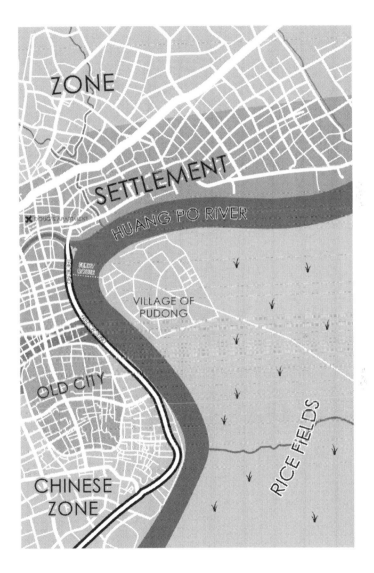

DOWNTOWN SHANGHAI

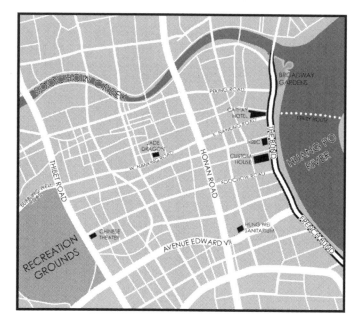

Historical Note

This story is set in 1935. Prior to the development of Pinyin in the 1950s, English spellings of Chinese place names were different than they are today (i.e. Peking versus Beijing, Nanking versus Nanjing, etc.).

I have used the old spelling for street names, since that is how they would have been spelled at the time of this story. When referencing cities, I have considered the speaker, and have used the old spelling when the person only speaks English, and the modern spellings (which are closer to the Chinese pronunciation) when the person speaks a Chinese language.

1

Saturday, May 25, 1935

The stiff breeze hit Douglas Bainbridge the moment he stepped onto the deck of the ocean-liner, whipping his dark blond hair back from his face. The wind was cool and crisp, and he enjoyed the feel of it on his cheeks. It tugged his necktie from inside his gray suit coat, and blew it over his shoulder. He stuffed it back down and kept his hand over the front of his coat, thinking he should have packed a tie tack.

He leaned against the rail and looked out over the blue East China Sea. As he'd heard in the dining room, the coast was visible several miles away, low and green and shimmering in the morning sun.

He tingled with anticipation. It seemed he'd been preparing for this his whole life.

He enjoyed the final moments of peace and quiet, then went back to his stateroom.

His trunk sat open at the foot of the bed, clothes neatly folded inside. His white dinner jacket still lay across the back of a chair where he'd tossed it last night; he found his black bowtie on the floor, and knelt to pick it up. He stared at it for a moment with a grin and tossed it into the trunk.

He retrieved his white trousers from the floor, and shook his head at how wrinkled he'd left them. He folded and hung them with the jacket, placed them in a suit bag, and folded it in the trunk.

The porter knocked as he finished packing his shaving kit.

"All ready for disembark, Mr. Bainbridge?"

"All ready, Xiao," Doug said, handing him a silver dollar.

The porter lugged his trunk down the narrow hall, and Doug followed with his valise in his right hand, his gray fedora in his left.

The deck was more crowded now as Doug set his valise beside his trunk with the rest of the First Class luggage, all with numbered tags. Seeing no available space along the rail, he strolled toward the bow of the ship. He nodded to the well-dressed matrons and their daughters who had made his acquaintance on the voyage, and returned their greetings, brief but polite.

He'd been a bit of a sensation the first half of the trip—an unmarried young man of twenty-five traveling alone in First Class—and the ladies of a certain age had sought his attention. Some were widows seeking a dance partner after dinner, but most were mothers only too eager to introduce him to their eighteen or nineteen-year-old daughters. Most of these gave him back his space once they learned he planned to stay in China for two years. This amused him immensely.

The most persistent, however, was Mrs. Herbert Kinzler of Chicago. Perhaps it was because her daughter Lucy was twenty-one, and Mrs. Kinzler could hear the clock ticking. At least Lucy was more amused than complicit, and took steps to aggravate her mother.

He'd enjoyed getting to know Lucy. She reminded him of a character right out of an F. Scott Fitzgerald novel—tall and blonde, witty and a bit sardonic, well-coifed but seemingly careless about it, and thoroughly modern right down to the cigarettes she hid from her mother.

Every night he danced with the kindly widows, always obliging them, taking them for a waltz around the ballroom; or if they felt a bit more daring, a foxtrot. But by the end of every evening, he would be dancing with Lucy.

They'd hit it off right away, discussing China, literature and music while strolling the deck. She shared his admiration for Fitzgerald and Faulkner, but disagreed with him on Hemingway.

"But he is without a doubt the greatest American writer of our time," Doug had said the first night after they'd tired of dancing and went out on deck for fresh air.

"His stories are all rather self-consciously 'manly,' don't you think?" she'd said. "It's as if he's overcompensating for something."

Doug had clasped his hands over his heart in mock pain, and took two staggering steps backward. This made her laugh.

"I know how you feel—Mother doesn't approve of my taste in books," Lucy said as she lit a cigarette. "I read a lot of Gertrude Stein for a while, and Alice Toklas, but lately I've been more drawn to Virginia Woolf."

"I confess I've never read any Virginia Woolf."

"Oh, you should! She's wonderful."

She leaned back against the railing and took a long tug on her cigarette. "I wish I could write like her. I rather fancy myself a writer," she said with a grin.

"And with rather a penchant for the British turn of phrase," Doug teased.

She blew cigarette smoke into his face, and they both laughed.

Stopping now just before the bow of the ship, Doug thought about last night's stroll, when Lucy had stopped in almost this exact spot and asked if he had a light. He'd taken a matchbook from the inside pocket of his dinner jacket and struck a match, shielding it with his hand while she lit the cigarette and took a long drag.

"Ah, that's good," she'd said. "Mother won't let me smoke, you know. For the last twelve days I've had to slip off to the ladies' to do it."

"Doesn't she smell it on you?"

Lucy grinned. "Why do you think I keep an atomizer in my purse? Vanity?"

He'd laughed with her.

"Mother likes to pretend the '20s never happened," Lucy said. "Nice girls don't drink or smoke." She'd stopped and stared into his eyes a moment. "Or do this."

She leaned in and kissed him.

He'd been so surprised, he hadn't kissed back. She pulled back and regarded him with a raised eyebrow.

"Too forward?"

"No," he replied with a nervous laugh. "I've just never had a girl kiss me first."

She grinned again. "Mother says the reason I'm still single is that I'm 'too bold and forward.' I say it's because I haven't found a man interesting enough yet." She leaned her elbow on the rail, cocked her hip, and looked up at him. "You're awfully interesting, though."

After twelve days of thwarting her mother's every attempt at match-making, this frankness surprised him. But only slightly. They *had* enjoyed each other's company.

And so he'd kissed her, and they embraced right there on deck, for several minutes. When they broke the kiss, she winked at him, took his hand, and led him down to his stateroom.

He shouldn't have; he knew he shouldn't have. And yet, he hadn't been able to stop himself.

As the ship moved into the wide mouth of the Yangtze River and to the left of a pair of islands, the salt smell of the air mingled with the sour smell of fish and dirty water.

The estuary was full of fishing boats, some no bigger than a dinghy, most with single sails raised, coming back from the morning catch. Occasionally a larger Chinese Junk floated past going the opposite direction, its multiple sails fluttering in the breeze. Doug watched them bobbing in the wake of the giant ocean liner.

"There you are!"

He turned around to see Lucy walking toward him. She was dressed casually in a light short-sleeved dress of pale blue, the sleeves sheer. The breeze billowed the hem around her legs just below the knees. Her hair was pulled back from her face by a pair of barrettes, and tied up in a hairnet at the back of her neck.

"Good morning," he said with a smile. He glanced over her shoulder and saw the plump middle-aged woman hurrying after her, and groaned on the inside.

"I thought I might find you here," Lucy said with a crooked smile, lowering her voice so only he would hear.

"No chance of a repeat performance," he muttered with a nod toward the woman just about to reach them.

"Mr. Bainbridge, how pleasant to see you," the woman said, attempting to hide her shortness of breath. Her hair was pulled back in a bun, and she wore a navy blue dress that hung almost to her ankles, and a small matching hat pinned to the top of her head. "I thought we might run into you at breakfast, but you must have risen early."

Doug forced a smile. "Good morning, Mrs. Kinzler. Yes, I did. I didn't want to miss our first look at China." He nodded toward the endless vista of rice fields stretching away from the river, dotted with the stooped figures of peasants in dark trousers and pale blouses, their heads hidden beneath conical straw hats.

Mrs. Kinzler's smile faded slightly. "Yes, it's quite something, isn't it?" Her tone sounded forced, and he suppressed an amused grin.

"I think it's incredible, Mother," Lucy said, leaning against the railing and looking out.

Doug had to look away so Mrs. Kinzler wouldn't see his smile; Lucy had said she'd insisted on Asia rather than Europe when her mother suggested a summer tour abroad, and wouldn't agree otherwise. He noticed Lucy had positioned herself between Doug and her mother; a tall barricade in blue pumps.

The older woman chattered about the fine restaurants and tea houses she'd read about in the guidebook. Doug barely listened, watching the low banks of the muddy river slipping past and occasionally casting a sideways glance at Lucy, who rolled her eyes.

The crisp breeze died away, replaced by a wall of humidity. Perspiration began to bead on his forehead, and the air felt heavy.

Like Washington in July, he thought. *Welcome to Shanghai.*

"Perhaps you could join us for lunch, Mr. Bainbridge?" Mrs. Kinzler was saying.

He shook his head and did his best to look regretful. "I'm afraid I have lunch plans already. Business to attend to."

Mrs. Kinzler's face showed disappointment mingled with a hint of skepticism. "On Saturday? Your company still observes the six-day workweek?"

"It's his first day in Shanghai, Mother!" Lucy said. "*Of course* he has business to do—that's why he's here."

"Oh, yes, of course." Mrs. Kinzler gave her daughter a frosty look. "Come dear, we must check on our luggage. God only knows what those Chinamen have done with it."

Doug cringed, but knew better than to criticize his elders for their prejudices. He glanced at Lucy and saw a pained look flash across her eyes.

"I'll join you in a moment, Mother."

Mrs. Kinzler's expression softened as she looked back at Doug. "Yes, I'll give you two a moment to say goodbye."

"God, I'm dying for a cigarette," Lucy muttered as her mother walked away.

Doug chuckled, and she regarded him thoughtfully.

"You could pretend it was yours if she came back, you know. It would be the gentlemanly thing."

Doug shook his head. "Wouldn't work. For twelve days we've been cooped up together on this boat, and she's never once seen me smoke. She'd catch you for certain."

She groaned. "Good God, why do you have to be right?"

He looked away, and watched the shore pass by. He thought back over their time together, the laughs, the easy familiarity—last night—and wished their timing had been better.

"Penny for your thoughts," she said, drawing him back into the present. He saw her looking at him, pencil-thin eyebrows raised.

"They wouldn't even be worth that," he said. What could he tell her that would change anything? That he wished circumstances were different? He looked back at the water. The ship had slowed considerably, and began a hard left turn into the narrower Huang Po River.

She looked away. After a moment's silence, she said, "You never give away much, do you?"

He said nothing. What could he say? That he wasn't allowed to? He stared at the filthy water of the Huang Po, littered with flotsam and the iridescent shimmer of oil, and tried to ignore the stench that now filled the air.

The breeze had stopped entirely, and the late morning sun beat down mercilessly. He took a step back from the rail and put his hat on.

"I knew all along that last night wasn't the beginning of something, you know," she said. "You needn't feel guilty."

"I don't," he said, quietly.

She straightened, looked toward the collection of luggage, which seemed to have gathered a collection of passengers around it. "Well, we had some laughs, didn't we?"

He smiled in spite of himself. "Yeah, we had some laughs."

He wished he didn't like her so much.

She hesitated, as if she had something else she wanted to say, but then she just smiled, and leaned in to kiss him on the cheek.

"If we see each other again, I'll thank our good fortune. If we don't, I'll always remember our conversations fondly."

She waved as she turned and walked away, and he watched her for a moment. A feeling of regret hit him, but he pushed it aside. *Duty first.*

He turned back toward the rail. The green fields of rice gave way to low brick buildings, packed together like sardines in a can. The rural vista disappeared, replaced by a modern cityscape of brick tenements with blackened chimneys on flat tar roofs, and iron fire-escapes along the sides. Warehouses fronted the river, workers swarming around them like ants.

The ship rounded a bend, and a skyline of clean limestone skyscrapers loomed on the far side of a wide boulevard filled with cars rushing past a planted median of potted palms and marble statues. Numerous docks jutted into the filthy river, sleek and elegant yachts moored to their sides.

Farther down, Doug could see docked naval vessels flying several different national flags—battleships mostly, a few destroyers, and one gigantic aircraft carrier flying the Japanese rising sun. He strained to get a better look.

The ship slowed to a crawl, and stevedores on the shore caught ropes tossed by the crew.

He straightened, squared his shoulders, and strode toward the crowd gathered near the First Class gangplank.

Porters moved the luggage to shore, and the First Class passengers disembarked. Doug stood near the back of the crowd, which gave him time to look out. Motor cars of every make imaginable, many quite luxurious, shared the road with bicycles and man-powered rickshaws. Businessmen and ladies in western fashions shared sidewalks with workers in plain trousers and tunics. There were even older Chinese men with long thin beards wearing robes of brightly colored embroidered silks and stiff square hats, looking as if they'd stepped off the pages of a school encyclopedia.

Car horns competed with the shouts of rickshaw drivers in the chaotic traffic.

As Doug stepped onto the gangplank, its canopy shading them from the intense midday sun, he spotted Lucy and her mother standing at the edge of the boulevard. A porter raised his arm, and a rickshaw stopped, its runner barely dropping the handles before reaching down to throw their trunks in the back of his cart. The porter helped the ladies into the seat, said a few words to the runner, and they were off.

Doug wondered if he'd run into them while they stayed in Shanghai. Even in a city of three million people, Mrs. Herbert Kinzler just might sniff him out. Part of him hoped so; part of him hoped not.

He reached the bottom and looked back. The First Class decks sat empty, only a few porters scurrying around. Below on the Second Class deck, a smaller crowd waited their turn to exit, carrying their own valises.

There wasn't much of a middle class left these days, Doug thought. He'd almost been with them, before he'd used his own money to upgrade his ticket the day they departed. Now that he was twenty-five, his parents could no longer keep him from his trust funds; could no longer punish him by withholding the money his grandparents had bequeathed to him.

Below in Steerage, the deck above the water line was packed with passengers. Most of their faces were Chinese—but scattered amongst them were the grimy faces of a few white men. They'd probably heard there was work in Shanghai, unable to find any in the States.

He turned back toward the city. Around him he heard conversations in at least five recognizable languages, plus several he didn't recognize. Most were in the local dialect, and he listened hard, trying to pick out words or phrases.

The customs officer at the front of the line was a pink-cheeked blond man with thin reddish-blond mustache, the emblem of the

International Settlement on the arm of his blue uniform, and a name tag that said "Johansson."

He gave Doug a pleasant smile and asked in English for his passport. He opened it, glanced at the photograph stapled inside, and handed it back. He took Doug's declarations form, gave it a quick look and marked it with a check. "Welcome to Shanghai, sir."

Doug chuckled at the ease of entry into Chinese treaty ports.

"Your luggage ticket, sir?" a Chinese porter asked in English. He handed it over, though he could have simply pointed out his trunk and valise in the dwindled collection. The porter hauled them to the sidewalk, and hailed a rickshaw.

"Where to, sir?" the porter asked, but Doug waved him off. "I'll tell the driver myself." He climbed in, and hesitated a second while trying to decide on Mandarin or Cantonese. It was a gross oversimplification, but Shanghainese was more or less in the middle. He opted for Mandarin, and directed the runner to take him to the Cathay Hotel.

The man replied in Shanghainese, and Doug had to give him a blank look and a shrug.

"Okey-dokey," the runner said in Pidgin, picked up the handles and pulled out into traffic without so much as a sideways glance at the motor cars.

It was just after noon when Doug approached the glittering art deco entrance of the Cathay Hotel, past the brass frieze of two whippets over a large stained glass window. A tall white man with a full beard, brown with twin streaks of gray, and deep-set blue eyes stepped forward and took his luggage from the rickshaw.

"Welcome to the Cathay, Sir. What room?" he asked twice, first in Shanghainese and second in English, with a thick Russian accent.

"Just lunch," Doug replied in English. "Please hold them for me for an hour." He handed the doorman a half-dollar and went inside.

The cavernous lobby was walled with gray and rose marble, with huge paintings of fantastical cities high on the walls. Sunlight streamed through stained glass of orange and red arranged in geometrical designs, softening the light from the giant crystal chandeliers.

He found the restaurant, and was about to ask the Chinese maître'd if Robert Hilliard was waiting, when a tall man of about thirty stood from a nearby table and raised his hand.

Doug assumed the wave was for him, nodded to the maître'd, and walked to the table, where the man extended his hand.

"Lt. Commander Bainbridge, I presume. I'm Commander Hilliard. Welcome to China."

2

"Thank you, sir," Doug said, shaking Commander Hilliard's hand. "I'm glad to be here." He resisted the urge to salute, taking his cue from the superior officer's civilian attire and handshake.

The restaurant was full, and he wondered how much they would be able to say.

"And welcome to ONI's immersion program," Hilliard continued after they sat. "We're very excited about this program. It's unusual for us to find an officer fluent in *both* Mandarin and Cantonese. That should make it easier for you to acclimate."

Doug felt his cheeks flush. "I have to confess, sir, so far Shanghainese has confused me. I've barely understood a word."

"It'll take a little while," Hilliard said. "It's as unique from Mandarin or Cantonese as Spanish is from Portuguese or Italian. We have a hell of a time getting the brass in Washington to understand that. But, in the same way that someone who speaks Portuguese and Italian can learn Spanish quite easily, I think you'll find that Shanghainese will come to you pretty quickly. You may wake up one day and it will suddenly make sense."

A tuxedo-clad Chinese waiter approached with a pair of menus, but Hilliard waved them off. "I hope you like seafood," he said to Doug.

"Yes, very much."

"Of course—you're from San Francisco." Hilliard turned to the waiter and rattled off an order in Shanghainese.

Doug listened closely, and was able to pick out a few words—shrimp, rice—even though the pronunciation was different. He made a mental note of how Hilliard had pronounced them.

After the waiter departed with a bow, Hilliard turned back to Doug. "I ordered Drunken Shrimp—a Shanghai specialty. They take them off the boat and throw them in rice liquor, let them drown and soak for a couple of hours, then cook them in a wok and toss them on rice. Delicious."

"I've never heard of it," Doug confessed. "I'm more familiar with the Cantonese food we'd get in Chinatown when I was a boy. My parents used to take us there often. It reminded them of their childhoods."

"Try everything," Hilliard said. "That's what we want you to do while you're here. You bought the recommended guidebook?"

"Yes, I did."

"Good, start with that. Then when you're comfortable, wander on your own. Try to memorize the boundaries of the International Settlement—not that you have to confine yourself to the IS. There are good restaurants in the French Concession, if you don't mind snobby French waiters. Remember French law applies there—the French opted out when every other western power consolidated their concessions." He shook his head. "Crime is higher in the Chinese municipality, so don't venture there at night if you're alone, but there are things to see in the old town."

He paused while the waiter returned with a pot of tea and two little porcelain cups, set them down, and bowed.

"Our first order of business," Hilliard said after the waiter departed, reaching into his white linen suit coat and removing an envelope. "That's your first month's stipend, less the month's rent we paid to your landlord. It's in U.S. currency, which you can use just about anywhere, but the merchants will gouge on the price. I'd exchange most of it for the local Shanghai dollar if I were you, but keep a few American

14

dollars in reserve. In the future we'll deposit directly into an account we've set up for you at the HSBC—that way no nosy neighbor sees a check from the United States Navy in your mailbox. You can find the bank on the Bund, a few blocks from here—it's the building with the dome on top."

"I passed it on the way here." Doug put the envelope inside his breast pocket without looking at the money. He knew how much the stipend was; he'd do the math later to figure out his rent.

Hilliard smiled. "Relax, your job is easy. Just soak it all in."

Doug realized his shoulders were tense, and he relaxed them and made an effort to breathe more easily.

"They probably told you before you left Washington that your immersion isn't really 'top secret'—I'm sure they said you could tell your family, if you asked them to keep it to themselves. We know mothers never do that, though—they brag to a couple of neighbor ladies, and swear them to secrecy, but the neighbor ladies tell a few more neighbor ladies and swear them to secrecy, and so on. It's fine."

Doug had difficulty imagining his mother bragging about anything he did. More likely she'd sit rigid in her high-backed parlor chairs, hands folded in her lap, and say vaguely, "Douglas is in China," if anyone asked about him. She'd no doubt let them assume he was working for his father's firm.

Lucy wouldn't have told anyone, he mused. He wondered what might have happened if he'd been more forthcoming with her. Then he scolded himself. He didn't really *know* her, after all. His instincts about her reliability might be spot on, but there was no empirical evidence to back that up. Best to have kept her out of it.

Hilliard continued. "This isn't cloak-and-dagger. You can write home as often as you like, socialize at will—enjoy the city. That said, it would be prudent not to broadcast your association with ONI, given the political climate toward foreigners these days."

This startled Doug. "Oh? I hadn't heard there was difficulty."

He knew only too well his maternal grandparents' stories of fleeing during the Boxer Rebellion thirty-five years before, full of references to friends—fellow missionaries—who hadn't survived. Not that his mother ever spoke of it, of course.

Hilliard held up his hands. "Don't worry, there hasn't been any unusual violence against foreign civilians in the International Settlement, or even in the Chinese municipality, but locals don't hesitate to show hostility to western authority figures. Chinese republican politics and public opinion are pressing for the return of the heart of the city to Chinese control, and some foreign residents in the Settlement have reported intimidation, mostly the British and Japanese."

The food arrived in a big steaming bowl, and the waiter set smaller bowls and chop sticks in front of them. He bowed and backed away without a word.

"Enough business," Hilliard said with a smile. "We can finish that up after I take you to your new home."

Tim McIntyre sat at the bar and dug into his bowl of noodles, bringing his mouth down to the chopsticks and chewing in the mass of noodles hanging from them. His shirt sleeves were folded up past his elbows, and he wore no jacket. His white straw hat lay on the bar beside his bowl, the sweat stains on the rim still wet. He washed down the bite with a gulp of hot tea from a little cup.

The stockier man beside him fanned himself with his hat and took a drink of his martini. Condensation dripped from the glass. He was about forty, with a thick brown mustache and round cheeks flushed red.

"I'll never understand how you can eat hot noodles and drink tea this time of year. You have definitely gone native, my friend."

"And I'll never understand how you can drink a martini *at lunch time*," Tim replied.

His companion chuckled. "When you've been in the business as long as I have, you'll have liquid lunches too. And if you're lucky, you'll have rich sources who buy them for you."

"Ha!" Tim's laugh was hard-edged. "I don't think I'd want to take any favors from the sources I've spoken to lately."

"Still digging into the underworld?" his companion asked, and shook his head with a 'tisk-tisk' expression.

"Something like that," Tim said through a mouth full of noodles.

"I hope you have a license to carry a firearm. And then *carry* one."

"I never took you to be a worrier, Jonesy."

"I'm not. I'm just practical. I carry a Colt .45 right here under my coat." He patted his side.

"Didn't anyone ever tell you 'the pen is mightier than the sword?' What kind of newspaperman are you, anyway?"

Jonesy chuckled. "The kind who didn't waste time studying 'journalism' in a classroom. Unlike you with your fancy junior college degree, I earned my chops working the labor beat in Detroit for sixteen years—where I learned there are all kinds of weapons mightier than a pen."

"Such as?"

"The almighty buck for one," Jonesy said, his expression growing stony. "I saw dozens of union men beaten to death by strike-breakers, and then had editors refuse to print the stories."

Tim made a little grunting noise as his only reply, and finished the tea in his cup. As he poured more from the teapot, something caught his attention and he overflowed his little cup.

"Whoa there! You haven't even been drinking," Jonesy said, throwing down his napkin where the overflow had started to drip off the bar onto his seat.

"Sorry." Tim nodded toward the lobby. "Believe it or not, I know that guy over there—the young one in the gray suit, who just came out

17

of the restaurant. Doug Bainbridge. I went to day school with him when we were kids. I used to caddy for his dad at the country club they belonged to."

"Well, well, well," Jonesy said.

"What? You know him, too?"

"Not him, his lunch companion."

Something about Jonesy's tone and expression piqued Tim's interest. "So are you gonna tell me who it is?"

"That's Robert Hilliard—*Commander* Robert Hilliard—one of the Assistant Naval Attachés from the U.S. Embassy in Nanking. I heard he was in town yesterday, touring a factory in Yangtzepoo. Apparently he stayed in town, and now he's had lunch with your boy."

"Interesting," Tim said. He remembered hearing something from a mutual acquaintance he'd run into in a little jazz club in San Francisco not long before he'd left, said in a gossipy whisper. Something about Doug joining the Navy after graduating from Stanford, she'd said. An odd choice for someone with his background, Tim had agreed, and then promptly forgot about it.

"I know that tone," Jonesy said with a knowing smile. "You want to know what's going on there. Reporter's curse, the insufferable need to know everything about everyone. Go on, then—go find out where they've gone. I'll buy your lunch, and you can owe me. Maybe a good tip sometime, huh?"

"Thanks, Jonesy," Tim said, retrieving his hat from the bar.

He hurried through the revolving door facing toward Nanking Road, but Doug and Hilliard had already gone. He put a few coins into the hand of the Russian doorman and asked in Shanghainese where the two Americans had just gone.

"They took rickshaw," the Russian replied. "I heard one tell runner in Shanghainese to take them to Huang Lei Road in North District."

Tim smiled. "Thanks, Ivan. I know just where that is."

** **

Doug listened closely when Hilliard gave directions to the rickshaw runner; the address he gave on Huang Lei Road would be home for the next two years. The runner was shirtless in the heat, and the sweat on his yellowish-tan skin gleamed in the bright midday sun as he hoisted Doug's luggage into the back. His faded blue trousers were cut off just below the knees, and the waist band was soaked. As he pulled them down Nanking Road, rivulets ran down his spine.

What a way to make a living, Doug thought. And not much of a living at that—Hilliard had paid him just twenty-five cents.

They came to a stop at a busy intersection—Honan Road, Hilliard said—where a tall, dark-skinned man with a thick black beard, in a blue police uniform and bright red turban directed traffic. A Sikh from India. Another stood at the corner and held the lever that operated the traffic signal.

"Strange that they have a stop light, but still have someone out in the road directing traffic," Doug remarked.

"That's Shanghai," Hilliard said. "The modern world meets the ancient orient, where no one gives a hoot about the color of the traffic signal."

As he spoke, a rickshaw runner on the other side of the intersection looked around and sprang forward, dodging the cross traffic, oblivious to blaring horns and shouts from other rickshaw drivers. The Sikh in the intersection pulled out his baton and struck a blow against the errant driver's thigh, eliciting a yelp, and went back to directing traffic.

The Sikh officer on the corner pulled his lever, their light turned green, and the Sikh in the road turned 90 degrees and motioned them on. Their runner rounded the corner and pulled them north along Honan Road.

They encountered a similar situation a couple of blocks farther, at the intersection with Peking Road—again with a pair of Sikh police officers. Doug commented about the anomaly.

"The British recruit from their colony in India for traffic duty and riot duty in the Settlement," Hilliard explained. "The British pretty much run the Shanghai Municipal Police. Technically they're supposed to cooperate with the American, Japanese, and other concessions represented in the IS, but in practice they run the SMP any way they want to."

They crossed a bridge over Soochow Creek. Doug gazed down the creek —really a small river—and saw women crouched in clusters, running clothes across washboards. Near the bridge dozens of Chinese boys were skinny-dipping in the slow-moving brown water, then shamelessly scrambling up the muddy banks and running down wood planks to jump back in, laughing and squealing like it was a Coney Island roller-coaster.

The street narrowed north of the creek, and they passed through a neighborhood of short brick buildings, three or four stories tall, with shops on the ground floor and tenements above. Fresh ducks and chickens hung by their feet from the open windows of butcher shops; street vendors shouted to passersby to buy pork dumplings or dried fish; and old women hung out windows and chattered with their neighbors in rapid Shanghainese. A pair of police officers—one white, one Chinese—strolled down the street, and the white one nodded to Doug and Hilliard and touched the rim of his hat as their rickshaw passed.

They made a couple of turns, and stopped in front of a building on the corner of two side streets. They stepped out and waited for the driver to remove Doug's luggage and set it down by the door; Doug fished a quarter from his pocket and tipped him, thanking him in Mandarin.

Hilliard had already entered the store, a laundry, and Doug hurried to join him. He found the commander speaking to a young woman with round cheeks at the counter, and when Doug entered she looked at him. Their eyes held for only a second before she looked down, and mumbled something to Hilliard with a quick bow.

A moment later a rail-thin man with deeply lined face came from the back, moping his brow. He greeted Hilliard with both a bow and a handshake—*East meets west*, Doug thought—then turned and gave Doug the same greeting.

"Doug, this is Mr. Hwang, your landlord," Hilliard said in English.

"Very nice to meet you," Mr. Hwang said in careful English, his words slow and deliberate. "Welcome to Shanghai."

Doug said 'thank you' in Mandarin. Mr. Hwang's face lit up. He said "Ahh!" and proceeded to correct Doug's pronunciation to the Shanghainese variant. Doug repeated it with a bow, grateful for the lesson.

Mr. Hwang led them out of the store to a second doorway at the corner of the building. Doug hesitated at the door, then lugged his trunk off the sidewalk and into the hall. It was hot and stuffy as they climbed up two flights of stairs, each flight turning at a landing midway between floors. At each floor the stairway opened to a small hallway with three doors. At the third floor, Mr. Hwang led them to a door and unlocked it.

"You have a flat on the top floor, with windows over the street *and* courtyard," he said in Shanghainese, slowly for the newcomer, enunciating carefully, and beamed as he stood aside for Doug to enter.

Doug hid his disappointment as he looked around. It was even smaller than his apartment in Washington, and not as attractive. The bare wood floors were plain and unlacquered, the wooden walls unpainted. There was one cushioned armchair in the corner, and a small table with two chairs in the middle of the room. A window stood open, with plain white curtains stirring in the occasional breeze.

There was a kitchenette near the back with a couple of cabinets, a small counter, an ice box, and a cast iron wood-burning stove. An open window looked down on a courtyard surrounded by other brick buildings, clotheslines strung from window to opposite window, most hung with damp laundry. Women in the courtyard chattered in Shanghainese as they chopped vegetables to prepare the evening meals.

A short hall led to the bedroom, with a little linen closet to the side. In the bedroom he found a bed with a wrought iron frame, the mattress sagging in the middle, covered with a blue cotton blanket. A little table stood next to it, a dresser faced the bed, and another window stood open with white curtains stirring in the slight breeze off the street.

"You like?" Mr. Hwang asked with an expectant smile.

It was smaller and plainer than he'd expected, and the furnishings left a lot to be desired—it was far from how he'd pictured living for two years—but the place was clean. Most Chinese lived in squalid conditions in one-room shacks or tenements, so Doug nodded and returned the smile.

"Yes, very much." He hesitated, mindful of Chinese manners. "Where do I find the toilet?"

"Ah, the toilet and bath are off the main hall," Mr. Hwang said, a proud smile on his lips. "One bath for every two flats, very nice."

"It is exactly what we had in mind, Mr. Hwang," Hilliard said, bowing. "Mr. Bainbridge will be very comfortable here."

"Your neighbor is English," Mr. Hwang said, pointing toward the door opposite Doug's. "He has lived here many years, speaks very good Shanghainese."

"Well, isn't that nice?" Hilliard said to Doug, with a smile for Mr. Hwang's benefit.

"Yes, thank you, Mr. Hwang," Doug said, careful to imitate the Shanghainese pronunciation. He bowed.

Mr. Hwang returned the bow and handed him the key. He bid them good afternoon and departed.

"We've put you in a middle-class neighborhood in the old American Concession," Hilliard told him, returning to English. "This will be a good place for you to get comfortable while you explore."

"Thank you, sir."

"First off, get yourself a lighter suit, something linen—every westerner in Shanghai wears linen—and some electric fans. This is typical weather for May, so you can imagine how hot it will be in a couple of months."

Doug nodded. He was wearing his summer suit, and he felt like he was roasting in it.

"I come to Shanghai several times a year, and I'll meet with you every three months during your immersion. I'll send you a telegram inviting you to lunch, and sign it 'Your friend Bob.' I'll give you a few days' notice.

"I'm sure they told you in Washington that completing the immersion doesn't guarantee advancement—and as a matter of fact, there are two others besides you who have already started the program here. If things go as we'd like, others will come. So there's competition. You won't know who they are, and may never encounter them. But let's be honest—do well in your immersion, and you'll get placed somewhere, either as an assistant Attaché in Nanking, or as on-board Intelligence officer in the Asiatic or the Pacific Fleet. You'll learn vital skills that ONI will need."

Hilliard paused and took a deep breath. "Which brings me to our last piece of business. It's no secret the Navy has concentrated its intelligence quite heavily on Japan for the last fifteen years."

"Since the Great War."

"Precisely. ONI has run a three-year immersion in Japan for nearly a decade, and we had to fight hard to get Washington to grant us an opportunity to run an immersion in China. How you and the others

23

do over the next couple of years will determine if this program continues. The Navy knows our next fight is going to be against the Japanese—even if the public would scoff—but *we* believe it's as likely to take place on the China coast as out in the open Pacific. So you can see how important your role is."

"Yes sir," Doug said, feeling the excitement building in his gut.

"Good. I'm confident you'll do well. You should have little trouble, but in case you do," he paused and took a card from inside his coat, and handed it to Doug. There was a number printed on it, but no other writing. "If you get into trouble and need help fast, call that number. It's classified, so memorize it and hand it back to me. Use it only in an emergency. If you need ordinary assistance, just call the Embassy in Nanking and ask for me, I'll get back to you when I can."

Doug memorized the number, and handed the card back.

Hilliard walked to the door, but paused with his hand on the doorknob. "One more thing—two years is a long time, and you'll get lonely. It's been said if God lets Shanghai survive, He owes an apology to Sodom and Gomorrah. There are prostitutes everywhere, not to mention gold diggers. Officially, fornication is against Navy policy—but we're realistic. You've probably read in the papers about the 'miracle drug' that cures infections: penicillin. It's not available to the public, but we've had it for five years. So just in case..." He let his voice trail off.

Doug felt his cheeks flush. "I understand, sir."

"Most of the prostitutes are Chinese or Russian. Not that you'd ever visit any, of course; just keep in mind the Chinese hookers are more likely to be infected with something than the Russians, but don't trust any of them."

Doug stiffened. "Understood, sir."

That's awfully racist, he thought, hearing it in his grandfather Bainbridge's voice. Grandfather had been a freethinker and an egalitarian, and Doug always wished he could be more like him.

24

"Good luck, Bainbridge," Hilliard said, returned Doug's salute, and walked out.

Doug relaxed his shoulders and let out a long exhale, tingling inside with a mix of excitement and apprehension.

He was on his own. Again.

DOUG'S NEIGHBORHOOD

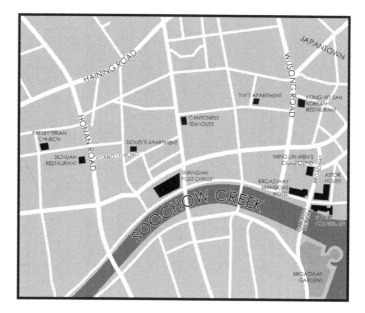

3

They collided as Doug exited the store with two boxes under his arm. The boxes fell to the ground, and he cringed at the sound of metal pieces clanging.

"I'm awfully sorry," the young man who ran into him said, in English with an American accent, looking at the boxes and kneeling to help pick them up. "I hope they're not broken."

"I'm sure they're fine," Doug replied. The voice sounded familiar, but he couldn't place it.

"Ah, Eskimo. That's the same brand I have," the man said, nodding at the boxes containing small desk fans. "You must be new to Shanghai."

He stood and handed a box to Doug, and they looked at each other.

Doug knew that face, but out of context it took him a second to realize who it was.

"Doug Bainbridge?" the man said, sounding surprised.

Something about his tone and the surprised look seemed a little put on. But that didn't make sense. He told himself to not be so suspicious.

"Tim. Tim McIntyre," the man said, and extended his hand.

"Yes, Tim, I remember you," Doug said, shaking the offered hand. "You attended Carlisle Day School, in San Francisco. It's been years. I didn't know you were in China."

"Couple years now," Tim said, smiling from ear to ear. "I write for the AP, one of their Far East correspondents. I don't live too far from here, actually. A few blocks that way. I've got a nice girl, and we've got an apartment just off Woosung, almost to Japantown in Hongkou."

"I'm around the corner," Doug said. "As a matter of fact, I just arrived this morning. Getting settled in." He nodded down at the fan boxes and raised the shopping bag in his right hand that contained a kettle, tea pot, and tea cups. "I'm going to be here a while. My family's been in the China trade for a long time, but we haven't had anyone on this side of the Pacific in thirty-five years."

"You don't say? Well then, I should take you out tonight, show you some of the good clubs. Shanghai's famous for its nightlife."

"Thanks, maybe some other night," Doug said. "It's been a big day, I'm not sure I'm up for a night on the town."

Tim nodded. "I understand. Maybe next Friday? I know a couple of great places."

Why not? Doug thought. "That would be swell, thanks."

Tim grinned. "Great! Here, give me your address, and I'll come get you at eight o'clock." He handed Doug a slip of paper and a pencil, then took it back with a smile after Doug had written his address on it. "It was great running into you. Perhaps I'll see you around the neighborhood. If not, I'll see you Friday."

Tim touched the rim of his hat and nodded as he turned away.

"See ya, Tim."

As he headed back to his apartment, fan boxes back under his arm, Doug wondered about the odds of running into someone from San Francisco on a neighborhood street in Shanghai.

After a nice cool bath in the claw-foot tub he shared with his third floor neighbors—whom he had yet to meet—Doug headed out at dusk to explore and find some dinner.

The neighborhood bustled with activity as the sun went down and the temperature fell from stifling to barely tolerable. All around him were conversations in multiple varieties of Chinese—most in Shanghainese, which he was beginning to recognize, but also several in Cantonese, a few in Mandarin, and some in other languages or dialects he didn't recognize at all.

Old men sat in groups on the stoops of every building, most playing Mah Jong with great intensity, but as Doug passed they looked up and stared at the new foreigner in the neighborhood. Doug knew they would watch his every move, until they grew accustomed to his presence.

There seemed to be a tea house on every corner, and at this time of day they were packed. He strolled by slowly, listening to the conversations through the open windows, and settled on an establishment that seemed to cater to a Cantonese clientele.

He found a seat at the counter along the side wall, and a waiter approached him immediately, bowed—polite but stiff—and handed him a folded paper menu. Doug thanked him in Cantonese and ordered an Oolong tea and a *bo luo bao*—a pineapple bun with red bean filling — eliciting a broad grin from the waiter, who then bowed and hurried to fill his order.

The other customers cocked their heads in curiosity and watched him a moment, then returned to their conversations and appeared to ignore him.

As he listened to them, Doug could pick out two distinct languages—Cantonese, and another that sounded a bit like Cantonese with its harsh nasalization, but incomprehensible to him.

When the waiter returned, Doug asked what the other language was. "Fujian," the waiter said.

Of course, another southern language. Doug knew people in the south of China felt distinct from the rest of the country—much like the Deep South in the United States.

29

The waiter was very attentive now that he knew Doug spoke Cantonese, and Doug decided to ask him for directions. Before he'd left San Francisco, his mother had given him the address of a Presbyterian Church on Tianjian Road—the pastor was an acquaintance of his grandparents—and said it would be good for him to go there on Sundays. Doug had no doubt she'd written to the pastor and told him to keep her informed of her son's attendance at Sunday services.

The waiter knew the address—Doug stifled his disappointment—and told him it wasn't far.

After his tea and snack, Doug wandered west a few blocks toward Honan Road. Twilight deepened, and the air was thick with the smells of garlic, soy, and peppers cooking. Doug could hear the muted sizzle of the woks and the chatter of the women cooking for their families, hidden from view in the courtyards behind the buildings.

Honan Road was brightly lit, and here he saw several white people in western dress among the Chinese on the sidewalks and in the street. He heard several conversations in English, with both American and British accents.

He considered several small restaurants for dinner, pausing as he passed to look inside, and waiters called out to him in Pidgin— "Wantchee good eat, Mister?"

He eventually settled on a Sichuan restaurant with a mixed clientele. He ordered *gong bao ji ding* in Mandarin, a spicy chicken dish, with hot and sour soup, and sat for a while in deep thought.

He felt an exciting touch of discomfort, and wondered if he'd ever be able to let his guard down here. He'd felt excited and apprehensive like this when he first moved to Washington—before he found he had nothing in common with any of his coworkers, and spent almost three years feeling alone. But he wouldn't think about that now.

Would he run into Lucy and Mrs. Kinzler somewhere? That thought gave him mixed emotions.

And finally, what about Tim McIntyre? Something about the interaction hadn't seemed natural. He supposed the fact that Tim was a reporter added to his unease, though he couldn't think of any other reason Tim would have anything other than friendly intentions.

It was an interesting crowd. A pair of tall Scandinavian-looking men in linen suits, blond and pink-faced, chatted at the table next to his in what he decided was probably Danish judging from their red and white ties. There were two tables of Americans—four businessmen in the front, and two couples to his right—who laughed and conversed quite loudly. Several Chinese families sat at long tables, usually three generations, conversing more quietly but with equal mirth. And in the back sat a group of seven young Chinese in somber gray clothing, boys and girls, with books open; their voices were quiet, but their faces were intense, and they leaned in close to one another. He presumed they were university students, but wondered about their drab matching clothes.

The door opened while he was eating his soup, and he looked up to see the round-faced young woman who worked at Mr. Hwang's shop. She was looking toward the back of the restaurant, but noticed him watching her and looked down. She hurried to the table occupied by the seven young people with books and serious expressions.

Doug stole glances her direction as he ate his chicken. She still wore the same outfit she'd worn at Mr. Hwang's—light blue tunic and dark blue trousers; she was pretty, and her expression was more passive than those of her companions. She seemed quiet, listening for long periods before uttering a few words that he couldn't hear, and then listening to the reactions.

She didn't have a book, and he wondered what her connection with these students might be.

Once, late in the evening as he was finishing an orange cookie, she glanced up and caught him looking at her. She gave him a curious look for a second, and then looked away quickly.

31

The students were still there when he left the restaurant, and as he stepped into the warm night he resolved to visit the shop downstairs on Monday and talk to her.

The stairwell was still hot and stuffy as he climbed to the third floor. He turned toward his door and nearly bumped into a white man coming out of the bathroom. "I'm very sorry," he apologized in English.

The man was in his early to mid-40s, with rumpled light brown hair turning gray at the temples, slight crinkles at the corners of his gray-blue eyes, and deep laugh lines around his mouth. He had the square build and broad shoulders of a man who had done plenty of manual labor in his time, and who might once have been svelte, but now had a bit of a gut. He wore blue boxer shorts and a sleeveless white tee-shirt, with a damp towel draped across his shoulders.

"Ah, an American!" he said in a working-class English accent, giving Doug a big grin. "You must be our new neighbor." He extended his hand. "Charlie Ford. Please excuse the way I'm dressed, just finished me bath."

"Doug Bainbridge." He'd noticed the plural pronoun; Mr. Hwang had only mentioned the Englishman. *Interesting.*

"Wouldja like to come in for a cuppa tea?" Charlie said, motioning toward his apartment. He bent his vowels with every word.

"Thanks," Doug said, and followed him.

"We have company!" Charlie shouted as they entered the apartment, which was a mirror image of Doug's, but better decorated— the walls were painted red, there were rugs on the floor, a gold screen stood in one corner, and black lace fans hung tacked to the walls. "Put the kettle on for tea, wouldja Love?"

A skinny young Chinese man appeared in the hall, wearing tan trousers cut off below the knees, shirtless and barefoot. He was younger than Doug, probably about twenty, and he stared at Doug for a few seconds before bowing.

"Doug Bainbridge, Li Baosheng," Charlie said.

"How do you do?" Doug said, returning the young man's bow.

"Doug's our new neighbor, Bao. Go put some tea on for us," Charlie said, and the young man went into the kitchenette without a word.

Who was this Li Baosheng? Doug wondered. He wasn't dressed like a servant, though it was late in the evening.

He gave Charlie an involuntarily curious look.

Charlie flushed when he noticed Doug looking at him, and a sheepish smile came to his lips as he looked down.

Doug silently scolded himself for showing such obvious curiosity. Usually he had a better poker face. "I didn't realize you had a servant. What time does he leave?" He noticed a veil seem to fall across Charlie's eyes, and regretted how stiff his tone had sounded.

"Bao's not my servant, he lives here with me—he's my man Friday, you could say," Charlie said, his voice quiet in comparison to his previous boisterousness.

Doug felt his gut tighten. He kept his face expressionless.

Charlie looked back up, and his smile seemed a little forced. "Well! It is certainly nice to have a fellow Anglophone for a neighbor, let me tell you. The Chinese are wonderful people, but they don't have that sense of neighborliness that we Anglo-Saxons have, do they?"

Doug nodded in agreement, but said nothing.

"We must have you 'round for dinner some evening, get to know you better," Charlie said. "Bao's a very good cook. Much better than me, that's certain."

"That would be nice," Doug said, politely.

"Won't you have a seat?" Charlie motioned toward an armchair. He took a seat in the other armchair facing Doug's. "So, Mr. Bainbridge, what brings you to Shanghai?"

"My father's company imports *chinoiserie* to the United States—porcelain, silks, art work, Ming vases. It's the family business, started by my great-grandfather over eighty years ago."

"And you've taken your place in the family business. How lovely."

Doug shrugged. "It's what was expected of me."

"Oh, quite, I'm sure," Charlie said. "I was expected to join me father in his business, too. Dad was a butcher, but I wanted no part in that. I ran off to sea when I was seventeen. A sailor for twenty-one years, I was, 'fore I decided to settle down on land. Almost stayed in New York, but decided on Shanghai instead."

Doug's interest piqued. "Were you in the Royal Navy during the war?"

Charlie shook his head. "Merchantman. I served on cargo ships during the war, keeping England supplied with war materiel. After the armistice I went back to work in private shipping. Get to see the world that way, and if you don't like a ship or its captain, you just leave at the next port and find another job. Always a ship hiring, no matter where's you are."

"Why'd you give it up?"

"Rheumatism." Charlie patted his knee.

"How did you end up here, in the old American concession?" Doug asked.

Charlie waved that off. "Those old boundaries disappeared a long time ago, mate. We live all mixed up here in the International Settlement nowadays. Well, except over in Japantown—they don't much like other foreigners living in the Japanese Colony. Good place to go for dinner, though—just don't stay too late, or you might get roughed up by Japanese marines on shore leave."

Doug frowned. "For what reason would they do that?"

Charlie chuckled. "Paranoid, the Japs are; think everyone's a spy."

Bao approached from the kitchenette, carrying a bamboo tray with a tea pot and three little porcelain cups. He set it on the little side table between the armchairs, and Charlie poured the cups.

"To new neighbors, new friends," he, said raising his cup to Doug. "Cheers, mate."

"Cheers," Doug echoed, and drank. It tasted like the Oolong tea he'd had earlier that evening, and he wondered if Li Baosheng were from the south of China.

They drank in silence for a moment. The Englishman and his companion both looked at Doug, and he became slightly uncomfortable. He crossed his legs and shifted sideways in the chair.

"So what do you do for a living nowadays, Mr. Ford?"

"Oh, Charlie, please," his neighbor said with a smile. "I do some backstage work at a little Chinese theatre off Thibet Road, near the race track. I do handy work, build sets, or whatever they need done. It's good honest work, but not so grueling as ship work."

"I see."

"You should come see a show there sometime. Maybe I can get you a free ticket. The company's quite good, and they're doing a lovely little production right now." He snapped his fingers a few times and looked up at the ceiling. "Oh, what is the name of that bloody show they're doing?"

After a few seconds he looked back at Doug with an apologetic shrug. "Sorry mate, can't remember what the bloody thing's called. Quite something, though."

"I wouldn't want to trouble you."

A shadow seemed to fall across Charlie's face. "Right. Well, if you're not a fan of Chinese theatre, you probably wouldn't understand what's going on anyhow. It's not like one of our plays."

Doug drained his cup and stood. "Thank you for the tea. It was a pleasure meeting you, Charlie, Baosheng." He nodded to them both.

"I'll see you to the door," Charlie said, and hurried forward. "Do come again, won't you?" he said with a forced smile as he held the door open.

"I'll look forward to it," Doug said, minding his manners, and crossed the hall to his apartment.

4

Doug woke early enough on Sunday to wash and dress in his nice suit, and walked to the Presbyterian Church on Tianjian Road for the ten AM service in Shanghainese. There were between eighty and one hundred Chinese in the pews, mostly families dressed in western-style suits or dresses. He noticed right away that he was the only white person in attendance, besides the fifty-ish pastor and the woman at the organ or similar age, whom Doug presumed to be the pastor's wife.

The Reverend Mr. Jonathan Allen had clearly been in country a long time—he delivered his twenty-minute sermon in the local language at a normal pace, not the typical slow speech of the foreigner. Doug was disappointed to realize he understood maybe a tenth of what the pastor was saying.

When the organ began the hymn—the number was posted on the board beside the pulpit—Doug turned to the page in the hymnal and realized that although he could read the words of the Chinese translation of "Nearer my God to Thee," he had no idea how to pronounce the lyrics. He listened as those around him sang and followed along with his finger, trying to learn. By the middle of the second verse he knew it was a hopeless exercise. Maybe a little bit would stick, anyway.

As he exited the sanctuary at the end of the service, the pastor greeted him in English.

"How do you do, young man? We're pleased to have you this morning. What made you decide to come at ten o'clock, instead of the English service at eleven?"

"Trying to master Shanghainese," Doug said. "I speak Mandarin and Cantonese."

"Oh, and how did you manage?"

Doug grimaced a little. "Not terribly well, I'm afraid. I didn't understand much of your sermon."

"Don't be too hard on yourself. Stick around, the English service starts in ten minutes. It's the exact same message. Wouldn't want you to miss it, now would we?"

Doug inwardly groaned, but just smiled. "I'm Doug Bainbridge. I believe my mother wrote to you."

"Ah, yes indeed. A very good lady, we've corresponded for years. I knew your grandfather Preston many years ago. He and my father went to seminary together, more than fifty years ago. Your grandparents were from Ohio, I believe. We're from Indiana. The congregation I grew up in—my father's church—we supported your grandfather's mission in Guangdong a couple of times a year; sent supplies—Bibles, hymnals, clothing, that sort of thing. After they got back from China in 1900, I heard your grandfather speak at our seminary. I was a divinity student then, and his speech inspired me to come to China on my own mission. My wife and I have been in Shanghai for thirty-three years now."

"I had no idea," Doug said. "Mother didn't tell me any of that." *Typical.*

Rev. Allen smiled. "Very thoughtful of her to let me tell the story."

Within days, Doug was in love with Shanghai.

He explored a different part of the International Settlement every day, setting out on foot from his apartment in the morning, and sometimes catching a streetcar downtown.

Having to sit through back-to-back church services aside, Doug had loved every moment of his time here. The people were friendly when he spoke to them in Mandarin or Cantonese rather than English or Pidgin, giving him big genuine smiles, and they patiently corrected his errors when they responded in Shanghainese. The street vendors gave him a couple extra dumplings when he bought lunch, the grocer gave him a generous measurement of dried tea—a touch more than a kilo for the price of a kilo.

If only the shop girl at the desk in Mr. Hwang's laundry downstairs had been as friendly when he spoke to her on Monday morning.

Doug had come in with no particular topic of conversation in mind, and he simply introduced himself with a smile and a polite bow.

"Have wash?" she asked in Pidgin, eyeing his empty hands.

He replied in Mandarin mixed with a little Shanghainese. "No. I'm new here, I just moved in upstairs, and I'm getting to know my new neighbors."

"Makee pidgin here," she said, curt. *This is a place of business.*

His guidebook had a glossary of Pidgin words, and Doug had memorized them on the ship. Pidgin was the Pidgin word for business, and the point of speaking Pidgin was to have a common language for commerce up and down the China and Indochina coast. A simple language with only one verb tense and slightly more than 400 words—a strange mix of English, several Chinese varieties, Portuguese and Hindi in roughly that proportion—it had become the stereotypical "chinaman-speak" of Hollywood movies.

Doug had resolved before arrival to never use it.

He answered in his own blend of Chinese—Shanghainese when he knew the word, Mandarin when he didn't. "I'll bring my wash down tomorrow, and we'll do business then. May I have your name, though?"

She gave him a curious look for a few seconds, then murmured, "Wong Mei-Ling."

Doug grinned and bowed. "I'm pleased to meet you, Miss Wong. Until tomorrow."

He spoke to her every day after that, bringing some laundry down on Tuesday morning even though he didn't have much that needed washing—he'd bought a new linen suit Monday at a high-end store on East Nanking Road downtown—and picking it up on Wednesday.

He went to the horse track and recreation grounds Monday afternoon, watching a baseball game with several other Americans while a raucous British crowd cheered on a rugby match nearby; on Tuesday he strolled the gardens on the Bund where Soochow Creek emptied into the river, then wandered Japantown in the Hongkou district.

Every evening he came home around the same time, and inevitably saw his neighbor Charlie Ford in transit to or from the bathroom for his nightly bath and shave. Doug silently cursed his luck that they seemed to be on the same schedule.

The Englishman always smiled and waved, saying "Good evening, neighbor!" and Doug would nod and mumble "Good evening" in reply.

He settled onto his bed every night—naked above the covers with both fans blowing on him—and went to sleep with a smile on his lips.

On Friday morning he sat in the Cantonese tea house eating a red bean pastry and drinking a pot of Oolong tea, reading the local English newspaper—he liked to read both the English and Chinese papers every morning—and on page three he saw Tim McIntyre's name on an article that took the entire top third of the page.

Friday, May 31, 1935
Provisional Government Seeks Freedom for Korea
By Tim McIntyre, Associated Press Shanghai

The story continued in a single column on Page Eighteen. Doug read the entire feature, fascinated. It described the workings of the Korean Provisional Government, operating out of Shanghai, as they sought international recognition, and also worked clandestinely with resistance cells inside the Korean Peninsula. It described their history—formed by exiles fleeing the Japanese invasion in 1910, and incorporated in Shanghai after Japan annexed Korea in 1911.

After a brief description of alleged atrocities and injustices perpetrated by the Imperial Japanese army on Korean civilians—nothing new there—the story relayed in depth the status of Koreans in China. *"Officially Japanese nationals, the Koreans are viewed as racially inferior by the Japanese, but superior to the Chinese. Thus, the Koreans hold an ambiguous status in China—paradoxically privileged and at the same time second-class."*

A source identified only as "Mr. Kim" was quoted as saying: *"If a Korean or a Japanese are accused of killing or robbing a Chinese, the Japanese court in Shanghai will never convict either; but if a Korean is accused of killing or robbing a Japanese in China, the Japanese court will always convict. Guilt or innocence does not matter."*

Farther down, Mr. Kim stated that their biggest threat was infiltration by Korean fifth columnists in the pay of the Japanese secret service.

"Well I'll be damned," Doug muttered when he'd finished reading. He'd have to remember to mention to Tim that night how impressed he was.

41

**

He came home early Friday so he could wash and dress up for his evening on the town. He caught himself whistling while he knotted his necktie, and realized with a bit of surprise that he was looking forward to the night's activities, whatever they might be.

He had just finished combing his hair when he heard voices in the hallway. It took a second to realize it was Charlie Ford talking to Tim McIntyre. Doug scowled, marched across his apartment, and threw open the door.

"Hello Tim," he said, stepping out into the hallway and locking his apartment door.

"Hello Doug," Tim said, smiling. "I was just meeting your neighbor, Mr. Ford."

"Yes, and I was telling your friend Mr. McIntyre how nice it is that you have someone to show you around," Charlie said with a big smile.

Doug shrugged, slightly annoyed. "I've been showing myself around pretty well for the last several days. I've explored quite a bit on my own."

Charlie seemed to deflate a little bit. "Yes, quite right. You have indeed, haven't you? Well, then, I'll just be on about me bath, and let you two go out and enjoy yourselves. Cheers, mates."

"Very nice to meet you, Mr. Ford," Tim said. Charlie nodded and waved as he slipped into the bathroom, and closed the door.

"What a nice fellow," Tim said.

"He seems nice enough," Doug said, not convinced. "Let's get going." He started down the stairs, and Tim joined him.

"You don't like him?" Tim asked, picking up on the tension.

Doug looked back over his shoulder. "He has a young man living with him," he said quietly. "A young Chinese man, younger than us." He paused, and grimaced like he had a sour stomach. "And there's only one bed."

Tim shrugged. *Who cares?* "He seems like a pretty nice fellow to me."

Doug looked exasperated. "I think he and the young man who lives with him are lovers."

"That doesn't bother me," Tim said, waving it off. "Why should it?"

Doug scowled. "It's not normal."

"Ha! Who is?" Tim said. "The way I figure it, they're not hurting anybody, so why should I care? Why should you?" He paused for a moment, and added as an after-thought, "Besides, I have a good friend who I think might be, you know, like that."

Doug didn't respond right away. After a few seconds he said, "I don't trust those kind of fellows. I never had any experience with that sort before I got to Washington. There seems to be a lot of them there, and they hide behind bushes in Lafayette Park and the National Mall, and have sex with each other."

"Wow, they should just do it in the back seat of a car, like everyone else!" Tim joked.

Doug didn't look amused.

Tim let it go. "So I thought I'd take you to some night clubs on Nanking Road, give you a real taste of Shanghai," he said.

"I've read about some of the nightclubs," Doug said. "The Paramount sounds like the biggest and most popular."

"And a bit occidental," Tim said. "Oh, it's a fun place, don't get me wrong—but I thought for your first Friday in Shanghai I'd take you to some of the Chinese clubs. Nanking Road west of Honan is more Chinese than the spots east of Honan, which are full of westerners. There are several fun places I like to go, and most of the crowd will be Chinese."

"What kind of places are these?" Doug asked.

Tim chuckled. "Don't worry, I'm not taking you to any dives. These joints are every bit as classy as the Cathay or the Paramount—good food, good drinks, decent cabaret shows—just not so many tourists, you know? It's the real Shanghai."

"Sounds like fun."

They exited the building, and Tim said they needed to catch the streetcar on Honan Road to take them downtown.

"So are you a short-timer, or a long-timer?" Tim asked as they walked to the streetcar stop.

"Pardon?" Doug asked.

"In Shanghai—are you here for the short term? Or are you staying long term?"

"Oh, I see what you mean. Long term."

Tim grinned. "Then it's a good thing I decided to show you the real Shanghai. No short-timers where we're going tonight." He cupped his hand around the side of his mouth and leaned closer. "That's what we long-timers call our fellow Westerners who come here for business or what not and stay a few months, then go back home."

"Thanks for the tip," Doug said.

"It's been a really long time since we knew each other," Tim said as they turned onto Honan Road and navigated its denser pedestrian traffic. "Fancy running into you on a street in Shanghai!"

Doug smiled, but his eyes stayed guarded. "Quite a coincidence, isn't it?"

"I don't think we've talked much since we were thirteen," Tim said. "After Carlisle Day School, I went on to public high school, and you left for boarding school, didn't you?"

"Yes, St. James Academy in Monterey."

"I remember seeing you around the neighborhood in the summertime, but you were always in the middle of a bunch of fellas and never saw me or my friends," Tim said. "I assumed it was your friends from prep school."

Doug nodded. "I had a group of really close friends at St. James, we were inseparable I suppose." He shrugged. "You know, you live with these fellows day-in and day-out for months, study together, play sport together, sit together in chapel—it's not like just going to school. It's hard to describe to someone who hasn't experienced that kind of environment."

Tim resisted the urge to roll his eyes. "So what have you done since prep school? We're all grown up now."

Doug nodded. "After St. James I went to Stanford."

"Yeah, I heard that," Tim said. In response to Doug's questioning look, he added, "I caddied for your dad at your country club for a couple of summers, working my way through junior college. He'd talk about you sometimes to the other gentlemen he played with."

Doug didn't respond to that. "I went to Stanford for four years, graduated in '32, and I've spent the last three years working for my father. The company decided we needed someone full-time in China, so I volunteered to come set up the Shanghai office."

Tim acted surprised and confused. "Really? I'd heard you joined the Navy after college. Someone told me—Mary Ellen Burris, I think it was—that you did that *instead* of going to work for your father. She said you'd been shipped off somewhere."

He enjoyed the uncomfortable look that came to Doug's face.

"You know rumors," Doug said with a nervous smile.

They'd reached the streetcar stop, and Tim looked him directly in the eye as they waited. "Yes, I know how rumors are. I'm a reporter, Doug, and a pretty good one—I don't take rumors at face value, but I don't dismiss them, either. I know how to dig for facts, and the facts are you didn't go to work for your father, as you just said, and you haven't lived in San Francisco for years. You *did* join the Navy, right after leaving Stanford as a matter of fact, and you got an officer's commission. Then last Saturday you had lunch with Commander Robert Hilliard, who's one of the Assistant Naval Attachés at the U.S. Embassy in Nanking."

The men stared at each other in silence for a moment.

"So do you mind telling me why you just lied to me?" Tim asked, unblinking.

Doug looked off for a moment. "I apologize if it offended you. I'm just not supposed to advertise my association with the Navy while I'm in Shanghai."

"Oh, I assumed that already," Tim said. "My sources couldn't find out what your job is—that seems to be classified."

Doug exhaled slowly. "It seems you've already got it all figured out, haven't you?"

"Not exactly," Tim said, continuing to stare at Doug, watching his eyes. "The easy assumption is that you're with Naval Intelligence in some capacity—but the problem with that assumption is Naval Attachés and Assistant Naval Attachés aren't classified positions, and the classified positions are all in Washington—which, by the way, is where I know you've been for the last two and a half years."

"You've got good sources," Doug said.

"I've made a lot of friends in the Associated Press the last few years, all over the world," Tim said. "Comes in handy sometimes. We do each other favors. It's a pretty tight club actually—a bit like your prep school chums, I would imagine."

Tim enjoyed the jab, and the brief reaction it brought to Doug's face.

"Everyone knows the Navy gets its intelligence through its attachés, which are not classified positions. Army's the same way. So my question to you is—what are you doing here in Shanghai?"

Doug looked suddenly tired. "It's not really that secret," he said with a half-hearted shrug. "It is classified, technically, but at the lowest level. I'm allowed to discuss it with my family, no questions asked. With others, I'm expected to use my judgment."

Tim raised an eyebrow. "And?"

Doug suddenly looked frightened, which took Tim aback.

"Listen, just don't publish it all over the place, will you? I don't want to read about it in the newspaper one day—like your piece on the Korean Provisional Government this morning. I could get in trouble if this gets publicized that broadly, understand?"

Tim looked him hard in the eye. "OK," he said at length. "But drinks are on you tonight. Dinner too, for that matter—the whole tab all night, got it?"

Doug nodded, looking resigned. "Got it."

He looked up the street at the sound of the streetcar's bell clang, leaned in close and spoke quickly. "Alright, in a nut shell—I've been working as an analyst for ONI the last few years, one of the China specialists. ONI's starting a two-year immersion program in China, and since I'm fluent in two Chinese languages I got one of the first spots. The idea is to develop Intelligence Officers who know China inside and out."

The streetcar came to a stop in front of them, its bell clanging.

"After you," Tim said, and followed Doug up the steps.

The streetcar was almost full, and they took the last two open seats together.

"So was tonight just a ruse to get me to give you a story?" Doug asked, brown eyes narrowed slightly.

Tim chuckled. "Not really. I was dying to spend an evening with you ever since I spotted you in the Cathay last Saturday afternoon."

Doug looked surprised. "Really?"

Tim laughed out loud. "Yeah, really. The rest was just...professional curiosity, I guess you'd say. Curse of the trade, I suppose."

"Why?" Doug leaned forward, looking genuinely interested.

Tim looked away for a few seconds, watched the buildings and storefronts flying by. Why not have it out?

"I suppose I wanted to prove to myself that I was good enough now. Even back in day school, your set looked down on me and my friends. We were as rich as the rest of you, but my father worked with his hands and yours' didn't, and somehow you all knew that. I still remember the jokes at hygiene inspection time—'Don't look under Tim's fingernails, Mrs. Alberts, he's trying to be like his father.'"

"I never said that," Doug said.

"No –but you sure laughed when your chums did, didn't you?"

Doug looked down at his hands.

Tim's anger softened. "You weren't a bad guy, Doug. You were pretty nice, over all. You just ran around with a snotty little clique, and you didn't much notice the rest of us. I liked your sister Francine a lot, though. She might have had a crush on me for a few years, now that I look back on it. She adored you, though."

Doug smiled. "Yeah, Frannie's a peach. She's getting married next month, did you know?"

Tim smiled. "No, I didn't know that. That's wonderful news."

Doug looked at the floor in front of them. "Yeah, it's wonderful. Great fellow. I'm sorry I'll have to miss it."

Tim was caught by surprise by the genuine tone of sadness in Doug's voice. He hesitated a second, unsure what to do, and then awkwardly patted Doug's shoulder. "I'm sure she understands."

Doug straightened, and a forced smile came to his face. "Oh, she understands. She always has."

"This is our stop," Tim said, rising from his seat as the streetcar slowed. Doug followed him, and they jumped off a few seconds before the streetcar came to a stop at the intersection of Honan Road and Nanking Road.

"This way," Tim said, motioning toward the west and starting to walk down Nanking Road. Doug hurried to catch up with him.

"One of my favorite places is just up ahead," Tim said. "The Jade Dragon, excellent place to start the evening."

**

"So I'm dying to know," Tim said, leaning forward with a grin. "Why did you join the Navy instead of going to work for your father's company?"

"You mean like I was expected to?" Doug asked.

"Well, sure. Why *the Navy* of all places?"

They were sitting at a table along the wall of the Jade Dragon, which was decorated in bright red and yellow patterns, with red paper lanterns hanging from the ceiling that muted the electric lights, and jade figurines sitting in little alcoves in the walls at regular intervals, lit by bright electric spotlights. There was a stage to their right with a bright red curtain, a giant gong to one side with a green dragon in the center, and a small orchestra booth beyond the stage. A cloud of cigar and pipe smoke hung above their heads, and the rich smells of many varieties of tobacco filled the air.

Doug shrugged. "It's not a very good story. They approached me at the beginning of senior year—September '31. They were recruiting intelligence analysts who could read Chinese. I turned them down flat. Not interested in the least. They were talking to all the white students studying Mandarin, as it turned out. When they found out I spoke fluent Cantonese, they pushed hard. The captain gave me his business card, even. I'm still not sure why I didn't throw it away. Maybe I thought he could be a business contact someday. Who knows?

"Anyway, things were going downhill fast in '31, you remember, and the economy was a big subject of debate on campus that fall. Four million American workers unemployed. Little did we know what was to come, you know? But we were all engaged. I listened to the arguments, read all the books and newspaper articles, and came to the conclusion on my own that President Hoover's policies weren't helping.

"I went home for Christmas vacation, and the first time my father brought up the subject of politics, and how the 'damned unions' were to blame for the economic woes of the country, I argued back about the failures of President Hoover's Trickle-down policy. Needless to say, that didn't go over well. I don't think I'd ever seen my father's face so red. Even Mother lost her composure at one point and told me, 'Shut your mouth, you vile little heathen!' I was furious, but I apologized anyway. What was I going to do? Disrespect my mother?

"Well, I went back to Stanford in January, and at Easter I said something to my father about what kind of position he had in mind for me, and he gave me the most humiliating look, like he couldn't stand the insolence of me asking about that, even though that's all he'd ever planned for me as far back as I could remember.

"I said, 'Maybe I could work in Will's department.' That's my older brother, William, if you didn't know him. Dad gave him a job when he graduated, and he'd become a manager."

Tim nodded. "I remember him."

Doug continued, the words pouring out of him now. "Father just looked at me like I was some kind of buffoon, like he had no words to express his incredulity. I asked him again, what did he have in mind for me, and he said, 'We don't have any positions open. The Depression, you know, we've had to let people go. I can't be seen giving my son a job when I've fired almost a quarter of the people who worked for me.' And he stormed out. He was really angry. I knew then it wasn't because of the employees he'd let go that he didn't want to hire me—it was because I'd defied him and his dogmas a few months before.

"So when I went back to campus after Easter I dug out the business card the captain had given me, and I telephoned him in Washington. Mother was not pleased when I broke the news. I pointed out that the Bainbridges were seamen for generations—Great-Grandfather Bainbridge was a Connecticut whaler who owned a pair of ships, and he had the foresight in 1855 to see that the China trade was where the money was going to be, so he picked up his family and moved to San Francisco. I thought that might win Dad over, but he didn't say a word. Not a single word."

Doug fell quiet for a moment, looking at his hands on the table, not sure why he'd opened up like that. Tim gave him a sympathetic pat on the shoulder.

"Family can be a hard group to please," he said. "My folks have always been supportive of me, but they never really understood why I came to China, even if there were no jobs back home. And I never have told them about my girl here. She's wonderful, and I adore her—but she's Chinese, and they wouldn't understand."

Doug cleared his throat and looked up, embarrassed. He resumed his erect posture and cleared the sad look from his eyes.

"Well anyway, a week after I graduated Stanford, I entered Basic Training. Six weeks later, I went to Virginia for Intelligence training. Then I moved to Washington, and stayed there until I heard they were looking for immersion candidates in China. I jumped at the chance, and here I am."

"Here you are," Tim agreed. He raised his tumbler. "I'd like to propose a toast—to Shanghai, and all the ways she helps us shock and dismay our folks. Cheers!"

That elicited a grin from Doug, and he raised his high-ball glass of gin and tonic and said, "Cheers."

After they drank, Doug leaned forward, and gave Tim a friendly expression. "So what's your story, Tim? What are you doing here in Shanghai? I know you're a reporter, but that's all."

Tim took a swig of his Black Thorn. "Well, I graduated from junior college five years ago with a certificate in journalism, and promptly learned that didn't mean much to a managing editor who had never taken a journalism class in his life. I did boring jobs like write up the night's arrest records before deadline for the morning edition, and eventually worked my way into slightly less boring assignments like covering City Council meetings in Oakland. Not thrilling, and not what I'd had in mind. I got laid off in February '32 with a whole bunch of other folks, including one fellow who'd worked at the Chronicle for thirty-seven years, and was just three years shy of earning his pension. He got nothing, poor bastard. I was outraged, you know, but what could you do?

"I looked for work, but there weren't any jobs. I even tried little country newspapers out in the valleys—nothing. I got evicted from my apartment in March, and was facing having to move back to my parents' house, and I couldn't stand the thought. Then I heard the AP was hiring foreign correspondents, and I sent them a sample. They hired me, and asked if I'd be interested in going to China. *Hell yes*, I thought, and I accepted. I came to Shanghai, and haven't looked back."

"I guess we both got lucky breaks when things didn't work out as we'd planned," Doug said.

"Yeah, I suppose so," Tim said. "I love the kind of work I get to do here. There's so much for a reporter with the soul of a social crusader to dig into. This city's a refuge for every outcast the world has to offer, and she's also a refuge for the worst scoundrels and pure scum you can imagine."

He leaned in close, a conspiratorial grin spreading across his face, and motioned Doug to lean in too. "Let me tell you what I'm working on now," he whispered, just loudly enough to be heard over the din of conversations.

Doug leaned in, curious. "What is it?"

"There's a whole lot of corruption in Shanghai," Tim said. "The Commissioner for Shanghai on the Chinese Government's Anti-Opium Board, he's the head of the Green Gang, the biggest organized crime racket in the country. They move more opium than anyone else in the whole of Asia. And as Commissioner, Du Yuesheng—Big Eared Du, he's called—he can eliminate his competition. They own half the police force. I've made some pretty shocking discoveries, let me tell you. For starters, I've learned—"

The banging of the gong drowned out all other sound in the club. The curtain parted, the orchestra began to play, and out stepped a long-legged white woman with wavy cinnamon-colored hair in a red sequined gown slit high up the right thigh, surrounded by Chinese chorus girls in white with red parasols.

"Gorgeous, isn't she?" Tim shouted over the orchestral intro, pointing his thumb toward the tall singer. "Her name's Tatiana Molonov. Her father's a Russian Count, for Christ sake. They lost everything to the Bolsheviks, came to Shanghai penniless. Now she sings here, and the Count is the doorman at the Cathay Hotel. After the show, she'll dance with you for a dollar."

Tatiana began singing—Gershwin's "I Got Rhythm," in Chinese—and Tim turned toward the stage, their earlier conversation forgotten.

After the song ended, and Tatiana bowed and exited to thunderous applause, the orchestra played a series of radio show hits, and the chorus girls tap danced.

The maître'd escorted four well-dressed Chinese—three men and a woman—to the table between Tim and Doug's and the dance floor. He swept away the "Reserved" sign from the table, bowed deeply, and held out a chair for the lady.

She caught Doug's eye as she sat, and he detected a hint of smile crossing her lips, which were painted ruby-red. She wore a green sequined evening gown, sleeveless with a plunging neckline revealing a touch of cleavage, and she had a matching green comb holding her black hair in place. In her delicate hand she carried a small green sequined purse that matched her gown. She was young—about Doug's age, he thought, or just a little bit younger—and her face was powdered white, in sharp contrast to the bright red of her lipstick and the black of her penciled eyebrows. She had a long neck and delicate facial features, tapering to a narrow chin.

She had come in on the arm of a middle-aged man, about forty, tall and broad shouldered for the Chinese, in a well-tailored black silk suit with a red rose in the lapel and a cerulean blue tie. Gold cufflinks

53

with little diamonds in a row sparkled in the light. Narrow strips of black mustache swept along the edge of his upper lip. His black hair was oiled and shiny, and perfectly parted on the left. He sat down next to the young woman, his right hand on her elbow.

The other two men also wore dark suits and narrow mustaches, but they were thinner and their hair was slicked backward; they sat after the bigger man and the young woman. All four watched the show for a while, and then the three men began to converse in low voices. On one occasion, Doug saw them glance at their table.

Tim seemed not to notice, he was watching the tap show on the dance floor. Doug watched the men out of the corner of his eye, and about five minutes later they looked over again. This time, it was plain that they were looking in Tim's direction specifically.

Doug nudged Tim's elbow. "Do you know those gentlemen over there?" he asked in Tim's ear.

Tim shrugged. "Never seen them before. Why?"

"They've looked over here a couple of times, as if they're talking about you."

Tim grinned, but Doug thought it looked forced. "I guess I'm more interesting than I thought!" He looked at the men, then faced forward again to watch the show.

Tatiana Molonov came back out to sing a set of Broadway numbers—all in Mandarin—and the waiter brought Doug and Tim a third round of drinks. It was hot in the club, and the drinks went down fast.

The show ended a half-hour later, Tatiana and the chorus girls disappeared backstage, and the curtain closed. The orchestra played a fox trot, and several couples got up to dance.

Doug noticed the three men at the table in front of theirs get up and leave the room, the man in charge whispering briefly in the lady's ear. She looked annoyed, but said nothing. Instead she picked up his half-drunk scotch glass after he left, and tossed back the rest. Then she retrieved her purse from the table, stood, and walked toward the ladies' lounge.

Doug watched her go, watched the elegant sway of her narrow hips.

"How do you like the Jade Dragon?" Tim asked, grinning.

"Very much," Doug said, returning the smile.

"There's not many places in the world where you can hear a Russian dame singing Gershwin or Cole Porter in Chinese, with a full stage production all around her. Pretty swell, huh?"

"I'm really enjoying this," Doug said. "Thank you for bringing me."

"Then maybe we can come here together again sometime," Tim said.

Doug smiled, a bit surprised at how much that appealed to him. It hadn't been easy to make friends in Washington, let alone Shanghai, and it would be nice to have someone to meet up with on the weekends.

"That would be real swell," he said.

"There's Tatiana," Tim said, motioning toward the side of the stage, where the singer had emerged and stood, statuesque, next to the dance floor, appearing to watch the couples doing the fox trot.

"Here," Tim said, slipping a dollar into Doug's right hand. "This one's my treat. Go dance with her. I've got to visit the men's room, then I'm going outside to get some fresh air for a little bit. It's like an oven in here." He fanned himself with his hat, then slipped it on his head and walked toward the exit.

Doug watched Tim disappear around the corner, and slid the dollar into his pocket. He'd find a way to slip it back to Tim unnoticed later on. If Tim had many more of those whiskey drinks he'd ordered, Doug figured it shouldn't be difficult.

He saw the Chinese lady return to the table in front of theirs, folding her arms and looking annoyed. He ignored the Russian singer standing by the dance floor, and instead he approached the elegant young woman sitting alone. He bowed and greeted her in Mandarin.

"Good evening, miss."

She looked startled for a second, but then her face relaxed, and a coy smile crept across her lips. "Good evening, sir."

"I can't understand why three gentlemen would leave a charming and lovely lady such as you all alone," he continued, still in Mandarin.

Her smile disappeared, and she glanced toward the door with a slight scowl. "They'll be back," she said with a tiny disapproving shake of the head. "They have business to conduct. They always have business to conduct."

She looked back at Doug, and this time she gave him a brilliant smile that showed even white teeth. "You speak excellent Mandarin, sir. I'm impressed. Not many Europeans speak it so well."

"I'm American."

"Oh? Even more fascinating."

"May I have a seat?" Doug asked, and she closed her eyes and gave him a genteel nod, her head cocked slightly to the left. He took the seat across from her. With her fine manners, elegant clothing, and crisp bell-like accent in Mandarin, he deduced that she was high-born and well-educated. "My name is Douglas Bainbridge, from San Francisco."

She extended her arm, wrist up in the European fashion, and he kissed her hand.

"A pleasure to meet you, Mr. Bainbridge. I am Ming Lin-wen. How long have you been in China?"

"Just a week," Doug said. "I like it very much."

Her smile became more fixed, polite. "Just a week? Are you staying long in our country?"

"Yes, a few years at least," Doug said. "I live in Shanghai now."

Her smile grew bright again. "Ah, that's wonderful. Hopefully we will see you again, perhaps often."

"Do you and your gentlemen companions come to the Jade Dragon often?" Doug asked.

"From time to time," she said, her smile once again turning coy, and she lowered her eyes, letting the dark lashes partially cover them.

"Who are the gentlemen you are with, may I ask?"

She glanced back at the door with a slight scowl, and waved her hand in the air dismissively. She turned back to him and smiled. "As you can see, I am not with anyone now—except for you."

He felt a tingle in his stomach, and he couldn't help but grin back at her like a schoolboy.

The music changed, and the orchestra played a slower jazz melody. Couples on the dance floor began to waltz.

"Would you care to dance?" he asked.

She cast a quick glance at the door, and then held out her hand. "I would love to."

He led her to the dance floor, and waltzed her around the floor. He noticed Tatiana Molonov waltzing with an older Chinese man, balding and probably late fifties, at least half a foot shorter than she; and yet she beamed at him the entire time he spun her around.

"Do you live in Shanghai, Miss Ming?" he asked.

"Yes. My family has a house on Broadway, near the Garden Bridge."

"I was in that area just yesterday," Doug said, recalling the enormous mansions that lined Broadway, at the entrance to the Hongkou district. "It's quite lovely. Do you live with your parents there?"

"My parents live in Nanjing now—my father is in the government, you see. They come to Shanghai on occasion."

"Besides going to places like the Jade Dragon, what do you do?" he asked, genuinely interested.

"I supervise the house and the gardens, manage the servants and the accounts. I entertain ladies for tea some afternoons, or go calling. And at least once a week I go downtown to shop on Nanjing Road. What do you do, Mr. Bainbridge?"

"I work for my father, and we import Chinese goods to the United States. I'm going to open a new office here in Shanghai."

She smiled, but he saw in her eyes that she wasn't really interested in his business, any more than she was interested in the business her gentlemen companions had left to discuss.

They finished the waltz, and returned to her table. He held her chair, and as she sat he saw the big-shouldered man returning without his two companions. Doug turned to her and bowed. "You are a lovely dancer, Miss Ming. I hope I have the honor again sometime."

He returned to his table as the large man passed, and the man looked him square in the eyes. Doug wasn't able to read his expression.

Another show started, with Tatiana singing the standards while the Chinese chorus girls tap-danced around her. Doug looked toward the door, surprised that Tim hadn't returned. He'd been gone more than thirty minutes.

After the second song, Doug asked the waiter for the bill, paid it, and collected his hat. Ming Lin-wen looked over as he stood, and their eyes met for a second before she looked back toward the stage. He went outside, and the sultry night air felt cool in comparison to the stuffy air in the club.

He looked around, but saw no sign of Tim.

Several people stood around, talking and smoking, some laughing. Almost all of them were Chinese. He approached groups and asked in his mix of Mandarin and Shanghainese if they had seen a slender young white man in a light blue suit. The first few groups shook their heads, but then a young woman and her boyfriend said they had seen that man a while ago.

"He was talking with two other men, both Chinese," the young man said. "They went around the corner a long time ago."

"I think they were having tense words," the young woman volunteered. "It was not friendly."

"They went that way?" Doug pointed east, and they nodded. He thanked them and hurried that direction, concerned, but not sure why. He turned the corner they had indicated, but saw no sign of Tim. This side street was not well-lit, and fewer pedestrians walked the sidewalks.

He began to call Tim's name, walking slowly, looking in all of the doorways and alley entrances.

Then he saw him, lying face-down between two trash cans on wet cobblestones.

"Tim! Are you alright?" he called, rushing toward him.

He reached Tim in a few seconds, knelt down and shook his shoulder. Then he realized with a start that the wetness on the cobblestones was a pool of blood—a pool spreading out from Tim's body.

He turned him over, and the air caught in his throat.

Tim's eyes were open and glassy, staring straight up at the night sky. A huge bloody gash stretched across his throat, deep and gaping. The blood no longer flowed from the wound, but had congealed into a thick goo that shined in the moonlight.

"Oh Tim," he breathed, feeling his own tense body deflate. Then he looked back down the alley toward the street, and shouted.

"Help! Please, somebody, I need the police! Help!"

5

The Detective sat across a metal table from Doug in a bare interrogation room at the Central District precinct, reading the statement Doug had given to the constables who arrived about ten minutes after he'd discovered Tim's body. The constables had interviewed him and the residents who had responded to Doug's shouts, and after the two detectives arrived—one white, one Chinese—the police had brought him down to the station, where he'd waited alone in this room.

The white detective had finally come into the room, introduced himself perfunctorily as Detective Sergeant Phillips, and sat down to read. He had a thick brown mustache and pocked cheeks.

To Doug it seemed that he didn't want to be there.

"So Mr. Bainbridge," he said in a working class English accent, looking up from the page. "It appears you were the last one to see Mr. McIntyre alive, other than his killer."

"No one in the buildings above the alley saw anything?" Doug asked, unable to keep the incredulous tone from his voice.

The detective folded his arms and took on an imperious posture. "I know that probably seems strange to a Yank, since interfering with your neighbors is a national preoccupation where you come from, but here in China people really do mind their own business—often to a fault, as in these unfortunate circumstances. It ain't always easy to find reliable witnesses to a homicide."

Doug's posture stiffened. The detective's attitude rankled, and he wasn't confident they were taking this as seriously as they should.

"Did your officers interview *everyone* in the buildings?"

"They knocked on all of the doors on the sides that faced the alley where you found Mr. McIntyre's body, talked to anyone who answered the door. No one saw or heard a thing. You'd be surprised how often we run up against that wall."

"How many people were interviewed?"

It was Detective Sergeant Phillips' turn to look annoyed. "I don't know exactly, can't remember the figure off hand. Quite a few."

"Detective, it was barely after ten o'clock. It was too early for everyone to be turned in for the night. Someone *had* to see something."

"Detective *Sergeant*, if you please, sir." Phillips wore a scowl and kept his arms folded across his chest. "Listen, Mr. Bainbridge—even if someone did see something, they ain't saying nothing, and I know from years of experience on this force that you can't force 'em to talk if they don't want to. The Chinese are the most bloody stubborn race in the whole damned world, if you ask me—an' every other white copper on the force. I tell ya, this happens all the bloody time. Yeah, it's frustrating, for all of us, but that's Shanghai, gov."

Doug took a deep breath, tried a different tack. He leaned forward, placed his hands on the table, and softened his eyes and his tone just short of pleading.

"Please, Detective Sergeant—this was my friend, my only friend in Shanghai, and I can't accept that you're unable to track down his killer."

Phillips sighed, and unfolded his arms. He stared Doug hard in the eyes for several seconds before he replied.

"Armed robberies happen dozens of times a day in the International Settlement. Sometimes they go horribly bad, and the victim winds up six foot under. Even if we manage to identify the robbers and give pursuit, nine times out of ten they cross the boundary out of the Settlement into either the French Concession or Chinese territory, and we have to stop chasing 'em. If we're really lucky, we can convince the police in the French Concession to take up the trail, but if it's Chinese territory, they're as good as gone. In your friend's case, we don't even know who the robbers were, and likely never will. I'm sorry, sir."

Doug nodded slowly, figuring this was probably true. "Why do you think it was a robbery?"

"Simple. His wallet was found in the trash down the far end of the alley, and it was empty. Only his identification papers, no cash. No coins in his pockets, no watch on his wrist. No cuff links, no ring, nothing a man on the town would be expected to have. Only thing he had on him was the key to his apartment."

Doug sighed and leaned back in the hard wooden chair. "So whoever killed him wanted it to look like a robbery."

"I'm tellin' you, it *was* a robbery. I've seen more of these than I care to remember, and I know a robbery gone bad when I see one."

"What about what that couple told me outside the Jade Dragon? They saw Tim talking with two Chinese men, and said the conversation was tense. Then he went with them around the corner—which is where I followed right before I found him in an alley off that street."

"We never located the two you say told you that story," Phillips said, his expression hard. "There were hundreds of people in and out of the Jade Dragon all evening, and any number could've fit the description you gave."

"That I 'say' told me that? I didn't make it up, Detective Sergeant."

"I didn't say you did, Mr. Bainbridge."

Doug took another deep breath, trying to fight the exasperation welling up. This was getting nowhere. "What's the next step?"

"Detective Sergeant Xiong and I will put feelers out for any leads, and let you know if we learn anything helpful. You just let us worry about that, alright?"

"Alright," Doug said, though he hardly agreed.

"I hate to ask you this now, I know this is difficult, but who's going to be in charge of Mr. McIntyre's personal effects?"

It occurred to Doug that he had no idea who should get Tim's things. He didn't know Tim's girlfriend, didn't even know her name. He didn't know exactly where Tim lived. But Tim's identification papers would tell him that.

"I'll take them," he said.

"You can pick up the body for burial at the morgue tomorrow after the forensics examination is finished, probably mid-afternoon. Bring whatever clothes you want him buried in—unless you don't mind the orderlies down there stuffing him into the coffin naked."

Doug found himself getting unexpectedly choked up. He wasn't sure why—he hadn't known Tim well, they weren't really friends—and yet, he'd really enjoyed Tim's company this evening, and it had made him feel free to be able to talk to him as he had. He kept his composure with effort.

"Where do I pick him up?"

"You come to the station, and tell the constable at the desk that you're picking up a body from the morgue. He'll walk you down there. You give the clothes to the orderlies, an' they'll dress the body. They'll provide your basic pine box, but if you want something fancier you've got to bring it yourself. You can provide your own transportation for the coffin, or for twenty Shanghai dollars one of our drivers will transport the coffin to the funeral."

Ten minutes later, a Chinese constable brought him a paper bag containing Tim's clothes, shoes, and wallet. He could see the rust-colored blood stains on the collar of the jacket and white shirt, the well-worn brown leather wallet lying on top of them.

Doug waited until he was out on the sidewalk before retrieving Tim's identity papers from the wallet and finding his address. It was late, but there were still a few rickshaws out on the main streets, and he hailed one a few blocks away on Nanking Road. He gave the coolie Tim's address.

It turned out to only be a few blocks from Doug's apartment, just a little to the east. So Tim hadn't been lying about that last Saturday afternoon outside of the store. Doug felt oddly comforted by that discovery. He paid the coolie two quarters and got out, carrying the paper bag.

He tried the front door of the building, and found it unlocked. He was about to go up the stairs when the door to his left opened, and an older Chinese man came out. He gave Doug a suspicious look. "Who wantchee?" he asked in Pidgin.

Doug answered in his mix of Shanghainese and Mandarin. "I'm going up to Tim McIntyre's apartment."

"No can do," the man answered in Pidgin.

Doug replied in Chinese, "I'm his friend. Is his girlfriend at home?"

The man stared at him for several seconds, seeming to appraise him. Then the suspicion left his face and he shook his head. "They are not home. What do you want?" he asked in Shanghainese.

"I went out with Tim this evening. Tim was killed. I need to speak with his girlfriend. Do you know when she'll be home?"

The man bowed his head and kept it there for a moment, standing perfectly still. When he looked up, his eyes were wet.

"That is very sad. Mr. McIntyre was a good tenant, a good man. We will miss him."

"Do you know when his girlfriend will be home?" Doug pressed, gently.

"Li Sung isn't staying at home right now," the man said. He seemed reluctant to go on.

"Do you know where she is? It's important that I talk to her. I have to tell her what happened to Tim."

Doug dreaded that conversation. In everything that had happened tonight, he hadn't stopped to imagine the reaction he'd likely get when delivering the news to someone who loved Tim.

And then he thought of Tim's parents in San Francisco. Who was going to tell them? That responsibility also seemed to be his. *Damn it!* How had he inherited these morbid tasks?

The older man in front of him nodded. "I am Chen Gwan, I am Mr. McIntyre's landlord," he said. "Li Sung is in a sanitarium downtown. Mr. McIntyre took her there after she got off the opium. She's been there two weeks, has one more week there."

That was unexpected, but Doug stayed calm. "Where is it?"

"Downtown somewhere. I don't know exactly. Tim found it from that white priest at the church on Tianjian Road."

Doug's eyes widened. "The Presbyterian church?"

Mr. Chen shrugged. "I don't know, they're all the same to me."

"Thank you, Mr. Chen. I'll speak to the minister there in the morning. May I go upstairs to Tim's apartment? I have the key."

Mr. Chen nodded. "I'll go with you."

Doug stepped aside to let the older man climb the stairs ahead of him. It was a four-story building, but Mr. Chen climbed all the way to the top floor without growing visibly winded. *Impressive for a man his age*, Doug thought.

Chen led him to the door, and stood aside for Doug to unlock it.

The apartment was dark, but Doug could hear the soft whir of an electric fan on the far side of the room—the same fan he'd bought, he recalled. A little bit of light spilled in through the open door from the hallway, and after a few seconds Doug's eyes had adjusted enough to see the shadow of a lamp on a table in the corner. He walked towards it, taking small steps lest some unseen object on the floor trip him, and pulled the cord.

The layout of the apartment was surprisingly similar to his own, and Doug figured most of the buildings in this neighborhood were built around the same time by the same builders, thirty-five or forty years ago. It was much better decorated, however, and Doug had no trouble imagining a feminine hand at work. The curtains were cerulean blue, which complemented the lighter shades of blue that patterned the wallpaper, reminiscent of the colors and patterns he'd seen on countless Chinese porcelain vases his father's company imported. A cabinet of blue china stood in the kitchenette.

He set down the paper bag in a corner. "I need to see if he has a suit for the burial," he told Mr. Chen before walking down the hall to the bedroom.

He turned on another lamp when he reached the bedroom. Signs of Tim's presence were visible everywhere. A half-full glass of water sat on top of the dresser, Tim's fingerprints visible on the outside. A damp white shirt was flung on the back of a chair next to a whirring fan on the bedside table, and a white sleeveless undershirt lay on the bed. A pair of boxer shorts and socks lay on the floor next to the bed. A slightly frayed towel hung from a peg on the back of the bedroom door, and it too was damp.

"Nothing ever fucking dries here," Doug muttered, too tired to care that he'd used such language out loud.

Doug opened the closet door, where he found a few hanging shirts that ranged from white, to off-white, to light blue. Three neckties hung from pegs on the wall. An empty suit bag hung next to the shirts; this must be from the suit Tim had worn that evening. He found another suit bag delineating Tim's side of the closet from the other side where a woman's clothes hung, and pulled it out.

He laid it on the bed, unbuttoned it, and was relieved to see a black suit inside. Doug assumed Tim had been brought up to know that every gentleman needed to own a black suit, and he figured Tim needed one even in Shanghai for business meetings. Doug got out a white dress shirt and a black necktie, put them inside the suit bag and buttoned it back up.

That task completed, Doug set about looking for Tim's address book. He'd need to send a cable to Tim's parents in San Francisco. He wasn't sure what he was going to say yet, but first things first.

He found Tim's address book easily enough in one of the desk drawers. He was about to slip it inside his coat pocket, when curiosity overtook him and he opened it to the B tab. He found his name and Shanghai address written neatly in pencil.

He glanced at the file drawer in the desk, and after a few seconds' hesitation he crouched down and opened it. He thumbed through the first several files—sorted alphabetically, as he'd assumed—and found one labeled "Bainbridge, Doug." It was a thin manila folder, and he pulled it out and opened it. It contained a single piece of notebook paper with a few scribbled notes:

> May 25 '35, Cathay Hot restrnt, DB lunch w/ cmdr Rbrt Hilliard (asst naval attaché)
> DB left San Fran June '32—not SF res (G Lloyd, AP SF Cal)
> DB – Lt Cmd Navy, job unk/classfd, res Wash DC (K Hartmann, AP Wash)

As Doug read the notes in Tim's shorthand, it occurred to him that the answer to Tim's murder might be hidden in the files in this desk drawer. The thought sent a shiver down his spine.

His mind began to race. There was no time to look through them all, not with Mr. Chen waiting in the next room. Would they be safe if he left them? Probably, but wasn't there a chance the killer might come here looking for something? If Doug waited until morning, might he lose vital evidence forever?

He looked around for some way to take them with him. He needed a large box, preferably one with a lid so Mr. Chen wouldn't see what was inside.

He looked in the closet, saw a couple of hat boxes. Not big enough, he decided. There was a coat closet in the short hall that connected the bedroom to the rest of the apartment, so he hurried there and opened the door to look inside.

"Almost finished?" Mr. Chen called from the main room. Out of the corner of his eye, Doug could see him standing by the open door.

"Yes Mr. Chen, I'm almost finished," Doug said. There was a large box on the floor, and he knelt down to look inside. He found a shoe shine kit, an electric iron, a sewing kit, and a few tools—hammer, screwdriver, wrench, pliers. He removed all of these as quickly as he could, and set them on the ground in the corner of the closet without making a sound.

He took the empty box and hurried back into the bedroom. He removed stacks of files and stood them in the box.

When he'd emptied the file drawer, he quickly looked through the other desk drawers for anything else that might prove informative, and he took Tim's date books for 1934 and 1935.

The box had no lid, so he draped the suit bag across the top. Pleased with the effect, he carried it to the main room. "All finished," he said.

Mr. Chen looked at the box for several seconds, but didn't ask about it. Still, Doug felt obligated to offer some explanation.

"Things to send to his parents in California."

"Ah, yes," Mr. Chen said, nodding. "You are a good friend to think of his parents."

Doug felt a slight pang of remorse for the lie, but it had been necessary, and he pushed the feeling aside.

"Thank you for your help, Mr. Chen," Doug said as they walked out into the hall. He set the box and suit bag on the ground, fished Tim's key from his pants pocket and locked the door. "I'll let you know when the funeral arrangements have been made."

"Tomorrow or day after, makes no difference to me and Mrs. Chen," the landlord said. "We will walk for Mr. McIntyre."

Not sure what that meant, Doug followed him down the stairs, and the landlord escorted him to the front door, bidding him goodnight.

He'd walked about two blocks when he realized he was being followed.

It was almost midnight, and the streets in this quiet residential area were nearly empty of people, only a few here and there , in pairs or trios returning home from a night out, and these walked the opposite direction than Doug, most likely coming from the streetcar stops on Honan Road.

But the footsteps behind him were alone, keeping pace with him, and they had started within a moment of leaving Tim's building.

The way home rounded two corners, and after turning the first one Doug listened closely to see if the footfalls continued his way. They did.

Doug turned around, but only saw a shadowy figure duck into a doorway. He turned back and picked up his pace. It was only a block to the second corner onto Huang Lei Road, Doug's own street. From here it was just two blocks to his building.

He heard the footsteps behind him again, and his heart pounded as he turned onto Huang Lei Road.

Ahead of him, strolling toward him down the middle of the street with his hands behind his back, Doug recognized the young English constable who patrolled his neighborhood most nights, Constable Billy Dickinson, and he began to breathe easier. Within seconds, the footfalls behind him stopped, then reversed.

"Good evening, Mr. Bainbridge," Billy Dickinson said, touching his fingers to his hat rim as he approached. "A bit later than usual this evening. Did you have a nice night out?"

"I did at first," Doug said, and stopped walking. "My friend Tim McIntyre and I went out this evening, to the Jade Dragon."

"Oh, very nice place," Billy said. "Went there with some blokes from the force a couple weeks back, lovely time, loads of fun."

"Yes, well...my friend left to get some air after the first show, but he didn't come back. I found him dead in an alley. He'd been killed, throat cut."

"Oh God!" Billy said, sounding genuinely concerned. "I'm dreadfully sorry to hear that, Mr. Bainbridge, sir. What a bloody rotten thing to happen. Is there anything I can do?"

Maybe get your colleagues at the Central District precinct to do their jobs, Doug thought. But he just shook his head. "Thank you for the offer, but I don't think there's anything you can do. I appreciate the gesture."

Billy Dickinson patted his shoulder. "Not a gesture, mate. I meant it, so if you think of anything I can help with, you just let me know. I pass by here every hour. Good night, Mr. Bainbridge."

Billy touched the rim of his police hat again, and resumed his patrol down the street.

6

Doug barely slept, tossing and turning on top of the covers, unable to get his mind to shut down, just dozing in and out of consciousness.

At one point he must have slept, for he had a disturbing dream about being followed down a foggy street, hearing the echo of footsteps louder and louder, until they were far louder than real life could ever be. He wanted desperately to know who was following him, but something kept telling him not to look around. He grew frightened, and began to run, and the steps behind him began to run also. Finally he found himself in a dead-end at the back of an alley, and he turned around. A giant dragon, green and shimmering, emerged from the fog. It opened its enormous jaws, sharp teeth as big as his face looming closer and closer.

He felt the dragon's hot breath on his face, then he awoke with a start, sitting up with a sharp cry, and saw that he was sitting naked on top of his bed, dripping sweat, and a sudden blast of hot summer breeze had come in the window and awakened him.

He lay back down, his heart pounding against his breast bone, and stared at the ceiling. When the pale light of dawn began to make shadows on the walls, he got up, dressed in last night's rumpled clothing, ran a comb through his hair, and left.

He kept his eyes and ears alert as he walked toward Honan Road, but there was no indication that anyone was following him. He hoped the streetcars ran this early on a Saturday morning; he didn't want to walk downtown. He was in luck, and he hopped off the streetcar at the Peking Road stop and walked to the American Express office.

It was ten minutes to seven when he walked through the door. A wooden sign on the counter with removable blocks announced that it was Saturday, June 1, 1935. There was only one customer at the counter at this early hour, but Doug thought he recognized the dress and the short plump figure.

Then he definitely recognized her voice.

"I'd like to send a message to the United States, please," she said in an exaggerated slow and loud voice. "I'm Mrs. Herbert Kinzler, and I need to send a cable to my husband, that's Mr. Herbert Kinzler, in Chicago, Illinois. That's I-L-L-I-N-O-I-S. Don't forget the 'S' at the end, we just don't pronounce it."

The tired-looking young man at the counter, who appeared to be of mixed heritage—half white, half Asian—answered her in an American accent. "Don't worry, Mrs. Kinzler, I know how to spell Illinois."

"Oh! You speak very good English!" she said, at normal pace this time, but still overly loud.

"I'm from Seattle, Mrs. Kinzler," the young man said, somehow managing to keep his patience.

Doug suppressed the urge to laugh out loud.

"What is your message, ma'am?" the young man asked, pencil ready. He wrote it down on a form as she dictated.

"Leaving Shanghai Monday AM. Stop. Taking Yangtze River cruise with Lucy, stop. No, make that just the letter "L," capital L, and stop. Arrive Chungking Sunday AM, stop. Will write. All our love, Lucinda."

The clerk finished writing, and turned the form around to face her. "Sign here please, Mrs. Kinzler, and I'll get that sent as soon as there's a free wire on the cable. That will be $26.70 U.S., please."

"Gracious, so expensive from here."

"It's a long way, ma'am."

"It's as expensive as two nights in our hotel." She removed a wallet from her purse and handed him three $10 bills. He went to the cash register and came back with change. Doug watched her take the change, and hand back just a dime as his tip.

"How soon will you be able to send that?" she asked.

"Probably within the next five or ten minutes, ma'am," the young man said. "There's more inbound traffic on the cable than outbound at this time of day, we shouldn't have too much trouble securing an open wire."

"Let me make sure I've got this right," she said, looking up in thought. "It's seven AM here, and the difference is 13 hours, so that makes it six PM there—Friday or Saturday night?"

"Friday night, ma'am," the clerk said, while slipping her message through a chute that would take it to the telegraph operator. He looked over her to Doug, and said "Next, please."

Mrs. Kinzler turned around to leave, and her eyes widened in surprise when she recognized Doug. She smiled at him. "Why, Mr. Bainbridge! What a pleasant surprise."

"Good morning, Mrs. Kinzler," Doug said, returning her smile. "How are you?"

"Very well, thank you. Lucy and I have enjoyed Shanghai this past week. I would love to stay here longer, but she insists we take a river boat up the Yangtze to see some gorges."

"Yes, the Yangtze Gorges are quite famous," Doug said. "I look forward to seeing them myself sometime."

"Well perhaps you can come along," she suggested, her face lighting up at the prospect. "I'm sure the river boat has state rooms still available, and I know Lucy would be happy to see you again."

Still her daughter's matchmaker, Doug thought with mild amusement. He wondered if Lucy would be annoyed to know about this conversation, or if she'd be eager to see him again.

"Unfortunately, Mrs. Kinzler, I have work to do. That's why I'm here, in fact; I have to send a cable to San Francisco before business closes. It's still Friday afternoon there, you see."

"Oh, yes of course. We're here until Monday morning, feel free to call on us at the Astor House Hotel. It's on Broadway by the Garden Bridge. Good day, Mr. Bainbridge."

The clerk had busied himself with the papers on the desk, but he looked up when Doug stepped up to the desk. "May I help you, sir?"

"I need to send a cable to San Francisco, but I confess I'm not really sure what to say. Perhaps you can offer some advice? You see, my friend was killed last night, and I need to let his parents know—but I've never had to tell someone that their son was dead, and I don't know how to do that delicately in a cablegram."

The young man looked startled. "Oh, I see. That is difficult. Well, during the Great War, didn't the War Department send telegrams to the families of soldiers killed in battle?"

"Yes, I suppose so," Doug agreed. "It just seems wrong to send them a short message that their son is dead, but there isn't really any other way, is there?"

"We do have a telephone, sir," the clerk offered, though his expression was doubtful. "But it's thirty-nine dollars for three minutes to call, and the sound isn't very good. And it can take thirty or forty minutes to connect."

Doug shook his head. "No, I'll send a cable."

"I'm very sorry sir," the clerk said, getting his pencil ready. "I can mark it urgent, so it will go on the next open wire, ahead of any other waiting messages. It's double the price, but that will also put it in line ahead of other messages received at the San Francisco office for the next available delivery boy. It would be in their hands in less than thirty minutes."

"That's fine, thanks."

"What name and address, sir?"

Doug gave the name of Tim's father, and their address on Russian Hill in San Francisco. *Just a few blocks from Mother and Dad's house.*

"And what is the message?" The clerk's tone was sympathetic.

Doug thought for a few seconds. "Terrible news from Shanghai, stop. Tim McIntyre killed Friday PM, stop. Unknown assailant, police investigating, stop." He paused, unsure. "I should probably give them my address to reply, shouldn't I?"

The clerk gave him a sympathetic look. "I would, sir. We can receive cablegrams for you at this office, but under the circumstances you probably want it delivered."

"Alright, then the last line is 'Deepest condolences, Douglas Bainbridge 118 Huang Lei Road, stop.'"

The clerk finished writing, counted up the characters, and said "That will be $25.34 U.S. for the message, plus another $25.34 for the priority delivery."

Doug handed him $51 and told him to keep the change. *More than triple Mrs. Kinzler's tip*, he thought with satisfaction.

"Thank you, sir. Sign here, please."

Doug signed it, and watched the clerk slip it into a chute marked "Urgent/Priority." *Well, that's that. No going back now,* he thought. He thanked the clerk and turned to leave.

"I've very sorry about your friend, Mr. Bainbridge," the clerk called after him.

Doug paused for a moment. "I'll get breakfast at the Cathay Hotel. If they reply quickly, would you deliver the message to me there? I'll be home by eight. After that, you can deliver it to me at home."

"Absolutely; my pleasure, Mr. Bainbridge."

**

Doug drank his tea, deep in thought. He barely picked at the red bean pastry in front of him. He was picturing Mrs. McIntyre—he thought he could remember what she looked like—receiving the cablegram at their home, bursting into tears upon reading it, and throwing herself onto a sofa, distraught. Then she'd probably pick up the telephone and call her husband at his office—it would be about four-thirty there now—and he imagined her bursting into tears all over again as she relayed the news.

Doug had no idea if Tim had any siblings, or nieces and nephews. Probably so. He wished he'd gotten to know Tim better when they were younger; perhaps they could have been friends.

He shook his head to clear that thought from his mind; no sense having regrets about things done or not done twelve years ago, when they were only thirteen.

He drained the tea in his cup, placed a few coins on the table to pay the bill, and got up. He was halfway through the cavernous lobby when he saw the clerk from the American Express office hurry through the revolving door, his eyes scanning the room and settling on Doug with a look of relief.

"Mr. Bainbridge, sir—I'm glad I caught you," he said, handing over a sealed cablegram marked "Urgent/Priority."

"Thank you, Mr.—"

"Thompson, sir. Dan Thompson."

"Thank you, Mr. Thompson." Doug handed him two quarters, which the young man accepted with a nod and spun around to hurry out the door.

Doug settled into one of the big plush armchairs and ripped open the cablegram.

RECEIVED NEWS OF TIM'S DEATH, STOP
WOULD LIKE TO SPEAK BY TELEPHONE, STOP

COST NOT IMPORTANT, CONFIRM AVAILABLE, STOP
F. G. MCINTYRE, SF CAL USA

Doug wanted to bury his face in his hands, but settled for a deep sigh of resignation. He had hoped he might go home for a few hours of sleep before having to go to the Presbyterian Church, locate and visit the sanitarium where Tim's girlfriend was staying, and perhaps have to pick up Tim's body from the morgue.

Instead, he took himself back to the American Express office, composed a cablegram reply to Mr. McIntyre, saying that he would indeed be available to speak by telephone at the American Express office, and settled in to wait.

It was 50 minutes before the clerk at the desk shouted his name, rousing him from a doze in a chair in the lobby, and called him to the telephone.

He took a deep breath. "This is Douglas Bainbridge."

"Mr. Bainbridge, I've had the pleasure of meeting your father on a couple of occasions. This is Frank McIntyre. Thank you for cabling us about Tim." The scratchy voice sounded as if it were shouting from the end of a long pipe.

There was static-filled silence, and Doug said in a near shout, "I'm terribly sorry about your loss, sir."

"Thank you, we appreciate that." Another few seconds of silence, and Doug imagined Mr. McIntyre trying to compose himself. Then the gruff voice returned. "It's a most difficult situation, you see, Tim's death being on the other side of the world and all. There's little his mother and I can do. I suppose he'll have to be buried there in China." His tone didn't sound pleased.

"I'd be happy to do anything I can, sir," Doug heard himself saying, and cringed on the inside. "I'll do anything I can to make things easier for you and Mrs. McIntyre."

"Thank you, Mr. Bainbridge. May I call you Douglas?"

"Doug, please."

"Thank you, Doug. I'd be happy to wire money to cover the costs, but I'm afraid I'm powerless to make any arrangements. Would you handle that for us?"

"Yes, of course," Doug said, quietly.

"What was that, son?"

"I said 'Yes, of course.' As a matter of fact, I'm meeting with the minister at the Presbyterian Church later this morning. I believe Tim had met him."

"That's good, thank you. Makes sense—we always went to Presbyterian Church on Easters. Tim wouldn't have objected, I'm sure."

Doug didn't know how to respond to that. Instead he just asked, "Is there anything in particular you want said or done at the service?"

"No, nothing specific. I'm sure the minister can say the appropriate things. Be sure to cable me with all the costs, and wire instructions to get you reimbursed."

"I will, sir. Um, about Tim's belongings..." Doug let his voice trail off.

"Yes, another difficulty," Mr. McIntyre said, and paused. "I don't know that we would want much, just some mementos. Perhaps some clothes, any photographs he might have—I think his mother would appreciate that. The rest you can do with as you will. Again, I'll be happy to reimburse you all costs associated with all of this."

"I'll take care of it, sir."

"One last thing before this call breaks the bank—what happened to Tim?"

Doug hesitated, unsure how honest to be. "He was killed. The police think it was a robbery gone bad."

"Do you believe that, Doug?"

Doug hesitated again, closed his eyes, and took a deep breath. "No, sir."

"I don't either. I know my boy, and he's an activist—*was* an activist. I like to think he got a little of that from me, but most of it is pure him. People like Tim do a lot of good in this cynical world of ours, but they also make a lot of enemies. Sometimes bad enemies. My boy was never good at protecting himself from that side of things. I'm afraid it's what got him in the end."

"That's very well put, sir. I couldn't have said it better myself. I'll make sure the pastor puts those words into the eulogy—what I mean is—"

"I understand what you mean, and we appreciate that more than you can know. Listen, we can't hold up the wire, and this call is costing a fortune, so I'm going to leave it to you to make the arrangements, and bill me the cost. We'll trust your judgment."

"Thank you, sir," Doug said, but the line had already gone dead.

He breathed a heavy sigh, glad that was over. The call had only lasted four minutes, but it had felt like an eternity. He thanked the clerk and hurried out the door.

The doors of the Presbyterian Church on Tianjian Road were locked, but the sign on the wall had a phone number "For Emergencies." Doug went back home, knocked on Mr. Hwang's door, and asked if he could make a phone call.

"If you pay me twenty-five cents, you may make a phone call," Mr. Hwang said.

Twenty-five cents seemed an awful lot for a local phone call— these were generally just a nickel back in the States—but Doug gave him a quarter and was directed to the telephone in the office of Mr. Hwang's store.

He closed the door but didn't latch it, and dialed the operator. He gave her the telephone number from the church sign.

A woman's pleasant voice answered, first in Shanghainese, then English. "Hello?"

81

"Yes, I'm calling for Rev. Allen," Doug said. "It's a bit urgent, someone has died."

"Oh, I'm terribly sorry! Just one moment, please."

Doug heard the telephone receiver on the other end drop and hit the wall. He heard the woman's muffled voice say, "Nathan! Telephone. It's an American on the line, saying someone has died."

Doug heard the shuffle of a chair moving across hard wood, and heavy footsteps approaching the telephone. Then he heard the receiver scrape the wall as it was lifted, and the minister's voice. "This is Rev. Allen."

"Rev. Allen, this is Doug Bainbridge. We spoke on Sunday."

"Yes, Mr. Bainbridge. It's a pleasure to hear from you—although I understand from Mrs. Allen that the circumstances aren't so pleasant."

"No, I'm afraid not. A friend of mine has died—been killed, actually. It's someone you've met, I believe—Tim McIntyre."

"Oh no!" Rev. Allen's genuine surprise startled Doug. "Poor Tim—just when he was making so many positive changes. What happened?"

"The police don't really know." *And aren't trying that hard to find out, either.*

"Oh, gosh. What a tragedy. He was a fine young man."

"You knew him well?" Doug asked, not prepared for the emotional response from the minister.

"Not terribly well, no—but we'd talked a few times over the last couple of weeks or so. He had a very strong moral compass, that was obvious. I enjoyed our conversations. He came here for Easter the last few years, and then for the last couple of weeks circumstances conspired to bring us together for a common purpose."

Doug appreciated that the pastor was keeping Tim's confidence, even in death. That was commendable—but not helpful under the circumstances. "Yes, I understand you may be able to help me with the location of the sanitarium where Tim's girlfriend is staying right now."

There was a momentary silence on the line, and then Rev. Allen said, "Yes, certainly. I didn't realize Tim had spoken of this to anyone."

"To be honest, Rev. Allen, he didn't tell me—I learned of it from his landlord, Mr. Chen. But unfortunately Mr. Chen didn't know the name or location of the sanitarium, and someone needs to inform Tim's girlfriend." He paused for a second, and then added, "It seems to have fallen to me to notify everyone."

"That's not an easy job. I'm very sorry to hear that burden has been placed on you, son. Is there anything I can do to help you?"

"Well, you can do the funeral. Also, I'm not really sure how to go about arranging Tim's burial, or even to get Tim's body out of the morgue."

"I can take care of Tim's body, from the morgue to the cemetery," Rev. Allen said. "You needn't worry about that part."

Doug felt his entire body sag with relief. "Thank you," he said, genuinely heartfelt. "I have clothes that he can be buried in. Should we schedule the funeral for Monday? Or for Tuesday?"

"Good heavens, no! Tomorrow at the latest, if not this evening."

This took Doug aback. "I'm not sure when the death will be announced in the newspaper. And I haven't arranged for a proper obituary." He wasn't sure how many friends Tim had in Shanghai, who would read the obituary and want to come to the funeral.

"No, it doesn't work like that here," Rev. Allen explained. "You see, once he leaves the morgue, the body will start to decay rapidly in this weather. There is no embalming to speak of around here. It's not like home. At the morgue, it's kept very cold, and his body will keep a day or two. Once it's brought out, it needs to be buried within hours."

"I didn't realize," Doug said, grateful that the minister would handle the arrangements, and especially grateful that he'd spoken with Rev. Allen before retrieving the body himself. That could have turned into a disaster.

"Well, how would you have? You haven't been in Shanghai long enough to have learned that."

"Thank you, Reverend. I'm terribly grateful to you."

"Don't mention it. I'm honored to be of service to Tim. He was a fine young man. It's such a terrible shame we won't get to see what great things he might have done."

Not for the first time that day, Doug thought how much he wished he'd gotten to know Tim better.

"I suppose there isn't time to write a proper obituary, then," Doug said. "How will all of Tim's friends know about the funeral? How will they even know he's dead?"

"Sung will know how to communicate with everyone who would want to know," Rev. Allen said.

"Tim's girlfriend?" Doug felt a little foolish admitting that he didn't know her name.

"Yes, Li Sung. A lovely young woman who fell into the trap of opium addiction, like so many others. She's staying at the Hung Wei Sanitarium on Avenue Edward VII. That's on the south end of downtown Shanghai, almost to the French Concession. I'll get you the address. I wish I had time to go with you."

Doug memorized the address, thanked the minister, and told him he would call again that afternoon.

Doug managed to locate the office of the Associated Press with the help of the telephone operator, and he caught the streetcar back downtown. He found the address, and told the Chinese elevator operator which floor. When he found the office, the door was unlocked, but he didn't see anyone.

"Hello?" he called, in English.

"Be right with you," a gruff man's voice replied in an American accent. A moment later, a burly bearded man with an open collar came out of an office in the back, a lit cigar clenched tightly in his teeth. "Help you?" he asked.

"You have a reporter by the name of Tim McIntyre," Doug said.

"Tim's not been in today," the man cut in, impatient. "He sometimes checks in on Saturdays though. Write down your message, and I'll give it to him." He turned away.

"No, I'm not looking for him. I'm here to inform you that Tim has passed away."

The burly man stopped mid-turn, and his eyes bored into Doug for several seconds. "How'd it happen?"

"The police don't know yet."

The man shook his head. "Went and got himself killed, finally, huh? Well, I can't say I didn't suspect this might come someday. Real shame, though. Hell of a reporter. We'll miss him around here."

"Is there anyone I should notify? Anyone at the AP who would want to attend the funeral?"

The man nodded. "I'll call Gladys; she'll get the word out. When's the funeral?"

"I'm not sure yet. Either this evening or tomorrow. I'm hopeful it's tomorrow."

"Who can Gladys call that will know?"

"Call the Presbyterian minister, Rev. Allen." Doug gave him the phone number, and the burly man wrote it down.

"I'm sorry, I didn't get your name," Doug said.

"Wainwright. Chuck Wainwright. I'm Tim's editor." He shook Doug's offered hand with a firm grip. "And you are?"

"Doug Bainbridge. I was a friend of Tim's."

"My condolences. Is there a phone number where Gladys can reach you?"

"I'm afraid I don't have a telephone," Doug said.

"Well then, Gladys will call that minister. I suppose he'll know everything?"

"Yes."

"Good. Now if you'll excuse me, I've got work." He turned and walked off without another word.

"I'll let myself out," Doug muttered, and left.

He found the Hung Wei Sanitarium, and asked the Chinese orderly at the front desk if he could see Li Sung. The orderly asked for his name, and then flipped through a notebook, found a page and ran his finger down the left hand side.

"I'm sorry sir; you are not on the visitors list."

"Is Tim McIntyre on the list?"

"You said your name was Bainbridge, sir."

"It is. I'm here on Mr. McIntyre's behalf. What I mean is—well, Mr. McIntyre died last night, and I need to inform Miss Li."

"You'll need to speak with her doctor," the orderly said, and disappeared behind a door.

Doug took a seat in one of the wooden chairs in the lobby. It was several minutes before the orderly reappeared behind the desk.

"Dr. Wong will speak with you. Wait there."

It was several more minutes before a man of about thirty-five wearing a white coat over a white dress shirt and black necktie came down the hall to Doug's left, a stethoscope draped around his neck. He gave Doug a shallow bow, and addressed him in English.

"I'm Dr. Wong. I understand you are here to speak with Li Sung. I am told that her sponsor, Mr. McIntyre, has died. Is this so?"

Doug found the directness of the Chinese almost amusing. If the circumstances hadn't been so tragic, he might have smiled. "Yes, sadly, Mr. McIntyre was killed last night. Miss Li is his girlfriend, and they lived together. She should know."

Dr. Wong stared at him for several seconds. "Li Sung is a very fragile woman. She arrived here addicted to opium. She has been here only fourteen days, and she has seven days more of treatment before she is cured."

Doug braced himself for an argument, and summoned up his best reasoning. "Miss Li has the right to know what happened to her lover. If she learns of his death more than a week after it happened, she will have missed the opportunity to grieve him at the funeral, and the shock and sadness will push her back to opium. If she learns of his death now, she will be able to grieve him with others, face the pain, and return to your care after the funeral, instead of returning to an opium den to forget the pain."

Dr. Wong's expression did not change, but Doug watched his eyes shifting as he weighed Doug's statement.

"We will speak to her together," he said at length.

Doug bowed in appreciation and thanked him.

Dr. Wong took him into a large room with big windows and more comfortable chairs. "Wait here."

Three little clusters of people sat around the room, talking in quiet voices—an elderly Chinese couple with a baby-faced young man who couldn't have been older than eighteen or nineteen; a young Chinese woman with two small children who all sat stiff-backed across from a young man about Doug's age; and a white woman with platinum blond hair and black pencil-thin eyebrows, sitting close to a white man with dark circles under his eyes, and uncombed brown hair. Doug saw her dab at her eyes several times before he looked away, not wanting to stare. A half-dozen orderlies stood around the room, all Chinese, with their hands behind their backs, observing.

Dr. Wong entered through a door with no window, followed by a pretty young Chinese woman and an orderly. The young woman glanced around the room eagerly, but her expression went blank a few seconds later.

She'd been looking for Tim, Doug realized. They hadn't told her. They had probably only said that she had a visitor, and she assumed it was Tim. Doug wondered if she had family in Shanghai, or if Tim was the only one who ever visited her.

Doug stood as they approached, and Dr. Wong gave him a stiff, shallow bow. "Mr. Bainbridge, this is Li Sung. Miss Li, this is Mr. Bainbridge, a friend of Mr. McIntyre."

Li Sung nodded her head at Doug, not meeting his eyes.

"Please sit," Dr. Wong said.

As they sat, Doug noticed that the orderly remained standing behind Li Sung, rather than along the wall with the other orderlies.

Li Sung sat with her hands folded in her lap, her eyes lowered.

"Miss Li, I knew Tim many years ago, when we were children in San Francisco," Doug said in Chinese, watching her face. "I recently came to live in Shanghai, and renewed my friendship with Tim. We went out together last night, to a place on Nanking Road called the Jade Dragon."

He hesitated, watching her eyes for any sign that she recognized the place, but she stared down at his feet, her face calm and stoic. What was going on inside her head?

"Tim stepped outside between shows to get some air, but he never came back. I went looking for him, and found him in an alley a few blocks away. He was dead. I'm very sorry."

He thought he saw tears welling in her eyes, but her expression remained utterly unchanged, her eyes still downcast. She muttered a word he didn't understand, and he looked to Dr. Wong.

"I didn't understand."

"She said 'Green Gang,'" Dr. Wong said, his lips pursing.

"I told Tim not to," she said, and a tear broke free from her left eye and ran down her cheek, dripping onto her pants. Her voice had sounded so calm.

"I don't understand," Doug said to her. "You told Tim not to do what?"

"Not to look into the Green Gang," she said, and wiped away at her right eye before a tear fell. "I knew they would get him. But he is stubborn."

Something told Doug not to press her on the subject, at least not in front of Dr. Wong and the orderly. He made a note to speak to her alone at the funeral.

"The minister at the Presbyterian Church is arranging the funeral. I've spoken to Tim's editor," Doug said. "Are there any other friends of Tim's that should be told about his death?"

Li Sung continued to stare down at Doug's feet. "Speak to Chen Gwan, our landlord. He will know."

"I've spoken with Mr. Chen," Doug said. "Is there anyone else?" She shook her head.

"It is time for Miss Li to go back," Dr. Wong said, his voice matter-of-fact. He looked at Li Sung and said, "Mr. Bainbridge will let us know when the funeral is, and he will take you to it and bring you back."

Doug had not volunteered to be Li Sung's chaperone, but he knew better than to argue. Just one more job he'd been given in this mess.

Dr. Wong turned to the orderly. "Please take Miss Li back to her room. I will escort Mr. Bainbridge."

The orderly gave the doctor a deep bow, took Li Sung by the elbow, and walked her out of the room. She did not look back.

"I will telephone when I know the time of the funeral," Doug told the doctor as they walked back to the reception area. "I hope to have that information soon."

"Who will take her to buy a funeral dress?" Dr. Wong asked.

Doug had no idea. "I'll speak to someone about that," he said, and bowed to the doctor as he left.

7

It was noon when Doug arrived home, though it felt much later. He was exhausted. He took off his suit coat, loosened his tie and opened his collar. He plopped down in his armchair with a cup of tea.

Before he knew it he jolted awake from a sound outside his kitchen window.

He glanced at his watch as he blinked the sleepiness from his eyes, and saw that it was quarter to one o'clock. He sat straight-backed and stared at the window on the far side of his kitchenette. The fire escape was through that window, and he was pretty sure the sound he had heard was metallic. But he was on the top floor, and the apartment across the hall had its own fire escape—there was no reason for anyone to be by his window.

He watched and listened for a full minute, sitting perfectly still. All he could hear was the normal sound of the city—birds chirping from the roofs of the buildings surrounding the courtyard, conversations on the street coming through his living room window, the shouts of street vendors—and he began to think that he'd dreamed it. Or perhaps a bird had flown into the fire escape and made the noise.

Then he saw a shadow move outside the window—too big to be a bird—and his heart began to pound.

He bolted from his chair and rushed toward the window. "Who's there?"

He saw the shadow slip away as he reached the window, and he thrust his head through the opening and looked left in time to see a pair of legs scrambling over the side of the roof above.

"Damn!" He clambered out onto the fire escape, stood, and reached for the ladder that led to the roof.

He reached the roof only to see the top of a man's head disappearing over the side of the next building over, presumably onto its fire escape. The head was covered with shiny black hair, so Doug presumed the man to be Chinese.

He ran to the edge of the roof, which was lined with a three-foot brick wall, and scrambled over it and the neighboring wall that sat flush against it, onto the roof of the neighboring building. He ran across to where he'd seen the head, and looked down.

All he saw was an empty fire escape, and an empty alley below.

"Damn!" He banged his fist against the top of the fire escape.

What in the hell was going on? Doug wondered as he hurried down the stairs inside his own building after locking his window. He'd been followed home from Tim's building last night, and now someone had spied on him from the fire escape—and he was pretty sure it wasn't an ordinary peeping tom. They didn't get away so skillfully.

He considered calling the embassy in Nanking and trying to speak with Commander Hilliard about it, but decided against that. He didn't know anything, and so there was no need to involve the Naval Attaché's office. He should call the police, but he suspected they would do nothing more than make a report and file it away, uninvestigated. He decided not to bother. Besides, there was too much still to do.

He paid Mr. Hwang a quarter and placed a call to Rev. Allen's home.

"Ah, Mr. Bainbridge, thank you for calling. I spoke with the morgue a short time ago, and they will release Tim's body at two o'clock. I have arranged the funeral for six o'clock this evening. You said you had clothes that he could be buried in?"

"Yes, can I bring those by the church?"

"Please do. I can meet you there at one-thirty."

Doug went back upstairs. Once inside his apartment, he went to the kitchen window and looked out on the fire escape, but it was empty. He closed and relocked it.

He went into his bedroom, got the suit bag he had taken from Tim's apartment the night before, retrieved Tim's shoes from the bag of clothes the police had given him, and walked to the church on Tianjian Road.

He stayed alert the whole way, but saw no sign of anyone watching or following him.

He got there a few minutes before the pastor. Tianjian Road was a side street, with light pedestrian traffic, but Doug still watched everyone who walked by.

Rev. Allen arrived a few minutes before one-thirty, and looked surprised when he saw Doug waiting. "I'm sorry to have kept you," he said as he unlocked the front door of the church.

"Not at all, I was early," Doug said. He followed the pastor inside.

"I'll take those," Rev. Allen said, taking the suit bag and shoes from Doug. "I have to go to the morgue to identify the body before they'll release it. They'll dress him for me after I identify him. I'm afraid we won't be able to have an open casket, so there will be no showing before the funeral."

"I understand."

"I received a phone call from a Miss Gladys Sherman, who said she worked with Tim at the Associated Press. I gave her the details, and she said several people from the wire service will attend. Is there anyone else I should call?"

"Yes, Chen Gwan, Tim's landlord," Doug said. "According to Li Sung, Mr. Chen will notify everyone who needs to know. I don't know the phone number, but I'm sure they have a telephone in the building, so the operator should be able to connect you." He gave Rev. Allen the address.

"Thank you, I will call him in a few moments. Will Li Sung be able to attend?"

Doug nodded. "I have to sign her out of the sanitarium myself, but I'll bring her, and take her back when it's over."

"That will be a few hours," Rev. Allen cautioned. "Chinese funerals are not short affairs. She'll have dinner with Mrs. Allen and me tonight, and we can take her back."

Doug was relieved to have one more thing taken off his shoulders. "Thank you very much, I appreciate that."

Rev. Allen shook his head. "The poor dear girl. I pray this doesn't push her back to the opium dens. I feel partly responsible for her, since I referred Tim to the Hung Wei Sanitarium. He loved her dearly, and cared so deeply for her wellbeing."

Doug wasn't sure he understood the pastor's concern. Just how well had he known them?

"Would you please bring her around a little early?" Rev. Allen asked, looking back up at Doug. "I think it will be good for her to have some alone time with the coffin."

Doug nodded. "I'll bring her by at five-thirty." He started to walk out, but turned in the doorway. "One more thing, Reverend—do you know anyone who could buy Miss Li a funeral dress?"

"I'm sure we have some in the donations," Rev. Allen replied. "Don't worry about that. Just bring her by at five-thirty, and Mrs. Allen will be here to help her."

"Thank you, Reverend—for everything."

**

Doug got home without being followed. The apartment felt stuffy, because the kitchen window was closed, and there was no cross breeze. He opened the window long enough to stick his head out and verify there was no one on the fire escape, then he closed and locked it again. Stuffy or not, he wasn't taking any chances.

He stripped out of his sweaty clothing and plopped naked onto the top of his bed, savoring the feel of the air moving over his body from the fans. Within minutes he had fallen asleep.

He slept hard for quite some time, in that deep slumber without dreams. But eventually his mind came back into that lighter sleep and he began to dream.

He was sitting in his armchair in the living room, naked, with the warm breeze from the windows lightly touching his bare skin, and the sunlight through the lace curtains dancing across the floor and walls. He could feel the caress of the breeze. The whole scene was quite pleasant, and yet there was a feeling of dread in the pit of his stomach that he couldn't banish.

Then he saw movement at the kitchen window, and he looked over to see a man climbing through. He was dressed like a common laborer in the street—shirtless, with dark blue trousers cut off at the knees, and he was thin and lithe—but his face was long in an extremely exaggerated fashion, and he wore a Fu Manchu mustache of the type that one saw in caricatures. He leered at Doug.

Doug tried to get up and run away, but he was glued to the armchair, unable even to lift a hand no matter how hard he willed his muscles to move. He tried calling for help, but no sound came from his mouth.

The man crawled across the kitchen table, and his leering face kept growing longer and longer, and his teeth also grew longer until they were fanglike. The next thing Doug knew, the man—now looking like some sort of monster—was at his feet, crawling up into the chair above him, hovering over Doug's naked form. His jaw, mouth and nose had grown into a sort of snout, and his teeth into giant fangs. His trousers had somehow changed to green. His yellow-brown skin faded into green as well, and Doug found himself face to face with a shimmering green dragon, the same dragon that had chased him through the fog in this morning's dream.

He tried to scream, but no air came from his lungs.

The dragon's gaping mouth dove toward Doug's exposed belly, from his groin to his ribcage, and the teeth began to sink in. Doug tried harder to scream, willing air from his lungs with all of his might.

Suddenly he bolted upright in his bed, an actual scream escaping his lips. His body was drenched with sweat. His heart pounded so hard in his chest that he could see the movement when he glanced down. His breath came hard and fast, and a bead of sweat poured off his forehead and stung his eye.

He swore he could feel deep wounds in his gut where the dragon's teeth had penetrated, but when he looked down at his sides he saw no marks. He felt with his hands, but the skin was unbroken.

Then he heard knocking at his door, persistent knocking, followed by a voice in English with a Chinese accent.

"Mr. Bainbridge! Mr. Bainbridge, sir—you alright? Mr. Bainbridge?"

Doug bolted from the bed, threw on his bathrobe, and hurried toward the front door, tying the robe tightly.

"Coming!" he shouted when he was still in the short hall from his bedroom to the living room.

The knocking stopped after he shouted, and he rushed across the living room, unlocked the door and opened it less than halfway.

Li Baosheng stood in the hall, looking at him wide-eyed.

"Are you alright, Mr. Bainbridge? I heard you scream."

"Yes—yes, I'm fine," Doug stammered, still flustered from the nightmare.

"Are you hurt?" Bao's eyes flicked down for half a second to the triangle of bare chest between the folds of the robe, then back up.

Doug hadn't failed to notice. He tugged the robe around his neck.

"I'm fine," he said, his voice more gruff this time. It occurred to him that he'd never heard Li Baosheng speak before—his English was excellent.

"Okay," Bao said, and started to turn away. "I am glad you are alright. I am across the hall if you need any help."

Doug heard himself mutter "Thank you" as he closed the door.

He walked back into his bedroom and looked at his watch, discovering with alarm that it was a few minutes after four o'clock.

"Damn!" he said, and grabbed his bath kit. He hurried out of his apartment, careful to lock the door behind him, and went to the bathroom. He thought of Li Baosheng next door as he closed the bathroom door, and he scowled as he turned the lock.

Imaginary dragons weren't the only things to fear, he thought as he turned on the hot water.

8

He dressed in his good summer suit instead of the cooler linen suit he'd bought the day after he arrived in Shanghai. A funeral required nicer attire.

He went into the shop downstairs to look for Mr. Hwang so that he could call the sanitarium to let them know he was coming, and he saw Wong Mei-Ling behind the counter. He realized that he hadn't stopped by to see her that day, after five consecutive mornings of seeking her out to talk to her.

"Good afternoon, Miss Wong," he said, her presence giving him cause to smile, a rarity that day. "I am looking for Mr. Hwang."

"He is not here," she said, without explanation.

"I wanted to use his telephone to make a local call. Usually he will let me use the phone if I pay him twenty-five cents."

She gave him a curious look, mixed with sympathy and a touch of incredulity. "He is over-charging you," she said, again without further explanation. She looked around the empty store, and then nodded her head backward in the direction of Mr. Hwang's office.

He stepped behind the counter and followed her. She opened the door, and stood aside as he went in. "Do not tell Mr. Hwang that I allowed you to come in here when he was not present."

"I won't, I assure you."

After placing the call, he stepped back out and closed the office door behind him. He found Mei-Ling sweeping the shop floor, a growing pile of dust in the center.

"Thank you, Miss Wong," he said with a bow. Then an impish grin came to his face, and he added, "Perhaps I should pay *you* twenty-five cents."

She scowled momentarily, but seemed to realize it was a joke, and a faint smile crossed her lips. "No, sir."

"Then perhaps instead you will let me take you to dinner tomorrow night," Doug said. "Do you work tomorrow?"

"Tomorrow is my day off," she said, her expression unreadable.

"Then where can I find you?" he asked. "I would very much like to see you."

"That is not a good idea," she murmured, her eyes cast down at the floor, and she resumed sweeping.

"Then perhaps one evening next week after you get off work?" he suggested. "What time do you usually leave here?"

But she just shook her head without looking at him. "I should not," she said, beginning to sweep the broom across the floor more firmly. "Good bye, Mr. Bainbridge."

He nodded in resignation, and gave her a polite bow before he left, even though she wasn't looking at him.

He suppressed the feeling of rejection and regret that sank into his belly, and focused on the task ahead. He had to transport a grieving girl to the funeral of her lover. That would require all of the steeling he could give to his nerves.

He took the streetcar downtown, and hopped off a few blocks from the Hung Wei Sanitarium. He walked through the door to find Dr. Wong waiting for him in the lobby.

The doctor gave him a stiff and formal bow. "Mr. Bainbridge, wait here please." He left, and returned a few minutes later with Li Sung and an orderly. Her face was freshly scrubbed, though her eyes looked red, and her hair was washed and neatly combed, its clean shine making it look soft and luxuriant. She wore a simple housedress and slippers.

100

"What time will you bring her back?" Dr. Wong asked.

"The funeral will probably end quite late, so the Reverend Mr. Jonathan Allen of the Presbyterian Church—I understand he was instrumental in placing her here—will bring her back tonight. I don't know what time."

Dr. Wong didn't look pleased with this new information, but he didn't argue. "Thank you, Mr. Bainbridge. Good afternoon." He bowed and walked away.

Doug turned to the girl standing next to him, her eyes downcast. "Miss Li?" he said, holding out his left elbow. She slid her arm through it, and he escorted her out the door and down the stairs to the sidewalk. They walked to the corner, and he stopped to flag down a rickshaw.

He helped her into the back, and told the runner in Shanghainese, "Tianjian Road a block west of Honan Road, in the North District."

The rickshaw would take longer than the streetcar, but it would be a more pleasant ride, and afford Li Sung a bit more privacy than an elbow-to-elbow crowd.

"I am terribly sorry about Tim," he said as the Sikh traffic constable waved them on, and they crossed Nanking Road heading north.

"Thank you," she said quietly, her eyes staying downcast.

"I wish we could have met under happier circumstances."

She nodded, but said nothing.

Mindful of the runner pulling the rickshaw, he switched to English. "Earlier you said something about the Green Gang, and that you told Tim not to look into them. What did you mean?"

She stiffened, and didn't answer immediately. When she did, her voice was very quiet, and Doug had to lean close to hear her.

"Tim very angry. He find me at one of their opium dens, and he wanna stop them. I tell him they not able be stop. He try anyway. He no listen to what I say. I tell him they never go jail long."

"What do you mean?"

Sung shrugged. "Tim call police after he find me, but he go back few days later and it again open. I tell him, 'Always same people there. Police bust in, arrest everybody, and few days later everyone back in business.' Tim ask how that be, I say 'Police take money, gang go free. Place go again open, police no look.'"

Doug stared at her a moment. "How do you know this?"

She shrugged again. "Everybody know that. I wonder why Tim not know. I say 'Gang has big money, can pay lots policemen.' He say he get to bottom of it, I say 'Don't! They hurt you!' He say he have to. He no listen to me."

Doug took a moment to digest this information. Why had he asked, anyway? What was he going to do with this?

Jesus, Doug, who do you think you are—Charlie Chan? He heard that in his brother Will's voice.

He put that thought from his mind. "When was this?"

"Few days after he put me in Hung Wei." She began to cry, and looked away.

They rode in silence the rest of the way to the church.

Doug felt awkward, not knowing if he should say anything. There was nothing he could say that would make her feel better, and he didn't know her well enough to talk about other subjects. So instead he stared at the passing store fronts, the pedestrians on the sidewalk, and the motor cars and rickshaws going the opposite direction.

He could feel her pain, even if she didn't express it. He saw it in her eyes when he picked her up from the sanitarium, and he heard it in the quiet sadness of her voice when she so briefly answered him when he offered his condolences. It amplified his own sense of regret at not having had the time to get to know Tim better, of really becoming his friend.

And, he had to admit to himself, her presence was a reminder that Tim had found happiness and love, and he had not. It amplified his sense of regret about Wong Mei-Ling, and about Lucy Kinzler, and even about Barbara Hancock back in San Francisco.

He sometimes still thought about her. Barbara had been his sweetheart from age seventeen until he was almost twenty-one. Their families belonged to the same country club south of the city, and he'd escorted her to dozens of dances and ice cream socials, even joining her parents' table in the dining room on many occasions. But he'd never asked her to marry him, no matter how many hints she dropped; and the summer after his twenty-first birthday, when he came home from his junior year at Stanford, he learned that she had started going steady with Chester Farnsworth, a chubby fellow with a high pitched voice who had been accepted to Yale Law School, and the engagement was announced at the club's Memorial Day barbecue.

In spite of the sharp feeling of betrayal the news had initially brought, within days he had surprised himself with how little sadness he'd felt about the whole thing. His mother made passive-aggressive comments about how Barbara couldn't have been expected to wait forever, and what a good provider Chester would be. Doug had paid little mind to his mother's vocal disappointment. She was always disappointed in something about him anyway. And as the summer of 1931 progressed, it became clear to him that he didn't want to get married at all, didn't want to be tied down, constantly answering to a wife the way his father had to constantly answer to his mother.

He looked hard at his parents' marriage—and at the marriages of so many of his friends' parents—and he saw people who were cool and polite to one another, not spending too much time in each other's company, and not seeming to enjoy it when they did. No, that was definitely not for him.

And yet, Tim had seemed to be happy. Why couldn't he?

At the church, he handed Sung off to Rev. Allen, who escorted her into the sanctuary to be alone with Tim's coffin. Doug waited in the pastor's office, and Rev. Allen joined him there a few moments later.

"I made a pot of tea," the minister said upon entering the room carrying a silver tray with a tea pot and two cups. "Would you care to have a cup with me?"

"Yes, thank you." Doug accepted the cup the minister offered, and took a sip. It was hot and slightly sweet.

"You've shown amazing fortitude through this trial, Douglas," the minister said. "May I call you Douglas?"

"Doug, please."

"Well, Doug, I've been quite impressed with the way you've conducted yourself throughout this sad business. I know a lot has been thrust upon your shoulders today, and I know it probably seems that this is all happening way too fast. I wish it didn't have to be this way, but this is the lot we have been given. The Lord sees your efforts, and He will give you the strength to persevere through it."

"Thank you, Reverend," Doug said, mechanically. He wasn't sure how much of the minister's sentiments he agreed with.

Rev. Allen patted him on the arm and smiled. "I'll be sure to write your mother next week, and tell her what a strong and upright young man you've been."

Doug forced a smile. He supposed the minister intended that as good news. "Thank you."

The minister took a drink from his tea cup, then set it down and cleared his throat. "Doug, I assume you have never been to a Chinese funeral before."

"No, sir."

"Well, the first part, here at the church, I will conduct as I would any funeral back home. I'll say words about the deceased, we'll have scripture readings, prayers—everything you're probably used to. Then pall bearers will carry the casket outside, and this is when it will become a Chinese funeral. There will be a walk of about a mile to the American and British cemetery, and everyone walks behind the casket—which, by the way, will be carried inside a twenty-foot carved dragon. There will be drums and rattles making noise to scare off evil spirits, perhaps even fifes playing Chinese music if Tim's landlord arranged for them."

He paused, a strange sort of smile coming to his lips, and he appeared to be searching for the right words. Then he spoke slowly, carefully. "And...there will be a great deal of, well, wailing and lamentations."

Doug didn't really understand. "I beg your pardon?"

"Well, as you're probably already aware, the Chinese are by rule a very stoic people, accepting fate as it comes without question. This is a Confucian principle that is deeply ingrained in their culture—and it doesn't run counter to good Christian theology, for that matter. But the one big exception to this is funerals—you'll see what I mean."

Doug counted twenty-two people in the sanctuary when the funeral began at six o'clock. Aside from Li Sung, Mr. and Mrs. Chen, and a few others sitting with them, the majority of the faces in the church were white. The white people present wore black clothes; the Chinese wore white.

Rev. Allen spoke in English. He spoke of the tragedy of Tim's death at such a young age, and how deeply he would be mourned by those who loved him—"Especially by his parents in San Francisco, and by his companion, Li Sung."

He nodded in Sung's direction, and Doug was impressed that the minister acknowledged the relationship publicly, given that she and Tim lived together outside of marriage. The clergy he had known in the States would have ignored Li Sung's presence altogether.

"In both his work and his personal life, Tim McIntyre was a tireless champion for social justice, whether that was for the city's homeless beggars, the opium addicts, or the oppressed people of Korea. He once told me that he became a reporter because he wanted to expose things that the powerful prefer to keep hidden. It went to the core of his belief system. In that way, he was not unlike our Lord Jesus, who also spoke truth to the powerful.

"Tim always considered the consequences of his actions, and that meant that sometimes he struggled with knowing the right thing to do. I had the privilege of walking that road with him recently, and know first-hand of his concern for doing the right thing.

"But above all, he was passionately dedicated to the truth, and spoke the whole truth, no matter the consequences to himself. He was a man of deep integrity, for whom the responsibility of exposing evil was taken quite seriously. I am proud to have known him."

Rev. Allen paused, took a deep breath, and stared down at the pulpit for a moment. When he looked back up, he gazed over the gathered mourners, and his eyes were full of compassion.

"Let us all take comfort in our grief by remembering what a good and courageous man Tim McIntyre was—and by remembering that this Earthly life, this mortal flesh and blood, is but a temporary vessel, and that the immortal soul of our beloved Tim lives on in the presence of God, and in our hearts as well.

"Let us consider the words of the Psalmist David, recorded here in Psalm 46:

God is our refuge and strength, an ever-present help in trouble. Therefore we will not fear, though the earth give way and the mountains fall into the heart of the sea, though its waters roar and foam and the mountains quake with their surging...Be still, and know that I am God; I will be exalted among the nations, I will be exalted in the earth."

There were other readings, and prayers said, and then the gathered mourners filed out of the sanctuary to the sound of Mrs. Allen on the organ playing "How Great Thou Art."

Outside the church, a large crowd of Chinese had gathered, all wearing white. Doug wondered who they all were. Several men carried a twenty-foot carved wooden dragon on poles, made of connected pieces, like the vertebrae of a snake. From behind, Doug could see a flat board in the dragon's head, which had two poles stuck out the sides, like a litter some ancient king would have ridden.

Other men carried placards in Chinese script proclaiming Tim's virtues—courageous, honorable, speaker of truth, etc.

Six white men carried the casket out of the church on their shoulders, and Doug recognized Tim's editor Mr. Wainwright among them. Rev. Allen walked behind them.

Mr. Chen seemed to have taken charge now, and he directed the pallbearers in Pidgin to carry the casket to the head of the dragon, and then slide it onto the empty board there.

One of the pallbearers walked up to Doug where he stood watching. He was about forty, slightly heavy set, with brown hair soaked wet at the brow, and a heavy brown mustache. His round cheeks were flushed from the effort of carrying the casket.

"We haven't met," he said in a flat Midwestern accent. "I'm Art Jones, one of Tim's colleagues. And I was one of his friends." His voice grew quieter as he said that last part.

Doug shook his hand. "How do you do? I'm Douglas Bainbridge."

"Yes, I know. I was with Tim last Saturday when we saw you at the Cathay with Commander Hilliard. I know you and Tim went out together last night. He was looking forward to it. I'm wondering if you have any thoughts about what happened to him—seeing as you were with him not long before."

Doug stood rigid, uncomfortable with how much this Art Jones knew, and also with the blunt directness of his manner.

"I'm not sure what I can tell you, Mr. Jones. I don't know what happened."

"Everyone calls me Jonesy. Tim called me that, so you may as well."

"Alright, Jonesy." Doug didn't let down his guard, in spite of the invitation to familiarity.

"You were the one that went to Chuck Wainwright this morning," Jonesy pressed. "Gladys called me, and she said you were making the arrangements for the funeral. So it stands to reason in my mind that you have a reason for taking responsibility for everything. In my experience, rich men don't just do things like that out of the kindness of their hearts."

Doug ignored the blatant cynicism in Jonesy's jibe. "I'm just trying to help out, for Tim's sake. We were friends, and it's the least I could do."

"No, you weren't friends. If anything, I would say Tim had a few scores to settle."

Doug looked Jonesy in the face; his green eyes never wavered from Doug's own, hard and unblinking.

"Well, we've known each other a long time, anyway. If Tim had a score to settle, it wasn't with me personally, so you're misinformed. And last night we really were starting to become friends. We had a good time, and good conversation."

"So tell me what happened last night."

Doug's instinct was to clam up, but he knew Jonesy wouldn't let it go. "Tim left between shows to get some air, and didn't come back. I went looking for him, some people in front of the club said they saw him go around the corner with a pair of Chinese men, and so I went around the corner and found him in the alley."

"No idea who the two men were?"

Doug thought of Ming Lin-wen's companions—they had gone out after the first show, and only one of the three returned to the table for the second show, the big one who had obviously been in charge.

Jonesy's eyes narrowed; he'd seen the proverbial wheels spinning. But Doug wasn't about to voice vague suspicions. He just shrugged and shook his head. "The police think it was a robbery that went bad."

The drummers around the dragon began to beat their drums, and several Chinese men shook rattles, creating an awful noise.

"I need to go back inside and fetch my hat before this parade leaves," Jonesy shouted over the din, spun on his heels and marched off.

The dragon moved off slowly, following behind the drummers, and suddenly dozens of Chinese people around it burst into tears and loud wailing, their faces contorted and their arms waving in the air like they were having spasms.

Doug's mouth dropped open for a moment before he recovered. He had never seen anything like this. He looked toward Li Sung, walking behind the dragon's head, her eyes downcast. She was not wailing, but the tears flowed freely down her cheeks and her lips quivered. Behind her, even Mr. Chen was wailing and shaking his fists, carrying on in the most unbelievable way, his face turned to the heavens as if he were cursing them.

The crowd of fifty or sixty Chinese fell in around the dragon, walking east down Tianjian Road to Honan Road, and followed as it turned left and moved slowly toward the Anglo-American cemetery to the north.

Doug fell in with the parade around the tail of the dragon. He was keenly aware that only some of the white people at the funeral had joined the procession.

A young woman who appeared to be in her early twenties, with brown hair perfectly shaped in finger curls along the side of her head—

whom Doug had noticed in the church dabbing at her eyes with a silk handkerchief—walked not far from him, her tears now flowing freely, and quiet sobs escaping her lips. A moment later, Jonesy appeared at her side, a brown bowler hat now on his head. He put an arm around her, and she leaned her head on his shoulder.

Doug supposed that was probably Gladys, the secretary at the Associated Press office. He wondered from her reaction if she had been secretly in love with Tim. It wouldn't have been shocking. He supposed she'd never told Tim, given that he was by all accounts devoted to Li Sung.

The procession moved slowly, and as they went crowds of Chinese gathered on the sidewalk to watch them go by, standing still and silent in respect. Doug saw their eyes move from the dragon to the placards accompanying it, reading the messages, and their heads bowed lower.

They began to pass the cemetery, enclosed in a wrought iron fence, with small simple sun-bleached headstones facing the road. Doug read many of them as they passed—mostly men, a few women, with dates of death in the 1850s and 1860s.

The procession turned and passed through the open gates, proceeding down a dirt lane. As they went deeper into the cemetery many of the stones grew larger and more ornate, with more recent death dates, and an increasing number of them representing a husband and wife rather than a single man. After a while there were even a few enormous above ground crypts, these generally marked with a family name in large block letters, and several individual names below in much smaller script.

Near the back of the cemetery, in a section with only a few modest grave stones, there was an open pit with a pile of fresh dirt next to it. A trio of skinny shirtless Chinese with shovels stood next to it, their bare torsos smeared with a mixture of sweat and soil. They stared at the

110

procession dispassionately, and from time to time wiped their brows with a dirty forearm, smearing mud across their foreheads.

The dragon head came to a stop beside the open grave, and the rest of the dragon wrapped around it, the tail stopping on the far side of the pile of earth. The men carrying the poles laid their sections on the ground—all except for the four men carrying the head, who kept the side poles at waist height.

Mr. Chen—who had mysteriously stopped wailing a moment before—now directed the pall bearers in Pidgin to remove the coffin from the dragon head and set it down on the ground beside the open hole.

The second the coffin hit the ground, the drums and the rattles fell silent.

Rev. Allen, who had been walking at the end of the procession, approached Li Sung and put a hand on her shoulder. He whispered something in her ear, and she nodded and walked with him to the head of the grave.

Rev. Allen carried a Bible in his right hand, and when he and Li Sung had positioned themselves at the head of the open grave, he opened his Bible, put on his reading glasses, and began to speak—two passages, each in English first, followed by the Shanghainese translation.

"From Genesis, the word of God to Adam: *'By the sweat of thy brow wilt thou eat thy food, until return thou to the ground, since from the ground thou were taken; for dust thou art, and to dust thou shalt return.'*

"And from the Book of Revelations, the words of Christ Jesus: *'Behold, I am coming soon! My reward is with me, and I wilt give to each according to what he hath done. I am the Alpha and the Omega, the First and the Last, the Beginning and the End.'* Amen."

The minister closed his Bible and nodded to the grave diggers, who walked to the coffin, slid it into the grave and lowered it slowly, and then picked up their shovels and began pitching dirt into the hole.

For several minutes the thud of dirt onto the wooden lid of the coffin was the only sound, accompanied by the occasional sniff from Gladys, who held her handkerchief to her face. Jonesy stood next to her with his hands clasped in front of him, his face stony as it gazed downward.

When the thud and echo had ceased, replaced by the quiet sound of earth landing on earth, the crowd walked away, the dragon moving listlessly back toward the cemetery gate. The quiet clink of rattles as they were carried at the sides of departing mourners, or the click of drum sticks hitting the sides of drums in beat to the footsteps of their carriers, the occasional chirp of a bird in a nearby tree, the steady swish of shovels throwing dirt—these were the only sounds.

Doug felt a deep melancholy fall over him. He remained beside the grave and watched as the procession left, all wailing ceased. Tears continued to stream down Li Sung's cheeks as she left on the arm of the pastor, but no sound came from her lips.

Gladys' sniffling had subsided, and Jonesy put his hand on her shoulder and guided her to the dirt path. Doug fell in beside them.

Jonesy made the introduction in a hushed tone. "Gladys Sherman, this is Douglas Bainbridge."

Doug saw the recognition cross Gladys' blue eyes at the sound of his name. "How do you do?" she said, extending her hand. "Thank you for notifying us about Tim this morning. I heard you were a friend of his. I'm sorry we didn't meet under happier circumstances."

"He was out with Tim last night," Jonesy told Gladys. "When Tim went out for some air and didn't come back, Mr. Bainbridge went looking for him, and found the body."

"Oh goodness, how awful that must have been!"

Doug nodded, surprised at the lump coming to his throat.

"Mr. Bainbridge said the police think it was a robbery," Jonesy said.

Gladys shook her head. "You read about such things, but you never think it will happen to anyone you know." She looked up at Doug. "Do the police have a suspect?"

Doug shook his head. "No. The detective said it's almost impossible. Truthfully, I don't think they're taking it very seriously."

"Oh, but they are," Gladys said.

"Excuse me?" Doug cocked his head, confused.

"I had to go into the office after Mr. Wainwright called to tell me about Tim—I don't usually work on weekends, and If the telephone rings whoever is there writes down the message on my pad and leaves it on my desk. Anyone who comes in knows to look there; otherwise I give them the message Monday morning. When I went in to make the calls, you know, about Tim, there was a message for Tim on my desk, in Mr. Wainwright's handwriting. It was dated this morning at 9:42, from a police captain—Captain Geoffries, West District."

"The police wouldn't leave a message for Tim if they were investigating his death," Jonesy said.

Gladys flushed. "Oh, of course not. It must have been about something Tim was working on, some story. How sad that he'll never finish it." Tears welled up in her eyes again.

"Did you work with Tim for a long time?" Doug asked to change the subject.

A weak smile crossed Gladys' lips, then faded. "I've been here just over two years. Tim had already been working here a while when I arrived. He was always a pleasure to work with. I can't say that about every reporter. They can be a very opinionated crowd, and sometimes a little intense. Tim was one of the nicest reporters I've ever known."

Jonesy snorted. They were exiting the cemetery gate now. "I hope you say I was always a pleasure to work with when I'm gone."

She swatted at his arm. "You know I always adored both of you," she said. "But Tim really was the nicest reporter I've ever worked with, and one of the nicest men."

Jonesy nodded and sighed. "Yes, that is true. He was one of a kind. We'll all miss him."

"You knew Tim in San Francisco?" Gladys asked Doug.

"Yes, we went to day school together. We grew up in the same neighborhood."

"Did you know his folks?" Gladys asked.

"A little bit," Doug said. "I cabled them this morning, and his father called me on the telephone."

"On the *telephone*?" Gladys looked at him wide-eyed.

"Yes, isn't it amazing? We only spoke for a few minutes, of course. They want me to send them some of Tim's things—clothes, photographs; things they can remember him by."

"That's very nice of you," Gladys said.

"I can't begin to imagine how painful this must be for them," Doug said.

"With the miracles of modern medicine, it's unusual these days for your children to die before you do," Jonesy said.

Doug and Gladys nodded in silent agreement.

They walked in silence for a block or so, and then Jonesy cleared his throat. "Gladys and I are going to dinner after this—would you care to join us?"

The invitation startled Doug, given the hostile nature of Jonesy's questions earlier. He didn't know what to say.

"Oh, please do," Gladys said, touching his arm. "You shouldn't go away from a funeral alone. Please join us."

Doug nodded. "Alright, I will. Thank you for the invitation."

Gladys suggested an Italian restaurant she frequented on Honan Road just south of the Soochow Creek Bridge.

Doug shook his head. "Why not a Chinese restaurant? Tim loved China, let's have Chinese in his memory."

"Sounds good to me," Jonesy said.

Gladys shrugged and nodded. "Alright."

"Swell, I know this great little Szechuan place in my neighborhood. It's just down the road," Doug said, using the usual English pronunciation of *Sichuan*.

Twilight was settling over the city as they reached the restaurant, the sky a deep blue, and the pedestrian traffic on Honan Road was thick as the dinner hour approached. Doug opened the door for Gladys and Jonesy, and followed them in. He asked the host in Mandarin for a table for three. It wasn't full yet, and they were seated right away.

"I ate here my first night in Shanghai." It occurred to Doug that it was exactly one week since that night. It seemed longer.

"I was surprised to see Sung today," Jonesy said after the waiter had delivered the menus, which were in English. "Tim told me about their situation, and when Gladys called this afternoon with the news one of the first things I thought was, *Poor Sung won't be able to be there.* But she was."

So Tim had confided in at least one other person besides the minister.

"The sanitarium let me check her out for the evening," Doug explained. "Rev. Allen will take her back."

"Sanitarium?" Gladys asked.

"Opium," Jonesy said.

"Oh! I didn't realize," Gladys looked embarrassed. "Oh, poor Tim!"

Well, at least I'm not the only one who didn't know, Doug thought with a touch of satisfaction.

The table fell silent as they looked over their menus. Doug saw movement in the back of the restaurant, and noticed one of the students from last week take a seat at the same table they had occupied then, dressed in the same drab gray. He opened a book and read.

He hadn't come in the front door, or he would have passed their table. Perhaps he worked at the restaurant—but this would be an odd time to get off work, right at the beginning of the dinner rush.

Doug watched him out of the corner of his eye, and a few moments later a second boy entered the restaurant from the kitchen, also dressed in the drab gray. He also opened a book the moment he sat down and began to read.

The waiter returned to take their orders, and while Jonesy was ordering the spicy shrimp dish, Doug saw a pair of girls in gray enter from the kitchen. The group of four whispered to each other for a few seconds before turning their attention back to their open books.

"Doug?"

Jonesy's voice startled him, and Doug realized he'd paid too much attention to the students and hadn't noticed that the waiter asked him for his order. He ordered in Mandarin— *Zhong shui jiao* as an appetizer for the table, and *Fu qi fei pian* for his dinner.

"What did you order, show-off?" Jonesy asked. His crooked smile bordered on a smirk. He pulled a cigar from inside his coat and struck a match.

Doug felt his face flush. "Pork dumplings with chili and garlic sauce for all of us to share, and for dinner I ordered the ox tongue with beef tripe."

Gladys made a face. "The dumplings sound good, anyway."

Jonesy was staring at him. He blew out a long stream of smoke, his eyes never leaving Doug's face. "Where did you learn to speak Chinese?"

"I learned Cantonese as a child," Doug said. "My father wanted us to learn it, and we went into Chinatown frequently. My parents both grew up near Guangdong—what we call Canton. My grandfather Bainbridge was in the China trade, and for twenty years he and his family lived in the American settlement in Guangdong. My father was little when they moved there from San Francisco; they sent him back for school when he was twelve. My mother's parents were missionaries in Guangdong Province. They left during the Boxer Rebellion, when Mother was a teenager."

"Was that Cantonese, then?" Gladys asked. "I don't know much about Chinese, but I didn't think they spoke Cantonese in Szechuan."

"No, that was Mandarin," Doug said. He paused, not wanting to sound like a know-it-all, but then figured they probably already thought that. "Mandarin is understood just about everywhere in China, by educated people anyway, and in many parts of the country it's beginning to replace the local dialects. Szechuan is one such province. I studied Mandarin in college. It's the language of government and the courts, and it's taught in the schools."

"How does Shanghainese compare?" Jonesy asked, his cigar clenched in his teeth.

"It's different," Doug said. "I'm having a difficult time learning it." He hoped this confession might lessen the know-it-all image.

"So then, why not speak Pidgin to them, like everyone else?"

"If I speak Pidgin, I'll never learn Shanghainese."

Jonesy made a brief grunt, took a long pull on his cigar, and blew out a thick cloud of smoke. "Tim could speak Shanghainese. He never liked to speak Pidgin, either."

"What about you, Gladys?" Doug asked. "Do you speak Shanghainese?"

"I know a few words," she said with an apologetic smile. "I can ask for the bathroom, and I can ask directions—beyond that I've never needed to. You can get by really well in Pidgin."

"That's what I've heard," Doug said.

The dumplings arrived, and Doug picked up his chopsticks while the other two took forks.

"What do you do for a living?" Gladys asked.

"I work for my father. I'm in Shanghai to open a China office for the firm. It will facilitate the shipping of goods."

"Imports-exports," Jonesy said, puffing on the cigar.

Doug couldn't read his expression. "Chinoiserie is very popular in the States."

"So it is."

The restaurant was filling up, with many people coming through the front door, but Doug noticed right away when Wong Mei-Ling entered, wearing her work clothes. *Just like last week.* She headed for the table in the back where the students sat, but as she passed she noticed Doug watching her. She appeared startled.

Doug stood and bowed. "Good evening, Miss Wong," he said in Shanghainese.

Her eyes widened, and he thought he saw fear in them for a second before she looked away; she mumbled "Good evening," and hurried to the table in the back.

He felt his cheeks flush hot as he sat down, embarrassed by her snub. He saw Jonesy staring at him with the same unreadable expression.

Gladys looked a little embarrassed, but covered it up with a smile and a question. "You know her? She's lovely."

Doug forced a smile. "Yes, she works for my landlord, in the shop downstairs. We've spoken often this past week. Ironically, I saw her at this very restaurant last Saturday night, and with the same group of friends over there." He nodded toward the table.

Jonesy glanced at the table, but then looked back at Doug as if trying to measure him up.

"What is it?" Doug asked, letting a touch of irritation show.

"She's a communist," Jonesy said, still clenching the cigar in his teeth.

Doug stiffened. "Oh? And how would you know that?"

Jonesy continued to stare at him, his expression calm. "That whole table is a communist student cell. The gray clothes are a dead giveaway. And the big books—easy way to hide contraband literature. The owner of the restaurant's probably a communist too, or at least a sympathizer. A bit unusual in a middle-class neighborhood like this one, but not unheard of."

Doug scowled, not wanting to believe it. "You seem to know an awful lot about the subject."

Jonesy shrugged. "The labor movement's been my specialty for twenty years. You meet a lot of socialists and communists in that line of work, and you learn real fast how they operate."

"Communists!" Gladys said, as much to herself as to them, and shuddered.

Doug looked back at the table by the kitchen door. The conversation seemed to have become heated—the voices were still low, but the expressions on everyone's faces were angry, and their body language tense. Wong Mei-Ling was shaking her head emphatically.

They're questioning her about me. They're suspicious.

A moment later they began to leave, one or two at a time, out the kitchen door. Within minutes they had all left, Wong Mei-Ling with them.

"You like her," Jonesy said.

Dinner arrived just then, allowing Doug to ignore the statement.

"She's lovely," Gladys repeated.

They spoke little the remainder of the meal. When they walked out the door, Jonesy asked Doug where the nearest streetcar stop was.

Doug pointed it out on the other side of the street. "What part of Shanghai do you live in?"

"Gladys and I both live uptown—West District—not far from each other, actually. I'm just past the race track and recreation grounds; Gladys is a little farther west, near the bubbling well."

"Have you been in that part of Shanghai yet?" Gladys asked.

"I've been to the race track and the recreation grounds, but I have yet to visit the bubbling well."

"It's not much to see," Gladys said. "But it's a nice neighbor-hood, and there's good shopping on Avenue Haig."

"He doesn't care about the shopping, Gladys," Jonesy said with a grin.

A sheepish smile spread across Gladys' lips. "Oh, of course not. How silly of me."

"I go to the rec grounds most evenings," Jonesy said. "Do some swimming, play some tennis, maybe watch a rugby game—perhaps I'll see you there sometime." He touched the rim of his bowler hat, took Gladys' elbow, and walked her to the streetcar stop.

Doug reflected on the evening as he walked home. Jonesy's manner had been strange, and Doug wondered what he knew. Had Tim told Jonesy about Doug's connection to ONI? Doug hoped not, but suspected otherwise—it wouldn't really be a problem, most likely, but an inconvenience anyway. The fewer people who knew, the better.

The full weight of the day seemed to settle over him as he climbed the stairs, and he realized how exhausted he felt. By the time he reached his floor, he could barely move his feet.

He hadn't left a lamp on, and the only light was a pale yellow strip from the front window. The stuffiness of his apartment reminded him to check the fire escape, and he opened the kitchen window long enough to look out and see that it was empty. There was no moon tonight, but there was enough light from windows around the courtyard that he could see the shape of the fire escape and know that no one lurked there.

He locked back up, and shuffled into his bedroom, shedding clothes as he went. He plopped onto the bed and was asleep within seconds.

9

Doug awoke with a start. It took his mind a few seconds to wake up enough to realize it was still the middle of the night. Had a sound awakened him? His pulse quickened, and he felt fear gnawing at the pit of his stomach as he threw on his robe and hurried to his kitchen window.

He looked out onto the fire escape, but saw nothing. He looked down into the courtyard, but the only movement came from a cat that was stalking something.

He decided to make a pot of tea, turned on the lamp, and saw on the clock that it was half past midnight—earlier than he'd thought. Too early for a pot of tea, or he'd be awake all night. Not that he felt all that sleepy at the moment, with his heart still pounding in his chest. He sat in his arm chair and took a deep breath.

I can't just sit here all night, staring at the clock. Or thinking about Tim. He needed a distraction, and it was still early enough to find plenty of distraction in Shanghai.

He got dressed, ran a comb through his hair, and caught a streetcar downtown. From there another streetcar took him to the West District—where Nanking Road became Bubbling Well Road—and out almost to the end of the International Settlement.

The Paramount was easy to see from blocks away, with its bright neon illuminating the street and reflecting off the surrounding buildings. The sidewalks were crowded with pedestrians of multiple races and nationalities in various stages of inebriation, and Doug navigated around them, sometimes barely avoiding collision. Several sleek limousines—Lincoln, Rolls-Royce, Duesenberg—sat idling in front of the Paramount, Chinese chauffeurs sitting in the front seat or lounging against the vehicle, invariably smoking cigarettes. Groups of people stood around the door, talking and laughing and sometimes smoking.

The noise of conversation and laughter increased the second he stepped through the door, and whatever cool breeze he had felt outside was replaced with a sweltering heat. Ceiling fans swirled the cigarette smoke, but brought little relief from the stuffiness.

He maneuvered his way through the crowd to the nearest bar, and ordered a gin and tonic. Then he stood for a moment, slightly overwhelmed. There were three floors of bars, ballrooms, and tables, and he felt momentarily paralyzed with options.

A white woman with wavy red hair, wearing a long red sequined evening gown sauntered up to him and asked in Russian-accented English if he would buy her a drink. He shook his head and shrugged as if he didn't understand, and she repeated the question in French.

"Español?" he asked, gambling that she didn't speak Spanish.

She gave him a look of disdain and sauntered away.

A Chinese cigarette girl, so tiny he wondered how she managed to carry her tray all night, wandered by, smiling at everyone and saying "Cigarette?" in English. He stopped her, and asked in his Mandarin/Shanghainese mix if she could tell him where most of the Americans were. It would be a lot easier to make small talk or friendly banter with strangers if they were fellow Americans.

"No wantchee cigarette?" she replied in Pidgin, her eyes narrowing.

"No," he admitted. He repeated in as much Shanghainese as he could that he wanted to find Americans.

"Catchee lift," she said in Pidgin with a scowl, nodded toward the elevator in the back, and walked away. Her smile returned the second she left him. "Cigarette?"

He heard American accents from a group of three young men getting on the elevator, and he followed them. "Third floor," one of them said. The Chinese elevator operator was about to close the gate when a short but broad Asian man in an expensive silk suit hurried on. He looked Doug in the eye as he stepped in, and held his gaze for a second before he turned toward the front of the elevator. He wasn't Chinese—Doug had been around Chinese people all his life, and the man's features were not Chinese. Probably Korean or Japanese.

As the elevator operator closed the gate and began their ascent, Doug spotted two faces in the crowd that he recognized, faces which at that moment appeared to be watching him—it was the two men who had sat at the table with Ming Lin-wen and her companion last night at the Jade Dragon.

Doug felt as if a cold stone had been dropped into his stomach.

The elevator stopped on the third floor, and the Chinese operator opened the gate. The Asian man in front of Doug exited, followed by the three American young men, and then Doug. He looked around at the crowds of partiers standing in clusters, drinks in one hand, and as often as not a cigarette in the other. Roars of laughter rang out from one quarter after another.

Everyone seemed to be having the time of their lives. *Too bad I don't feel the same*, Doug thought. *Damn you, Tim!* He felt guilty for that almost as soon as he thought it, but it was honest.

He downed the last of his cocktail, and went to the bar for a fresh one. As he waited, he leaned against the bar and watched the dancers on the ballroom floor. The orchestra was playing a fox trot, and most of the dancers were young.

As he watched, he was stunned to see Lucy Kinzler dancing on the arm of a young man about her age. He was talking quite animatedly, and she seemed to be making a valiant attempt to look interested. Doug chuckled. He walked away from the bar without ordering another drink and went straight to the dance floor.

"May I cut in?"

The young man looked startled, then his eyes dropped as he mumbled "Yes, of course," and stepped back. Doug saw the look of relief cross Lucy's face, followed by a dazzling smile as he took her hand and her waist.

"Hello, stranger," she said. "Isn't this a pleasant surprise?"

"I have to say you're a sight for sore eyes," Doug said, returning her smile.

"Mother told me she ran into you this morning."

Doug's stomach clenched at the thought.

Lucy must have seen a look cross his eyes before he could stop it, for she laughed and said, "Don't worry, she's not here. She's in bed fast asleep by now."

"She let you out on the town by yourself?"

This brought another burst of laughter from Lucy. "No, of course not. I have chaperons—but they're German, so I can drink and smoke to my heart's content. They're our neighbors across the hall at the Astor House, a nice older couple, about my parents' age. They can speak a bit of English, which is good because my German is atrocious, and Mother's is even worse. They speak perfect French, however, and since Mother made me take French lessons ever since I was ten years old, that's what we speak."

"Kinzler's a German name, isn't it?"

"Yes, and of course they noticed that right off. They might've been a little disappointed when they found out I don't really speak much German—Mother wouldn't let Father teach us any when we were kids. I'm sure it was because of the war. Father's grandparents were all from Germany, but I never knew them."

"I'm afraid I don't speak French or German," Doug admitted.

She cocked an eyebrow. "Does that imply you want to meet the Von Elslanders?"

He chuckled. "Well I'm not going to waste an opportunity to spend time with you just because your chaperons barely speak English."

"Oh, they know some, and I can translate if we have to go back to French."

The song ended, and the orchestra began a slower waltz. "Another dance?" Doug asked.

"Absolutely." The intensity in her eyes as he pulled her closer held him spellbound, and for a few moments he forgot all about the last twenty-six hours.

Then he caught sight of the two Chinese men from last night, moving through the crowd near the bar, scanning the room. He spun Lucy to the far side of the dance floor.

"What's so interesting over there?" she asked, following his eyes.

His cheeks flushed, embarrassed that she'd noticed. He tried to brush it off. "Oh, just a couple of fellows I met last night at the Jade Dragon, whom I'd rather not run into again."

"Ah, I see." Her tone sounded unconvinced, but then she smiled. "I've not heard of the Jade Dragon—is it a club? Or a restaurant?"

"A Chinese nightclub."

"Not a nice place?"

"Quite the contrary. I enjoyed it very much."

"Then you'll have to take me there sometime, when we come back to Shanghai later in the summer."

He perked up at the thought. "I didn't realize you were coming back. When will you be here?"

"Sometime around the end of July. It just depends on how long we spend in other places. Our ship back to the States leaves from here on August 10th."

"How will I know?" Doug asked. He didn't want to risk missing her.

"We'll be staying at the Astor House again," she said. "Of course, you *could* give me your address so I can write to you."

He hesitated only a second. "I will. And I'll look forward to your letters."

"Will you write me back?"

"If you tell me where you'll be, I'll write to you there." He couldn't believe how giddy he felt.

Then he spotted the two Chinese goons leaning against the bar, both staring in the same direction. He couldn't tell what they were looking at, but at least it wasn't him.

The song ended. "Let's take a break," he suggested.

He followed her to a booth along the far wall, where a white couple in their fifties sat with three glasses of champagne. The woman wore an evening gown of silver silk with elbow-length white gloves; diamond earrings and diamond pendant sparkled in the light. The man wore a black dinner jacket and black bow tie, with little pince-nez glasses. His hair—more silver than black—was slicked down and neatly parted on the side.

The man stood and said something to Lucy in French, and she replied "Merci." Then she made the introductions in English.

"May I present Douglas Bainbridge? Doug, this is Herr Von Elslander, and Frau Von Elslander."

Doug inclined his head in a polite nod. "How do you do sir, ma'am?"

The man returned Doug's nod. "How do you do?" He reached into his jacket and handed Doug a calling card; on it was printed only his name, in bold letters:

Heinrich Wilhelm Eugen, Ritter Von Elslander

Doug slipped the card into his jacket pocket.

"Doug is from San Francisco, California." Lucy slid into the booth next to Von Elslander, and took a sip of champagne. "We met on the ship to Shanghai."

She pulled a cigarette from her purse, and Von Elslander struck a match.

As he sat next to Lucy, Doug noted that the booth would shield him from view by the two Chinese goons, who continued to lounge at the bar and stare at something or someone. He didn't want that attention turned on him.

"We order the drink for you?" Von Elslander asked.

Doug smiled at the mangled grammar. "Yes, thank you. I'll have what everyone else is having."

This must have confused Von Elslander, for he looked to Lucy, who said something in French. He nodded and chuckled. "Ah, of course." He motioned for a waiter, and rattled off an order in French.

"How long have you and Frau Von Elslander been in Shanghai?" Doug asked, speaking slower than normal.

Von Elslander inclined his head as he listened, and formed his words carefully. "We have been from August."

This surprised Doug, who had assumed they were wealthy tourists. "Oh, you're Long Timers, then." It felt good to use the expression Tim had taught him.

Von Elslander didn't seem to understand, and Lucy translated to French. "Yes, long time," he said with a nod.

"How long do you plan to stay here?"

This brought a grand shrug from Von Elslander. He spoke to Lucy in French.

"He says it's not so good in Germany these days. Maybe they'll go back when it gets better."

This really surprised Doug, who had never dreamed that wealthy Germans—who were clearly not Jewish with a name beginning in 'Von'—would be displeased with the Nazi regime. He played dumb to learn more.

"Oh? What's not so good?"

Lucy gave him a look that told him she knew exactly what he was doing, but she suppressed the amused smile that briefly crossed her lips, and turned back to Von Elslander to translate the question.

He gave her a long answer. She giggled for a second as she turned back to Doug.

"He says that right now the country is being run by a bunch of common Bavarian street thugs who beat up anyone who gives them the slightest offence; and they're led by an uncouth Austrian corporal who speaks gutter German and shouts all the time."

Doug couldn't help the grin that spread across his lips.

Von Elslander's lips pursed, and he continued in French, with Lucy translating. "All the silly uniforms, the salutes, the outrageous parades and book burnings, the silly grandiose titles of their paramilitary officers—they're a bunch of spoiled little boys playing a deadly game."

Mrs. Von Elslander said something in French, her voice quiet.

"She says their two sons are still in Germany, and she worries about them. They're students at Wittenburg," Lucy translated.

The Chinese waiter arrived with an open bottle of champagne and another glass. He bowed before departing.

"Will your sons join you in Shanghai after they finish school?" Doug asked, sipping the champagne.

Von Elslander shrugged again after Lucy finished translating. "If Germany is still run by madmen, then we will send for them—but hopefully the people will remove them before then."

Doug was fascinated. "Do you think they will?"

Von Elslander looked sad. "Who can say? Right now, business is good, and the people seem willing to tolerate the madness."

Doug nodded agreement, and then turned back to Lucy. "Where do you plan to visit the next several weeks? Your mother said only that you're taking a river cruise through the gorges to Chongqing."

Lucy's face lit up. "Yes, I'm excited to see the gorges. We'll stay in Chungking a few days, then take a train north to Peking. I'm eager to see the old Imperial capital, and we can use it as a base to see other things, such as the Great Wall and the Marco Polo Bridge. It's all very exciting."

"I could suggest other sights to see while you're in China," Doug said.

"That would be lovely!" Lucy gushed.

"I'll put a list in the first letter I send to you. It'll be waiting for you when you get to Chongqing, if you tell me what hotel."

"The Imperial. I wish you could meet us at some of these places."

"I wish I could, too," Doug said. He changed the subject. "What have you done in Shanghai?"

Lucy exhaled a stream of smoke. "Mostly we've gone shopping in the nicer stores on Nanking Road, or dining in the French Concession. I managed to convince Mother to go into the Old City yesterday. It was fascinating! So different. I bought a few souvenirs from street vendors, and tried some Chinese food. Mother wouldn't eat anything. We went to the temple and watched the worshippers lighting incense in front of a giant gold Buddha; I thought it was beautiful, but Mother wouldn't let us stay long. She called them pagans."

Doug chuckled. "Well, I hope *you* had a good time at least."

"I did." Lucy put her elbow on the table and leaned her head on her hand. He couldn't read the glint in her eyes. "I'd say running into you tonight was definitely a good omen. I figured I wouldn't see you again. I'd hoped I would, though."

She sat up and laughed at herself. "Sorry, didn't mean to get sentimental. Let's just drink to friendship, shall we? Cheers."

"Cheers." They clinked their glasses and drank their champagne.

"So how are things going with your business?" she asked.

Doug shrugged, not sure what to tell her. "It started out well, but I've had some problems recently. I had to make a telephone call today, across the Trans-Pacific cable."

"Really?" she looked amazed.

He nodded. "The sound wasn't very good, even worse than cross-country long distance calls."

"Well it's amazing you can even *place* a phone call across the ocean," she said. "Must've been pretty important."

"It was."

He took another sip of champagne, and noticed Von Elslander watching them. Doug smiled at him, a little embarrassed. "We were just catching up," he explained.

Von Elslander looked confused. "Catching up? What is?"

Lucy translated into French, and Von Elslander nodded. He said something to her, and she grinned. "He says young people should be dancing instead of sitting with old folks like them."

Doug thought of the two Chinese thugs he'd seen, but just returned Lucy's smile and stood, holding out his arm for her. "Shall we, then?"

They danced several numbers, talking and laughing as if they were still back on the ship. Doug enjoyed every moment of it.

He saw no sign of the two Chinese men from last night, and put them out of his mind.

After a while, Lucy begged for a rest. Doug walked her back to the Von Elslanders' table, and then excused himself and walked to the men's room.

A couple of dark-haired men stood by the sink as he entered, conversing in French. Doug nodded as he passed them on his way to a stall. He heard them leave a moment later.

The room seemed empty as Doug walked to the sink. As he turned from the sink to dry his hands, he was startled by the presence of the short Asian man from the elevator, standing barely two feet from him. He hadn't heard him enter, or heard his footsteps across the floor.

"Where are Korea files?" he asked in heavily-accented English.

"I beg your pardon?" Doug asked, startled by the harsh edge to the stranger's voice.

"Korea files!" the man hissed.

"I don't know what you're talking about," Doug said.

The man jabbed a finger into Doug's chest, the surprise move pushing him back against the sink. "You took Tim McIntyre files. Where are Korea files?"

"I honestly don't know," Doug insisted.

He heard a click, and glanced down to see a stiletto in the man's hand, pointed at his gut.

"Korea files missing. You know?" he jabbed the stiletto just far enough to poke into Doug's shirt, pulling it back before making contact with Doug's body. It was a warning.

Doug forced himself to remain calm. The man said something was missing from the files he'd taken from Tim's desk—had this man broken into Doug's apartment and searched the files? It seemed the only explanation. Was he the one who had followed him home last night? He thought of the figure on his fire escape, and realized it had been someone far younger and more nimble than this man.

"Please, I honestly don't know what files you're talking about. I did take files from Tim's desk, but I don't know anything about them. I had no idea any were missing. Please believe me."

The man's eyes narrowed and he grunted, a short breathy sound through the nose.

"You find, you give me," he said, giving Doug another quick warning jab with the stiletto. "My name Kawakami. We speak soon."

Doug sighed in relief as Kawakami turned away and strode to the door. Then his breath caught in his throat as Kawakami opened the door and nearly ran into the two Chinese thugs from last night.

They both stood taller than Kawakami. One of the men pushed him back into the men's room, while the other closed the door behind them, remaining outside.

"We have been looking for you, Kawakami *san*," the man said in Shanghainese, seeming oblivious to Doug's presence. "You have been avoiding us."

Doug inched his way along the sink toward the door.

"I have seen you watching my place of business today," Kawakami replied in the same language. "I know who you are."

"Then you know why we are here."

Doug reached for the door, but the thug inside the bathroom grabbed him by the shoulder, never taking his eyes off Kawakami.

"You stay," he said in English.

"What is this about?" Doug asked in English. He decided it would be best if they didn't know he understood what they'd said in Shanghainese.

The man ignored him, but kept his grip on Doug's shoulder.

"We need to know what you are after, Kawakami *san*," the man said in Shanghainese.

"What I want is of no concern to the *Juntong*," Kawakami replied, his words short and clipped.

The Juntong—the Chinese government's secret police. Doug thought back to the previous night at the Jade Dragon, how these two and the big man who was clearly in charge arrived shortly after he and Tim; how they left at intermission right after Tim did, and only the big man returned for the next show—were the secret police somehow interested in what Tim was working on?

"Everything is our concern," the *Juntong* man said. "Now tell us what you are after, Kawakami *san*, and perhaps we will let you alone."

132

What happened next was so fast that Doug hardly even knew what was happening. Kawakami's right hand chopped at the side of the *Juntong* man's neck, sending him crumpling to the ground. Kawakami leapt onto his back, driving his stiletto deep and twisting it.

Doug stood as if frozen by the door. Kawakami glared at him, held the bloody stiletto toward Doug as he backed toward the door, and kicked it open. With a soft cry he threw himself against the second *Juntong* man, driving the stiletto into his midsection in two rapid thrusts, then pulled it upward and out. He closed the knife and slipped it into his pocket in the blink of an eye, and was gone.

The second *Juntong* man slumped to the ground in a sitting position, his back holding the door open. He gasped for breath for a few seconds, his eyes moving around without focusing on anything, and then he went still.

Doug's heart felt like it had stopped for the last several seconds, but now it began to pound against his chest, and he broke out in a cold sweat.

"Someone help!" he shouted in English. Then he had the presence of mind to repeat it in Mandarin. He bolted out the open door, looking around for any sign of Kawakami.

He was nowhere in sight.

Two swarthy white men in expensive silk suits who had been waiting for the men's room stared at him with wide eyes and open mouths. "These men need help," Doug said to them, first in English, and then in his mix of Mandarin and Shanghainese.

One of the men turned to the other and said something in what sounded like Italian. The only word Doug understood was "*polizia.*"

Others nearby had begun to take notice of the tall Chinese man slumped in the open doorway, eyes open, his white shirt soaked in blood and torn in two places. Within seconds the air was filled with shouting in multiple languages.

Doug stepped back into the bathroom and kneeled next to the first *Juntong* man, lying face down on the tile. He put his fingers on the side of the man's neck, but felt no pulse.

A Chinese waiter appeared in the doorway, holding onto the door frame and effectively making himself a barricade. He stared at Doug with wide eyes.

"Both of them are dead," Doug explained in Mandarin.

The waiter's stare turned accusatory, and Doug shook his head. "I saw it happen," he explained. "Someone needs to stop a Japanese man named Kawakami from leaving the building." He described Kawakami, but the waiter continued to stare at him with hard, accusing eyes.

"Go! Tell someone, before he gets away!" Doug insisted.

The waiter looked to his side and rattled off in Shanghainese what Doug had said. Doug heard the rapid shuffle of feet, followed by running, but the first waiter remained in the doorway, staring at him.

Doug sighed, stood and waited for the police to arrive.

10

For the second time in as many days, Doug found himself sitting in an uncomfortable metal chair in a plain room, across a table from a police detective. Different precinct, different detective, but it still felt like déjà vu.

The thirty-ish red-haired man had introduced himself at the Paramount as Detective Sergeant Wallace, and he'd been very polite when he insisted Doug come to the West District police station. He'd been gracious enough to allow Doug to go to the Von Elslanders' table and explain to Lucy that he had to leave. She'd looked startled when he told her he'd witnessed two men get stabbed to death, and had to go with the police. He assured her he was alright, and scribbled his address on a scrap of paper, telling her to write to him with her upcoming locations; then he hurried back to where the detective waited.

"I have to tell ya, Mr. Bainbridge," Wallace said. Doug couldn't place his accent, though British—not exactly English, and not exactly Scottish. "My partner, Detective Sergeant Lu, is convinced you killed those two Chinamen. We couldn't find no one who could swear to seeing the Japanese man you described. The only other witnesses are those two Italian men who saw you coming out of the men's room. Detective Sergeant Lu, he thinks I should arrest you."

Doug couldn't help the sweat that broke out across his brow and his upper lip. He swallowed hard, trying to stay calm.

"But I have to say, I don't think you did it," Wallace continued. "You don't seem to have no motive, for one thing; that, and you were awful specific with the events you described to us, right down to that name you gave."

Doug felt his hands trembling, and clasped them together to hide it. He'd only told Wallace and Lu what he'd seen after the *Juntong* men arrived at the men's room; he'd kept his own conversation with Kawakami to himself. "I'm sure you can track down Mr. Kawakami. It's not a common name, and he can't have had enough time to leave the city."

"If he has left, well that implies he's guilty of something, don't it?" Wallace grinned briefly, then his face went serious and he leaned back, folding his arms across his chest as he did. "But that ain't our problem you see, him escaping that is. You understand how extra-territorial rights work?"

Doug nodded.

"He's Japanese—so even if we catch him with the bloody knife in his goddamn pocket, and arrest him for the murders, he goes to the Japanese Court. The Japanese Court will release him tomorrow morning, guarantee it. He probably won't even go to trial, and if he did they'd acquit him in no time. I've been on the force here for seven years, and I can't recall a single case where the Japanese Court convicted one of their own for killing a Chinese.

"If we arrest you instead, like Detective Sergeant Lu wants, you'll go to the American Court. Now *probably* they won't convict you, seeing as how the evidence against you is pretty flimsy, but just maybe they would, given that you were the only one witnesses can put at the scene."

Doug could see where this was going. "So Sergeant Lu doesn't even want to try to find the Japanese man who's guilty, and since he's Chinese he wants *someone* to pay for murdering two of his countrymen —so that falls on me, is that it?"

Wallace chuckled. "I didn't say that, now did I?"

"Not in so many words."

136

Wallace's face grew serious again. "Now keep one thing in mind—if these two corpses turn out to be *Juntong* like you said, well, let's just say the Chinese Government isn't going to let the crime go unsolved. As long as the secret police had no interest in you, you should be fine."

Doug breathed a little easier. "I can't imagine why they would have any interest in me, Sergeant."

"*Detective* Sergeant."

"Sorry, Detective Sergeant." He had to get used to using the British titles.

"That's not to say they won't come knocking on your door, asking questions about what you saw," Wallace cautioned. "In fact, I'd count on it."

Doug knew Wallace was right. "There is a little more that I haven't told you, Detective Sergeant. Those two men who were killed, I saw them last night—Friday night, that is," he added, glancing at the clock and realizing it was nearly three AM—"at the Jade Dragon with my friend Tim McIntyre, who was killed later that night."

He saw a look cross Wallace's eyes, but disappear almost immediately.

"They had the table next to ours, and when Tim went outside for intermission, they went out, too. There was a third man with them— a big man, also Chinese, very well-dressed—and he came back after intermission, but Tim never did, and neither did the two men who were killed tonight."

Wallace's posture was stiff, and his expression serious. When he spoke, his tone was matter-of-fact, but his volume just a touch too loud. "The Jade Dragon, that's a Chinese club on West Nanking Road, isn't it? Central District, that would be. Who are the detectives at that precinct working your friend's homicide?"

"Detective Sergeants Phillips and Xiong."

Wallace wrote the names with more concentration than was necessary. "I'll get in contact with them this morning, see if any of this affects their investigation, or if they have any leads that could help us with ours. I don't suppose you saw this Kawakami at the Jade Dragon?"

"No, I've never seen him before tonight." Even after bringing up Tim's name and death, something told Doug not to disclose what Kawakami had said about Tim's files—or that he had most of them.

Wallace gathered his papers, stood and walked toward the door. "I suspect we'll be able to let you leave shortly," he said, facing the door. "We'll send in an officer to let you know. I'll be in touch with you, Mr. Bainbridge."

He closed the door hard behind him.

After a Chinese constable came for him some twenty minutes later and escorted him to the door, Doug looked around. There was a street light directly across from the station door, but deep shadows separated its ring of light from similar ones down Chengtu Road.

It was a few blocks to the bustle of Bubbling Well Road, and Doug felt deep apprehension as he walked that direction. His heart pounded, and he kept looking over his shoulder and glancing to both sides. He held his breath every time he passed a corner, wondering if anyone was waiting in the darkness there for him to pass.

Sitting in the interrogation room after Wallace left, he'd had time to mull over the events of the last two nights. It was clear that Kawakami had to be some sort of Japanese agent, perhaps in the secret services. Why else would he be interested in Tim's files on the Korean resistance, and the Chinese secret police interested in him?

One more thing was clear—Doug needed to find those Korea files. If they hadn't been in Tim's apartment the night he was killed, then he'd hidden them somewhere.

And if he'd hidden them, then he must have known someone was after them.

Would Kawakami have killed Tim over the information in those files? It seemed as plausible an explanation as any. Perhaps he should have said something to Wallace about it; but again he had a feeling in his gut that he should keep it to himself.

Might Tim have given the files to his friend Jonesy to hide for him? Doug wondered. He rounded the corner onto Bubbling Well Road, relieved to see it crowded with people even at this late hour. The crowds made him feel safer, more anonymous. Jonesy had said he lived somewhere near here, Doug remembered; too bad he didn't know exactly where. Not that he could just go knock on a man's door at three o'clock in the morning, anyway.

But he needed to find Jonesy, and quickly, before Kawakami came back.

He hailed a motor cab and rode home in silence, thoughts tumbling around his head. Even so, he nodded off during the ride, and was awakened by the driver in front of his building. He paid the fare, and hurried upstairs to his apartment.

His heart pounded as he checked the fire escape outside the kitchen window, but he was relieved to find it empty. He made sure the window was locked before stripping off his sweat-damp clothing and falling onto the bed.

He slept hard, dreamless, and awoke to bright sunlight streaming through his window. The clock said it was just past eleven o'clock, and he cursed as he jumped out of bed. He hadn't intended to sleep away half the day. He tugged on his robe and hurried out to the hall, nearly colliding with Li Baosheng in the bathroom door.

"Good morning, Mr. Bainbridge," Bao said with a polite bow. "You sleep late this morning."

Doug forced a smile and nodded.

"Fun party last night, Mr. Bainbridge?"

"You could say that," Doug said, stepping into the bathroom and closing the door. He looked in the mirror and realized how bad he looked—blond hair askew, brown eyes bloodshot, a hint of dark circles under his eyes, his robe barely fastened at his waist from the way he'd hurried into it.

"I didn't even drink that much," he muttered to his reflection.

He washed quickly, returning to his apartment as soon as he could. He was relieved not to run into his neighbors, and once inside he hurried back to his bedroom, got out the box of Tim's files, and began laying them out on the bed. He sat cross-legged on the bed in his bathrobe and went through the files, not really sure what he was looking for, wondering if anything would jump out at him.

He was an Analyst, this is what he did—he took raw data and searched for patterns, sifting clues from the minutiae.

He didn't find any patterns that would seem to shed any light on Tim's death, but he jotted down some names of informants that Tim used on various stories. Tim seemed to use the same informants frequently, so there was no mention of contact information until Doug managed to find the first time Tim had used that particular source.

It was tedious, and he rubbed his tired eyes frequently, but he pushed through until he'd gone through every file in the box.

He looked back over the page of notes he'd written—nothing about the Korea story in any of the files, and never a mention of the name Kawakami.

He put the files back in the box and folded the notes. He got dressed, combed his hair, and put the page of notes into his jacket pocket. He checked his kitchen window before going downstairs, paid Mr. Hwang to use the telephone, and asked the operator in Mandarin if there were a residential listing for Arthur Jones in the West District. Doug figured as a reporter, Jonesy would probably want to have a telephone where sources could call him.

The operator responded in Shanghainese, and he had to ask her to repeat it. She repeated in English, "There many Arthur Jones in West District. What one?"

"I'm looking for an Arthur Jones residence near the recreation grounds. Can you help me?"

There was a pause in the line, and the operator said, "This one near there. Hold line, I connect." The line rang several times, and then the operator said, "There no answer. Try call again later."

"Operator, could you please give me the address for that listing?"

She gave him the address, and he jotted it down, thanked her in Shanghainese, and hung up.

He caught the streetcar downtown, and from there took another streetcar west, past the intersection at Thibet Road where Nanking Road became Bubbling Well Road, past the towering Park Hotel to the far side of the recreation grounds. He hopped off two blocks farther at Chengtu Road. From there he could see the bubbling well a few blocks to the west. Several groups of people clustered around the well, most of them westerners, a couple of the men carrying small personal cameras with which they snapped a picture of their girlfriend posing in front of the well.

Doug walked into a small store, and asked the elderly man behind the counter how to find Li'er Street. The man gave him directions in Shanghainese, and Doug listened carefully, repeating them twice—as much to practice the words in the local language as to memorize the directions.

He backtracked east a block toward the recreation grounds, then north a block, and found the building easily enough. It was brick with elaborate stone masonry around the door and windows. The buildings in this part of Shanghai were newer than in his neighborhood, less than twenty years old.

He knocked on the concierge's door, and a short middle-aged woman answered. She smiled when he greeted her in Shanghainese and bowed, and she returned both. He asked her where to find Arthur Jones' apartment, and her expression changed, stiffened a little, and a wariness came to her eyes.

"Up two floors, door on the right," she said.

He thanked her in Shanghainese with another bow, but she returned it with a silent nod, and watched him walk up the steps until he turned at the first landing.

As he started the second flight of stairs, he heard a door open above him, and two male voices exchange a few quiet words in what sounded like English, though he couldn't make out what they were saying. When he rounded the corner to the last half-flight, he saw a tall, big-shouldered blond young man standing at the top of the steps, just turning away from the open door where Jonesy stood. The big blond was dressed in khaki pants and a white button-down shirt, the top three buttons open, with the sleeves cuffed above the elbows, revealing thick-muscled arms. He looked startled, and his cheeks colored.

Doug saw Jonesy scowl in the open door. He noticed that Jonesy's collar was open, he wore no tie, and his cuffs were unfastened; that seemed odd.

"Mr. Bainbridge, I wasn't expecting you." Jonesy's tone was gruff, irritated.

"I called on the telephone, but there was no answer," Doug said, and glanced back at the big blond young man, who stood there looking as if he didn't know what to do.

Jonesy stepped out into the hall. "Douglas Bainbridge, this is Sean Nolan, the rugby player," the mumbled introduction tumbled from his lips as if he couldn't get it out quickly enough. Then Jonesy's posture stiffened. "Mr. Nolan was good enough to grant me an interview about last week's championship game. He made a key score for the local

British club, helped 'em beat the local French club. You may recognize him from his photo in the papers."

Doug turned to the young man with a smile. "Really? Congratulations."

Sean Nolan looked embarrassed, mumbled "Thanks, mate," and looked down at his feet as he hurried down the stairs.

It occurred to Doug as Sean Nolan's rapid footfalls fell away behind him, that Sunday morning was an odd time for a sports interview. And Jonesy's apartment a strange place to conduct it. And Jonesy was not wearing a tie or cufflinks, let alone a jacket.

Doug's eyes narrowed as he looked back at Jonesy and came up the last steps.

"I didn't know you did sports reporting, Jonesy. I thought you said you did labor stories."

Jonesy squared his shoulders. "I do a bit of everything," he said, tone defensive. "I'll do any story that earns me a commission. And I happen to enjoy rugby. Now why are you here uninvited?"

"I'm hopeful you can help me with something," Doug said. He described his encounter with Kawakami last night at the Paramount, and the absence of any Korea files among Tim's things.

Jonesy's brow furrowed as he listened, and midway through Doug's story he ushered him into the apartment, glancing around before closing the door.

It was smaller than Doug's, just a single room with an alcove for cooking, and an empty cut-out in the wall where a murphy bed would be stored during the day; Doug noticed with irritation that the bed sat folded out in the middle of the room, sheets rumpled. Not something any conscientious reporter would have out while interviewing someone. Doug's stomach clenched, and a deep scowl came to his face, but Jonesy didn't seem to notice.

"That's very interesting," Jonesy said, looking off in thought. "Tim's big story about the Korean Provisional Government ran on

Friday, he was killed Friday night, and now some Japanese man is demanding his files. At knife-point no less."

"There's more," Doug said, forcing himself to focus on the situation at hand, and not what had happened here before he arrived. He told Jonesy about the three men who had occupied the next table at the Jade Dragon, how they left shortly after Tim went out for air, that only one of them had returned; and how the two others had been at the Paramount last night, confronted Kawakami, and that Doug had watched as Kawakami stabbed and killed them both.

"Good God, man!" Jonesy exclaimed when he'd finished. His eyes had grown wide, and he shook his head in awe. Then he muttered, "Tim my boy, what the devil did you get yourself into?"

"I wondered if you knew where those files might be," Doug said, watching Jonesy's face.

"Well, I don't have them, if that's what you're asking," Jonesy said, his tone gruff. "But I'd bet anything Tim locked them up somewhere—maybe a safety deposit box at a bank."

"I suppose I might find a key somewhere in his apartment," Doug thought out loud.

"I can help you look for it," Jonesy said. "Let's go."

Doug stiffened, not pleased that Jonesy was insinuating himself into the situation. "That's not necessary, I'm sure I can find it myself."

"Oh no," Jonesy said, a half-smile turning up one corner of his mouth. "You're not leaving me out of this. I was Tim's friend, and we both know you weren't, so don't even argue."

Doug's brows knit so tightly together it almost hurt. His eyes narrowed and his lips tightened. "Don't you have to stay and write your 'story?'" he asked, his tone biting with sarcasm.

Jonesy stared him in the eyes without speaking for several seconds, unblinking. "That is none of your business."

Doug's posture stiffened further. "Even so, I can handle this by myself. I don't want your help." *Not anymore.*

Jonesy's sudden chortle surprised Doug. The sardonic half-smile returned and grew into a strange grin.

"Don't act so proper with me. I've known rich boys like you before. Went to prep school, didn't you? Made some good friends there? Trust me, pal, I've heard what kind of things go on in the dormitories of those all-boy schools."

A flash of rage rushed through Doug's body. His fists clenched so hard his fingernails dug into his palms, and his cheeks burned hot.

Jonesy's expression was bitter. "Yeah, I thought so."

Doug's arm pulled back, but Jonesy stepped up and clamped his hand on Doug's forearm.

"Don't." Jonesy's voice was hard as ice, his green eyes locked on Doug's in an intimidating stare.

Doug looked away, focusing his attention on Jonesy's grip. "Let go of my arm."

"If you'll behave," Jonesy said. "Try a sucker punch, and I'll knock your lights out, understand?"

Doug nodded in silence, and Jonesy released his arm. Doug immediately took two steps backward. Jonesy continued to stare at him.

"Alright," he said after a moment's consideration. "Maybe I don't want to help you anymore. Maybe I'll let you face this Kawakami fella by yourself. But remember, pal—you came to me."

He strode to his door and opened it, then made a sweeping motion with his arm toward the hall.

Doug didn't look at him as he walked out.

"I still want to know what happened to my friend, though," Jonesy said.

Doug glanced back as he turned at the top of the stairs. Jonesy was watching him.

"Just why are you doing this, anyway?" Jonesy asked.

Doug wasn't really sure. Something compelled him to find out what had happened to Tim Friday night, and for some reason he couldn't put his finger on he didn't trust the police to find the truth. He shrugged, but said nothing.

"You're not exactly the Sam Spade type," Jonesy said. "What's in it for you?"

Doug stayed silent.

Jonesy's mouth set. "I'll stop by and check in with you this evening."

Doug's expression must have amused him, for he chuckled. "Don't worry, I'm a reporter—I'll know how to find you."

The thought sent a wave of unease through Doug's belly as he started down the stairs.

His temples pulsed with barely-suppressed rage at Jonesy's insult of his boarding school.

Brent Aleshire's face seemed to flash before his eyes, with his toe-head blond hair and classic good looks, his old roommate teasing him and wrestling with him in their underwear on the floor of their dormitory room.

His hands fisted, uncomfortable at the memory, and he slammed the door shut as he marched from the building. But then he squared his shoulders. They'd only been fourteen after all; at that age, a boy got an erection any time the wind shifted. They'd laughed about it, childishly thrusting their hips forward to exaggerate the tent effect in the front of their boxer shorts. Brent had been the first to take his in both hands and wave it around, shouting "I'm d'Artagnan! You be Rochefort. *En guard!*"

They'd had many 'sword fights' that year, leaping from bed to bed chasing one another until the cornered one was forced to defend himself in a fencing match with their erect members. *We were only horsing around*, he always reminded himself.

146

He remembered a couple of occasions when someone would accidently get a woody in the shower, and after a bit of nervous laughter someone else inevitably popped one too; and then the discomfort was masked with a full sword fight, every other boy in the shower gathered around to laugh at the horseplay, and even place bets on the pretend outcome.

"Twenty cents says Roger wins!"

"Oh yeah, I've got twenty-five that says Henry takes him."

"You're on."

None of this meant Jonesy was right, of course. He was just a jerk who enjoyed getting a rise out of Doug.

And he was ashamed to admit he had let him.

Doug saw the folded piece of paper as soon as he opened his door. It sat on the floor a foot inside the apartment, where someone had slid it under the door. He stooped to pick it up. On it were scrawled a few lines in English:

"Important--House of Singh restaurant tonight at 6:00, off Bubbling Well Rd behind the Park Hotel. Back corner, must speak in private. IMPORTANT."

It was a man's scrawl, and it was unsigned. He immediately thought of Jonesy, but it couldn't be from him—Doug had come straight home from Jonesy's place, in a motor cab, and there was no way Jonesy could have gotten here first; certainly not in enough time to slide a note under the door and disappear. So who could it be from?

He hesitated a moment before walking across the hall and knocking on his neighbors' door.

Li Baosheng answered. "Hello, Mr. Bainbridge."

Doug's reply was stiff. "Hello Bao. Did you by any chance see anyone at my door today?"

Bao nodded. "A man came by while back, knocked on your door. I said you weren't home. He said he'd leave note."

Doug's heart quickened. "What did he look like?"

Bao shrugged. "Didn't see his face. He no turn around, and kept hat on."

"What did his voice sound like?"

"He was English," Bao said.

Behind Bao, Doug saw Charlie Ford enter the living room. He smiled when he saw Doug at the door.

"Mr. Bainbridge! How are you? We haven't seen much of you this past week. Finding your way around the city?"

Doug nodded. "Yes, thank you."

Bao turned to Charlie. "Mr. Bainbridge ask about that man earlier."

"Ah, yes, Bao mentioned you had a visitor while you were out." Charlie nodded to the folded note in Doug's hand. "Plans for this evening?"

Doug suppressed his irritation. "Yes, dinner plans." He hesitated, then asked. "Do you by any chance know the House of Singh restaurant? It's near the Park Hotel."

Charlie nodded. "Yes, it's not far from the theater where I work; other side of Thibet Road. I've had lunch there a few times. Small place, Punjabi food."

Doug thought of the Sikh traffic officers. "Is it popular with the police from India?"

Charlie shrugged. "I've seen a couple of constables come in while I was there, but mostly it's ordinary citizens. Mixed crowd—Indians, whites, some Chinese. It's good food."

Doug nodded. "Thanks."

He had an idea who might want to see him, and wondered about the cryptic request for privacy.

"If you're not familiar with Indian food, I can give you some recommendations," Charlie Ford offered as Doug turned back toward his own door.

Doug forced a smile. "Thank you, but that won't be necessary. Good afternoon."

Doug told Chen Gwan that he needed to go through the rest of Tim's things. "His parents want me to send them his photographs and some clothes," he said in his blend of Mandarin and Shanghainese.

Mr. Chen took him upstairs and opened Tim's door. "Would you like me to help?" he asked in Shanghainese.

"No, thank you, Mr. Chen."

Chen bowed and walked away. Doug watched him go down the stairs before closing and locking the door.

"Where would Sam Spade look first?" he muttered to himself, remembering Jonesy's reference this morning. He'd never been a fan of the gritty detective, but he had read a couple of dime novels when he first moved to Washington, including The Maltese Falcon.

He first re-checked Tim's file cabinets, to be sure he hadn't left anything behind, and was glad to see he hadn't.

He opened all of the drawers in the dressers, searching under the stacks of clothes for a key or paper with a safe combination, then feeling with his fingers in the crevices above and behind the drawers, but came up empty.

He did the same with the kitchen drawers, but found nothing of use.

In the closets he emptied every box—and in the process found photos that Tim's parents might want; he set them aside, since that was the reason he'd given Mr. Chen for being here. He shook the shoes to see if a key might be hidden inside, and grew increasingly frustrated at his lack of success.

He felt under furniture, under window sills, over windows, behind the kitchen sink; after a while he concluded his original suspicion that Tim had given the files to someone else had to be correct. But if not to Jonesy, then to whom?

Doug could think of few possibilities—Chuck Wainwright or Gladys Sherman at Tim's office, perhaps, though Jonesy would have been more likely than either of them. Who else?

He decided to put it out of his mind for a bit, and focus on the personal items that he had indeed promised to send to the McIntyres. Besides, Mr. Chen would be suspicious if Doug walked out without such things.

Mr. Chen! The landlord and his wife had been among the most grieving of mourners at the funeral, and Mr. Chen had organized the Chinese funeral march. Would Tim have trusted Chen with his most sensitive files?

It was possible, Doug concluded. The trouble would be finding out for certain. He doubted Mr. Chen would just tell him if he asked.

He rehearsed possible questions in his mind as he gathered up photos and other personal things in a small box for Tim's parents; he discarded some ideas as hopeless, and weighed the possibility of response to other lines of questioning.

Mr. Chen must have been listening for him to come down the stairs, for he opened his door while Doug descended the last flight. He nodded to the box in Doug's hand and asked, "All finished?"

"Nearly," Doug replied. He hesitated, trying to look uncertain.

Mr. Chen looked at him with a passive expression, waiting.

"I'm sorry, but do you happen to know where Tim banked?" Doug asked. He saw a quick flash of suspicion cross Mr. Chen's eyes, and he hurriedly added, "His parents have authorized me to close his accounts, but I confess I don't know where his accounts are, and neither did they."

The bluff seemed to satisfy Mr. Chen, though a touch of suspicion remained in his eyes. "I do not know. Mr. McIntyre would not have told me such things. Ask Li Sung."

Doug faked an embarrassed laugh, and gave Mr. Chen a gracious bow of the head. "Of course, thank you. I will speak with her soon. But perhaps you can tell me if the building has a safe where Mr. McIntyre might have kept valuables?"

Doug noticed a quick look of uncertainty cross the old man's eyes before they narrowed with renewed suspicion. "Our tenants are responsible for their own valuables."

But there's something more you're not saying, Doug thought. He gave Mr. Chen another gracious head bow. "He probably kept such things at the bank, then."

Chen motioned toward the door and put the other hand behind Doug's back, suddenly in a rush to see him out.

"Just one more question, Mr. Chen—did a Japanese man visit Mr. McIntyre recently?"

Chen Gwan stood bolt straight at the mention of a Japanese man, and his lips pressed into a tight line. He said nothing.

"He did, didn't he?" Doug said. "A Japanese man came calling not long ago. What happened?"

Chen looked around, and then motioned Doug to follow him.

The Chens' apartment was large, wrapping around the back of the hall stairs in a U shape to include nearly the entire first floor of the building. The living room into which Doug stepped was as large as Tim's—or his own— apartment, with plush furniture, multiple standing screens, and paintings of Chinese peasants stooped in rice fields under green conical mountains, with puff-ball clouds in the sky.

"A Japanese man came here Saturday morning. It was before you came to tell us that Mr. McIntyre was dead. My wife and I saw him from the front window, and when he came inside, my son and I went

151

out to meet him. I asked whom he came to see, but he said he had the wrong building and left."

"What did he look like?"

Mr. Chen shrugged. "Big, wide shoulders. He had a mustache, and he wore a silk suit—three piece—and a silk hat, red carnation in his lapel, gold watch on a chain. Only Japanese dress that way, and he had a Japanese accent."

Kawakami. "Is that the only time you saw him?"

"Yes, only time we saw *him*," Chen said.

Doug's breath caught. "Who else?"

"Two Japanese marines attacked Mr. McIntyre outside the building on Wednesday night. They punched and kicked him, and shouted in Japanese, then ran away. I saw it from that window, and helped Mr. McIntyre come inside."

"How do you know they were marines?" Doug asked.

"They were in uniform," Mr. Chen said. "Everyone in this part of Shanghai knows what Japanese marines look like. Japantown is just two blocks from here, other side of Wusong Road."

Doug took a few seconds to ponder why Japanese marines had attacked Tim. At Kawakami's orders, most likely. The reason must be in Tim's files.

"Did Mr. McIntyre say why they attacked him?"

Chen shook his head. "The Japanese think they can boss everyone. I told Mr. McIntyre he did something they didn't like. They're like that. 'No good calling the police,' I said, 'they won't touch the Japanese for anything these days.' I told him 'go home, put some ice on your side, drink some tea, you'll feel better in the morning.'"

"Anyone else?" Doug asked.

Chen shook his head again.

"Thank you, Mr. Chen," Doug said, giving the landlord a deep bow in gratitude. Mr. Chen returned the bow, opened the door, and bid him good day.

Kawakami was definitely a Japanese spy, Doug reasoned as he walked home. There was no other reason he could think of that a pair of Japanese marines would have attacked Tim, and Kawakami himself have come calling early the morning after Tim died—especially with the suspicious way he left when Chen Gwan confronted him.

But Doug was no closer to getting ahold of Tim's missing files, and finding a connection to Kawakami.

Doug needed time to clear his head and think things over, so after stopping by his apartment to drop off the box of things to send to Tim's parents, he took a walk.

He headed to Honan Road and took it south, past the temple and over the Soochow Creek bridge into downtown. At Nanking Road he turned left and walked east toward the river.

When he reached the Cathay Hotel on the corner of the Bund, he went inside, relishing the feel of the air conditioning in the enormous lobby. He decided to sit in the restaurant with a pot of tea and think, but when he neared the maître'd station he saw the large *Juntong* man from the Jade Dragon sitting at a table with another Chinese man.

Doug ducked behind a potted palm and looked at them for a moment, but he didn't recognize the second man. Deciding the Cathay might not be the best place for him to be, he exited and headed back west.

Expensive stores lined this part of Nanking Road, and he walked slowly, pretending to look at the items in the window displays.

I shouldn't be doing all of this. He felt like he owed it to Tim— owed it to him for the past, owed it to him for being the only one in Shanghai who seemed willing to give his death more than a passing inspection. But he was also in over his head. He had no idea how to convince Chen Gwan to let him look at Tim's hidden files—and even if he did, what was he looking for? What kind of smoking gun might he find? And what if he didn't?

"Hello, Mr. Bainbridge of San Francisco," he heard a refined female voice say in Mandarin, and he looked up to see the smiling face of Ming Lin-wen in front of the revolving door of a high-end women's boutique, shopping bags in each hand. She wore a blue silk dress cut in the western style, with matching pumps, and a strand of pearls around her neck.

"Good afternoon, Miss Ming," he replied in Mandarin, giving her a polite bow.

"It is a pleasure to see you again," she said, her smile dazzling. "Are you shopping today?"

"No, I'm just coming from the Cathay."

"Ah, then it is good fortune that I should encounter you."

Her eyes seemed to twinkle, and Doug lost his train of thought for a second as he stared at them. He found the scent of her Chanel perfume intoxicating. Good fortune, she'd said? Had she hoped to see him again? He couldn't help but smile back at her, slightly giddy. "Yes, I suppose it is good fortune, isn't it?"

"My chauffeur won't be here for twenty minutes. Escort me to the next shop?"

"Yes, of course."

He took the packages she was carrying, she took his arm, and they strolled a block, making small talk until she pulled at the door of a hosiery store. She laughed as he blushed after entering, and turned to speak to the clerk, requesting a dozen pairs of silk stockings.

She took a seat after the clerk had gone into the back to put together the order.

"You like silk stockings?" she asked, touching her leg below her hem. "Very smooth to touch, no?"

His eyes moved from her fingertips lightly touching her shin, to the gentle curve of her calf. She crossed her legs just then, and he caught a flash of thigh before she smoothed her skirt over her knee. He

154

felt a familiar flutter in his belly, and his throat seemed to have gone dry.

"Yes," he replied, his voice croaking.

Her crooked grin and the glint in her dark eyes seemed to turn devilish.

The clerk returned from the back with a brown paper package. Ming Lin-wen handed her some cash, took the package, and then took Doug's arm. She leaned close to him as they walked out, and he could feel her warmth through his linen suit and shirt.

A black Rolls Royce limousine idled a short distance away, and a Chinese chauffeur in a black suit got out and opened the back door. He didn't look directly at them, but took the shopping bags from Doug and put them in the car without a word.

"You should come for tea," Lin-wen said. "Tuesday, four o'clock." She handed him a calling card. It bore her name and an address on Broadway.

He knew she wanted more than tea, knew he should say no; but he found himself unable to speak, his throat completely dry.

She reached out and touched his arm, then got into the back seat of the limousine. The chauffeur closed it and got into the driver's seat without ever glancing at Doug.

Doug continued walking west. The next intersection was Honan Road, and on the other side Nanking Road took on a more Chinese feel, with all of the signs posted in Chinese script, porcelain and jade objects in the store windows, small restaurants serving inexpensive stir fry, and tinny Chinese music coming from open windows. The sidewalk was more crowded, and all around him were the sounds of animated conversations in Shanghainese. Occasionally he saw a white woman in a grocery store, negotiating the cost of produce with a Chinese grocer in Pidgin.

None of this distracted him from what had just happened. He didn't have to go to tea on Tuesday, he thought. He hadn't committed; he hadn't said anything at all. He could simply not go. That was it, he decided—he would just not go.

Even as he came to that decision, he still thought about what it would be like if he did, and certain arousing images wouldn't just go away.

He paused when he passed the front door of the Jade Dragon, dark and quiet at this hour. How was it possible that it had been less than forty-eight hours since he came here with Tim? So much had happened, it seemed like at least a week.

He came to the intersection at Thibet Road, jammed with traffic. Shouts and blaring car horns nearly drowned out the sharp whistle blasts from the Sikh traffic constable. Doug saw the marquee of a Chinese theater a block to his left, and wondered if that were the theater where Charlie Ford worked. At the thought of possibly running into his neighbor on the street, he tugged his fedora lower on his face.

The twenty-two-story tower of the Park Hotel loomed in front of him as he crossed Thibet Road and continued west. Motor traffic zoomed by here, some vehicles moving as fast as forty miles per hour on the long unbroken stretch of road. On his left was the horse track, and beyond it the green lawns of the recreation grounds. A cricket match was underway on one of the fields—the local British club versus the local Australian club, judging from the flags on display in the audience.

He noted with mild surprise how refreshingly cool the shadow of the Park Hotel felt as he walked through it. He must be getting used to the climate, he mused.

He turned right at the corner just past the hotel, and found the House of Singh restaurant a half-block down. He looked at his watch—it was only quarter past five. He had passed a noisy English pub on the corner beside the hotel, so he back-tracked a half-block and went inside.

Several young men stood in the back, singing a bawdy song in unison at the top of their lungs, half-full pint glasses raised. Many in the crowd were singing along from their seats, while others watched the line of young men with grins and the occasional shout of encouragement.

At the end of the line Doug recognized the big blond rugby player he'd met exiting Jonesy's apartment this morning. He realized with irritation that Jonesy's apartment was little more than a block from here. Sean Nolan's eyes met Doug's a few seconds later, and quickly averted. He threw his arm around the black-haired young woman standing a few feet from him, and tugged her to his side, his fingertips dangerously close to the underside of her breast. She squealed with delight, put one arm around his neck and the other hand on his chest and beamed at him.

There wasn't a single Chinese person in the place—only white folks, more men than women, and they all looked very English. The big Union Jack tacked to the back wall was the final not-too-subtle clue that this was a British establishment.

Doug stepped up to the bar, noted that beer on tap seemed to be the only option, and asked for a pint of Bass.

The bartender set a tall glass of the pale ale in front of him, foam spilling down the sides. He flicked drops of it off his fingers and said, "You're a Yank? Thought so. We don't get many Yanks in here." He hurried to the other end of the bar where a buxom blonde held up an empty pint glass.

"You must be new to Shanghai," a man said to him in an English accent that seemed refined compared to most of the voices raised in shout around the pub. Doug turned around to see a smiling round-faced man, late thirties with thinning brown hair, his black necktie loosened and the collar of his white shirt unbuttoned.

"Yes," Doug admitted with a nod. The man looked familiar, but he couldn't place him. "Just over a week now. That obvious?"

The man chuckled. "Well, when an American walks into a place like this, one assumes he hasn't been here long enough to find the American entertainments. We may live all mixed together in Shanghai, but the different nationalities keep to themselves when it comes time to socialize."

"I was at the Paramount last night, and there were quite a few different nationalities present."

The man nodded. "Yes, I suppose the Paramount is a bit of an exception—the exception that proves the rule, you might say." He extended his hand. "I'm Will Geoffries. Welcome to Shanghai."

"Thank you. I'm Douglas Bainbridge."

"Pleasure to make your acquaintance, Mr. Bainbridge. And please don't let my words keep you from staying and enjoying the atmosphere here at the Black Horse. It's a friendly crowd, by and large."

He seemed to notice Doug looking toward Sean Nolan and the other singing revelers. "Those are our newest champions. Our ruggers beat the bloody Frogs in the spring championship a week ago, and we're still celebrating."

"I recognize the one on the end, I think," Doug said.

"Ah, Mr. Nolan, the rookie full back. You probably saw his mug in the papers. We're very pleased to have him here. He arrived at the start of the spring season, from Belfast in Northern Ireland. He drove for a long score in the championship match."

"I think we may have a mutual acquaintance," Doug said, and took a long drink of beer.

"Well, cheers!" Geoffries took a drink from his beer. "What brings you to Shanghai, Mr. Bainbridge? Business or pleasure?"

"My family is in the China trade, and I'm here to open a local office," Doug said.

"Ah, business must be good, then. Unusual to hear such good news these days. Mostly one hears how horrid business is, what with the global Depression and all."

"We mostly serve a high-end market—silks, porcelain vases, that sort of thing. Our customers continue spending even when the economy is bad." This was partly true, though the severity of the Depression had actually cut into his family's business; but he wasn't about to admit to that. "Besides, the economy here in Shanghai is booming."

"Yes, it is at that," Will Geoffries said. "Bit of a bright spot, what?"

Doug took another long drink of his beer. He hated small talk with strangers. He looked up at the clock on the wall, disappointed to see only ten minutes had passed. He looked back to see Geoffries watching him, and his cheeks flushed in embarrassment. "Sorry, I'm meeting someone for dinner in a little while."

"Don't mention it. Let me buy you another beer while you wait. No, no—I insist."

"Alright, thanks."

Geoffries raised his hand to get the bartender's attention, motioned to Doug and to his own glass without a word, and a moment later the bartender handed over two pints of Bass without overflowing either.

Doug noticed the difference, and wondered if it was because he was an American in a British hang-out, or if Will Geoffries were a local VIP. Geoffries was dressed in a nice gray suit, more nicely-dressed than most of the men in the pub.

"Since you're new to Shanghai, allow me to recommend some of the finer dinner establishments," Geoffries said. "The restaurant at the Park Hotel next door is quite good, but the restaurant at the Cathay downtown is better. I go there often."

"I've eaten at the Cathay. I enjoyed it very much."

"Oh, excellent! I'm a bit partial perhaps—I live in the Sassoon House next door to the Cathay."

This surprised Doug slightly—the Sassoon House was one of the most expensive addresses in Shanghai, a glittering skyscraper only a few years old. If Will Geoffries lived in a tony location like the Sassoon, and ate at fine restaurants, what was he doing in a basic English pub such as the Black Horse?

Geoffries continued with his recommendations. "There are excellent French restaurants on Avenue Joffre in the French Concession; my favorite is a place called Le Chateau de Vert. Tell the maître'd Jean-Claude that I referred you, and he'll seat you at a good table—they like to sit Americans near the kitchen door, so they won't linger too long—but if you use my name he'll give you a better place."

As Geoffries continued to list the best places to dine, Doug wondered what had prompted this burst of friendly advice to a stranger.

"If you like the Black Horse, come 'round next Sunday. We usually have a good time on Sundays."

"Thank you, that's very kind of you."

"Don't mention it. Well, I will leave you to your dinner plans. Cheers."

Geoffries walked off, leaving Doug slightly bemused by the interaction. He downed the last of his beer and set the glass on the bar.

The last thing he noticed as he exited the pub was Sean Nolan in a booth, necking with the black-haired girl he'd grabbed during the singing.

He was a few minutes early at the House of Singh, and the restaurant was mostly empty. He asked for the table in the back corner, and sat facing the door. He ordered tea and settled in to wait on his mystery companion.

Six o'clock came and went, and no one joined him. A turbaned black-bearded man in a police uniform came in with a woman in a sari and three small children, but otherwise the place was quiet.

"Mr. Bainbridge, thank you for coming."

Doug looked up to see Detective Sergeant Wallace standing behind him, by the kitchen door. He slipped into the seat across from Doug, his back to the front door.

"Did anyone know you were coming here?" Wallace's voice was low.

Doug thought of Charlie Ford and Li Baosheng, but he just shook his head.

"Good." Wallace was quiet a moment, looking as if he were trying to decide what to say. "I'm terribly sorry about your friend, Mr. McIntyre."

"Thank you. Have you learned anything from the detectives investigating his death?"

Wallace stared at him hard for several seconds. "Mr. Bainbridge, I'm going to ask you something, and it's critical that you answer me honestly—just how much do you know?"

"I beg your pardon?"

"Your friend's death wasn't a robbery. How much do you know?"

Doug took a breath. "Very little for certain. Why?"

"Tell me what you do know."

Doug hesitated, and stared back at Wallace. "Why are you asking me that here, instead of at the police station? Why the need for privacy? What exactly do *you* know, Detective Sergeant?"

"More than you, I'm certain. But what you need to understand is that this is dangerous business. You are in danger if you know too much about certain things. I need to know how much you know."

Doug was still suspicious. His eyes narrowed as he stared back at Wallace. "Why should I trust you, then? If I'm in danger—and you haven't said from whom—how am I to know that I can trust you?"

"I suppose you don't. But let me ask you this—why do you suppose I didn't want to meet at the police station?"

A puzzle piece seemed to fall into place in Doug's mind. "Because you don't trust the other police."

Wallace nodded. "And neither should you, Mr. Bainbridge. Now, tell me what you know."

11

It took a while for Doug to recount everything that had happened since the last time he'd seen Tim alive. No one disturbed them as they sat, not even the staff. Wallace just leaned back with his arms crossed and listened, nodding occasionally. A pained expression came to his face when Doug mentioned the Green Gang, and how Li Sung thought Tim should have left them alone.

"So, now that I've told you what I know, tell me why I'm in danger," Doug said.

"What do you know about the Green Gang?" Wallace asked.

"That they're the largest drug syndicate in China, and that they have connections in the government that keep them safe from prosecution," Doug said.

"Any specifics?"

"Their leader, Du something—"

"Du Yuesheng."

"Yes, Du Yuesheng—I've been told he's a government anti-opium commissioner."

"That's correct. Big-eared Du. He's close to President Chiang Kai-shek. That makes him untouchable. What else do you know about them, specifically?"

"That's it."

Wallace laid his hands flat on the table, and took a deep breath. "There is a lot of dirty money flowing around Shanghai, Mr. Bainbridge, and lots of officials are on the Green Gang's payroll. Your friend Mr. McIntyre came to speak with me about it—the corruption, that is.

"He'd tracked down police arrest records, and noticed that I'd arrested Green Gang members twice—once in 1933, and once in 1934. He knew that was the second most in my precinct, after Detective Inspector Greenlee, who had arrested their gangsters five times. He'd also noticed we arrested Green Gang members a lot less often than other gangs, even though there's lots more of 'em. Mr. McIntyre asked to speak with Detective Inspector Greenlee, and I told him the detective inspector had been killed by a bullet to the chest in March of this year."

Something stirred inside Doug—excitement or dread, he wasn't sure. It all sounded like the organized crime mafia in the States during Prohibition. He wondered just how deep Tim had gotten himself.

"When exactly did Tim come to talk to you about all this?"

"Thursday."

Doug's eyebrows rose. "Thursday?" *Just three days ago?*

"That's right—and he was killed about thirty hours later. I told him the Green Gang was a touchy subject; maybe I should've discouraged him more. Was one of their blokes what shot up Detective Inspector Greenlee, ya know. I still think he was targeted specific-like, but the inquest ruled it 'a normal consequence of a raid on a gambling house and the resultant fire fight.'"

The look on his face implied Wallace didn't agree.

"I didn't know Mr. McIntyre'd been killed until you told me last night at the station."

Doug took a moment to consider this.

"Detective Sergeant, would you mind telling me everything you told Tim?"

Wallace shook his head. "I'd leave it alone if I were you, mate."

I probably should. But something inside him wouldn't let it go. He owed it to Tim, he supposed; and besides that, it just wouldn't be right. Someone needed to seek justice.

"Let me ask you this, Detective Sergeant Wallace—what are the odds the detectives working Tim's case are going to pursue any of this?"

"None," Wallace said, his expression stony.

Doug nodded. "That's what I expected. I think you and I need to start at the beginning—tell me what you said to Tim, and what he said to you. I want to know everything."

Wallace looked at him hard for a moment. "Your funeral, mate—just make certain it's not mine, too."

He leaned forward, lowering his voice even more. "I told Mr. McIntyre that they—the Green Gang—ain't so easy to catch by surprise. Almost every time we get information about something they're up to, and we go out to raid one of their joints, they're ready for us. Either they've cleaned house and there ain't nothin' left for us to find, or they're firing down on us with bloody Tommy Guns. Someone always tips 'em off. Maybe that someone's the informant who told us about the joint in the first place, settin' us up and gettin' double payment for it; or maybe it's someone on the inside, a dirty copper. I used to hope that weren't it, but I ain't stupid, neither. I told him all of that.

"And I told him If we *do* arrest some of the bastards, it's even harder to get anything to stick. They always seem to get off Scot free. Chinese judges ain't known to be lenient, or inclined to hand out Not Guilty verdicts, you know? But them Green Gang boys always get released, and almost never go to trial."

He shook his head, a look of disgust on his face.

"Your friend Mr. McIntyre asked if I had any direct evidence of corruption. He asked if I'd ever witnessed a bribe to anyone in the police or the courts. I told him 'No, course not. But the fellas talk, it's no secret some of 'em are on the take.' I told him it's usually small-time operators that hand out bribes, but sometimes it's the big fish—the ones with the deepest pockets."

"And that's what Tim was interested in," Doug said, as much to himself as to Wallace.

"He seemed pretty interested. Typical reporter, he asked if I'd mention any names, and told me he'd keep it off the record. I just laughed at him." Wallace chuckled again at the memory. "I said 'Hell, that wouldn't save my arse! I'd find myself in a cold grave like Detective Inspector Greenlee, God rest him.' He asked how anyone would know it was me, if, as I'd told him, the fellas talk, so couldn't any of them be the ones who'd leaked the names?"

He stopped, and looked at his hands on the table.

"And what did you say?" Doug prompted.

Wallace took a look around. A large Indian family had come in and taken a table near the front, but the restaurant was still mostly empty.

He leaned in and whispered. "I said it's because none of the others have ever got a visit from their captain, ordering them to let their perpetrators go, just walk out the door, with no explanation gave other than 'That's an order!' I told him that happened to me twice. *And* I said 'Everyone knows I was close to Detective Inspector Greenlee, so they'd suspect me in a heartbeat.'

"It only took your Mr. McIntyre a few seconds to catch what I was telling him—I wasn't naming names, but he got my meaning."

It was a few seconds before Doug understood. "And who is your captain?"

"I'm still not naming names, mate."

Doug's head was swimming. Powerful crime lords, corrupt police and judges—any number of potential killers.

And there was still Kawakami—how did he figure into it? Clearly he was not hesitant to kill. Doug felt more confused now than he ever had.

Wallace was watching him.

"So what you're telling me is that if Tim was killed by the Green Gang, there's no chance the police will find the killers," Doug said.

Wallace nodded. "That's right. It's bloody lousy, I know—but there ain't nothing you or I can do about it."

"Tim must have thought he could do something about it," Doug mused, as much to himself as to Wallace.

"Yeah, and look where that landed him."

"Hmm," Doug grunted, his heart sinking even as his mind grasped for any hope of justice. Clearly Tim had been looking to make a difference through exposing the corruption in the newspapers— perhaps a similar strategy would bring Tim a modicum of justice for his death. If the police and the courts wouldn't do anything, the newspapers surely would.

That meant finding Jonesy. Doug hated that, but he couldn't think of anyone else.

"Thank you, Detective Sergeant," Doug said, rising from his seat.

Wallace didn't rise. "You best leave this alone, Mr. Bainbridge. Don't put yourself—or me—in any more danger." His eyes narrowed. "I won't take too kindly to that. Understand?"

Doug felt his insides go cold at the sight of Wallace's menacing glare. "I understand."

"Good. I'll keep an eye on you, Mr. Bainbridge." Wallace raised his hand to signal to the waiter as Doug walked away.

Back on Bubbling Well Road beside the Park Hotel, Doug briefly considered going straight to Jonesy's apartment—it wasn't even two blocks away, just west of the Recreation Grounds—but instead opted to cross the street into the park, remembering that Jonesy had said he went to the Rec grounds most evenings. Doug figured if he couldn't find Jonesy there, he could easily walk over a couple of blocks to his apartment house.

The sun was getting low in the west, but the cricket match was still going, and Doug walked an arc around it, scanning the crowd. Beyond the Cricket field were the tennis courts, where several people still played, but not Jonesy. A large number of English women chatted at the lawn bowling grounds, and there were several shouts of "Well done!" when one threw a particularly good pitch. Beyond them another group of well-dressed English women played croquet.

The football/rugby field stood empty for the summer, and Doug cut across it toward the Administration building, which divided the Recreation Grounds from the horse track and its grandstand.

Inside, signs pointed right for the basketball courts, up the stairs for the offices of the Shanghai Racing Club, and to the left for "Men's and Women's swimming baths."

It took him a few seconds to decide that Jonesy was more likely to go for a swim than to play a vigorous game such as basketball. He turned left. At the end of the hall signs pointed right for the "Women's swimming baths" and left for the men's.

It didn't surprise him that the Shanghai Recreation Grounds still had old-fashioned swimming facilities—the sexes separated, no bathing suits— since the clubs seemed to all be run by wealthy old men, and the older generation was still suspicious of mingling the sexes in such an "intimate" activity.

The thought made Doug uneasy. It wasn't the nude swimming that made him uncomfortable—he had grown up with that—but the idea of finding Jonesy in such a setting gave him pause.

Doug had been eleven when their country club had put in an outdoor "family" pool. His parents never used it. Father said "Public bathing is vulgar, simply vulgar." Mother had refused even to speak of it. He and his brother Will, fifteen at the time, had taken their allowances and gone downtown to buy bathing suits—one-piece affairs, short trunks connected to a sleeveless top, in seamless synthetic fabric that was slightly stretchy. Will bought a black one, and Doug a red and white stripped one. They were stylish and slightly daring.

Doug had had butterflies in his stomach the first time he put it on and walked out to the pool area—he'd never shown bare legs, arms, and shoulders in public before. He somehow felt more exposed in the bathing suit in public than he had naked in the men's pool.

"But girls will see our arms and legs!" he'd said to Will.

"That's the idea, dummy!" Will had replied.

Then he saw the way the girls at the pool gathered around Will, flirting with him while eyeing his arms and shoulders, and Doug decided this wasn't so bad.

That first summer, no one older than twenty used the outdoor "family" pool; but slowly that changed. The last time Doug had visited the country club—right before he entered the navy three years ago—there had been a considerable number of young parents in their 20s and 30s, swimming with their children at the outdoor pool. And many of the teenage boys now wore trunks only, with bare torsos—something that would have gotten Doug and his friends kicked out of the club when he was younger.

Even now, Doug didn't think he'd be comfortable in bathing trunks—it would feel like walking around in his underwear. Ironic, perhaps, but skinny-dipping in a men-only area would feel less exposed.

But he'd never worried about men like Jonesy in those environments. What would he do if he did encounter Jonesy here? As he entered the men's lounge and saw the young Chinese attendant, he thought he might not have to.

The white-coated Chinese attendant bowed and smiled when he came in. "Help you, sir?" he said in English.

"I hope so," Doug said in his Mandarin-Shanghainese blend. "I'm looking for someone, a friend of mine. His name is Art Jones, an American. He's about this tall"—he held his hand flat, level with his forehead—"and a bit heavier than me. His hair is brown, and he has a big mustache."

"Jonesy?" the attendant replied, in English. "He write for newspaper?"

Doug couldn't help but be surprised. "Yes, that's him," he said in English. "Is he here?"

The attendant was silent, so Doug handed him a dime. "He here. You go for swim too? Forty cent."

"Would it be possible to send him a message?"

The attendant shrugged, and Doug handed him another dime. "I give him message."

Doug asked for paper and pen, and wrote a short note; he folded it in half and handed it to the attendant. He took a seat as the attendant disappeared.

A pair of middle-aged men came out the door speaking French. They gave Doug a curious look as they passed, but resumed talking before leaving the lounge.

It was several minutes before the attendant returned. Doug stood as he approached.

"Jonesy say he meet you outside, ten minutes."

Doug thanked him and bowed. The attendant seemed to be waiting for something, so Doug fished another dime out of his pocket and handed it over. The attendant smiled and bowed.

The sun had dropped below the buildings to the west by the time Jonesy came outside a short while later, his hair wet and recently combed. He kept his hat in his hand as he approached.

"I didn't expect to see you again so soon," he said. "It seemed you couldn't get away from me fast enough, and now you track me down at the pool and send me a note that you need to speak to me right away."

Doug's jaw tightened at the reference to earlier. "Yes, I apologize for my manners this afternoon. I should not have been so dismissive."

Jonesy grunted. "I've come to expect it. Now what is the nature of your need to see me—business, or personal?"

Doug's gut clenched at the implication. *This was a bad idea.* "Business," he said, unable to keep the irritation from his tone.

Jonesy nodded. "Let's walk," he said, and they headed west across the empty football/rugby field. "Is this concerning our conversation earlier?"

"Yes, I have new information."

"Mr. Chen had the files?"

Doug scowled. "I never found out." He hated admitting that.

"Did you *ask* him?"

Doug's scowl deepened at Jonesy's accusatory tone. "It's not that easy. If I asked him directly, he would never tell me."

From the corner of his eye he saw Jonesy shaking his head. "I'll ask him, then. I'll bet you five bucks he'll tell me."

Doug ignored the bet.

"So then, Sherlock Holmes, what did you learn that's so important?"

"Mr. Chen did mention that Tim was attacked by a pair of Japanese marines in front of his building a few nights before he was killed."

"Japanese marines, huh? Yeah, they don't fool around. So you're probably thinking this is connected with that Kawakami fella from last night, the one that killed those Chinese secret police."

"I can't believe it's not."

"I think it's a good lead, anyway. Something to look into. So why rush over to tell me that? Do you need my advice on how to follow a lead?" Jonesy shook his head again. "Sam Spade you are not."

"No, there's more."

"Tell me, then."

"There was a note slipped under my door when I got home this afternoon, unsigned," Doug said, and recounted his meeting with Detective Sergeant Wallace at the House of Singh, and everything that had been said.

171

Jonesy listened in silence. When Doug had finished, he looked down and shook his head. "Damn it, Tim," he muttered.

"What?"

Jonesy grunted. "Tim never was one to back off from a story, for any reason. Seems that did him in, doesn't it?"

Doug shrugged. "The question is, which one?"

"If you want my advice, focus on that Kawakami character. He said he's coming back, didn't he? So find out what's in those files he's looking for. I can get them from Mr. Chen."

Doug didn't argue. "So you think it was Kawakami, then, and not the Green Gang?"

Jonesy chuckled. "I have no idea. Could've been either of them. But my advice to you is to leave that Green Gang strictly alone. You go digging into that too far, and someone's going to want you dead, too."

"I was thinking you would want to write the story exposing the corruption."

Jonesy guffawed. "Not on your life."

"Don't you think Tim deserves that?"

Jonesy stopped, faced Doug, and stared him hard in the face. "Don't talk to me about what Tim deserved, Mr. Johnny-come-lately."

Doug nodded in resignation. "Sorry. I meant no offense." He turned and resumed walking. "Do you want to go see Chen Gwan now?"

"No, tomorrow. I've got dinner plans."

Doug felt his chest constrict. "I don't need to know about your personal life."

Jonesy's brow knit. "I wasn't telling you anything about my personal life. I just said I've got plans."

Doug felt the irritation rising, and he let himself respond without pushing it down. "Your friend Mr. Nolan, the rugby player—he was with a woman tonight. I saw him at a pub, and they were necking." He felt a touch of *schadenfreude* delivering that news.

172

"Boy, you are a piece of work," Jonesy said. "You think I don't know the score? I'm not some tenderfoot, I've been around. It happens all the time. And what do you care, anyhow?"

"I don't," Doug said, defensive.

Jonesy stared at him hard for several seconds. "You're too young to be bitter."

"I beg your pardon?"

"You and your nasty attitude. You're alone, you're not the loner type, probably not too happy, and, well—you know what they say, 'Misery loves company.' I'll see you tomorrow, ten o'clock at Mr. Chen's."

Jonesy put his hat on and crossed the street from the Recreation grounds into his neighborhood.

Doug's hands fisted at his side as he watched Jonesy storm away. He was *not* bitter. He loved his life. And how dare Jonesy judge him?

The Recreation grounds were deserted now as he stomped north across them to Bubbling Well Road. His stomach growled, reminding him that he hadn't eaten. He wondered if Lucy Kinzler were eating dinner somewhere, on her last night in Shanghai, or if she and her mother would order room service while they stayed in and packed.

He hailed a motor cab and climbed in the back. "Astor House Hotel, Broadway."

12

Doug asked the desk clerk at the Astor House to dial Mrs. Kinzler's room. His fingers drummed on the desk as he listened to the line ring. He hoped they were there. He hoped Lucy was the one to answer the phone.

He got the former, but not the latter.

"Good evening, Mrs. Kinzler," he said, forcing himself to sound friendly. "This is Douglas Bainbridge. We met on the ship, and then at the American Express office yesterday."

"How are you, Mr. Bainbridge? So good of you to call. You wish to speak with Lucy?"

He smiled for real at her enthusiasm. "Yes, please."

He heard her set the phone down, followed by some muted conversation; then Lucy's frantic voice said, "Doug? Are you alright? What's going on?"

Her concern touched him. "Yes, I'm fine. I'll tell you all about it—can you meet? I'm downstairs in the hotel lobby. Have you eaten?"

There was silence on the line for several seconds, and then he heard Mrs. Kinzler's voice in the background saying, "Yes, of course dear."

"Yes, I can meet you," Lucy said. "Let me freshen up, and I'll be down in a few minutes."

When she came down the red-carpeted stairs fifteen minutes later, her long fingers gliding down the intricately carved wooden banister, she wore a long silver evening gown, diamond earrings, and her hair was curled. Doug felt shabby in his wrinkled linen suit as she came up and kissed his cheek.

"You look beautiful." It was an understatement, but he couldn't think of anything better.

"Thank you." Her dazzling smile made a tingle run up his spine.

"Can we get dinner?" He gave her his arm and led her toward the dining room. "I hope you haven't eaten."

"We ordered room service, but it hadn't arrived yet when you called," Lucy said. "Mother cancelled my dinner."

They walked through a set of dark wood doors and entered the long, colonnaded dining room; they were met by a white maître'd in a black tuxedo, with slicked-back hair and a pencil-thin black mustache.

"May I help you?" he asked in a snooty tone, in a posh sort of lockjaw New York accent. He glanced at Doug's suit with a look of disdain.

Doug already felt underdressed next to Lucy, but in response he squared his shoulders and lifted his chin. "Table for two, please," he said in his most commanding tone.

"I'm sorry sir, but we have a dress code."

Doug was irritated at himself for not thinking of that. He'd been too hasty coming straight here from the recreation grounds—he should have stopped by home to change into his white dinner jacket. Why had he been in such a hurry? "Do you rent dinner jackets?"

"Come with me, sir."

Doug apologized to Lucy and excused himself, following the man around a corner into a long closet. Five minutes later he was dressed in a white jacket and black tie; not as nicely fitted as his own, but it would do.

They followed the maître'd down the long dining hall with a domed ceiling of stained glass, all of the tables full, even on a Sunday evening.

"There are the Von Elslanders," Lucy said as they passed a table, and the older German couple gave them a polite nod as they passed.

The dining hall opened into a circular room, brightly lit by four enormous crystal chandeliers hanging from carved metal arches in a scalloped ceiling of frosted glass, with panes of stained glass in the corners of each scallop. Doug imagined the place in the daytime, filled with sunlight.

They were given a table near the back.

"I was so worried last night," Lucy said after the maître'd departed. "What the devil is going on, Doug?"

He loved that she spoke that way, like a man. It was amusing, and oddly charming.

"Everything's fine," he assured her. "You don't need to worry."

"How could I not? Doug, you left with the police because you'd seen two men get killed. What happened?"

"They just wanted to ask me some questions. I told them what I could."

"They could have done that right there at the Paramount," Lucy said, her eyes skeptical. "Why did they have to take you with them? Do they think you killed those men?"

"No, of course not," he said, putting on a smile for her behalf. "I'm here, aren't I? Clearly they didn't arrest me."

The Chinese waiter arrived, interrupting their conversation. Lucy ordered the veal, and Doug the duck and a bottle of Bordeaux.

"How long were you there?" Lucy asked after the waiter departed. "At the police station, I mean."

"Not much more than an hour." He tried to sound nonchalant.

"Did you know those men—the ones who were killed?"

"Not at all." It wasn't a complete lie.

She stared at him for several seconds, her eyes searching. Then she leaned back and crossed her arms. "You're not telling me something."

"There's nothing more to tell."

She gave him an exasperated sigh and shook her head. "I know you and I don't owe each other anything, but I had hoped—what I mean is, I thought you at least cared enough to be honest with me."

He stiffened. "Who says I'm not being honest with you?"

"I do. Not completely honest, anyway. There's more you're not saying, and maybe I don't have a right to expect you to, but I don't know why you came here tonight if you don't want to talk to me."

Doug hesitated, torn between not wanting to involve her in something that might prove dangerous, and wanting to confide in her.

"It's a long story," he finally said.

Her shoulders seemed to relax, and she unfolded her arms. "We've got all evening."

He nodded, a sense of relief already starting to wash over him. "The day we arrived in Shanghai, I ran into an old childhood acquaintance of mine from San Francisco..."

He told her about his interactions with Tim, and their night at the Jade Dragon, and she listened in silence until he came to the part where he found Tim dead.

"Oh my God, Doug!" she said, putting her hand on top of his and the other hand to her chest. She wrapped her fingers around his hand and squeezed, and he felt a tingle run through him.

He told her of his concerns that the police weren't taking it seriously, and he stopped when their food arrived.

"I'm not sure I can eat now," she said, looking down at her plate. "It smells divine, but I'm not hungry anymore."

"Please eat," he said. "I'd feel terrible if you went hungry because my story upset you."

She nodded and took a few small bites of her veal. "Your poor friend," she said after a while, and took a long drink of wine. "Please go on."

"Well—I'm not sure why exactly, but I haven't been able to ignore it. I'm not sure what I'm doing, or what I think I can do about it, but I keep trying to figure out what happened, who did this to Tim."

"I think that's very noble of you," Lucy said, reaching out to touch his forearm. He looked up from his plate, and she gave him a weak smile.

"Those two Chinese men who were stabbed last night at the Paramount—they were at the Jade Dragon Friday night, at the table next to ours. They were the ones who went out after Tim did, and didn't come back. They were probably the two Chinese men the witnesses in front of the club said they saw Tim arguing with before they all went around a corner. I followed, and that's where I found Tim's body."

She looked stunned.

"There's more—at the police station, I found out the two men were *Juntong*—Chinese secret police."

"Secret police?" She looked away, and began to think out-loud. "You were in the men's room when they were killed there—were they trying to kill you, too? Because you'd seen them when your friend was killed?"

He shook his head. "No, they weren't there for me. They were there to confront a Japanese man—and *he* was there to confront me, about some files I had taken from Tim's apartment a few hours after he was killed; but I don't have the files he wants. The Japanese man killed the two *Juntong*."

She stared at him in wide-mouthed silence.

He shrugged. "I don't know what I'm doing, or even why. It's really none of my business, and I'm not exactly Charlie Chan."

Her expression hardened. "It sounds to me like Inspector Chan is exactly what's needed. If not you, then whom? You said the police aren't looking into it."

"Exactly—so what can I do?"

"Find the truth."

"And then what?"

"I don't know—but I'm sure you can figure that out."

"I'm not sure it's wise for me to get involved."

She nodded, and reached out to squeeze his forearm. "You're concerned about the danger? I am too. You should be very cautious, but I'm sure you can find the truth. You're a smart man, Doug; I have confidence."

"It's not the danger," Doug said. He wasn't afraid for his safety, but he was concerned about his responsibilities.

She looked confused. "Then what is it?"

He took a deep breath. "I haven't been completely forthcoming with you. I couldn't be, I hope you understand."

She leaned back from the table slightly, and a veil seemed to come across her eyes. "You're married."

"No."

"Engaged? Promised to some heiress in San Francisco?"

He smiled and shook his head. "No, nothing like that."

She seemed to relax a bit, and he plunged ahead. "I told you I work for my father's company, and that I was coming to Shanghai to open a local office—well, that's not true. That was my cover story, as I'm not really supposed to broadcast what I'm actually doing. I work for the Office of Naval Intelligence."

She guffawed. "Oh, that's rich. A *spy*? Really Doug—I've heard all kinds of brush-off lines, but that's a doozy."

Her disbelief stung. She must have seen the look on his face, and a glint of uncertainty came to her eyes. "A spy? For the Navy?"

"No, I'm not a spy." He chuckled at the image she must have from cloak-and-dagger dime novels. "The U.S. Navy doesn't have spies. We gather our intelligence more-or-less openly, through naval attachés at embassies, or through Intelligence Officers attached to the fleets. That raw intelligence is sent to ONI in Washington, where Intelligence Analysts such as myself piece through it, and try to make sense of the puzzle. I've been sent to China on a two-year immersion, so that in the near future ONI can have Intelligence Officers who are completely versed in Chinese culture and politics. It's classified—not exactly top secret, but I'm not supposed to talk about it."

He couldn't comprehend the scowl he saw on her face. "And yet you're talking about it now, to me."

He nodded. "Yes. It's part of the reason I don't think it's wise for me to get more involved in this whole thing with Tim than I already am."

She crossed her arms, and her scowl deepened. "Then why were you even looking into it at all? Why didn't you leave it alone from the beginning? Turn your back completely?"

That stung. "I can't explain it. I just feel like I owe Tim something. I can't just turn my back, but I can't really do anything, either. I just—"

"Just stop."

The sharpness of her tone startled him, and he stared at her.

"Don't sit there and equivocate. Either do something, or don't. Make up your damn mind."

"I don't understand why you're so upset—"

"You don't understand why I'm upset?" She stared at him, Incredulous. "I don't even *know* you, Douglas Bainbridge. Everything you told me on the ship was a lie."

He stiffened. "Most of it was true. I only lied about why I was coming to Shanghai, and I told you I had to."

"And you don't think that changes everything?"

"No, not everything. Why should it? You still know me— everything else was completely true."

"What does that matter?" She looked away, her eyes burning.

He watched her in silence, wondering what she meant. When she looked back at him a moment later, he thought he caught a touch of sadness behind the anger in her eyes.

"I guess I thought perhaps—oh, I don't know what I thought." She picked up her fork and stabbed at her veal, shoving a bite into her mouth.

"Thought what?" he prodded. "Tell me."

She let out her breath hard and re-crossed her arms. "It makes me sound like a foolish girl," she said.

"I don't think you're foolish."

"I like you, Doug. I really like you. And I like Shanghai. I was starting to imagine what it might be like to come back here next year, after I finish at Vassar—" She stopped, looking down at her hands.

His heart raced.

"I thought perhaps if I came back here, for good, that you and I might have a future. But now..." she let her voice trail off.

"What?"

She looked back up, shaking her head. "It's nothing. If you were actually working for your father, like you said—well then, perhaps it could have worked out. But under the circumstances, it's not possible now."

He didn't know what to say. Part of him wanted to tell her it didn't matter, it could still work out; but another part of him knew she was probably right. So why had he come here tonight?

Because Jonesy had goaded him. He suddenly felt defiant.

"I'm not the marrying kind." He realized belatedly that he'd just quoted Sam Spade. His earlier conversation with Jonesy had put the cynical detective in his thoughts. *Damn you, Jonesy!*

"Neither am I," she said, her voice sounding a touch defensive.

He didn't know why that stung. He forced a nonchalant smile. "Well, we've had some laughs, haven't we?"

She stared at him in silence, a strange look on her face, almost searching.

"Listen, sweetheart—my situation doesn't mean you can't come back to Shanghai next summer. Look me up when you do, I'd like it.

We'll go dancing, have some more laughs." He wasn't sure whose voice was coming out of his mouth.

Her expression grew cold. "Aren't we the man about town?"

He shrugged. "I'll be here, you can look me up if you want to."

They finished their meal in silence. As they sat, Doug found himself falling into a malaise. By the time he paid the check and took her arm to escort her from the dining room, he felt very foolish. He tried to think of something to say, something that would fix it, but nothing came to mind.

When they reached the lobby and came to the bottom of the stairs, she removed her arm from his and looked at him with an unreadable expression.

"Would you like to get a drink somewhere?" he asked, hopeful. "I can get a cab to take us to the Cathay."

She shook her head. "No." She extended her hand as if to shake in farewell, but he didn't take it.

"Listen, about earlier—"

She cut him off. "I understand."

"No, I don't think you do. You see, I'm not sure why I said any of that earlier, or acted that way toward you. You've been really swell toward me, and I treated you like some nobody. I'm sorry."

She gave him a weak smile. "Thank you for the apology. Now I need to get back upstairs, and help Mother finish our packing. Good night, Doug."

Fear swept through his belly like a flock of birds, and his heart began to race. "May I write to you still?"

She hesitated a second, and then nodded. "Of course you may."

"And may I see you when you return to Shanghai in August?"

"We'll see." She hesitated again, then leaned in and kissed his cheek. "Be careful, Doug. Good night."

He watched her climb the stairs, his hands trembling. He balled them into fists.

13

The temperature had dropped while he was with Lucy; a stiff breeze from the northwest tugged at his jacket, and it felt cool for the first time in his eight days in Shanghai. As he walked west up Soochow Road along the north bank of the wide creek, he heard the low rumble of distant thunder.

The houseboats lining the creek rocked in the wind, and scrawny men emerged from inside to shutter the windows, then hurry back in.

It was four blocks from the Astor House to Kiangse Road, his route home, and he picked up his pace as the wind grew stronger. It began to rain as he reached Kiangse Road, large heavy drops, and he tugged his hat lower over his face and tucked his chin to his chest. He hurried the last few blocks, but shortly before he reached Huang Lei Road the heavens opened and rain poured down, drenching him.

He sprinted the last half-block to his building on the corner, and as he reached the door he saw Constable Billy Dickinson dashing from the street to the relative shelter of the awning over Mr. Hwang's store window. He grinned and waved as he saw Doug opening the door a few feet away.

"Good evening, Mr. Bainbridge!" he shouted over the din of the rain. "Nice night, huh?" A steady drip fell from the rim of his police hat.

"Come inside," Doug said, motioning with his hand. Billy Dickinson dashed the 10 feet from the awning to the open door, laughing.

"Thank you, Mr. Bainbridge, sir. Very kind of you."

"The awning isn't much shelter."

Billy laughed. "No, it's not at that." The awning snapped in the wind. Billy looked up at the dark sky, the clouds illuminated by the occasional flash of lightning. "I hope this blows over soon—this is ruining my schedule."

Doug looked at the young man, thinking. "How long have you been with the Shanghai Police, Constable Dickinson?"

"Call me Billy," the constable said with a grin. "I started with the SMP in January. My class trained in London a couple weeks, and we arrived here mid-February. You might find this hard to believe, but it was bloody cold here then. We had a big ice storm the week after I got here, made a nasty mess of things."

"How do you like it on the force?"

"Beats any job I ever had," Billy said with a grin. "It ain't too hard work most of the time, and we get some excitement now and then. I like the blokes I work with, we have a grand time of it. I've got used to working nights now, in fact I like it. Didn't think I would, but I do. What do you do, Mr. Bainbridge?"

"I export Chinese luxury goods to the States, for my family business."

"Now that sounds like right interesting work, sir."

"You can call me Doug."

"Oh, now that wouldn't do at all, Mr. Bainbridge, sir."

Doug considered a moment; Billy had been in Shanghai less than four months—probably not enough time to have learned anything useful regarding the Green Gang or its protectors on the force, but also not enough time to have been sucked into any corruption. He was at the North District precinct, and the detectives Doug was interested in learning more about were Central District and West District. Still, he could be useful.

"Billy, when you said a couple of nights ago—the night my friend was killed—that if I could think of anything you could help with, to let you know—you meant that?"

"Of course, sir." Billy's expression looked earnest. "What can I do?"

"Do you and your pals ever socialize with cops from other districts?"

"Oh sure. When we get nights off, we go to pubs downtown sometimes, places where other cops go. There are some nice friendly blokes from other precincts, and we all socialize together. It's a bit of a fraternity, being on the force."

Just what I was hoping for. "When are your nights off this week?"

"Why, I got me a regular schedule, sir—every Monday and Tuesday night off. I lucked into that—most first years ain't got a regular schedule."

Doug grinned and patted the young constable on the shoulder. "I wonder if I might ask you to do something for me."

"Of course, sir."

"Can you keep it confidential?"

"On my honor," Billy said, crossing his heart.

The hall was empty, but Doug still lowered his voice to just above a whisper. "There's a possibility my friend may have been killed by gangsters who are being protected by cops they've bribed—would you let me know if you hear anything about any cops on the payroll of the Green Gang? Anything at all, no matter how small."

Billy looked doubtful. "I don't know about that, sir. The force has been cracking down on corruption for a while. They say it's a pet cause of the commissioner. There ain't much talk about things like that in the barracks no more; not like there once was, from what I hear."

Doug nodded. "I understand. Still, if you hear anything, even off-hand—would you let me know?"

"I'll do what I can, Mr. Bainbridge, sir."

Doug patted Billy's shoulder. "I appreciate that, Billy. And remember—keep this between us."

His wet clothes clung to him as he climbed the stairs. He couldn't wait to get inside his apartment and change, but as soon as he stepped inside he saw rain blowing in his front window, and water puddled on the floor.

"Damn it!" He rushed to the window and lowered it, leaving it open just a crack to let some of the cool breeze through. Then he hurried to the kitchen to get a dish towel, and laid it across the puddle.

He peeled off his linen jacket, heavy with rain water, draped it across a kitchen chair and put it in front of a fan. He followed it with his shirt and pants on a second chair.

He grabbed a towel from the linen closet on his way to the bedroom, drying himself as he walked. He spotted the rain blowing in his bedroom window, and lowered it like the first one. He laid the towel down on the puddle under the window and walked to his dresser.

He stepped out of his soaked boxer shorts and opened his top drawer to get a fresh pair, when he spotted the corner of one of Tim's date books.

He'd completely forgotten about them. He wished he'd remembered them when he was going through Tim's files last night—

He remembered the notes he'd written, folded and put in his jacket pocket. He ran to the living room where his linen jacket hung on the chair-back, and thrust his hand into the pocket. The paper was damp, but at least it wasn't so wet it fell apart in his fingers. He pulled it out and unfolded it.

"Damn!" he muttered. The ink had smeared. It wasn't completely unreadable, but parts of it were. Would he be able to trust his memory? He thought so, and if worse came to worst he could always search through the files again; he just didn't want to spend that much time.

He took the notes back to the bedroom and laid them on the bed while he slipped into his bathrobe. He got more paper and a pen, sat cross-legged on the bed, and flipped through Tim's 1935 date book to the beginning of June—the day after Tim died. There were a few appointments entered for the following week—Doug wondered briefly if Gladys knew to cancel them—but nothing connected with anything Doug had seen in Tim's files.

He flipped back slowly, a day at a time. The first thing he saw made his breath catch.

Friday, May 31 – 8:00 PM – meet Doug Bainbridge, 118 Huang Lei Road

He shook it off and looked at the previous entries. He jotted down a list, including everything; he could always cross out the dead-ends later.

The entry right before his name was in pencil rather than pen, and the scribbled script seemed a bit more carelessly put down than the usual careful letters. It said, "PM, talk to Rev. Allen"—the minister hadn't mentioned that he saw Tim the day he died; Doug would have to see him tomorrow to find out about that conversation.

Some of Tim's entries had specific times; others had only 'AM' or 'PM,' seeming to be reminders to do something. Still other entries seemed to be scribbled notes—perhaps something Tim had learned at an appointment and wanted to follow up on.

After a half-hour of tedious note-taking and winnowing, Doug had the following list:

Friday, May 17 – Corporal Dunegan, North District Precinct
Rev. J Allen, Presbyterian Church, Tianjian Rd

189

Saturday, May 18 – Dr. Wong, Hung Wei Sanitarium

Monday, May 20 – noon—Mr. Kim, Kang Ho San (Korean) Restaurant, Wusung Rd
    Friday, May 24 – 7:30 PM – Mr. Kim, at the Paramount
    Saturday, May 25 – noon – lunch w/ Jonesy at the Cathay
        10 PM, alley behind the Docks
    Sunday, May 26 – 8 PM, Haining Rd Bridge
    Monday, May 27 – 3 PM, AP office
        8 PM, Haining Rd Bridge
    Tuesday, May 28 – Licensing & Registration office, "<u>Donghu</u> <u>Lu,</u> French Concession"
    Thursday, May 30 – Memorial Day (U.S.)
        AM, North District police, Hongkou X
        AM, East District police, Yangtzepoo X
        PM, Central District police, downtown X
        PM, West District police, uptown—<u>Wallace</u>*-- <u>W.F. Geoffries</u>**
    Friday, May 31 – run date for Korean Prov. Gov. story (repay loan to Gladys)
        Noon, lunch w/ Mr. Kim, Bistro Morais, Rue de Montaubon
        [pencil] PM, talk to Rev. Allen

Tim's entry for last Thursday had the names 'Wallace' and 'W.F. Geoffries' both starred and underlined. Doug remembered Gladys saying on Saturday night that there had been a phone message for Tim that morning from a Captain Geoffries at the West District precinct. This had to be the same person.

Then Doug felt the hair stand up on his arm, as if lightning were about to come through his window. The friendly Englishman at the pub that afternoon, his name had been Geoffries. What had he said his first name was? Will—that was it, Will Geoffries.

Doug's mind began to spin. Detective Sergeant Wallace had hinted about his captain and the Green Gang; Gladys had mentioned a message for Tim from "Captain Geoffries;" the Black Horse Pub was only a few blocks from the West District police station.

Will Geoffries—W.F. Geoffries. It couldn't be a coincidence.

But what did it all mean?

Tim's files had to hold the answer. He hoped to God he and Jonesy could get ahold of them tomorrow morning.

Monday, June 3

Despite all the questions rolling around in his head—or perhaps because of them—he fell into a hard sleep, and barely moved until his alarm clock rang on the bedside table at seven-thirty. After a quick bath and shave he dressed and went downstairs, where he found Mr. Hwang in his office. He asked to make a phone call.

"Twenty-five cents," Mr. Hwang said with a slight bow.

Doug shook his head. "Five cents."

"No, Mr. Bainbridge. If you want to use my telephone, you pay me twenty-five cents."

Doug stood as straight and tall as he could, and scowled down at the diminutive proprietor. "I'll pay you five cents, and I won't tell Mr. Hilllard that you overcharge and we need to rent an apartment somewhere else. You want my rent money, you'll take five cents for phone calls."

Mr. Hwang stared up at him in silence for several seconds, as if weighing the seriousness of the threat. "Ten cents."

Doug shook his head, and folded his arms for emphasis. "Five."

After another second's hesitation, Mr. Hwang nodded and took the nickel Doug gave him. He looked sullen as he walked away.

"Hello?" Rev. Allen answered, first in Shanghainese and then in English.

"Rev. Allen, this is Douglas Bainbridge."

"Good morning. Very nice to hear from you. What can I do for you?"

"I wonder if you have a few minutes this morning to talk about Tim McIntyre. It's important. I can be there in ten minutes."

There was silence on the line for a few seconds. "Yes, of course. I'll be here. What is this about?"

"I'll explain in person. Thank you, reverend."

The minister was waiting for him at the front door of the church.

"Thank you for seeing me on such short notice," Doug said as they walked back toward the office.

"Certainly. You said it was important; something about Tim."

"Yes. I hope you can shed some light on something. Did you speak with him on Friday afternoon?"

The minister's eyes widened momentarily, but the look of surprise was fleeting. "Yes, I believe I did. He came by to see me that afternoon. It was a private, personal matter—I wasn't aware that Tim had shared it with anyone else. In fact, I'm quite surprised that he would." His expression became slightly suspicious.

"He didn't. I saw that he scribbled a note in his date book to speak with you. Given it was just hours before he was killed, and knowing you said at his funeral that you had helped him with some sort of moral dilemma, I figured there's a good possibility it's not unconnected."

The minister looked wary. "Our conversations were confidential."

"He's dead, reverend—I don't think you're bound by confidentiality anymore."

Rev. Allen still looked skeptical. "You have to understand, what Tim and I discussed was rather sensitive. I don't know you well enough to entrust you with details."

Doug didn't try to disguise his growing impatience. "A man is *dead*, reverend. He was probably killed because of what he'd found out, or was close to finding. If what he spoke to you about had to do with his work concerning the Green Gang, or his story on the Korean Provisional Government, I need to know what he said—and I need you to tell me *now*."

He took a step forward with that last part, and made his expression and voice as menacing as possible.

Rev. Allen took an involuntary step backward, but his expression remained calm. "I'll tell you what I can. Have a seat."

Doug sat, staring unblinking at the minister's eyes.

"Tim came by without an appointment. It was early in the afternoon—perhaps two o'clock or a little after. He asked if I'd seen his feature article that morning in the Shanghai Times, about the Korean Provisional Government operating in exile, their resistance activities in Korea, and their activism within the Korean community here. I said that I had, and I complimented the story. He seemed reluctant to say something, so I asked if there were a dilemma he faced related to that article. He was very hesitant, but replied in the affirmative.

"He said he sympathized with the Koreans' struggle against their Japanese overlords, as inferred by his story, and during his investigation he met a young man that he later learned, by accident, was a spy for the Japanese. He'd seen the young man talking with a Japanese man in Japantown, and their behavior suggested to him they didn't like that he had seen them together. He told his main contact in the Korean hierarchy, and was told they would take care of it."

Doug wondered if Kawakami were the Japanese man that Tim had seen with his Korean acquaintance. It seemed the most plausible, especially if he were Japanese Secret Service, as Doug supposed.

"Go on."

Rev. Allen's eyes grew sad. "Tim looked uncomfortable with this, so I asked if he assumed they would do serious harm to the man he suspected of being a spy for the Japanese; and he said he was certain they would kill the young man, without trial or presumption of innocence. He was worried that he had 'signed the man's death warrant'—to quote his figure of speech.

"He tried to minimize it, but I could see on his face that this weighed on Tim's conscience. He knew the man deserved consequences for betraying his friends, and he admitted it was not for him to decide what those consequences should be; but he wasn't sure how to feel about a man being killed because he had informed on him. He worried that he was responsible for the man's death."

Doug nodded. He could understand that, though it had seemed to him that Tim was the kind of person who was always certain of the justness of his actions.

"What did you advise him?"

Rev. Allen sighed. "I agreed it was a complicated situation. I asked him what would have been the consequences of doing nothing; he said that Korean resistance operatives in Seoul or Pusan or Pyongyang would have been betrayed to the Japanese—they would have been arrested, killed, and perhaps even tortured.

"Then I asked if he had told his contact the whole truth—leaving nothing out, and embellishing nothing—and he said that he had. I told him that he had no moral or ethical reason to feel guilty."

Doug sat in silence for a moment, thinking over what he'd been told. This added to his suspicions that Kawakami would kill to get his hands on Tim's files—it was no longer just a matter of wanting to know who the Korean resistance cells were; it was a matter of finding the men who had killed his agent.

"Was there more he said?"

The minister smiled. "Not about that. We talked about the Lord Jesus for a bit, and how He had shown righteous anger at the complacency of the powerful. Tim—like most people, I'm afraid—had never thought of Jesus as being much like us; but of course, He was. He had His doubts and fears, His worries and heartaches, just as we do."

Doug didn't want to get pulled into that same topic, so he thanked the minister and stood to leave.

"You know, Tim was a very interesting person," Rev. Allen said, causing Doug to pause. "He didn't hesitate to tell me that his parents—though they would go to Easter services—were not actually fans of the institutional church. Tim said they thought the church was not a terribly moral place." The minister chuckled. "He said his father always said the church was full of self-righteous and self-congratulatory hypocrites. His mother taught him that Jesus was charitable, but that few Christians are. I agreed that's all too often true."

Doug cocked his head, unsure what to think of that.

"I told Tim that his parents sounded like the sort of people I would enjoy meeting. They clearly instilled Tim with a strong moral compass."

The look on Doug's face must have amused the minister, for he laughed. "Tim was just as incredulous. I told him that one of the reasons I've been here in China for so many years is that I couldn't stand the complacency of middle-class Americans who acted as though God's grace was their birthright because they'd been raised in the Church. After I came here, I saw how rewarding it is to reach those who don't take it for granted that they're one of God's favorite people."

Doug allowed himself to smile. "Yes, that's very true."

"Of course, Tim and I disagreed on the purpose of mission—he said that God's love should be unconditional, so why should we hand out food and clothing to the poor, and require the recipients to hear a Gospel lesson? It's a perspective I've heard before. But I think our mission here is two-fold—to ease the suffering of the poor and forgotten, as Jesus did Himself; but also to fulfill the Great Commission that the Lord gave to His apostles to 'Go forth and make disciples of all nations, baptizing them.' So when people come here for the services that we can offer—food, clothing, warm blankets, sometimes a place to stay for the night—we take the opportunity to preach Christ's love to them while they're here."

Doug shifted on his feet, uncomfortable. This reminded him too much of the preachiness he'd heard from ministers growing up. "Yes, well, thank you for the information, reverend."

"I hope it was helpful."

Doug forced a smile. "Yes, very helpful. Thank you." He put on his hat and hurried out the door.

14

Doug arrived at Tim's building a few minutes before ten o'clock; he waited outside. Jonesy arrived a few minutes after ten.

"You're late."

Jonesy ignored him, and motioned toward the door. "Shall we?"

Doug opened it and followed Jonesy inside. Jonesy rapped his knuckles hard on the Chens' door. Mrs. Chen answered, and she smiled when she saw Jonesy.

"Hiya, Mista' Jonesy. What wantchee?"

Jonesy replied in Pidgin. "My catchee pidgin Mr. Chen. Him have got?" *I have business with Mr. Chen. Is he home?*

"Him have got, okey dokey," she said, and motioned them inside. She called out in Shanghainese toward the back of the apartment, too rapid for Doug to catch more than a quarter of the words. Mr. Chen answered, and appeared a moment later.

"Hiya, Mista' Jonesy, Mista' Bainbridge," he said. "Wantchee go topside?" *You want to go upstairs?*

Jonesy took the direct approach. "My wantchee paper b'long Mista' McIntyre. My know you have. What side?" *Where is it?*

"Bottomside," Mr. Chen replied. *Downstairs.*

Doug was incredulous at how readily the landlord told them that information.

"Pay my?" Jonesy asked. *Will you give it to me?*

Mr. Chen looked grave. "No can do, Jonesy."

Jonesy scowled. "What fashion no can? No b'long plopper. Mista' McIntyre no walkee walkee, paper b'long my pidgin."

Doug had spent hours studying the Pidgin-to-English glossary in his guide book, but it still took him a few seconds to decipher what Jonesy had said: *Why not? That's not right. Mr. McIntyre's dead, the papers are my business.*

Chen seemed to weigh this. He stared at Jonesy for a moment. "My no watchee bad pidgin." *I don't want trouble.*

Jonesy shook his head. "No catchee bad pidgin."

It surprised Doug to hear Jonesy rattle off phrases in Pidgin as rapidly as if it were English. He'd clearly had lots of practice—so then, why not just learn Shanghainese? Doug thought of angry Americans raging against immigrants who could barely speak English. *We're the immigrants here, Jonesy*, he thought with a touch of contempt.

After a moment's consideration, Chen nodded. "Jonesy, you plopper mista'. Okey dokey, you can look-see. Us go bottomside."

Jonesy cracked a small smile. "Catchee chop chop." *Let's hurry.*

Jonesy winked at Doug as Mr. Chen walked out and headed toward the basement stairs, and there was a glint in his eyes that seemed to say *I told you so.* They followed the older man toward the basement door, hidden in shadow at the back of the hall under the main staircase.

The narrow wooden stairs creaked as they went down, and Mr. Chen reached up to pull the cord of a bare light bulb at the bottom. The musty smell of mildew and dust assaulted Doug's nostrils as he descended. It felt cool and slightly damp down here.

Doug wondered at the familiarity he'd witnessed—Mr. Chen had even told Jonesy he was a good man. "Do you know him well?" Doug asked in Shanghainese as they reached the bottom.

Chen grinned and answered in Pidgin. "Mista' McIntyre say, Eve'body know Jonesy."

Jonesy chuckled and nodded. "Talkee plopper." *That's true.*

Mr. Chen crossed the large room, which was scattered with boxes, a pair of old rusty bicycles, and other dusty odds and ends. On the far side of the room was an open door that led to the coal room behind the furnace, empty this time of year. In a dark corner on the other side of the furnace stood another wooden door, closed with a heavy brass latch. Mr. Chen opened it and walked through, pulling a metal chain to illuminate a light bulb on the low ceiling.

In the sudden flash of incandescent light, Doug saw dozens of colorful paper lanterns, and a pair of giant paper dragons neatly folded on shelves.

Chen crossed to a large trunk in the corner. He fished a tiny key out of his pocket, unlocked the trunk and lifted the lid. "My takee Mista' McIntyre key Sata'day."

The rich smell of cedar hit Doug's nostrils, overpowering the musty stench of the basement.

Chen reached in under the stacks of sweaters, woolen mittens and scarves, and pulled out two fat manila folders.

They each took one. Doug looked at the folder in his hand, labeled "Kor Prov Gov." He glanced at the one in Jonesy's hand; it was labeled "Green Gang / Du."

"How long have you had these here, Mr. Chen?" he asked in his Mandarin/Shanghainese blend.

This time, the proprietor answered him in Shanghainese. "Since Friday. Mr. McIntyre asked me to keep them safe for him."

That was wise, Doug thought. Then he realized that was the day Tim was killed. "Did he by any chance tell you why?"

"He worried someone would break into his apartment, looking for them. He said it was important they not find them. It was a good thing he brought them down here—a few hours later someone ransacked his apartment."

Doug immediately thought of Kawakami. But, he had to admit to himself, it could just as easily have been those two *Juntong* agents.

"Did you see anyone in the building that afternoon?"

Mr. Chen shook his head. "Mr. McIntyre asked me that, too. I told him no one tried to get into the building—I'd promised him I would watch out—but I told him there were two loafers standing by the stoop about an hour before he asked me. I knew they were up to no good—probably thieves watching the neighborhood to find good places to rob—so I told them to leave, and showed them my pistol. They scurried away like the rats they are."

Doug noticed Jonesy scowling at him.

"Are you going to let me in on any of this?" Jonesy asked, testy.

"Sorry, I don't speak Pidgin, and I assumed Mr. Chen doesn't speak much English, since you two conversed in Pidgin," Doug said, terse. *You could learn Shanghainese, since you live here, Jonesy.* "Tim was worried someone would break in looking for these, so he asked Mr. Chen if he could hide them. Then later that day someone did break into Tim's apartment and ransacked it. Mr. Chen said he'd chased off a couple of loafers from the stoop, but no one came into the building."

Jonesy grunted. "They probably came in through the fire escape, from the courtyard. The loafers were probably decoys."

Doug thought of the figure he'd spied watching from his own fire escape, and felt his stomach drop.

"That was the day he was killed," he said.

Jonesy's eyebrows rose, but he said nothing.

"Mr. McIntyre said they didn't take anything," Mr. Chen said in Shanghainese. "He said they were looking for those." He nodded at the files in their hands.

Doug translated for Jonesy.

"Then let's not take them with us," Jonesy said to Doug. "We'll go up to Tim's apartment, make our notes there, and then lock 'em back up."

Doug nodded in silence. He wished he'd thought of that.

Jonesy looked to Mr. Chen, "Us takee paper topside."

"Okey dokey, Jonesy."

Doug still wasn't thrilled that Jonesy was here at all, but he had to admit it was a relief to have some help.

Chen let them into Tim's apartment, which felt closed off and stuffy. Jonesy marched to the front window and threw it up. Then he went to the kitchen window and did the same.

"We can sit at the table here and make our notes," he said, pulling out a wooden chair.

"I'll sit over here," Doug said, taking a seat in the arm chair and balancing the thick file on his knees.

Jonesy stared at him for a few second, then shrugged. "Suit yourself." He opened his file and spread out the pages on the table.

Doug opened the file on his knees, read through the top pages, and realized he didn't have paper to jot notes on. He'd assumed he would take the files back to his own apartment and keep them with the others. He looked toward the kitchen table, where Jonesy sat with a pencil jotting notes in his reporter's notebook.

He hesitated, feeling foolish, but then cleared his throat loudly enough that Jonesy looked over.

"Could I trouble you for a pencil and a few sheets of paper?"

Jonesy chuckled. "Sure." He pulled a pencil from his inside pocket, tore a few sheets from the back of his notebook, and held them out.

Doug got up, left the file on the seat, and walked over. "Thanks."

"You sure you wouldn't be more comfortable at the table?"

"No thanks."

Jonesy shook his head and went back to work.

Doug opened the file across his knees, and set the blank pages on the arm of the chair. He flipped to the back of the file and began reading Tim's notes from a trip to the Shanghai Municipal Library more than a month ago. Finding nothing of interest, he flipped forward to his earliest interviews.

He recognized the name "Mr. Kim" from Tim's date book, and he took a blank piece of paper to jot down some notes, trying to balance it on his knee, but the page tore under the pencil. He tried again, three more times, and got the same result.

He glanced over at Jonesy at the table; he sat looking down at his file, not looking at Doug—but Doug noticed the hint of amused smile on the reporter's lips.

He swallowed his pride, gathered his work, and marched over to the table without a word.

Jonesy said nothing, but moved part of his work so that Doug could have half the table.

Doug tried to concentrate, but Jonesy's apparent smugness got under his skin.

"Why did you say that yesterday?"

"Say what?" Jonesy kept his cigar clenched between his teeth, and didn't look up from the pages in front of him.

"Why did you say what you did about my school days? You don't know me. Just what were you trying to prove?"

Jonesy looked up and gave Doug a scrutinizing look. "Why do you care?"

Doug stiffened. "Because you insulted me, for one thing—"

"Who said it was an insult?" Jonesy interrupted.

"—and it's not..." Doug stopped mid-sentence. It wasn't often that someone surprised him into silence. He shook his head and gathered his thoughts. "Anyway, I wonder why you had to say those things."

"Because I know something you probably don't know."

"Oh? About me? Not likely."

Jonesy ignored him. "I had the opportunity to interview a Freudian psychiatrist about five years ago, back in the States, and he told me some interesting things."

Doug wondered where this was going. "Such as?"

"For starters, he guessed about me. I don't know how, and I didn't ask, but he knew somehow." Jonesy looked off for a second, his eyes distant. Then he looked back at Doug and stared hard into his eyes.

"He told me that lots of people hate what I do, and think it disgusting and unnatural—he said this very matter-of-factly—but they don't spend a whole lot of time thinking about it. He told me the fellas who get really bothered by it, and especially the ones who get violent, have spent a great deal of time thinking about it, maybe even obsessing about it. I am a living challenge to them exactly *because* they are insecure about themselves in that regard."

"That's ridiculous."

"Oh? Ask yourself why it bothers you so much, and then think about what I said about your all-boys boarding school." Jonesy jabbed his cigar in Doug's direction. "And if you tell me it didn't happen, I'll tell you you're a liar."

Doug sat in stony silence.

Jonesy just grunted and looked back to the papers on the table in front of him.

Doug looked down at the file in front of him, but had even more trouble focusing his attention on them than before.

Jonesy's words drug up memories he'd rather ignore. As he and Brent Aleshire got older, the childish—and innocent—swordfights stopped happening. Then it became a matter of being awakened in the middle of the night by the sounds of your roommate masturbating; teasing masked the embarrassment. "Cut it out, you big pervert!" Doug had said as he wacked Brent over the head with his pillow.

Brent had started the dare game then. "I dare you to watch me." Followed by, "I dare you to do it, too." And Doug had.

It was just adolescent curiosity, nothing more. Fifteen-year-old boys are curious.

But he began to doubt that justification as he remembered how the dare game had escalated when they were sixteen. "I bet you're not man enough to let me do it to you," Brent had teased him. "I dare you to let me."

"Cut it out," Doug had said, shoving Brent on the shoulder.

"Why not? You afraid you'll like it too much, you homo?"

"No I won't!"

"Oh yeah? Prove it."

So he'd taken the dare, and Brent rubbed one off on him. He couldn't help it; it had felt good. Afterward, Brent smacked him up the back of the head and gave him a disgusted look. "I knew you were a damn homo."

"Am not! Maybe *you* are—you're the one who did it."

"But I didn't like it," Brent said, retreating to his bed where he pulled the covers over his head and turned his back.

A few minutes later Doug was certain he saw the motion of Brent's masturbation under the covers, and heard the muted sounds of his roommate's self-pleasure, no matter how quiet Brent tried to be.

"You're the homo," he muttered as he turned over and tried to go to sleep.

"You're not getting much work done," Jonesy said, irritated.

Doug snapped back to the present, his face flushing hot, and saw Jonesy staring at him with narrowed eyes.

"I was just thinking about something," Doug mumbled, and turned his attention back to the pages of the file.

"Must've been something interesting," Jonesy said.

Doug scowled, wondering what his expression had looked like. "It was nothing important."

"I wonder if Tim left anything to drink," Jonesy said, pushing back from the table.

Doug glanced at the clock on the wall; it was just past ten-thirty. He hoped Jonesy meant tea.

After a few minutes of rustling around in the kitchen, Jonesy said, "Looks like our only choices are tea, and a whiskey bottle with a couple fingers left."

Doug didn't respond. After a several seconds, the silence seemed suddenly uncomfortable, and he looked up to see Jonesy staring at him.

"Got a preference? Or would you rather die of thirst than have a drink with me?"

Doug felt his cheeks flush again, and he started to scowl before consciously forcing a neutral expression. "I'll take a cup of tea, if you're making a pot."

Jonesy snorted. "Yeah, I'm making a pot. I don't care for whiskey straight up, gotta mix it with something. You care for a shot in your tea? Might wake you up from those daydreams you're having."

"No, thanks," Doug said, keeping an indifferent façade with effort. He concentrated on the pages in front of him.

He read through Tim's notes, and most of what was written there had found its way to one degree or another into the story Tim had written, which appeared in Friday morning papers. There was little new information—until he came across a two-page description of a meeting of the Korean Provisional Government, written free-form in Tim's handwriting, almost like a journal entry.

It was dated Friday, May 24—the day before Doug arrived in Shanghai.

Mr. Kim met me at the roulette table on the ground floor of the Paramount, a little after 7:30. He was dressed for a night on the town, wearing a white dinner jacket with a black bowtie, a black silk scarf draped over his shoulders, and crisply-pressed black trousers.

"A pleasure to see you again, Mr. McIntyre," he said with a bow. "Would you be so good as to join us at our table?" As usual, he spoke in Shanghainese.

"I would love to, thank you," I said, bowed, and followed Mr. Kim to a dimly-lit booth on the far side of the room.

Five grim-faced men sat around the table, all between 30 and 35 years old I would guess, all similarly got out in white dinner jackets, black trousers, black bowties; all Koreans with flat, broad faces.

Mr. Kim introduced them by last names only, and each nodded in turn as he was introduced. Kim spoke to them in Korean, and then told me in Shanghainese to take a seat.

Mr. Kim slid into the booth after me, so I was hemmed in.

They conversed in Korean, and Mr. Kim quietly translated into Shanghainese, just loud enough for me alone. It was mostly conversation about people I never heard of, dry conversation about responsibilities, and who was assigned to them.

After about five minutes, I interrupted and asked if everyone at the table spoke Shanghainese, since I don't understand a word of Korean.

They all stared at me in stony silence, and I got the uncomfortable feeling I'd committed some sort of faux pas.

"Yes, we all speak Shanghainese," the gentleman who had been introduced as Choi said in Shanghainese. "We have all lived in this city for many years, and we speak the language. However, Korean is our mother tongue, the tongue we prefer to use amongst ourselves—plus a tongue that is not commonly understood by the strangers around us. You understand."

I was mortified, and apologized. I don't know why I never thought they might use Korean as much to keep their conversation secret from 99% of bystanders as anything else.

The conversation resumed—in Korean. Mr. Kim resumed quiet translation.

After a while, one of the men looked at his watch and muttered something. Choi looked at his watch and nodded.

"It is time to go," Mr. Kim whispered to me in Shanghainese. It was five minutes to 8:00.

We slipped out of the booth, and walked in a tight group through the club toward the front door. I stayed next to Mr. Kim.

Waiting at the curb was a sleek black Lasalle. A chauffeur in a black tuxedo opened the door. Mr. Choi got in the back with two others, and Mr. Kim motioned me to join them. The others crowded in the front with the chauffeur.

Mr. Choi gave an order, and the car sped away. We drove east all the way to the Bund, turning right and heading south along the river front. When we crossed into the French Concession a few minutes later, the man next to me tapped my shoulder and said in Shanghainese, "We must blind-fold you now, Mr. McIntyre."

I let him tie a black blindfold tight across my eyes.

The car continued straight at high speed for a minute, then slowed to turn right, heading away from the river. We had to be still in the French Concession, because we hadn't been heading south long enough to reach the Old City. Since the car didn't make a turn every few seconds, and was clearly not creeping along, we couldn't have been in the narrow winding streets of the Old City—so it had to be the French Concession.

The car made a few turns, but I can't remember the sequence of lefts and rights, and no idea how far we went in between—so I was lost, even though I know the big streets of the French Concession.

The car stopped, and I heard voices outside, speaking Korean. Then I heard a gate open, and the car crept forward. It stopped after a few seconds, and the driver killed the engine. I heard the doors open, and they grabbed my shoulders and pulled me out.

They led me by the hand for several paces, and turned to the right. After a few more steps, we stopped again. They untied the blindfold, and I could see a courtyard in the moonlight, between a large carriage house and a huge white mansion, with a high brick wall all around.

"Aren't you almost finished yet?" Jonesy said, setting a cup of tea in front of Doug.

"Soon," Doug muttered, not looking up.

"I thought we'd compare notes, and work on a plan of action—if you ever finish."

Doug didn't like the idea of working with Jonesy, let alone telling him what he was learning from Tim's Korea file—he didn't exactly trust men like Jonesy—but he had to concede that he needed to know what Jonesy had learned from Tim's file on the Green Gang. *One hand washes the other, after all.*

"Just a few more minutes."

Jonesy didn't say a word, but audibly sipped from his tea cup.

Mr. Choi seemed to be in command here, too, barking orders to several men, who bowed deeply and rushed off to do his bidding. It must be his compound.

Everyone who had come in the Lasalle hurried inside the mansion. Mr. Kim took my elbow, and ushered me inside. "Time for the meeting," he said.

We went through a back door into a kitchen, then down a corridor into a cavernous hall with marble floors, potted palms, big porcelain vases, and expensive plush wallpaper. A big open staircase led up from the center of the hall, and men of all ages—and a few young women—were making their way up the stairs.

We went upstairs with everyone else, Mr. Kim still holding my elbow. At the top of the stairs we walked down a hall to an enormous room with a long mahogany table—I imagine it looks like a corporate boardroom, though I've never seen one. I noticed everyone greeted Mr. Choi with deep deferential bows, and waited for him to sit at the head of the table before taking their own seats.

Choi spoke first, and Mr. Kim translated for me.

After Choi opened the meeting, a fierce argument started, with several of the young men shouting angrily and motioning my direction. Kim translated for a while, but eventually stopped, just summarizing their opposition to my presence. Older men in calmer voices urged patience and openness, citing the hoped-for benefits of western support, and how public opinion swayed policy in western democracies.

After a long debate—the clock on the wall said less than five minutes, but it seemed an eternity—Mr. Choi raised his hand, and it got silent. He spoke in an even, commanding tone, and Mr. Kim translated it.

"He says it is right for you to be here, and you will not be sent away. He proposes that I not translate secret details, and reminds everyone that there is always danger of spies amongst us, which is why our most sensitive subjects are always discussed in code anyway, so that they are only understood by those present who know the code."

The table was silent, and I noticed all eyes were on me. I wondered if I were expected to say something, but then the young man sitting directly opposite me said a string of words at me in Korean, and while I had no idea what the words were, there was no mistaking the biting tone.

Everyone watched my reaction, but all I could do was stare back blankly.

Then the room burst into laughter. I looked at Mr. Kim, hoping for an explanation, but he was laughing as hard as the rest of them. I looked at Mr. Choi at the head of the table, and saw our host watching me with an amused smile.

When the laughter stopped, Mr. Kim whispered in my ear. "He insulted you in a most intimate way, and I would not repeat it for all of Mr. Choi's money. It was a test, and you passed."

"What test?" I asked.

"To prove that you do not understand any Korean. They are satisfied."

The meeting lasted about an hour, and from time to time Mr. Kim would stop translating and sit quietly. I never asked why. I took notes in shorthand whenever I felt a detail would be significant to my story, but mostly just impressions of the group, their goals, and their internal dynamic.

Shortly after 9:00, Mr. Choi stood and pronounced the meeting adjourned.

Mr. Kim took my elbow again, and we went downstairs with the others—all except for Mr. Choi, who stayed upstairs.

At the bottom of the grand staircase I came face to face with one of the young men who had argued against me at the beginning of the meeting. He had a square, flat face and heavily hooded black eyes. I stared at him in what I hope was subtle defiance, but he bowed politely and spoke to me in Shanghainese.

"I hope you found our meeting informative, Mr. McIntyre. I am Kwan Jong, from Pusan." He turned to one of the men beside him and spoke in Korean. That man nodded, turned to Mr. Kim and the others, and said something in Korean before leaving with Kwan.

"What was that about?" I asked Mr. Kim in Shanghainese as we went back through the kitchen to the back door.

"They went to discuss an operation in private," Kim said. "Time to blindfold you again."

They led me back to the car, and a while later they dropped me off at the corner of Nanking and Honan Road downtown. I took a streetcar back to Hongkou, and came home to change clothes before I go back to Yangtzepoo.

Together with what Doug remembered from Tim's newspaper story, this journal almost made him feel like he'd been there at that meeting. He mused that Tim might have had a future as a cloak-and-dagger novelist like Graham Greene.

There were only a couple of things in the file after that, Doug noted. The first was a short note about spotting Kwan Jong in a hibachi restaurant in Japantown on May 29th, lunching with a Japanese businessman. Tim spoke to them, Kwan was very uncomfortable; and Doug felt a chill run up his spine when he saw the Japanese man's name—Kawakami.

Then on Friday, May 31st—the day Tim died, Doug noted—Tim had lunch with Mr. Kim in the French Concession, and told him about seeing Kwan Jong with a Japanese man named Kawakami, and how uncomfortable they were that he had seen them together. Kim said they would "take care of it."

"Bingo," Doug whispered with a satisfied smile as he jotted that down in his notes, and closed the file.

"Learn something important?" Jonesy asked, looking at him over his tea cup with raised eyebrows.

"Yes, as a matter of fact," Doug said, and recounted what he'd learned.

Jonesy listened, nodded a couple of times; but when Doug had finished, Jonesy just said, "Hmm."

Expecting a more enthusiastic response, Doug didn't hide his irritation. "What does *that* mean?"

"Well, it gives Kawakami a motive, definitely—but that's about it. No solid evidence linking him to what happened later Friday night. Not even any evidence that Tim saw this Kawakami fellow more than the one time."

"But put it together with what Mr. Chen said, about the Japanese marines who beat Tim up on Wednesday night—that was the day he saw Kwan with Kawakami. It can't be a coincidence."

"No, of course not—I didn't say it was," Jonesy said with a scowl. "All I'm saying is, it's possible that was all the action this Kawakami fellow took against Tim."

Doug didn't buy that, and he shook his head. "No, it was a warning. Kawakami was trying to intimidate Tim to stay silent about Kwan. But Tim *didn't* stay silent, he met with Mr. Kim on Friday and told him. It's pretty obvious this Kwan fellow got killed over his association with Kawakami, so he would have felt the need to escalate his reaction. A death for a death."

Jonesy nodded, looking up in thought. "That's definitely possible," he said, and looked Doug hard in the eyes. "But how are you going to prove it?"

"I don't know," Doug admitted, angry that he didn't have a better answer to Jonesy's challenge.

Jonesy grunted. "Seems to me the only thing you can do is wait and see if this Kawakami fellow comes back for Tim's file, or if he lets the whole thing go now that he eliminated the threat Tim posed."

Doug kept quiet, not about to admit that Jonesy was right.

"The other file had a lot of new information in it," Jonesy said, looked down at his sheets of notes, and began reading.

"There was this woman named Yung Mai, that Tim saw getting arrested the night he reported Sung missing—May eleventh. Tim saw her downtown on May sixteenth, turning off West Nanking Road. She told Tim that she had seen Sung at an opium den on Fao Sho Lane in Yangtzepoo, and he got her to take him there.

"It was in the middle of a real slum. Tim got inside, and the place was full of strung-out addicts. He found Sung, and she was pretty out of it, but he got her home. The next day—that was Friday the seventeenth, he reported the opium den first thing in the morning. A

Corporal Dunegan at the North District police precinct called in the report to the East District station, and told Tim they'd take care of it."

Doug recognized the name Corporal Dunegan of the North District precinct from Tim's date book.

Jonesy continued. "Tim went back to Fao Sho Lane that afternoon, and found the place busted up and empty, obviously raided. But then the next week—Thursday the twenty-third, he was in Yangtzepoo checking on a homicide investigation on a beggar who'd been found found killed before midnight on Wednesday, a couple blocks from the wharves, and after talking to some witnesses there he went by Fao Sho Lane on a hunch, and found the opium den back in business, with the same fellow manning the door.

"He asked around, talking to the prostitutes and beggars in the area, and got little snippets of info on the place—not much consequential, really—but he learned from someone named Chong that a man named Wong Ju runs the joint, and that he bribes the captain of the local police precinct.

"Tim paid the man to find out more about this Wong Ju—so on Saturday he goes back, and Chong tells him that Wong Ju works for Jiang Kao Lo, who's pretty high up in the Green Gang. He told Tim the Green Gang has hundreds of suppliers, and brings their opium into the city by boat and train, and they don't hide it in vegetable carts like the smaller gangs do. Chong says he won't do any more work for Tim, afraid of the Green Gang."

Jonesy stopped and looked up from his notes. "Pretty smart if you ask me," he said.

Doug ignored that, and Jonesy went back to reading aloud.

"Tim finds some teenage boys in an alley behind the wharves, and hires them to watch the joint on Fao Sho Lane, and follow anyone who leaves with any bags or boxes. He meets them that night at the Haining Road Bridge over Hongkou Creek, and they tell him about a house on Siping Road where some men went with heavy bags.

"He gets them to watch both places the next day, and meets them at the Haining Road Bridge again the next night. Only one of the boys shows up, and he's hiding in the shadows. He warns Tim that they're being watched, he's figured out they're Green Gang, and he won't work for Tim anymore."

Jonesy looked up again. "Seeing a pattern here, partner?"

"I get it," Doug said. *Don't beat a dead horse, Jonesy.*

"But the boy does tell Tim that he saw the men load a whole bunch of heavy bags into a big black car at lunchtime and drive toward downtown. He hired a rickshaw to take him downtown, and though they lost the car on the way, the kid spotted it in front of the HSBC bank a little while later. Lucky break, I guess.

"Anyway, on Tuesday Tim's sitting on a bench in front of the HSBC, and he sees a late model black Rolls Royce Phantom II park right in front of the building, and three fellows start unloading about twenty big bags and take them into the bank, while a fourth stands guard at the car.

Jonesy paused for a moment, and took a deep breath. When he continued, his voice carried a hint of sadness. "Evidently that fellow saw Tim watching him, and stared him down, even after Tim looked away. Tim managed to get the license number as the car drove away, though, and he went to the License and Registration office, where he bribed one of the girls there to give him the registration."

Jonesy looked up. "This is where it gets really interesting. The car was registered to Jiang Kao Lo, it was an International Settlement registration—but the address was on Donghu Lane, in the French Concession."

Doug was confused. "Was there a mistake?"

"Nope—but you'd think that, wouldn't you?" Jonesy said. "So later on, Tim's talking to Sung at the sanitarium about what he's been up to, and she tells him Du Yuesheng himself lives on Donghu Lane in the French Concession. She also tried to tell Tim not to mess with the

Green Gang, telling him all about Du's connection with Chiang Kai-Shek—but of course, as we know, Tim didn't listen."

He shook his head, his green eyes suddenly heavy with sorrow. He looked away for a second, then cleared his throat and looked back down at his notes.

"Tim thought it sounded an awful lot like Al Capone in Chicago—at least, before J. Edgar Hoover's G-men got him—and he wanted to expose it. He went to the French Concession, found Du's mansion on Donghu Lane, and watched it for a while. He didn't really learn anything there, though.

"He went to the library and did a bunch of research on Du Yuesheng—lots of details I won't bore you with—and he tried to talk to police detectives who had arrested Green Gang members. Only one would speak with him though—and you got to know him recently. It was your friend, Detective Sergeant Wallace at the West District precinct. You know the rest from what he told you."

Doug had to admit, Jonesy had gathered together a lot more information than they'd had before.

"I'll need to copy your notes, if you don't mind," he said.

Jonesy snorted. "The rich kid needs to copy the poor kid's notes. Why am I not surprised? Sure, go ahead."

Doug had had enough, and he snapped. "Why do you always say that? You don't know anything about me, Jonesy. You make these presumptions that I'm some arrogant jerk, but you don't really have any idea what kind of man I am, or what I'm like. Did you call Tim a rich boy all the time? His family has about as much money as mine, in case you didn't know."

Jonesy glared at him. "But his father earned his money with his own hands. Tim told me his father was a builder, and he made a fortune after the 1906 earthquake. Even so, he kept working on the building sites. Your father didn't work with his hands. Then you went to boarding school, and Tim didn't; you went to Stanford, and Tim went to junior college. That's the difference."

Doug shook his head. "Rich is relative, by the way—my last name isn't Rockefeller or Carnegie, you know; or Astor or Vanderbilt either. And Ivy League types look down their noses at Stanford, so that's relative, too. So drop the line and back off, will you?"

Jonesy crossed his arms and glowered at Doug, but he didn't say anything.

Doug reached out and took Jonesy's notes, and copied everything there. When he was finished, he shoved them back to Jonesy, folded his own notes, and slipped them into his jacket.

"We have a lot of leads to follow up. How do you want to split them?" Doug asked.

Jonesy snorted. "Unlike you, I have a job to do every day, so I can't spend all my time following up on something that don't get me a story."

Doug was tired of arguing. "Fine. I'll look into everything myself."

Jonesy held up his hands. "Now hold on—I didn't say I had *no* time, just that I can't spend my whole day on this stuff. But I've got a few sources I can call on, see if they can tell me anything. For now, tell me more about the night at the Jade Dragon, and don't leave out anything."

Doug took a deep breath, and started retelling the story. Jonesy stopped him multiple times, asking him questions about anything and everything, much of which Doug either didn't remember or hadn't noticed in the first place.

"You're not very observant for a junior spy," Jonesy said at one point.

Doug controlled his anger with difficulty. "First of all, I am *not* a spy; and second, this isn't a Charlie Chan movie, and I'm not Inspector Chan."

"Well, that's obvious," Jonesy said with a snort. "Unfortunately, Inspector Chan is just who we need right now."

Doug stood so fast he knocked over the chair. "You know Jonesy, I've had about enough of your insults. This is a waste of time. Let's just take the files back to Mr. Chen and be done with it."

"Fine by me."

They went downstairs in silence. When Mr. Chen opened his door, Jonesy handed him both files, thanked him, and bowed.

Out on the street, Jonesy put on his hat and pulled a cigar from inside his jacket. "Let me know if you learn anything big," he said, and paused to strike a match to light his cigar. "If you don't get yourself killed acting like an amateur."

He turned and walked away.

15

Doug was still irritated as he walked away from the building, and instead of going back to his apartment, he turned east at the corner. It was one block to Wusong Road, with Japantown lying on the opposite side of the street.

He paused to look across the wide street. The contrast with this side of the street was stark and instantaneous. As Doug looked up and down the east side of Wusong Road, he saw no signage in Chinese—only Japanese. None of the pedestrians on the opposite sidewalk looked Chinese to him; most looked Japanese. It was as if crossing Wusong Road took one through a magical portal to Japan.

He glanced to his left, searching the store fronts for Kang Ho San Korean Restaurant. It should be a block or two north of here, according to the address in Tim's file.

Kawakami was somewhere over there. He might even be nearby. The sudden thought that Kawakami could be watching him at this very moment sent a shiver up Doug's spine, and he turned away and walked south along the west side of the road.

It was a half-mile to the intersection where Wusong Road teed onto Soochow Road, on the north bank of Soochow Creek. Japantown had ended a block to the north, and here it felt more like his neighborhood—though a block to the east loomed the nineteen-story Broadway Mansions, and across Broadway stood the Astor House hotel, facing onto Broadway a block north of the Garden Bridge.

Lucy and her mother would have already checked out by now, he knew, looking at the hotel as he strolled that direction. Their boat was leaving at noon, she'd said.

A crazy thought occurred to him, and his pulse quickened. He looked at his watch—eight minutes to noon. He might just be able to make it, if their boat weren't too precise in its departure. He hurried to the corner, then dashed across Broadway the moment the traffic cop changed the signal.

He walked at a near-run along Huang Po Road, overlooking the river; below him on the right was an endless row of docks lined with yachts gleaming in the midday sun, and the occasional riverboat interspersed among them. The heat was stifling, and he could feel his back growing damp as he hurried.

He heard the double blast of a steam whistle from one of the riverboats, sounding final boarding. He could see crowds of passengers lining the three levels of decks running the length of a boat still a thousand feet in front of him, and he broke into a sprint, weaving around slower pedestrians on the walkway. Sweat ran down his face, stinging his eyes, but he ignored it.

The gangway had been pulled away by the time he reached the departure area below the Pearl of the Orient. The steam whistle, incredibly loud here, blasted three long notes, and the boat began to inch away from the wharf. Well-heeled Chinese passengers in western-style clothing waved down to other well-dressed Chinese on the shore, who shouted out best wishes for good travel in Shanghainese.

Doug stopped at the edge of the crowd, breathless, and removed his hat so he could mop his brow with his handkerchief. He fanned himself with his hat for a moment before returning it to his head.

He spotted Lucy standing along the rail of the third-level balcony, looking to her left, toward downtown Shanghai. She was wearing the same blue dress that she had worn the day they arrived, and Doug thought she looked amazing. He stood and stared at her, hoping she would look his way and see him.

After a moment, she looked across the crowd, and her eyes came back to him. The boat was twenty or thirty feet from shore by now, and picking up speed, but he could still see the surprise on her face. He smiled and waved at her, and she returned both in a half-hearted way.

Her faint smile faded within seconds, and he thought he could see sadness in her expression as she stared back at him—though at the distance he had to admit to himself that he couldn't be certain.

It's enough that she saw I was here. It showed her I care.

That would have to be enough for now.

He stood on the shore and watched the river boat paddle downriver, until its decks had fallen from his sight and all he saw was the back of the boat sinking away on the horizon.

He felt a little melancholic as he trudged back toward Broadway. He wasn't sure why he thought he might find Lucy and talk to her before she got on the boat, or what he would have said to her if he had.

Still, he'd had hope.

He would go home right now and write to her, tell her how sorry he was at the way they had left things after dinner last night, and how much he wanted to see her again. Perhaps he could even tell her how he felt about her, how much he really liked her.

Or more than liked her.

He scowled and scolded himself for even considering getting sappy. What a ninny she would think him. *Don't be a damn fool.*

Still, he *would* tell her again how sorry he was, and that he looked forward to seeing her again. She would like that. If he wrote her as soon as he got home, he could get it out in today's mail, and it would be waiting for her in Chongqing before her boat got there.

As he reached the intersection at Broadway, his gaze ran up the street at the walled compounds of the wealthy, with their three and four-story mansions rising behind big iron gates.

Ming Lin-wen lived in one of those mansions. She had invited him to tea, tomorrow afternoon; he still had her calling card with the address. But he probably wouldn't go, he told himself.

So why wonder which one was hers?

He turned around and looked back at the Astor House Hotel, replaying in his mind the scene in the lobby after dinner, when he'd tried to apologize to Lucy. He dwelt on the uncertain way she had left him. And his melancholy shifted to irritation that she hadn't accepted his apology. Why couldn't she understand? Why did she insist on punishing him?

Maybe he *would* go to tea at Ming Lin-wen's tomorrow afternoon.

He turned back toward the river, deciding to cross the Garden Bridge into downtown and go to the Cathay for a drink. Maybe he would still write to Lucy—later. Or maybe he wouldn't.

As he crossed the street, with the gleaming white walls and bright red roof of the Soviet Consulate in front of him, across from the Astor House, he saw someone come out of one of the side doors, and he did a double-take. It was a thin, young Chinese man, probably nineteen or twenty years old, with short hair, wearing a gray tunic and black trousers—one of the students that Wong Mei-Ling had met with on both occasions that Doug had dined at the Sichuan restaurant in his neighborhood.

Jonesy had said they seemed like Communists; judging by the young man's departure from the Soviet Consulate on a Monday afternoon, when he might otherwise be at classes at the University, and the way he looked around as he walked away, Jonesy had probably been right.

It galled Doug that Jonesy had been right.

He didn't want to think that Wong Mei-Ling was getting mixed up with a Communist cell. He reminded himself that she had not been dressed as they had, so perhaps she was only just being drawn in. Perhaps there was time to prevent her from being pulled too deep.

Maybe if he found out what the young man was up to, Doug thought he might persuade Wong Mei-Ling that he and the others were trouble.

He held back, and followed the young man from a distance as he crossed the Garden Bridge, walking south into downtown.

Broadway turned into the Bund here, and the young man stayed on the riverfront side of the boulevard as he continued south past the public gardens, the skyscrapers of downtown Shanghai looming over them to the right.

It was almost a mile along the Bund through downtown, and the young man continued south along the river at a brisk pace the entire distance; Doug actually felt a little winded following him, and sweat poured down the side of his face. It took them less than twenty minutes to reach the intersection at Avenue Edward VII, which marked the boundary between the International Settlement and the French Concession.

The young man continued south along the French Bund, and Doug kept following at a distance.

It occurred to him that in his nine days in Shanghai, this was his first time venturing outside of the International Settlement.

The French Bund, formally the Quai de France, was not so different from the Bund in the International Settlement, Doug observed—minus the granite and limestone skyscrapers, the buildings here being mostly five to seven stories tall. Cars of every make and vintage still competed with rickshaws for space on the wide boulevard, and the sidewalks were crowded with both Chinese and white pedestrians, speaking several Chinese and European languages. The wharfs here were busy with barges more than steamships.

It was less than a half-mile to the Rue Montauban, the boundary of the French Concession with the Chinese city, and the young communist continued south along the Chinese Bund into the Nanshi District. It was every bit as bustling with activity as the French Bund, but Doug noticed that he was conspicuous here as one of the few non-Chinese in sight.

There was a definite industrial feel to the commerce here, with massive dockyards on his left, and the offices of shipping, timber and rice merchants on their right. The conversations here were mostly Shanghainese, though Doug heard some in Mandarin.

After about a quarter mile, the young communist crossed the boulevard and took a narrow side street west from the Bund. Doug held back several seconds, to make sure the young man didn't look his direction, and as soon as his quarry disappeared behind the corner of a building, Doug dashed across the boulevard and followed.

Two blocks inland, the street passed through an arch in a remnant of ancient stone wall—a granite plaque carved in ancient Chinese script announced this to be the Great East Gate—and instantly narrowed to half its previous width. The edges were jammed with wooden stalls selling ivory figurines, sandalwood, bright Chinese fans, brassware, pewter or porcelain, and fine silks. The remaining space was packed with Chinese pedestrians shouldering their way past one another. Short, timbered buildings crammed wall-to-wall behind the stalls in shades of white and red, some with carved wooden dragons beside the doorways.

Doug could see the young communist about twenty feet in front of him, weaving through the crowd like a fish through the stems of water lilies. He hesitated—it would be easy to lose sight of the young man in this crowd, and with the way the narrow street turned to and fro at odd angles, with side streets shooting off haphazardly, there was a good possibility he could get hopelessly lost.

What was he hoping to accomplish, anyway? He wasn't entirely certain. It wasn't only about Wong Mei-Ling, though—if the young man was on some sort of clandestine mission for the Soviets, Doug felt a duty to find out all he could. Plus, wasn't it his job to observe while he was here?

He plunged into the crowd.

They passed a large temple on the left, and the air smelled rich with incense. The young communist took a sudden turn to the right, and Doug hurried through the throng to reach the turn off.

The side street was even narrower, though less crowded, and Doug could see the young man about thirty feet ahead. He seemed to be hurrying now, and Doug picked up his own pace to keep him within sight.

His quarry took a left turn, and Doug followed, finding himself in a narrow alley with a central gutter running with filthy water. The air reeked of human waste, and scattered litter lay on the stones of the alley. He could have reached out his arms and brushed his fingers along the pocked walls of the ramshackle houses on either side. Men and women in tattered clothes, their faces and arms covered in grime, stared at him in deep suspicion.

Just before reaching the point where this alley teed onto another side street, his quarry suddenly ducked to the right, into an open doorway.

Doug slowed, approaching the house cautiously, his eyes darting around for any sign of trouble. There was no door in the opening, only a tattered and faded blue curtain that didn't quite reach to the ground, hanging from a wire just inside the doorway.

Doug held back, and pressed his back against the wall a foot from the opening. He wasn't entirely sure what to do next, but supposed the best he could do would be to wait here for the young man to come back out. He recognized that could be a while.

225

He nudged his ear closer to the opening, and listened carefully for conversation. He could hear whispering, different male voices, but couldn't make out what they were saying. His proficiency in Shanghainese was still wanting, and the whispers were indecipherable.

Suddenly an arm reached out and grabbed a fistful of his linen jacket, tugging him into the opening. Caught by surprise, he wasn't able to struggle until he had fallen to the dirt floor, half inside the portal.

Several arms grabbed him then, and though he writhed fiercely there were too many to resist, and they stood him up and pushed his back to a wall. Someone held a fistful of his jacket in one hand, pushing against his breastbone in a slightly painful way.

The interior of the house was dim, the only light coming through the tattered curtains on the doorway and one small window high on the opposite wall, and it took Doug a few seconds to register that six or seven men stood around him, glaring.

"*Wǔ'ān*," he greeted them in Mandarin, struggling to keep his voice steady. *Good afternoon.*

"Shut up," the large one holding him replied in Shanghainese.

Doug closed his mouth. The men continued to glare at him, silent, for a long moment.

After a while, one of the men, a tall skinny fellow with a thin mustache and sunken cheeks, shirtless and glistening with sweat, pointed at the young communist Doug had been following. "You know this white man, Dai Chi?" he asked in Shanghainese.

"I've seen him."

"Who is he?"

Dai Chi shrugged. "Some American. Mei-Ling knows him."

The skinny man backhanded Dai, the smack echoing around the small room. "Foolish boy! You have allowed your feelings for the girl to cloud your judgement. Americans sell guns to the Nationalists, which they use to kill our comrades. You should not have allowed yourself to be followed."

"Wong Mei-Ling works for my landlord," Doug said in his peculiar blend of Shanghainese and Mandarin, hoping the honesty would earn him some leeway. "I do not know her well."

The skinny man regarded him with narrowed eyes for several seconds.

"Why are you here, American?"

Doug wasn't sure how to answer. He couldn't admit that he'd been following Dai Chi since the Soviet Consulate—they might kill him for that—so what could he say about why he'd been following him?

"I—I thought he might lead me to where Wong Mei-Ling lives," Doug said, hoping they'd buy the love-sick puppy explanation.

The skinny man continued to appraise him with narrowed eyes, silent for a long moment. Then he glanced back at Dai Chi.

"Bring the girl here."

Doug felt his heart skip a beat. "She'll be working now," he blurted out before thinking.

A curious glint came to the dark eyes of the skinny man in charge; otherwise, his expression remained unchanged as he stared at Doug.

"Tell the bourgeois pig that she works for that her brother has had a bad accident," he said, his eyes never leaving Doug's. "If that bourgeois pig gives you any trouble, break one of his legs. Warn him we'll break the other if he calls the police."

Dai Chi bowed, and hurried out the door.

The skinny man finally looked away from Doug; he turned to the men behind him and ordered, "Tie him up and gag him until they arrive."

Doug only struggled for a moment as they yanked him away from the wall, pulled his arms behind his back, and bound him with a length of rope. It was pointless to resist, and as the rope began wrapping around his wrists he grew still. He didn't resist at all as they bound his ankles together, then stuffed a rag into his mouth and set him down on his butt beside the wall.

16

Doug wasn't sure how long he sat there. It felt like hours, and with no clock, little daylight in the room, and no conversation to speak of, he had no way to track how much time passed.

He wondered whether they would kill him. Or if they would torture him first. Would they see him as an enemy, or just an inconvenience to be done away with? Perhaps an asset to be bargained? He couldn't be certain, and nothing in their manner gave anything away as they silently went about their business.

After a long while, Dai Chi parted the curtain and entered the house, followed by Wong Mei-Ling. She stared at Doug with an expression that he couldn't read.

The men in the room stood, and watched as the skinny leader approached the two arrivals, who both bowed their heads to him in deference.

"Wong Mei-Ling, do you know this white man?" the leader asked.

"Not very much," she said. "His name is Bainbridge Douglas, he is an American, and he rents an apartment from Hwang Lo, my employer."

"You have spoken with this American?"

Mei-Ling's expression remained passive. "A few times, when he has come into the shop while I worked. He has been here less than two weeks."

"What have you observed about him?" the leader asked.

A slight frown came to Mei-Ling's face. "He is a bourgeois pig, a typical American, throwing around money needlessly. He takes rickshaws and over-tips the operator, he rides streetcars one mile, and I have seen him get out of a motor cab. He pays Hwang Lo a quarter-dollar to make a local phone call. And he has expensive clothing, which he brings to Hwang Lo's shop to have laundered."

Doug had not been expecting that kind of assessment from Wong Mei-Ling, and his eyes grew wide as he listened. His heart raced, as fear sank into his belly.

The skinny leader looked at Doug and studied him for a moment, then addressed himself to Wong Mei-Ling while still looking at Doug.

"Can he be re-educated?"

"I don't know."

"Elaborate."

She shrugged, and a crack in her expression—a slight furrow of the brow—hinted that she was struggling with the question. "He is young enough—but he is American, and they are hopelessly capitalist."

"There have been limited socialist reforms in America recently," the leader said. It sounded more like he was playing devil's advocate than making a sincere argument.

Wong Mei-Ling stiffened, seeming aware that she was being tested. "They have not gone far enough, and there has been stiff resistance even to limited reform."

"There is always resistance to reform," the leader said, his tone sharp, and he turned back toward her. "All depends upon how it is dealt with. One must know when to be the tiger, and when to be the panda."

Mei-Ling nodded and lowered her eyes.

"What can you tell us about his associations?" the leader asked, turning back to look at Doug.

"I have not seen him with very many," Mei-Ling began, hesitant.

"Tell me what you have seen."

"He speaks with the white constable who patrols the neighborhood at night. He associated some with a reporter who died, and he attended the funeral. I have seen him associate with another reporter since then. That is all."

Doug was amazed at how much Wong Mei-Ling had observed—some of it long after her working hours had ended. Did she live in the neighborhood? It seemed reasonable that she might, though he wondered if she could afford the rent. Perhaps she shared an apartment with some of the communist girls he had seen her with at the Sichuan restaurant.

Still, that would only explain her observation of some of what she'd just said—other things would have required investigation. For example, how did she know that Tim was a reporter? Or that Jonesy was a reporter? And how did she know about Tim's funeral?

They had been watching him. Probably since he'd spoken with Mei-Ling at the restaurant Saturday night.

The leader arched an eyebrow, just a hint of expression on his passive face. "Tell me about the reporters, Wong Mei-Ling."

Mei-Ling took a deep breath, and Doug thought he could see a faint tremble in her lips. "The reporter who died was young, and they say he was an activist for social justice. He wrote about the Korean resistance last week, in the English newspaper. The other reporter is middle-age, fat—but they say he is a socialist, and a champion of the trade unions."

Clear evidence of an inquiry on their part. It surprised Doug a little to hear Jonesy referred to as "fat"—he was a bit stocky, perhaps ten or fifteen pounds overweight, but not what a westerner would call "fat." For half a second, he was amused at the thought of how Jonesy would react to the description.

The skinny leader's arched eyebrow rose a touch more. "That is interesting, Wong Mei-Ling," he said without elaboration.

"And two men came looking for him this afternoon," Mei-Ling added, staring now at Doug, her dark eyes unreadable. "Not white men—Chinese, dressed in western suits. They asked when I had last seen him, and when he would return."

This clearly piqued the leader's interest, for his eyes widened a touch, and his brow furrowed in surprise. "Did they say what their business was?"

"No."

The leader made a slight shrug. "Pity—but not surprising." He took a step toward Doug, and looked down at him from above. "Do you know who those men were, Bainbridge Douglas?"

Juntong, Doug surmised—but he just shook his head.

The leader's eyes narrowed. "You are lying, Bainbridge Douglas. I do not take kindly to lies. I will ask again—do you know who those men were?"

Doug shrugged this time, and tried to look uncertain.

The leader's face turned cold, he glanced back at the men standing around, and gave a quick jerk of his head in Doug's direction.

Three of the men grabbed Doug by the shoulders and hauled him into a standing position, though a somewhat unsteady one since his ankles were bound together. Two of them continued to hold his shoulders tightly, while the third pulled the gag from his mouth, then took hold of Doug's jaw and pried it open.

The leader stepped close. "I told you I do not take kindly to lies." His words had a sharp edge. Then he reached down to remove a knife that had been sheathed to his right calf, previously hidden from view by his pant leg. He held it up in front of Doug's face.

Doug broke out in a cold sweat.

The leader called to Dai Chi, his eyes never wavering from Doug's. The young man came alongside the leader, reached into Doug's forced-open mouth, and pulled out his tongue.

His fingers tasted of dirt and oil, and a hint of stale fish. Doug tried to wiggle away, but the hand on his jaw held his head still. He fought the panic.

Oh God, no, please no.

"In China, we cut a liar's tongue from his mouth," the leader said, cold as ice. "You have one last chance, Bainbridge Douglas. Tell me the truth, and your tongue will be spared. Who were the two Chinese men who came looking for you today?"

Doug tried to say that he wasn't certain, but it all came out as indecipherable sound with his tongue held tight between Dai Chi's dirty fingers.

The back of the leader's hand flew backward and made contact with Dai Chi's cheek, and the young man released Doug's tongue and took a step back.

"Speak, American," the leader commanded.

"I don't know for certain," Doug began, but as he saw the leader's knife inch closer to his face in response, he chose frankness. "They were probably *Juntong*."

His breath came hard and fast, and his heart pounded against his breastbone.

The leader's eyes narrowed even further, and he exhaled hard, making a little growl. "Why were the *Juntong* calling on you, Bainbridge Douglas? You were expecting them?"

Doug shook his head emphatically. "No, I wasn't expecting anyone today—but I witnessed two of their men get stabbed at the Paramount on Saturday night by a Japanese man, so I'm sure they want to talk to me about that."

He tried to calm his breath, and prayed the skinny leader would believe him.

For the first time since they'd pulled him up from the floor, he allowed himself to look past the leader, and his eyes locked for a few second's on Wong Mei-Ling's. She watched with a face like stone, her eyes hard and emotionless.

Doug was stunned. She wasn't horrified by what she was watching. Not even a bit squeamish. How could he have misjudged her so?

He looked back at the leader, whose eyes seemed to bore right into his head. They stared at one another in silence for several seconds, and Doug began to wonder if he had saved himself with his honesty, or if he had merely signed the death warrant with his own words.

Then a hint of sardonic grin came to the corners of the leader's mouth, and Doug felt his knees go weak. He might have dropped to the ground were it not for the two sets of hands holding him against the wall.

"You understand, do you not, that the *Juntong* are our deadliest enemy? If you were to be found to help them, or to be their agent, we would have no choice but to end your life, painfully—you understand my words, Bainbridge Douglas?"

Doug nodded. His mouth had gone too dry to speak.

"If the *Juntong* want to speak to you about two of their men who were killed, but then you turn up dead—it would be inconvenient for us. We do not want their interest in you to grow beyond what it already is. So you will go, and you will speak to no one of this, and you will give the *Juntong* no reason to ask questions. Is that understood?"

Doug nodded again, and managed to croak out "Yes" through his dry throat.

"We will be watching."

With those chilling words, the leader turned away. He paused beside Wong Mei-Ling to say something to her under his breath, and then he exited the house, followed by all of his men. Dai Chi took up the rear, and he glowered at Doug as he slipped past the tattered blue curtain.

In a matter of seconds, Doug stood alone in the room with Mei-Ling. They stared at each other without a word for several seconds.

He teetered on his bound feet, and she stooped down to untie the rope around his ankles. When she had finished, she ordered him to turn around, and then she untied his wrists.

"Come with me," she said, and walked toward the doorway without looking to see if he followed.

He followed her without hesitation.

She turned right—the opposite direction from which he had come earlier—and led him the short distance to the next narrow side street. She took him in a roundabout way through a maze of little side streets, probably deliberately to get him lost and confused.

He had absolutely zero intention of telling anyone about that communist safe house—it wasn't worth his life, for one thing, and they would almost certainly stop using it now in any case. Still, it wasn't surprising that Mei-Ling would try to confuse his sense of direction.

After a while they came to another ancient gate through another remnant of the fourteenth century wall— so this had to be the North Gate, Doug reasoned, since he had already seen the Great East Gate, and they were the only two that remained.

Here, the street widened and was lined with modern storefronts. A large sign posted on the corner of the nearest building announced this to be Rue Montauban—so they were back in the French Concession.

"I can find my way home from here," Doug said to her in his Mandarin-Shanghainese blend. "Thank you for guiding me out of the Old City."

She barely glanced at him before replying in a flat tone, "I am to stay with you until we reach Hwang Lo's building."

"Can we stop to eat along the way?" Doug asked, realizing that it was mid-afternoon and he hadn't eaten since breakfast. "I'm famished. May I buy you lunch?"

He realized in a flash that this might confirm her earlier accusation of being a 'typical American' who threw around money, so he hurried to add, "To thank you for guiding me safely home."

She remained silent, but he thought from the faint change in her expression that she seemed to be considering it.

"Follow me," she said at length, and picked up her pace. They were almost to the corner of Avenue Joffre, the busiest thoroughfare in the French Concession, and she turned left and guided him west for several blocks. They turned right onto an unmarked alley lined with tiny shops and restaurants that catered to an exclusively Chinese clientele.

She picked a little restaurant halfway down on the left. There were four small tables inside, only one of which was occupied at this hour. A middle aged Chinese man in a dirty white shirt and black pants came out and greeted them in Shanghainese.

His speech was so rapid, Doug had trouble understanding all of it, and when the man looked at him expectantly, Doug had to smile apologetically and ask him in Mandarin if he could repeat the question.

Wong Mei-Ling interrupted that they wanted cuttlefish with rice noodles, and tea. The man bowed his head and hurried back to the kitchen, shouting in rapid Shanghainese as he pushed through the swinging door.

"Is that the house specialty?" Doug asked, smiling at Mei-Ling. "I didn't see the menu."

"There is no menu," Mei-Ling replied, her voice flat.

"You know this place well, then?"

She stared at him for a second. "Well enough."

"Do you come here often?"

"No."

Doug tried one more time to make conversation. "How often do you come to the French Concession?"

"Rarely."

"So how do you know this place?"

236

She scowled a bit, and he wondered if his over-curiosity had offended her. She waited several seconds before replying. "I have known the owner since I was a little girl."

Her expression forbade further conversation, so he passed the minutes looking around at their surroundings in silence.

The food came a few minutes later, and the owner bowed as he set the steaming bowls in front of them.

Doug took the chopsticks that stuck out from the mount of noodles topped with pieces of cuttlefish in a dark sauce, and dug in. It smelled wonderful, and the taste was different from anything he'd ever had, but he loved it. He finished the entire dish, only noticing at the end that Mei-Ling had eaten barely half of hers. She had probably eaten lunch only a couple of hours before.

When the owner returned to take away their bowls, Doug complimented him on the dish, and asked what the sauce was.

"Soy and ginger with the black ink from the cuttlefish." The owner bowed his head with a smile and took the dishes.

After he had paid the bill, Doug followed Mei-Ling out the door and up the street. "Is he one of you?" he asked quietly, leaning close so she could hear him over the shouts and laughter of the people around them.

She scowled. "You should not ask that."

He took that as a yes.

"How did you come to those politics, Miss Wong?" he asked, still keeping his voice low.

She didn't answer.

"If you'll excuse me for saying so—you don't exactly seem the type."

She stopped, turned to him with a deep scowl, and crossed her arms. "What do you mean?"

"I meant no offence," Doug said, holding his hands up in front of him in a conciliatory gesture. "I meant only that you seem like a hardworking and traditional kind of girl; not the typical communist recruit."

Her eyes narrowed even further, and her lips pursed. Her eyes burned with such fury he thought they might burn a hole in his head. When she finally spoke, her words were sharp as razors.

"You Americans are so stupid. You know nothing about life in China. My father was the hardest working man I ever knew, but he was paid a pittance for his labor. When I was nine years old, my mother got very sick, and we could not afford a doctor. She died after three days of fever, delirious and miserable, with no relief but death. So my father began working to unionize the labor at his factory. The owners hired thugs to beat him and his friends, but that did not stop them. My father was brave. He became a communist when he learned that they were the only ones concerned about the welfare of Chinese workers.

"Then eight years ago, the tyrant Chiang Kai-shek sent gangs of *Kuomintang* loyalists into the streets of Shanghai to massacre anyone suspected of being a communist. For two days in April, the Nationalist thugs went from street to street, murdering thousands. They broke down the door of our apartment and killed my father with a machete in front of my brother and me."

Her voice cracked as she said that last part, and tears mixed with the rage in her eyes. Doug felt his cheeks flush hot with a combination of embarrassment, and anger on her behalf. His hands fisted at his sides, and he didn't know what to say.

After a few seconds pause, she continued, her words still cold and hard-edged. "They stole the little bit of money my father had saved in a clay jar. I was twelve years old, left to take care of my little brother all by myself. We had no food, no money. We went to my uncle's home, and found my uncle and aunt had both been murdered. I don't know where my little cousins went. My brother and I were left to live on the streets, eating scraps from trash cans and begging for pennies. I begged for work everywhere, odd jobs, but there is little a skinny twelve-year-old girl can do that will earn decent money. We were starving. That winter, my brother caught the flu and died."

Doug was horrified, and as he contemplated her agonizing story, he realized his mouth was hanging open.

"How did you get off the street?" he asked.

"The next spring, almost a year after they killed my father, I was begging for work when Hwang Lo offered to hire me as a shop assistant. He paid more than the odd jobs I had been doing, so I kept the job. I have worked for him now for seven years."

"Miss Wong, I am so sorry to hear about your suffering."

Her eyes flashed, and a sort of snarl came to her face as she spat out an angry tirade. "I do not need your pity, Bainbridge Douglas, you bourgeois American pig! What do you know of real suffering? What do you know of the plight of the Chinese people, suffering under a capitalist system that would make us slaves to wealthy western nations? We do not need your pity, either—none of us!"

She spun away from him, and marched down the street. She waved him forward with an impatient jerk of her hand, not looking back to see if he followed her.

He did, his head hanging a little in shame and embarrassment.

They walked the rest of the way in uncomfortable silence.

It was a long walk, and after a full afternoon of walking the length of Shanghai, Doug really wanted to catch a streetcar as they crossed into the International Settlement and passed through downtown, but he resisted the urge and kept walking alongside Wong Mei-Ling.

When they finally reached the door to his building, outside of Mr. Hwang's shop, he turned to her and bowed his head in deference.

"Thank you for escorting me home, Miss Wong. And I apologize for misjudging you, and for everything that has happened to you. I wish you the best, and I look forward to seeing you again at Mr. Hwang's laundry."

She returned the polite head bow, said "Good day," and walked away.

17

As Doug reached the top of the stairs, Li Baosheng exited his apartment, locking the door.

"Good afternoon, Mr. Bainbridge," he said in English with a smile and a polite bow.

"Hello, Bao." Doug turned away from the young man as he fished his key out of his pants pocket.

"I go to the fish market, to buy fish for dinner tonight," Bao said, sounding cheerful. "You come along? There is great many fish there, you find anything you like. I will show you."

"No, thank you," Doug said, trying to sound polite. "I just ate cuttlefish an hour ago."

Bao's face lit up. "Oh! Cuttlefish is very good. You like it?"

Doug forced a smile. "Yes, I did." He turned back to his door and turned the key in the lock.

"Charlie says I am a good cook," Bao continued. "I cook fish three or four times a week. You come for dinner tonight?"

Doug tried to think of an excuse why he couldn't go over for dinner, but he was both physically and mentally exhausted, and nothing came readily to mind. Feeling exasperated, he sighed and turned around. "What time?"

"We eat when it get dark—you come at nine o'clock?"

Doug nodded in resignation. "Sure, nine o'clock."

As he walked into his apartment and began closing the door, he saw Bao beam and wave as he bounded down the stairs. "Bye, Mr. Bainbridge! See you tonight!"

Doug suppressed a groan as he closed the door. He tossed his hat onto the table, loosened his necktie, unbuttoned his collar, and poured himself a glass of cold water from the pitcher in the ice box. The apartment was stuffy with no cross-breeze, and he downed the water and refilled it. After wiping the sweat off his brow with his handkerchief, he opened the kitchen window long enough to poke his head out and verify that the fire escape was empty.

He hated closing it again, but he didn't feel safe leaving it open anymore. Not until he got to the bottom of who was stalking him.

He sipped his water as he walked into the living room and plopped down in the armchair. He saw Ming Lin-Wen's calling card sitting on the side table, and he picked it up and contemplated it for a second before setting it back down.

He probably wouldn't go to tea tomorrow, he told himself. He should probably throw the calling card away.

But he left it on the table.

Twilight was settling over Shanghai as Doug crossed the hall, dressed in his nice gray summer suit instead of the new linen suit he wore every day now, and knocked on his neighbors' door.

"Coming!" he heard Charlie Ford's jovial voice call from inside, and a moment later the door opened. Charlie greeted him with a broad grin, wiping his hands on a small hand towel. He was dressed in a white linen shirt and a black necktie, and light gray linen slacks, but no jacket, and the sleeves of his shirt were rolled up and cuffed at the elbows.

"Mr. Bainbridge, welcome," Charlie said, stepping aside and motioning for Doug to enter. "Bao and I are so happy you were able to join us at last. We feel terrible bad you've lived across the hall for *nine days* now, and this is the first time we've shared a meal together."

242

"Thank you for the invitation," Doug said, forcing himself to sound polite.

"Do come in and sit down," Charlie said, motioning toward an arm chair beside one of the decorative partitions. "May I get you a cocktail before we eat? We have a full bar, so I can mix you anything you'd like."

"I'll take a gin and tonic, thank you."

Charlie's grin never faded. "I'm a gin man myself. We also have lime and sugar, if you care to make it a gin Rickey?"

"Just a gin and tonic, please."

Doug's tone made Charlie's grin fade, but his host nodded his head and hurried off. He returned a few minutes later with Doug's gin and tonic in a tumbler, and a gin Rickey for himself in a highball glass.

"To good neighbors," Charlie said, and clinked his glass against Doug's.

Doug raised his glass in silent acknowledgment of the toast, and took a long drink. It was a good gin and tonic—Charlie Ford obviously splurged for good liquor.

"Bao is cooking us a lovely fish stew—called *Geng* in Fujian—and he's added squid and oysters to supplement the fish cakes, since this is a special occasion."

That answered the question of Li Baosheng's origins—he was from Fujian province, to the south; and that explained his presence at the tea house around the corner that catered to Cantonese and Fujian customers, and the Oolong tea he and Charlie had served Doug on his first night in Shanghai.

"Does Bao cook for a Fujian restaurant?" Doug asked, just to make conversation.

Charlie shook his head and smiled. "No, he's not formally trained. He learned to cook by watching his mother when he was a child—" Charlie's smile faded, and a sad look came to his eyes "— though his father and uncles did not approve, and forbade him to cook.

When he came to live with me two years ago, I told him the kitchen was his, and he's blossomed into a wonderful cook."

Doug forced a smile. "How nice."

Charlie patted his slightly rounded tummy. "This is why I'm not so fit as I used to be, when I worked shipboard. If I had to live on me own cooking, I'd be skinnier than you, Mr. Bainbridge." He chuckled, but then flushed with embarrassment. "Oh! I beg your pardon—I didn't mean to imply you were *skinny*. You're certainly not. Oh, dear me."

Doug waved him off. "Think nothing of it."

A sheepish half-smile crossed Charlie's lips. "Thank you. What I should have said is—I don't know how Bao stays as slender as he does, the way we eat. The advantages of youth, I suppose."

"Yes, I suppose so," Doug said, and unconsciously tugged the seams of his jacket to cover his own slender midsection.

An awkward silence fell over them for half a minute, until Bao came into the room and announced that dinner was ready.

"Excellent!" Charlie smiled, and motioned for Doug to take a seat at the dinner table.

The table was set with blue patterned china, and in the center Bao set a large porcelain bowl of steaming soup. Charlie ladled it into bowls, setting the first one in front of Doug, while Bao brought out cups of Oolong tea.

The *Geng* was delicious, with a light but rich broth, and full of large braised cakes of some type of white fish, Chinese cabbage, boiled pieces of squid, and boiled oysters.

He complimented Bao on the seafood. Bao smiled and nodded in acknowledgement.

"Where is the fish market where you got all of this?" Doug asked. He had not seen any fish market large enough to sell all of these different things, and he had walked the riverfront from the Hongkou docks all the way down the Chinese Bund.

"On the river in Yangtzepoo, other side of Hongkou Creek," Bao explained. "Not far, thirty minutes on foot. Outdoor market, biggest fish market in Shanghai."

"The freshest seafood in the city," Charlie said.

"I haven't been that far east yet," Doug said. "Is that the East District?"

Charlie nodded. "Yes, the East District. Locals call it Yangtzepoo, though."

"I used to live near the fish market," Bao said.

Doug noticed Charlie's posture stiffen. He thought back to what Jonesy had found in Tim's Green Gang file that morning. "Isn't it mostly dockyards and warehouses in that area?" *And slums*, he thought, remembering the view from the deck of the ship as they sailed into Shanghai.

Charlie's smile seemed forced. "It's not all warehouses," he said, sounding a little hurried. "There are several sailors' taverns all along the waterfront over there. That's where I first met Bao."

"You worked in a tavern?" Doug asked, looking at Bao.

"Yes," Charlie said, too quickly.

Doug dropped the subject and concentrated on eating his soup.

"So tell us, Mr. Bainbridge—how have you enjoyed your time in Shanghai so far?" Charlie asked, though Doug wondered about the quick return of his jovial tone.

Doug hesitated, not really sure how to answer that question. "I like Shanghai very much," he finally said.

"You don't sound very enthusiastic," Charlie said, looking back at Doug with one eyebrow slightly arched. "You look a mite conflicted, if I may say so."

Doug shifted in his seat, uncomfortable. "The last three days have been difficult."

"Oh?"

Charlie's expression looked genuinely concerned, and Doug hated being evasive.

"My friend Tim died unexpectedly on Friday night. Killed, actually."

Charlie and Bao both looked stunned. "Do you mean that nice Mr. McIntyre who came here on Friday evening?" Charlie asked.

Doug nodded, but said nothing, surprised by the lump that formed in his throat as he pictured Tim's head lying in a pool of blood in that alley.

"Good lord!" Charlie said, his hand clutching at his throat in an almost feminine sort of way. "What on Earth happened?"

Doug started to tell the story about what happened at the Jade Dragon, and before he knew it he was spilling details about everything that had happened since. He castigated himself for being indiscreet about Kawakami and the *Juntong*, but for some reason he just couldn't stop the flow of words that spilled out of his mouth.

Charlie and Bao listened with sorrowful expressions, letting him speak uninterrupted.

"I am so terribly sorry, Douglas," Charlie said after the story ended, putting his hand on Doug's forearm.

Doug flinched at the contact, and at the presumptuous use of his given name, but he didn't pull back or say anything.

The sympathy felt like a relief, actually.

"What will you do now, Mr. Bainbridge?" Bao asked.

"I don't know," Doug said. He wondered if Jonesy had found anyone waiting for Tim at the Haining Road Bridge at eight o'clock. Probably not, after three days.

Then he thought about Tim's notes concerning meeting someone in the alley behind the dockyards in Yangtzepoo, and his mind went back to their earlier conversation about the sailors' taverns there. Charlie had clearly been uncomfortable when Bao mentioned that he used to live there—Doug wondered if he should ask about the area again, and risk increasing Charlie's discomfort.

"I found some notes in Tim's files, that he had recently interviewed some sources in Yangtzepoo for a story he was working on," Doug said, choosing his words carefully. "Multiple stories, perhaps. I know he was looking into the opium trade, but he seems to have also interviewed prostitutes about the murder of a crippled beggar in the area."

Charlie looked pained, but Bao seemed suddenly interested. "It was probably one of..." he paused, glanced up, and his face screwed up. Then he looked at Charlie and said, *"Jyutping?"*

Charlie flinched. He looked at Doug with an apologetic look. "He means a pimp, if you'll pardon the expression."

Doug felt a flush come to his cheeks, but he looked back at Bao. "Does the Green Gang traffic in prostitution, too?"

A horrified look came to Charlie's face, but Bao just shook his head. "No, not Green Gang. The—pimps?—they are local thugs. They mark territory, certain streets belong to one pimp. They don't like beggars coming into their territory, say it interfere with business. I saw them beat many beggars, very bad beatings."

"I would imagine prostitutes often worked the sailors' taverns," Doug said. His cheeks flushed again, and he looked at Charlie with a sheepish expression. "I apologize for the impolite conversation."

"No apology necessary," Charlie said, a little too quickly.

"Why impolite?" Bao asked, looking at Charlie with his brow knit.

Charlie smiled at the boy. "Westerners aren't comfortable discussing such topics in public."

Bao scowled. "We're not public, we are home."

"Yes, but—well, you see—"

Doug interrupted Charlie's search for words, addressing himself to Bao. "Did you have trouble with prostitutes in your tavern?"

247

Bao looked perplexed. "Trouble? No trouble—different type for different tavern. Everyone kept their place, no trouble."

Doug nodded, surprised at how uncomfortable he was feeling. Still, this was for Tim.

"Tim had a note about someone he spoke with in an alley behind the dockyards, and he used a name or a word I did not know—*Nán jì*?"

Charlie's face was beet red.

Bao was unfazed. "That word mean prostitute who is a boy."

Doug felt his stomach clench, and he was unable to keep the look of distaste off his face.

"The *nán jì* work in the alley behind certain tavern—that is their territory, where the *jyutping* no bother them. Sailors who want a *nán jì* know where."

Doug, mouth open, couldn't help but look at Charlie, who stared down at his bowl of soup. He looked back at Bao, who was staring at Charlie with a concerned expression.

"How old are you, Bao?" Doug asked, his words coming out stilted in spite of his best effort to sound relaxed.

"Nineteen years," Bao said, but he continued to look at Charlie.

"Bao is very trusting," Charlie said, quietly, still looking down. He paused a second, and when he looked up at Doug his eyes held both sadness and fear. "Your friend Mr. McIntyre seemed a decent sort, so perhaps Bao thought you and he were like-minded chaps."

Doug said nothing, but sat stiff-backed and uncomfortable. He thought about Lafayette Park in Washington, and felt disgust for the likes of Charlie Ford.

"You don't understand how tragic it is for those boys," Charlie said, his expression pleading. "Hated by their own families, when they're still frightful young. If they show no interest in girls, their fathers and uncles beat them, and take them to prostitutes to force them into shagging a chit. When it don't work, they take the poor boys and sell

248

them to the Tanka—that's the boat people who sail the Junks up and down the South China Sea coast. The Tanka bring the boys to Shanghai, and sell 'em on the black market—some of them as young as thirteen."

"I was fifteen years," Bao said, very serious. "My father showed great patience before he lost hope."

Doug felt a wholly unexpected flutter of sadness for Bao, and those like him. He didn't know where that came from, or why.

Charlie looked horrified. "Bao, please…"

Bao scowled at Charlie. "I not ashamed. You tell me not to be ashamed, and I listen."

Doug felt like he should say something, but no words came to mind. "I'm sorry that happened to you, Bao," was the best he could come up with.

"It happens all over the world, sadly," Charlie said. "But it seems to be more institutionalized here in China. It's a matter of dishonor here, and the families toss off some of the dishonor when they sell the boys. Once they get to Shanghai, though, those poor boys got no choice but to offer their bums for money—else they don't get to eat. Every seaport of any size, on every continent, got boys like that working the alleys behind the sailors' pubs. They got nowhere else to go."

"Charlie gave me home," Bao said. "I got lucky."

Charlie looked back at the young man with such a look of affection, Doug had to look away. It seemed so sweet, that he had to remind himself that it was unnatural and disgusting.

Charlie cleared his throat then, and looked at Doug with embarrassment. "Since this is probably the last time you'll ever come here for dinner, let me just say how sorry I am that your friend Mr. McIntyre got killed. He seemed a very decent chap. Such a shame."

Doug nodded, but said nothing.

An uncomfortable silence fell over the table, the only sound in the apartment the whirring of the fans or the occasional snippet of conversation on the street. Doug picked at his soup, but had lost his enthusiasm for eating.

After several minutes of unsuccessful attempts at small talk, Charlie stood and began clearing the table. As Bao joined in, Charlie made a half-hearted attempt to offer Doug a cup of *mǐjiǔ*—Chinese rice wine.

"We have a nice *Ang Jiǔ*," he said. "That's a Fujian red rice wine, if you're not familiar. Very tasty. Nice way to finish off a meal."

And very strong. "No, thank you. I'd best return home and not impose on your hospitality."

A sad look fell over Charlie's face. "Of course. We don't wish to detain you." He walked Doug to the door and opened it for him.

"I do hope you will forgive us for the improper topics of conversation earlier," he said in a lower voice as Doug walked past him through the door. "Bao don't always understand western manners, you see. And, well—he don't really have any mates to talk to, you see, so it's easy for him to get a little, um, *overenthusiastic* when making new friends. I really regret making you uncomfortable."

Doug's mouth tightened, but he resisted the urge to frown. "Yes, well—apology accepted. Good night."

He didn't look back as he crossed the hall, unlocked his apartment door, and slipped inside.

18

He was standing on a rocky outcropping on the coast of California, waves crashing against the boulders below, and he was looking out over the entrance to a large bay. This was Monterey Bay, his mind told him, though it didn't look familiar; he looked along its edges, and saw the outlines of a sizeable town that might sort of look like Monterey. He imagined he saw the bell tower on the grounds of St. James Academy, on the edge of that town, and he assured himself it was indeed Monterey.

Then he saw a boat in the middle of the bay that hadn't been there a moment before. It looked like a riverboat, long and narrow, bobbing on the swell. Then it was in front of him, heading out to sea, and he was staring at the stern as it steamed away. He saw Lucy standing on the top deck in the middle of the stern, staring at him. He felt like he was being pulled through the air toward her, as if her startlingly blue eyes were pulling him like magnets.

Then he was in the water, several hundred yards from the rocky shore. A towering finger of rock jutted out of the water not far to his left, a sort of island dotted with seagulls nesting in its nooks and crannies. The water was cool, with a steady swell that bobbed him up and down as it came in from the ocean, though it was not rough and he had no trouble treading water. He glanced down, and realized that he was naked, though the water was so murky and dark that he couldn't see his feet, or barely even his knees.

He detected tiny movements in the water, and thought to himself that there were fish all around him. Then he felt the strange sensation of little bumps accompanied by something between a tickle and a prick, and realized fish were nibbling at his toes, though he couldn't see that deep in the dark water. Then he felt them nibbling his fingers, and then at his penis and scrotum; though when he looked at his hands, or down at his penis, he couldn't see them even though he could feel them still nibbling.

He kicked harder, and waved his arms harder in the water, trying to avoid the fish, but they wouldn't leave and wouldn't stop. He thrashed in the water now, trying with all of his might to scare or push the fish away, but they kept at it, now nibbling at his buttocks and his back, and eventually all over his body. He swam for shore as hard as he could, but it didn't seem to draw closer.

He thought it might be the swell holding him back, so he dove into the water and propelled himself through the darkness toward the shore, feeling the rush of movement all around his body, hearing the swish of water moving past his ears.

And he knew he was making progress, even as his lungs began to burn from lack of breath.

Doug awoke feeling disoriented, as if he had risen slowly from sleep, as one might float to the surface after being submerged in water. It took him several seconds to realize he was lying on top of his bed in the dark, staring at the ceiling as it reflected the small amount of light that came through his bedroom window from the streetlights outside. The whirring of the fan on the nightstand nearby sounded remarkably like the swooshing sound of the water he'd been swimming through just a few seconds ago.

But wait—he hadn't really been swimming a few seconds ago, had he? No, he couldn't have been; how could he have gotten from the water to his bedroom so quickly? He must have gone swimming earlier today. No, that couldn't be, either—he couldn't have gotten from California to here in such a short time.

As his mind slowly awoke to reason, he finally concluded it had been a dream, albeit a strange one. He wasn't sure what to make of it, so he lay still for several minutes, pondering every element of the dream, while the movement of air from the fan tingled the nerves on his bare skin.

Eventually he gave up trying to make any sense of it, and got up from bed, walking to the open window that looked out over the street. He parted the white curtains enough to look out and see that there was no one out in the neighborhood at this hour. He concluded it was still the middle of the night, and he should go back to bed.

He heard a clicking sound down the street just as he turned away from the window, so he turned back long enough to see an Indian police constable rounding the corner and strolling down Huang Lei Road, spinning his night stick in a rhythm known only to him. Doug watched for a few seconds, and then stepped back from the window before the policeman could look up and see him standing there in his birthday suit.

He took the clock off the nightstand, and held it out into the dim beam of light that came through the window, turning it until he could read the face. Quarter to four. No wonder the neighborhood was silent.

His mind drifted back to the image of Lucy staring at him from the back of that boat in his dream, and how close he had come to her face for a second before she disappeared.

He felt an ache in his chest.

He wouldn't think about Lucy. He called to mind the image of Ming Ling-wen in the boutique, rubbing her hand along her silk-stockinged legs. This brought up more salacious images from his imagination, as he'd hoped it would, and he spent the next few minutes pleasuring himself until his body stiffened and tingled, and then fell back in exhaustion; and he drifted back to sleep to the hypnotic whir of the fan.

Doug rested in the shade of a large oak tree, as much for respite from the intense mid-morning sun as for the relative obscurity of standing in the shadow. Like most streets in the French Concession, he noticed, Donghu Lane was lined with large shade trees.

He stood partly behind the large trunk of one of the French Oaks on the corner, looking across at the massive complex that belonged to Du Yuesheng—better known in Shanghai as "Big-eared Du." A tall stone wall surrounded the complex, and through a large gate he could see a circular drive in front of a pillared portico, behind which stood a four-story stone mansion with huge front windows; two five-story towers framed the portico, with bay windows on every floor pushing out from the façade of the mansion.

This palatial home, along with several smaller mansions all along the block, belonged to the most notorious crime boss in China.

Doug wasn't sure what he expected to see, but he stood and watched for a while.

For what reasons would a man own multiple mansions on the same street? To house family, perhaps. To make a grand display of his wealth, probably. But none of these reasons seemed entirely right. Much more likely Du owned multiple mansions on the same street as a base of operations for his empire.

Doug stood there for what felt like an hour, with almost nothing happening on the quiet residential street. When a gray-haired Chinese man in traditional silk robes, red and yellow, with a wispy gray beard, walking a little Pekinese dog on a leash, stared at him as he passed, Doug realized how suspicious—and conspicuous—he looked. He turned and walked back the way he had come.

After a few blocks, Donghu Lane entered a commercial district, with stylish stores and restaurants lining the wide sidewalks. There were many people going about their business here, Chinese and white, most well-dressed in the latest western fashions.

The cafes and bistros bustled with activity as the lunch hour approached, and Doug found an outdoor table at one of the French bistros and ordered a glass of Beaujolais and a plate of coq au vin from the Chinese waiter.

A French sommelier brought out a glass and a half-full bottle of Beaujolais, showed him the bottle label and asked him something in French. Not familiar with more than a handful of words in French, Doug just nodded. The sommelier poured a glass with a haughty sneer and walked away without another word.

As he sat and sipped his wine, he mulled over all he'd learned from Tim's notes. Tim's theory about police corruption enabling the Green Gang's success did fit with what Detective Sergeant Wallace had hinted at on Sunday evening. And it seemed logical, Doug thought as he watched two French Concession police officers stroll by; one was white— probably French—and the other Chinese. They made their way slowly on foot down Donghu Lane, nodding respectfully to the most stylishly dressed passers-by.

Yes, the police had to be part of Du's empire. There was no other way it could function right under their noses in both the French Concession and the International Settlement without significant hindrance. The police—or at least a fair minority of them—had to be on the Green Gang's payroll.

But was *that* why Tim was killed? A corrupt police officer trying to cover his tracks by silencing a nosy reporter? Doug couldn't discount that possibility, but if that were the case, how on Earth could he prove it? And there had to be hundreds—if not thousands—of police offers on the take, if what he'd learned about the scale of the Green Gang's operations were true.

The thought made him melancholy.

This brought him back to what Jonesy had said yesterday—the best way to honor Tim was to work for justice in the world, as he had, and not waste time chasing windmills.

Jonesy. Doug felt his temples pulse with irritation just thinking about the cynical reporter. Where did he get the nerve to sit in judgement of Doug and his life, when *he* was the deviant? It made Doug furious.

The Chinese waiter arrived with a steaming plate of coq au vin, set it on the table with a quick bow, and backed away. It smelled delicious, and Doug concentrated on his food and wine, interspersed with casual people-watching.

He was sopping up the last of the sauce on his plate with pieces of baguette, when he noticed a young Chinese man in workman's clothes on the other side of the street, standing at the corner of a storefront, staring at him.

Doug recognized his face from the communist safe house the day before.

The leader had told him they would be watching, but Doug hadn't thought much of that warning in the nearly twenty-four hours since. They had to have been watching him all morning—how else could they have found him here, in a city of three million, the first time he had been here on only his second visit to the French Concession? The thought sent a chill up his spine, in spite of the ninety-degree weather.

He stared back at the young man for a moment, but the young communist never looked away, apparently undeterred that Doug had noticed him.

A moment later, the Chinese waiter appeared beside his table, took his plate and laid down the bill in one movement, and departed with a bow.

Doug paid the check and left, conscious that the communist across the street began to move when he did. He wondered how long they would watch him before deciding that he wasn't worth their time.

Probably not soon—but not forever, either. They couldn't afford to waste their resources.

It was only a couple of blocks to the boundary of the International Settlement, and he crossed from the French Concession into the West District—or Uptown, as the IS locals called it—and his tail followed. It was less than a half-mile to Bubbling Well Road, but this was in the far western reaches of the International Settlement—not far from the Paramount, actually. He was more than a mile west of the Recreation Grounds, with downtown beyond that.

Too far to walk. If he waited for the trolley, his tail would get on it with him, and if he hired a rickshaw, the young communist would just grab the next one; but if he took a motor cab...

Doug walked east on Bubbling Well road, and after just a block he spotted an empty cab approaching, and he raised his arm to hail it at the last moment. The cab driver slammed on the brakes to pull over a short distance ahead of Doug, who ran and scrambled inside.

"Take me to 118 Huang Lei Road, and hurry. Go!"

After the cab had sped away from the curb, and Doug had looked back to see the young communist frowning, he exhaled hard and relaxed for the first time in hours. Only then did it occur to him that when he had given the cab driver his instructions, he'd said the entire sentence in Shanghainese. He hadn't had to use a single word of Mandarin.

A small smile spread across his lips as it dawned on him. "Atta boy, Dougie," he said to himself.

By the time the cab stopped in front of his building, it had occurred to Doug that perhaps it hadn't been such a great idea to ditch his tail in such an obvious manner. They could well interpret his action as an attempt to hide his activity from them, and that would inherently make them suspicious. If they were anything like the Soviets, they were suspicious of everyone as it was.

The thought weighed heavily on his mind as he climbed the stairs and unlocked his door. Once inside his apartment, he went to the kitchen window and opened it long enough to check the fire escape; finding it empty, he closed and locked it again.

Then he saw Ming Lin-wen's calling card. Her house on Broadway was just a block from the Soviet Consulate, where he'd started following Dai Chi yesterday. If he went there for tea this afternoon, as invited, and the communists followed him—he was certain they would—that could provide a less-suspicious explanation for why he'd followed Dai Chi; as it was now, they almost certainly assumed he'd been tailing the young man for a while.

Yes, he told himself, tea at Ming Lin-wen's house was his ticket out of the hot seat.

He had two hours until tea time. Two hours to nap, bathe, and make himself presentable to his hostess.

An hour later, as Doug walked from his apartment door to the bathroom, Bao came walking up the stairs.

"Oh, hello, Mr. Bainbridge," Bao said with a smile.

Doug returned the smile half-heartedly. "Good afternoon, Bao." Why did Bao always seem to catch him in his bathrobe?

"I went to see old friends today," Bao continued, his expression growing serious. Then he leaned close and whispered, "My old friends who work as *nán jì*, they remember your friend Mr. McIntyre."

This grabbed Doug's attention, and he stopped in the hallway and turned to fully face Bao, only half-caring that his robe was tied loosely enough to leave most of his chest exposed.

"They do?"

Bao nodded.

"Were they working with Mr. McIntyre on one of his stories?"

"I don't know what story, but they say Mr. McIntyre pay them five dollars to watch a house on Fao Sho Lane. He offer *ten* dollars if

258

they can follow the men there when they leave for the bank, and tell him where they go. He say if they catch the boys watching or following, the deal off. He say the men sell dope, and he tell the boys no buying— just watch until sundown, then meet him at the Haining Road Bridge over Hongkou Creek."

Doug felt like two puzzle pieces from Tim's notes suddenly fit neatly together.

"I told them Mr. McIntyre dead now. Nobody surprised by that."

"Would they meet with me?" Doug asked, excited. Then he hastened to add, "Only for information, nothing else."

Bao looked faintly amused, but he bowed his head. "I will go with you. When do we go?"

That wasn't what Doug had in mind, but he supposed it was probably safer for Bao to accompany him.

"I don't know—this evening after dusk, maybe?"

Bao nodded. "You come by at eight o'clock, and we'll go then. Thirty minute walk to the alley."

Doug was afraid that was where Bao had meant. He muttered thanks, and hurried into the bathroom.

He walked out of the building about forty minutes later, dressed in his nice summer suit rather than his linen one, walked to the corner, and waited a couple of minutes for a rickshaw to come by. He paid the coolie twenty-five cents to run him the half-mile to Broadway, and drop him off at the gate to Ming Lin-wen's compound.

Doug glanced at his watch, pleased to see that he was exactly on-time.

A man in a dark blue uniform stood at the gate; Doug gave him his name, and explained in Mandarin why he was there. The man bowed deeply and opened the gate.

"The mistress of the house is in the drawing room with the other guests," the man said. "Greta at the front door will show you in."

Doug chuckled at the Germanic name as he walked to the front door, which opened as he approached.

A young white woman in a maid's uniform curtsied as he entered the enormous hall with gleaming white walls and a ceiling that had to be at least thirty feet high; she addressed him in German-accented English. "Good afternoon, sir. I am Greta, please follow me."

She led him past the twin staircases that rose on either side of the hall to a balcony above—their black wrought iron railing contrasting with the bright white of the walls—to a large room off to the side with tall windows, a grand piano in the corner, and several small tables of dark wood, with matching chairs. On a small secretary in another corner sat an ivory and gold telephone—the modern kind with a receiver that rested in a brass cradle atop the base, rather than an old-fashioned upright.

Five of the chairs were occupied—Ming Lin-wen and four other Chinese women, all but one about the same age, in their early twenties, he judged. The other appeared a little older, perhaps early to mid-thirties, and this one gave him an appraising look as he stood in the doorway.

He gave them all a polite bow as the German maid curtsied and disappeared, and he greeted them in Mandarin.

Ming Lin-wen gave him a dazzling smile. "Welcome, Mr. Bainbridge. I am so glad you could join us. Won't you sit down?" she said, motioning toward an empty seat next to hers. She wore a white sleeveless gown, cut just low enough in front to show a tiny hint of cleavage, and elbow-length white gloves.

Once he'd sat, she introduced the four women sitting opposite him. They exchanged pleasantries for a few minutes, until the maid brought another guest.

A white man in his late thirties stood in the door, with thinning brown hair, dressed in a white suit with a black necktie. Doug was startled to recognize the round-faced man as Will Geoffries, who had spoken to him at the Black Horse Pub on Sunday afternoon. He looked equally surprised to see Doug, but he smiled, and then bowed to the ladies, greeting them in Mandarin.

"You are very kind to greet us in our language, Mr. Geoffries," Ming Lin-wen said in good English; Doug had no idea she could speak it at all, let alone fluently. "We will converse in English, for the benefit of you and Mr. Bainbridge. May I introduce you?"

"We've met, actually," Geoffries said, his British accent sounding deliberately refined, not quite natural.

Ming Lin-wen raised one thin eyebrow. "Oh? I did not realize. How fortunate a coincidence. Please sit."

"Well, Mr. Bainbridge, I see you have made some excellent company here in Shanghai," Geoffries said, taking the seat next to Doug and nodding toward their hostess, who had turned to the lady next to her.

"I'm afraid Miss Ming and I are only slightly more acquainted than you and I," Doug said, taking the cup and saucer that the maid Greta handed to him. Another maid, this one Chinese, poured tea from a porcelain pot into his cup.

"Well, you've only just arrived, so that's to be expected," Geoffries said with a broad smile. "Miss Ming has excellent taste in everything, including people—so I interpret your presence here as a ringing endorsement of your character."

Doug felt his cheeks flush. "That's very kind, thank you."

"How are you getting on in Shanghai?"

"Very well, thank you," Doug lied. "I've had the chance to visit the French Concession on a couple of occasions, but I have not yet tried the restaurant that you recommended the other day."

261

"Oh, Le Château de Vert ? You must dine there soon. Best French cuisine in China."

"I had a nice meal at the Astor House a couple of nights ago," Doug said, willfully ignoring the tension with Lucy at that dinner.

"Yes, that's another fine place to dine, with a rather elegant dining room." Geoffries appeared slightly bored with the topic, and changed the subject. "I hope you've allowed yourself to enjoy our famous nightlife here in Shanghai. I believe you mentioned the Paramount the other night."

"I confess, I've only been out on the town just two nights," Doug said. "I went to the Paramount on Saturday, and found it very enjoyable. I went to a Chinese nightclub on Friday night, called the Jade Dragon."

Geoffries' smile seemed a touch stiff. "I'm familiar with the place. I live off Nanking Road myself, so I pass by there frequently. Mostly natives, I believe?"

"It was a mostly Chinese crowd there, yes," Doug agreed with a nod. He couldn't tell if Geoffries had meant that as a condescension.

Geoffries smile brightened. "Well, I'm having a bit of a soiree tomorrow evening, at my flat in the Sassoon House—you should stop by, have a cocktail and mingle. I have a bit of an eclectic mix of friends— eccentric, some of them, but all people of quality. You seem like a man of refinement, Mr. Bainbridge; you should spend time socializing with a quality crowd."

The sudden invitation both surprised and pleased Doug. It would indeed be a refreshing change of pace. And perhaps he would actually have an easier time making friends in Shanghai than he ever had in Washington.

"That sounds really swell, thank you. What time?"

"The party will start at nine o'clock. Mid-week, we can't carry on too late, now can we?" Geoffries said with a smile and a mischievous gleam in his eye.

"I'll be there," Doug said.

The tea party ended after an hour, with the ladies rising to bid everyone good afternoon. Doug and Will Geoffries stood as the ladies took their leave, and in turn thanked their hostess for a lovely time, and began to leave.

As Doug was following Geoffries out of the room, Ming Lin-wen called out to him in Mandarin. "Mr. Bainbridge, please wait a moment."

Doug turned back and looked at her, but she just stood by the little table and waited, staring back at him. After a few seconds, he walked back to her. "Yes, Miss Ming?" he asked, also in Mandarin.

She glanced over his shoulder, and then looked back at him with a dazzling smile. "I am so glad you joined us this afternoon. I was happy to better make your acquaintance. Would you like a tour of the house?"

Doug knew what she meant, that this wasn't about seeing the house. He also knew he probably shouldn't, but he felt himself nodding and heard himself agree.

She sauntered past him, and he followed her into the hall, aware that everyone seemed to have disappeared, including the servants. As they moved from room to room, he barely listened to her descriptions in Mandarin of the furnishing and art work, his heart racing. He said niceties about everything, and hoped she didn't notice him casting glances at her buttocks. As she guided him back to the central hall and up the stairs, he could hear the blood rushing in his ears. The second floor was a parade of one large bedroom after another, and as they walked through the door of each he couldn't help but wonder if this was where the "tour" would end.

And then in one of the rooms, she turned to him, put her hands inside his jacket at the shoulders, and pushed it down his arms until it fell to the floor. She took a step closer, loosened his tie, and unbuttoned his shirt without a word. He felt his heart pounding as she pushed it off his shoulders, and it joined his jacket on the floor.

He reached out to touch her shoulder, but she shook her head and gave him a look of mock disapproval, a sly smile on her lips. She unbuckled his belt, unbuttoned his pants, and tugged them down, followed by his boxer shorts. Then she took several steps back, stood at the corner of the four-poster bed, and stared at him.

He swallowed hard, not sure what to do, and slightly uncomfortable under her gaze. Then he used his right foot to kick off his left shoe, and then vice-versa, and hurried to step out of the pants that were bunched at his ankles. He took a step toward her, but she scowled and barked "No!"

He stopped.

"Men do not like taking orders from women," she said, her eyes never leaving his body. "But this is my house, and I give the orders here."

He stood as if frozen, and let her eyes roam. After a moment, she sauntered up and slunk around him slowly, inspecting him up and down. When she was behind him, she smacked his bare buttocks, hard.

He jumped. She smacked again, even harder.

It stung, and he didn't like it at all. He crouched down, grabbed his clothes, and held them in front of himself as he stood again and faced her.

"I think you may have the wrong idea," he said in Mandarin, but she smacked his face, then clawed his clothes out of his hands and pushed him backward toward the bed.

"I do not tolerate insolent back-talk," she said.

Putting her hands on both of his shoulders, she held him down as she climbed astride him, hiking her dress above her knees. He didn't resist.

"In my house, you will do what I tell you to, and we will both enjoy ourselves," she said, moving forward to straddle his chest and lifting her dress up to her hips. He watched her, mesmerized.

A wicked grin spread across her face as she reached back to take hold of him, and moved her hips toward his face.

She told him exactly what to do, and he obeyed.

Thirty minutes later, a child's happy squeal reached them from downstairs. Ming Lin-wen jumped from the bed, pulling her dress down and smoothing the skirt. She straightened her stockings, adjusting the hooks on her garters, and stepped into the white pumps she'd left in the middle of the floor. She paused only a second to glance back at his naked form lying on top of the wrinkled bed covers.

"Get up, straighten the bed clothes, and get dressed," she said, her tone serious and quiet. "Then do exactly what I tell you."

His initial bewilderment at her actions faded into a modest bemusement as he got up. Someone had arrived home—someone that she didn't want to find them in here—but who? Members of her family, he supposed.

He did as she ordered, smoothing the bed cover until there was no obvious evidence that anyone had lain on it. She watched him with obvious impatience as he pulled on his boxer shorts, followed by his pants, then his shirt, and finally his socks and shoes. "Hurry!" she hissed as he finished tying his shoes and slipped on his jacket.

He started to slip his tie under his collar, and she grabbed him by the hand and tugged him toward the door. "There is no time for that. Come!"

"From whom are you hiding me?" he finally asked, his irritation at her impatience overcoming any misgivings he had about angering her.

"The nanny," she whispered, tugging him down the hall toward a smaller room. "If she sees you upstairs, she will tell my husband."

Doug stopped cold, and it jerked her to a stop. "Your *husband*?" The incredulity momentarily outweighed any outrage he would soon feel.

She scowled and tugged at his arm. "Yes. Now come along, quickly."

"Why didn't you tell me you were married?" he asked as they stopped in front of a window looking out over the back gardens, careful not to speak too loudly, but not disguising his anger, either.

She gave him a look of contempt, which made him recoil slightly. "What business is it of yours?"

He squared his shoulders, and stared down at her in what he hoped was an intimidating scowl. "I had a right to know I was cuckolding someone," he said.

"Don't be a fool," she said, opening the window and motioning for him to step through to the small balcony on the other side. "Go, before you put us both in danger. Climb down the rain spout, and step off onto the wall above the garden. You can slip down into the alley on the other side and follow it to the street. Don't walk past the house—go north instead. Do you understand?"

"Yes." He let his insolence show.

"Do exactly as I say, and go *now*." She pushed him through the window, and closed it the second his fingers left the windowsill. Then she disappeared.

The balcony was barely wider than the length of his feet, with a two-foot stone rail encircling it. He climbed over the right side, and reached for the downspout attached to the wall a few feet away. There were foot holds jutting from the sides of the downspout at regular intervals, presumably for workmen to use should they need to climb to the roof.

He scrambled down, stopping when he became even with the top of the garden wall, which was only a few feet away at this spot. He held on as he reached one leg toward the wall, found firm footing, and shifted his weight there. Once crouched atop the wall, he could jump down five feet to the gravel alley that ran between the walls of neighboring compounds.

Taking a second to look around, he saw an elderly gardener standing beside a hedge of rose bushes, a pair of pruning shears in his hand. He was staring at Doug.

Damn! Doug leapt into the alley. Turning to the right and keeping his head low, he hurried down the alley about fifty feet to where it crossed the sidewalk along Broadway.

He turned left and walked along Broadway for a block until it teed onto Tiantong Road—the southern edge of Japantown. Wusong Road was only two blocks to his left, and he hurried there, only stopping for breath when he reached the corner of the busy thoroughfare.

His anger seethed inside of him. She was an adulteress—but that was her business, he decided. What angered him most was that she had turned *him* into an adulterer without his consent.

The thought made his skin crawl. He felt filthy. He may have consciously thrown off the outmoded Victorian morality of his youth—he and almost every other member of his generation—but he'd never imagined he could *ever* commit adultery.

It wasn't his fault, he assured himself. She hadn't told him. He thought only that he was having sex with a beautiful woman—a beautiful *single* woman. But deep down he doubted that made a difference. Willingly or otherwise, he had committed adultery, plain and simple.

There was still enough of his mother's stern old-fashioned Presbyterianism in the recesses of his mind to make him fearful of divine retribution, either in this life or the next. He was tainted.

He rushed home, barely paying attention to the people and things around him, and bounded up the stairs of his building two at a time. Relieved to find the bathroom empty when he reached his floor, he practically ran inside and slammed the door. Tearing off his clothes, he turned on the faucet of the bathtub, and stood in the bath scrubbing every inch of his body until his skin was bright pink.

19

Doug wasn't in a particularly good mood as he crossed the hall and knocked on Charlie and Bao's door. The events of the day tumbled around in his mind, unbidden, and always came back to one thought—*I'm an adulterer.*

Bao answered the door in dark blue trousers and a light blue linen shirt, open at the collar. "Hello, Mr. Bainbridge. All ready to go?"

"Yes, Bao, let's go." *And get this over with.*

"Charlie!" Bao called over his shoulder. "Mr. Bainbridge is ready."

Charlie appeared around the corner, tightening his necktie. He wore a holster over his white linen shirt, and he stopped and unlocked a cabinet in the corner and removed a small handgun. He checked the chamber, and stuffed the gun in the holster at his side. Then he tugged on his linen jacket.

"You're coming with us?" Doug asked, partly irritated, but also partly relieved to not have to go with Bao alone.

"Yes, I'll keep watch while you and Bao talk to the boys," Charlie said.

"And is *that* really necessary?" Doug asked, pointing toward where the gun sat hidden under Charlie's jacket.

"It might be," Charlie said. "Hopefully not, but where we're going can be a pretty rough area after dark. Better safe than sorry, mate."

"You have a license for that?" Doug asked as Charlie locked their apartment door. He knew from his pre-trip briefings that it was difficult to get a firearm license in Shanghai, and it had to be renewed every three months. That was the main reason he didn't have his officer's pistol with him in China.

"I certainly do," Charlie said, turning to go down the stairs. "In our situation, Bao and I can never be too certain of our safety."

Doug didn't respond. He'd never thought of that from their perspective. He followed Charlie and Bao down the stairs and outside in silence.

The street sat in deep shadow, while the tops of the buildings glowed in the reddish light from the sun as it sank, out of sight beyond the roof lines.

He followed them as they took side streets north through the neighborhood, past the Cantonese tea house, to Haining Road. The busy street was packed with pedestrians at this hour, as the setting sun eased the temperature down a few degrees. They followed Haining Road east, past Wusong Road, skirting along the north edge of Japantown, and then came to a bridge over a wide creek.

Bao turned toward Doug as they crossed. "This bridge is where Mr. McIntyre would meet my friends in the evening to find out what they saw."

Doug looked down at Hongkou Creek, the water dark in the gathering dusk. Bright lanterns hung from the eaves of houseboats that lined both sides of the creek, rocking gently in the current. Not nearly as wide as Soochow Creek, it was still substantial for a mere "creek"— about sixty feet wide, and apparently deep enough for houseboats.

The east side of the creek did not look much different from the west side, at first—the same brick buildings with stores on the ground and apartments on the next two floors. But after a short distance the buildings came to look somehow grimier, less well-kept. The men sitting on the stoops playing Mah Jong wore tattered clothing, and were as often as not shirtless.

After a while they began passing machine shops on the corners, radiating heat out their open doors, bright light spilling onto the rapidly darkening street, and loud with clanging metal and the shouts in Shanghainese of the men working the second shift.

They must have crossed into the East District, better known as Yangpu to the Chinese, or Yangtzepoo to everyone else. It occurred to Doug that after almost two weeks in Shanghai, this was his first time venturing into Yangtzepoo.

They had gone almost a mile past the bridge when they turned right onto a narrower side street, and headed south toward the river. The street was dark, illuminated only by the lights coming from the windows of the crowded tenements above them. In the twilight he could barely make out the suspicious glares the men on the stoops gave to him and Charlie, and Doug was suddenly glad his companion was armed.

He wished he were as well.

To their east several nearby factories belched smoke from tall stacks into the deepening twilight—mostly paper and textile mills, and the air was filled with their sour smell. Beyond them, to the northeast, the electric power plant glowed in the dark, its stacks sending thick black smoke into the night.

After several blocks, the tenements around them gave way to large warehouses, and the stench of oil, dirty water, and rotting fish filled his nostrils. The hum of ship engines grew as they neared the riverfront.

Scantily-clad young women, in pairs or trios, stood on every corner here, and they struck poses as the three men passed. Some called out to them in Pidgin, "Wantchee good love-love, mister?"

Doug noticed that the prostitutes in this area were all Chinese, but as they approached the river front he could see a couple of white women strutting along the river road in short dresses, tall-heeled shoes, and bright makeup.

They turned into an alley behind the buildings that lined the river road, and the air stank of the garbage that overflowed from the trash cans that stood next to open back doors. From inside, Doug could hear the raucous shouts and laughter of drunken conversations in several languages. The conversations in English were heavy with profanity. These must be the sailors' taverns.

After about fifty yards, Doug could see groups of boys lounging in the alley, just on the edges of the circles of light from the back doors.

Charlie stopped, and turned back to face the way they had come. "I'll keep watch from here," he said under his breath.

Bao looked at Doug and nodded ahead. "You come with me, Mr. Bainbridge."

As they approached, Doug counted almost a dozen boys, whom he judged to be between the ages of about fourteen and twenty, all shirtless and most of them shoeless, wearing short trousers that were cut off at the knees.

His heart raced and he felt a nervous tingle in his belly as they stood and stepped near, staring at him. Some ran their hands over their chests, and a few bolder ones over their crotches; others, even bolder, turned around and slid their trousers down to show their backsides.

Then from up ahead, someone shouted "Li Baosheng!" A group of five boys hurried toward them, clasping Bao in hugs, chattering in a language Doug didn't understand.

Fujian, I'd bet. Bao had said most of the boys were brought here from the south, by the Tanka people who lived on the Chinese Junks that sailed along the coast of the South China Sea.

After Bao had hugged and greeted all of them in Fujian with a big grin, he half-turned toward Doug, and said to the group in Shanghainese, "My friend Mr. Bainbridge wants to talk to you about his friend Mr. McIntyre—the one who paid you to watch the house on Fao Sho Lane."

The tallest of the boys, who appeared to be about eighteen, gave Doug an appraising look. "You speak Shanghainese?"

"Some," Doug said. "I speak better Cantonese."

The boy shook his head. "No Cantonese. Pidgin?"

Doug shook his head. "No Pidgin. Speak to me in Shanghainese. He will help if I need." He nodded toward Bao.

The boy shrugged, and rattled off a rapid string of words. Doug held up his hands to stop him.

"Slowly, please."

The boy shrugged again, and repeated it more slowly. "Your friend came here about two weeks ago, said he had business for anyone who knew Fao Sho Lane. Then he got scared and ran away." He laughed. "I don't think he knew our business. He came back though, next night."

"The scared ones always come back," one of his companions said, laughing. He appeared to be about sixteen, Doug thought, lanky and long-limbed. The others laughed with him.

As if on cue, a sailor came around a corner about twenty yards ahead, looking around nervously every direction before hurrying down the alley toward them. He was short and dark, with thick black hair—middle-eastern, Doug thought. A group of three boys fanned out around him, and the man swallowed hard, but then pointed a shaky hand at one of them; the boy he indicated took his hand and led him off into the shadows between warehouses.

Doug felt the acid rising in his throat, and had to force it down. He saw Bao's friends watching him with amused expressions, and his face flushed hot.

"What did Mr. McIntyre say when he came back?" Doug asked, harsher than he'd intended.

"He paid us five dollars to watch a house on Fao Sho Lane until sundown. He said he'd give us ten dollars more if we follow the men there when they leave for the bank, and tell him where they go. 'They'll be big fellas,' he said, 'carrying bags or boxes.' He said he'd pay us five dollars every day to watch that house, and he wanted to meet every night at the Haining Road Bridge, far side, to hear what we saw."

The boy shrugged again. "We don't do much business during the day, so we said we'd do it."

"What happened?" Doug asked.

"We watched the house all day, four of us. Only junkies came and went. Then at six o'clock two big men came out the back door, carrying bags. We followed them. They went six blocks, to a house on Siping Road in Hongkou. Big house. They stayed inside a long time, then they come out the back door, no bags now. We followed them back to Fao Sho Lane. They went in the back door, and didn't come out again. Then we went to meet your friend at sundown."

"Your friend asked us to show him the house on Siping Road," the lanky boy said. "We made him pay us ten dollars more, but we showed him." He grinned, and Doug realized what a huge sum of money that must be to these boys, even split four ways.

For that matter, it was probably a lot of money to Tim, living on a reporter's income. He must have really been desperate to nail the Green Gang.

Siping Road was in Tim's notes. His pulse quickened as he connected dots. "What happened after that?"

"He offered us five dollars for two of us to watch the house on Siping Road, plus five dollars for the other two to watch the one on Fao Sho Lane," the lead boy said. "Plus ten for following the men, if they don't see us."

"Then what?" Doug asked, trying not to be impatient.

"Same thing happened," the boy said with a shrug. "Same two men took bags from Fao Sho Lane to Siping Road, about six o'clock—but then instead of going back to Fao Sho, they stayed on Haining Road and watched the bridge."

Doug felt his breath catch. "They saw you," he whispered.

The lead boy laughed. "No—but that's just what your friend said, too. We told him they didn't see us—we're certain of that—but they saw *him*. Everyone sees white men when they walk alone through a Chinese neighborhood. So, they were watching for him. Maybe they were already onto him."

The boy shrugged again. "He got killed, right? So probably they were. We knew they were Green Gang, so too dangerous to meet at the bridge. I went alone, everyone else stayed here, and I waited a block away until I saw Mr. McIntyre at the bridge. I watched him wait a while, maybe ten minutes, before he came over the bridge looking for us. When he came close I whistled to him, and had him meet me behind a corner, where the big Green Gang men wouldn't see us."

He took a step closer to Doug, and leaned in. Everyone else around leaned in close, too, as if they were about to share a conspiratorial secret. Doug felt his pulse quicken and his breath come short.

"I told him if they saw us talking to him at the bridge last night, it was not safe for us to go there. I told him we wouldn't watch the place on Fao Sho Lane anymore, either."

He leaned in even closer. "But I also told him what I saw at Siping Road," the lead boy said, quiet. "Middle of the afternoon, several men got into a big black car with big heavy bags, and it drove downtown. I hired a rickshaw to follow, but it couldn't keep up. The rickshaw coolie ran me downtown, and dropped me at Nanjing Road and the Bund."

"By the Cathay Hotel," Doug said, almost absently. His mind was racing, and he pictured the crude sketch of a Rolls Royce in Tim's file.

The boy nodded. "Then I got lucky—I saw the big black car waiting in front of the bank with the big dome."

The HSBC.

"I waited at the corner until I saw the men come out and get in the car—the same men I saw leave Siping Road."

"What did they look like?" Doug asked, breathless.

"Chinese, but dressed in fancy suits like white men," the boy said.

"Then what?"

The boy shrugged. "They drove away in their big car. I told Mr. McIntyre we wouldn't watch them anymore, not safe. He paid me the twenty dollars he owed us for that day's work, and I never saw him again."

There had been two entries in Tim's date book for "*Haining Road Bridge, 8:00*"—May 26th and 27th. Then he'd been killed on the 31st. That gave the Green Gang four days to track him down and kill him.

The boys were watching him with curious expressions, and he realized he'd been staring up in thought. "Is there anything else?"

The boys shook their heads, but continued to stare at him.

Bao said something to them in Fujian, and the lead boy answered, sounding irritated. Doug reached into his pocket and took out some quarters and handed them out. The lead boy stared at the quarter in his hand, not putting it away. Doug realized he probably owed him more, since he'd provided most of the information, and gave him another quarter. The boy shoved them into his pocket.

"You got two dollars, mister? I'll take you somewhere and suck you for two dollars."

Doug's stomach clenched, and he scowled. "No," he said, his voice cold and biting.

The boy just shrugged again, said something to Bao in Fujian, and walked away.

Doug looked at Bao, who motioned down the alley with his head. "Let's go, Mr. Bainbridge."

They had almost reached where Charlie stood, when a trio of sailors came barreling around the corner from the direction of the riverfront, and stalked down the alley, two-by-fours in their hands and menacing glares on their faces.

Boys scattered, running away at full tilt.

"Yeah, you better run, you little faggots!" one of the drunk sailors yelled after them in English with a harsh Boston accent. They began chasing, raising the two-by-fours in the air.

Doug froze in place, aware that Bao had taken refuge behind him, and was holding his shoulders. His heart seemed to have stopped, and the air caught in his throat before he remembered to breathe.

Then the alley echoed with the crack of a gunshot, and he glanced over to see Charlie with his pistol in the air, a thin trail of smoke coming from the end of the barrel.

"You blokes best get going, and leave these lads alone," he shouted to the three sailors. "I got five more bullets, which is two more than I need to send you off to meet your maker."

The three men stopped in their tracks and stared at Charlie for a moment. Charlie lowered his arm, and leveled the gun at the nearest one. "I'm not joking, mates," he said, his voice hard.

From the corner of his eye, Doug became aware of several faces—Chinese faces—peeking out from the back doors of the taverns.

The man with the gun pointed at his chest swallowed hard, then turned tail and ran from the alley, his two companions hot on his heels.

Doug could hear Charlie exhale hard, and when he turned toward Doug and Bao a few seconds later, he had broken out in a sweat.

"I told you it could be dangerous around here," he said, his voice shaking in spite of the grin he forced.

Bao came out from behind Doug, and tugged on his sleeve. "Come on, let's go."

They hurried out of the alley, and back the way they had come, silent for several moments.

"Do things like that happen often?" Doug asked when they had almost reached Haining Road.

"From time to time," Bao said.

"It's not widely known what, um, business goes on in that alley," Charlie said. "Nobody goes there what don't already know."

He paused a second, as if weighing how much to say. "Men like me, we learn after a while which taverns are friendly to us in every port, and the barkeeps there have a sort of code they use. You start to hear which alleys have the, um, male prostitutes—there's at least one in every port city, mate—but sometimes that news falls on the wrong ears."

Doug held his lips in a tight line. "Perhaps if they didn't engage in that sort of behavior where they can be seen, that wouldn't happen."

He pictured a public restroom on the edge of the National Mall in Washington. An old man holding a cane, leaning against the wall near the entrance, had cleared his throat overly loudly as Doug approached; and when Doug went inside, he saw a pair of young men in office attire—slacks, white dress shirts and neckties, but no jackets—standing at the sinks. They washed their hands the entire time he was there, and made eye contact with him in the mirror when he washed his own hands. It had made him uncomfortable, and only as he was drying his hands did he realize that both men—still holding their hands under the running water—had their flies unbuttoned.

It took him a moment to realize what he'd interrupted. He'd bolted from the restroom, scowling at the old man, and ran off to find a policeman.

Charlie stopped, and Doug turned around to look at him, but couldn't make out his expression in the darkness. "Where else are they supposed to go, mate?" he asked.

"I don't know," Doug said irritated. "To a hotel room? Someone's apartment? Anywhere but out in public."

Charlie shook his head. "You think there's less risk getting a room at some *inn* with a male companion? They wouldn't be left alone five minutes, if they even got a room in the first place. They'd get beat senseless, dead to rights, maybe even stabbed."

He paused, staring off in the distance, and slowly shook his head again. "Those alleys are as safe as it gets for those blokes, mate. There ain't no other options."

Doug felt ashamed, but didn't really understand why.

"You know that if you'd shot that man, the police would be able to identify your gun from the bullet," Doug said. "Is it worth that?"

Charlie forced a half grin. "I'd go to the British court, you know—I'd just tell the judge I'd shot a violent drunk American, and they'd drop the charges."

Doug didn't react to the attempted joke. It wasn't funny. But, there might be some truth to it.

"Won't those men just come back later?" he asked.

"My friends will tell their *Jyutping*," Bao said. "The *Jyutping* will send some big thugs to stand guard at the entrance to the alley. Bullies are bad for business."

They continued on in silence for several blocks. Charlie spoke again as they reached the Haining Road bridge.

"You know, Bao and I are lucky. Most of those blokes back there could never imagine the life we live—" he paused, as if searching for words—"having someone as a companion, someone who makes you happy. It's just not possible very many places, you see—too dangerous."

Doug didn't say anything.

After a moment Charlie continued, his words coming fast, as if he felt some urgent need to explain himself. "Bao and I—we can pass, you see. Folks assume he's my manservant, because he's young and Chinese. Usually, I just let them believe it, and that keeps us safe most of the time."

"You didn't just let me believe that," Doug said, his voice coming out sharp-edged.

Charlie gestured with his hand in circles for a moment, seeming to search for words again. "Sometimes I just can't help meself," he said. "It's not right, you know—letting folks think of Bao that way. He ain't nobody's servant. And you—well—I guess I thought, since you was clearly an educated man, that you wouldn't find it so shocking. I've been to New York, mate—I know educated Americans have all read up on that Sigmund Freud, and how he says problems come from repressing sexual urges. So I thought, with you being an educated man, you'd understand why we don't repress ours."

Doug took a moment to contemplate Charlie's words. He felt a small pang of guilt that Charlie spoke highly of him, and that he'd placed some trust—*mis*placed some trust—in him because of that.

He pushed that thought from his mind. He hadn't asked for such trust, had never wanted it. And while Charlie Ford's comprehension of Freudian psychology was clearly pedestrian, Doug had to admit that he'd made a salient point about repression. Doug had just never applied such thinking to the more deviant expressions of sexuality.

He felt a headache coming on.

He realized with growing irritation that he hadn't learned all that much from their outing this evening—a few items in Tim's notes made more sense now, with context—but he didn't feel any closer to identifying who had killed Tim.

Perhaps this whole endeavor was a colossal waste of time.

"Are you alright, Douglas?" Charlie asked.

Doug nodded, his mouth set in a grim line. "I just have a headache."

"I make you some tea when we get home," Bao said.

Doug shook his head. "I have tea, I'll make my own pot, thank you."

They walked the last several blocks in silence. As they rounded the corner onto Huang Lei Road, Doug almost ran right into Constable Billy Dickinson.

"Ho, there! Terribly sorry, Mr. Bainbridge, sir," Billy said, touching the rim of his police hat and nodding. "Good evening, Mr. Ford, sir. Good evening Bao."

"Good evening, Constable," Charlie said, jovial.

Doug felt his cheeks flush, embarrassed that their neighborhood policeman had seen him in the company of Charlie and Bao—who were possibly known for what they were. Doug feared being associated with them.

It took him a second to realize that Billy had called Bao by his given name, and not "Mr. Li." Was that a subtle racist reaction? Or based on the assumption that Bao was Charlie's servant?

He hoped the latter.

"I'm surprised to see you tonight, Billy," Doug said. "I thought Tuesday was your night off."

"Usually is," Billy said. "Nice of you to remember, Mr. Bainbridge, sir. I switched nights with me pal Anush Patel, what usually walks this route on Monday and Tuesday nights. He's walking the route tomorrow night instead. Best get back to it now, good night, sirs." He touched the rim of his police cap and resumed his patrol.

When they reached the front of their building a moment later, Doug saw a shadowy figure lurking at the corner of the street. He held the door open for his companions while he stared. One of the communists, keeping tabs on him.

He wondered if they'd watched him all evening with Charlie and Bao. The thought of them watching him at that alley behind the sailors' bars, knowing what business went on there—he wondered why that bothered him more than the fact that they always seemed to be watching. Perhaps it shouldn't—but it did.

Then he wondered if he had put his neighbors in danger this evening, as he followed them up the stairs.

"Thank you for your help," he said as he turned toward his apartment.

"Glad to be of help, Douglas," Charlie said.

20

Doug could tell something was wrong even before he turned on a lamp. There was enough light from the street coming through the front window for him to just make out that the furniture was askew.

When he turned on the lamp, it was obvious—someone had ransacked his apartment.

The kitchen window was still locked, and unbroken. The thief must have picked the lock.

For once, he was glad that he didn't have many belongings. It only took fifteen minutes to clean up the mess. He was most irritated that his clothes were strewn all over the bedroom floor, wrinkled and dusty.

As he was putting clothes back in his dresser it hit him—Tim's 1935 date book was missing.

"Damn!" he shouted, and frantically looked for all of his notes.

Gone. All of them.

Kawakami. It had to be him. He'd said he'd be back soon, and It had been three days. And now he had Doug's notes from Tim's Korea file.

He thought of the names in those notes, and had to fight back the panic that slowly rose up from his belly. Tim had not used full names, he reminded himself. There wasn't enough information in his file to positively identify anyone. And Doug had only taken notes, not the file itself.

He took deep breaths. His carelessness hadn't cost anyone's life, he told himself.

But would he remember enough of what he'd learned to continue his quest to identify Tim's killer? Possibly. Even as he wondered, though, he knew he'd never remember everything.

"Damn it!" he said again, banging a fist against the top of his dresser.

He went downstairs, and knocked on Mr. Hwang's door.

The landlord answered the door personally. He looked at Doug with a strange expression for half a second before giving him a polite bow.

"Good evening, Mr. Bainbridge," he said in Shanghainese. "How may I help you?"

"Good evening, Mr. Hwang," Doug said, returning the landlord's bow. "Did you see anyone in the building this evening who does not live here?"

"Why do you ask?" Hwang said, evasive. There was touch of wariness in his eyes that didn't escape Doug's notice.

"My apartment was robbed sometime after eight o'clock."

"I am sorry to hear that, Mr. Bainbridge. Did they take anything valuable?"

The landlord's tone was stiff and formal, his face expressionless—which Doug found strange.

"Nothing of great monetary value. But they made a mess looking."

Hwang inclined his head in a stiff bow. "The spirits of your ancestors were protecting you," he said. "You should give them thanks and make an offering to them."

Doug had noticed that the landlord never asked if the thief broke the window or the door—legitimate concerns for the owner of the building.

He had also never said that he had not seen anyone. Nor had he offered to call the police.

Doug felt a cold sweat break across the back of his neck, in spite of the stuffy heat. His instincts told him to say nothing about his concerns.

He forced a smile and bowed deeply to Mr. Hwang. "I will do as you suggest, thank you." He turned and went back upstairs.

As he reached the third floor landing, he glanced at Charlie and Bao's door. They would have noticed someone strange going to his door, had they been home. They would have stopped the break-in.

He didn't expect the sense of guilt that came over him.

Or how reluctant he was to admit that he'd been wrong.

It took him a long time to fall asleep. It was hot and stuffy, even with the fan blowing, but no more so than any other night. Unable to sleep, though, his mind fixated on it, and that kept him awake for hours after he lay down on top of the covers.

When he finally drifted off, he slept fitfully, tossing and turning, in and out of semi-consciousness. He was vaguely aware of dreaming, as surreal images came and went in his mind's eye, but he felt detached from it, as if he were watching a moving picture show, but not paying much attention to it.

At one point, he saw Tim standing in front of him. They were in the central hall of the Public Library in San Francisco, and Tim was holding something out to him. It wasn't a book, but Doug couldn't make out what it was exactly. The image was fuzzy, and as he squinted he could barely make out an irregular shape. Tim said something, but his voice was muted and echoed, as if he were talking through a lead pipe.

He held the object out toward Doug, and Doug squinted at it harder, trying without success to determine what it was.

I'll be able to see it when I'm holding it in my own hands, he thought, and reached for it. As he extended his arm, though, the floor between them seemed to stretch as if it were rubber, and his fingertips barely brushed against Tim's. He stretched his arm farther, but the distance continued to grow, and his fingers wiggled in the air an inch from Tim's hand. He stretched his arm so far he was conscious that his shoulder hurt, but Tim's hand—and the object it held—remained just out of reach.

He heard a noise behind him, as if a bookshelf had fallen against another, and all the books had spilled onto the floor. He turned around, and saw the shimmering green face of a dragon emerging from behind the toppled bookshelf. It slithered out, snake-like, from the burrow formed by the one shelf leaning against the neighboring one. Its jaws were open, revealing long, sharp teeth that glinted in the spotlight from the library ceiling.

Several people stood around it, their noses in books, oblivious. Doug shouted at them, "Look out! It's behind you!"—but none of them moved. The dragon writhed in place, its big round eyes surveying everything.

"It's a dragon!" Doug shouted, louder, but still everyone seemed not to notice.

Then one man turned around, a tall, stocky fellow, and Doug recognized Jonesy. He scowled at the dragon as if it were a moment's irritation. He set his book back on the shelf, and slammed his fist into the dragon's nose.

The dragon's head fell to the floor. It lay there for several seconds, still, and then slowly vanished.

Jonesy looked at Doug, and shook his head. "You couldn't take care of it?" he asked, and turned back to the bookshelf.

Doug's mouth opened, but he couldn't form any words.

Then it began to rain, and Doug's first thought was that he didn't know where his hat was. As his suit got wet, he thought how strange it was that it would rain inside the library. He looked up toward the ceiling, and saw rain drops coming through stained glass as if it were a mosquito net.

Then he was standing in the middle of a park—the Broadway Gardens in Shanghai, he realized—and the rain fell slow and steady, almost soothing. He was conscious that he no longer felt the cling of wet linen, and looked down almost absently to see that he was naked. He looked around, momentarily panicked to be naked in the park, but he saw no one. He looked toward the river, but it too was empty.

A sense of calm slowly returned, and he held his arms out to the sides and felt the rain on his skin.

His eyes drifted open, and he saw the curtains dancing inward on a gentle breeze coming through the window. A gray light filled the room, and over the whirring of the fan he could hear the soft patter of rain drops.

The rain continued all morning, and Doug stayed in. He sat at his kitchen table, drinking a pot of tea, and trying to think of any option that didn't involve asking Jonesy for help.

Around eleven o'clock he went downstairs to Mr Hwang's shop. Wong Mei-Ling stood behind the counter, organizing sales slips. She looked up as the door opened, but her expression turned hard when she saw Doug.

He bowed and greeted her in Shanghainese.

She returned neither.

"I'm sorry you became involved on Monday," he said.

She didn't respond, just kept staring at him with a blank expression, but cold eyes.

"I regret any difficulty I have caused you," he continued, hoping she would see his sincerity and offer him some sliver of forgiveness. He glanced around, and lowered his voice. "I know you were put in a difficult position because of me—dangerous even—and I apologize for that. I never meant to cause any trouble for you, and if there is anything I can do to make it better, I would—"

"You've done enough," she said, her voice quiet but her tone sharp.

He bowed again, resigned. "I apologize again. I wonder if I might use Mr. Hwang's telephone?"

She stared at him in silence for several seconds before nodding her head toward the back of the shop. "He is in the office, ask him yourself."

After a brief reflection on last night's interaction, Doug decided that wasn't a good idea. He bowed again and said, "Thank you, but I'll find another telephone. Good day." He touched the rim of his hat as he turned away.

He'd bought an umbrella his first day in Shanghai, so after going upstairs to his apartment to retrieve it, he walked in the rain the few blocks to Tim's building, and knocked on Chen Gwan's door.

"Good morning, Mr. Chen," he said with a bow when Tim's landlord answered his knock. "I need to speak with Mr. Jones, about a matter concerning Mr. McIntyre. I wonder if I might use your telephone to call him?"

"Yes, you may call Jonesy," Chen said, and led Doug to the telephone.

Doug gave the operator Jonesy's name and address in Shanghainese. After the line rang ten times, the operator said in Pidgin, "He no answer."

Doug stifled a sigh, asked in Shanghainese if he could call another number, and asked her to put him through to the Associated Press office downtown.

Gladys answered on the second ring.

"Hello, Miss Sherman, this is Douglas Bainbridge—we met at Tim's funeral, and I went to dinner with you and Jonesy on Saturday night."

"Yes, how are you, Mr. Bainbridge?"

"I am well, thank you. Listen, I need to speak with Jonesy, is he available?"

"No, but he usually checks in later in the morning. Shall I give him a message?"

Doug hesitated, not sure what to do. He couldn't be reached by return call, unless he stayed here at Mr. Chen's apartment, and he didn't have any excuse to do that.

"Mr. Bainbridge?"

"Yes, I'm still on the line. Listen, I wonder if you know if he's free to meet me somewhere today. It's important."

"Well, I don't know his schedule, but he usually lunches at the Cathay during the week. You can usually find him eating at the bar around noon."

"Thank you, very much. If he checks in before noon, would you please tell him I'll meet him there?"

"I certainly will. Good day, Mr. Bainbridge."

Doug hung up the receiver, and as he turned around, Mr. Chen stood a short distance away, watching him with a tentative smile. "Is Jonesy coming here?" he asked in Shanghainese.

Doug shook his head. Chen hadn't understood a word of his conversation with Gladys, since it had been in English.

"No, he's busy this morning. I'm going to meet with him later." Doug fished a nickel from his pocket and held it out to Mr. Chen. "For the telephone call."

Chen put up both hands and shook his head. "No charge to call Jonesy."

Doug put the coin back in his pocket and bowed.

A thought occurred to him as he was leaving, and he turned in the doorway. "Mr. Chen, I wonder if you've seen any strangers in the building over the last two days? Anyone trying to get into Tim's apartment?"

Mr. Chen shook his head. "No, my son and I have been watching. There has been no one."

Doug bowed his head and thanked him.

I guess Kawakami only looked for Tim's files at my place, he thought as he left the building, and started walking downtown.

He reached the Cathay shortly before noon, and walked straight to the bar.

"Can I mix you a drink, sir?" the Chinese bartender asked in perfect English.

Doug shook his head. "Tea and a lunch menu," he said in Shanghainese. "A friend will be joining me in a few minutes."

The bartender bowed and backed away, then disappeared behind a door. While he waited, Doug reflected on how strange—and uncomfortable—it had felt to refer to Jonesy as his 'friend.' He hadn't meant it, of course—it had been just a facile moniker, easier than trying to explain the much more complicated truth.

The bartender returned a few minutes later with a pot of tea and a cup, and handed Doug a menu—in English.

Doug had just decided to order the shrimp with basil and spring vegetables when Jonesy appeared and took the barstool next to him.

"Fancy running into you here," Jonesy said, with a slight smirk. "We've got to stop meeting like this, or people will talk."

Doug scowled, but then reminded himself that Jonesy was deliberately toying with him. "I'm actually here specifically to meet with you."

"I know. Gladys told me." Jonesy raised his hand, and the bartender came over with a smile.

"Good to see you, Mr. Jonesy," the bartender said. "Martini?"

"Yes Lo, two olives, please. And the usual for lunch." He turned on his stool to face Doug. "So did you learn something?"

Yes and no, Doug thought. "Kawakami came back—last night, while I was out. He took all of my notes, plus Tim's date book for this year. Made a mess of my apartment."

Jonesy nodded, slowly. "So…now you need my help, is that it?"

Doug paused to take a breath. "Yes, I suppose I do. I think I can remember most of what was in my notes, but I'm sure I won't remember everything."

"So the rich boy wants to copy the smart fella's homework, huh? Again?"

Doug pushed aside his irritation, and forced a smile. "I just thought we could collaborate. Two heads are better than one, after all." He hoped he didn't sound over-eager.

Jonesy snorted. "OK, I'm game—for Tim's sake, not yours. For starters, tell me what you've learned since Monday."

"Not much, really—just a little bit." Doug recounted what had transpired since Monday afternoon, not going into great detail. He omitted his encounter with the communists, and his tea with Ming Lin-wen.

Jonesy looked amused when Doug described his trip to the alley behind the sailors' taverns with Charlie and Bao, even though Doug didn't say a word about the profession of the boys there.

"You *do* know what kind of business is conducted in that alley, don't you?" Jonesy asked with a sly grin and one raised eyebrow.

Doug nodded in silence. *And apparently, so do you.*

Jonesy chuckled and shook his head. "You're braver than I gave you credit for. Go on."

After Doug finished telling what he had learned there about Tim's investigation into the Green Gang, Jonesy leaned back, looked at the ceiling and stroked his chin.

"You're right—that's not all that much more than we had before. And those boys were smart to back off once they learned it was the Green Gang they were watching. I gave you pretty much that same warning, remember?"

"I remember," Doug said, trying not to sound as irritated as he felt. He hated smug 'I told you so's.'

Jonesy sighed. "Well, I guess I didn't give you enough credit. Ignoring my advice is something Tim would have done—and I'll have you know, that's pretty damn high praise in my book." He took a swig of his martini.

"I think it's a moot point now, anyway," Doug said. "I'm not sure what my next move should be. Nobody's going to talk if everyone's so afraid of these fellows."

A funny sort of half-grin spread across Jonesy's mouth. "Now let me tell you what *I've* learned since Monday."

Doug's eyebrows shot up in surprise, and Jonesy chuckled. "Unlike you, I know how to be careful with my inquiries. It helps to have friends in high places."

He took another sip from his martini, pulled his notebook from inside his jacket, and flipped it open. "That lady at the Jade Dragon who was with those *Juntong* men—you said her name was Ming Lin-wen, and that her father was some sort of government man. I made a call to a friend of mine at the American Embassy in Nanking, asked him to do a little digging for me. Sure enough, he struck gold.

"She's old imperial aristocracy—yep, *that* Ming family, as in 'Ming Dynasty.' Descended from some fourteenth century emperors, and cousin to some later ones. The family was high up at court in Peking during the final years of the Manchu Dynasty—but that's when things get *really* interesting. Her father knew Dr. Sun Yet-sen from his university days, and defected to him when the revolution came in 1911. Denounced his own father as a counter-revolutionary, and watched when he was beheaded in 1912. Cold bastard."

Doug couldn't hide his incredulity. Jonesy seemed not to notice as he looked down at his notebook and read aloud.

"Ming Lin-wen was born October 29th, 1911 in Peking, daughter of Ming Xiwen and his wife Yang Luo. The family moved to Nanking in 1912 when the capital was moved, and she grew up there. Educated at various top-notch academies—then in January '31 her father married her off to Wu Shan, a nephew of warlord Wu Peifu. It was a political move—the Wu controlled the entire region surrounding Shanghai.

"Wu Shan was fifteen years her senior. His first wife had died a few months before, and she became step-mother to his son and daughter. Apparently she balked at first, and in order to avoid shaming the family, her father bought her a mansion over on Broadway—not far from here, actually."

Doug felt his face flush hot, and he swallowed hard, trying to look nonchalant.

"A little bribery goes a long way, I guess—she married him," Jonesy said with a wry grin, and then continued reading. "One son born December '31—" his voice trailed off, and he looked up at Doug with a bigger grin. "After that, it gets darker."

He flipped his notebook closed and put it back in his jacket pocket. Taking another drink from his martini, he motioned Doug to lean closer.

Doug hesitated, uncomfortable, but then scooted his stool closer to Jonesy's and leaned toward him.

"Wu Shan is a captain in the *Juntong*," Jonesy said, keeping his voice low. "Safe bet he's the one you saw at the Jade Dragon. A real nasty character, responsible for the torture and murder of countless 'enemies of the state,' whatever that means. Sometime in 1932, during a street battle with some local communists he was trying to destroy, he was captured and interrogated for almost twenty-four hours, no sleep, fair amount of physical torture. In the end, his fellows busted in and killed all the insurgents and rescued him—but not before the reds inflicted some rather embarrassing injuries on his family jewels."

He leaned back, and seemed to enjoy the look on Doug's face.

293

Doug realized his mouth was hanging open, and consciously closed it and looked away, draining his teacup and pouring himself another cup.

"How would a consular employee at the embassy know *that*?" he asked, skeptical.

"The government gossips in Nanking detest the regional warlords—beyond the political sensitivities, they think them crass and uncouth—so according to my friend, it's not hard to get someone to spill about the extent of Wu Shan's, um, injuries. Fathering children isn't the only thing he's not able to do anymore. And according to the more vicious gossips, Ming Lin-wen has taken that lying down, so to speak. They say she gets around like a carrousel horse."

Doug's face burned hot, and his forehead beaded with sweat despite the air-conditioning inside the Cathay.

Jonesy chuckled. "That embarrasses you? I didn't take you for a prude."

Doug scowled, and sipped his tea. "I'm not fond of gossip, that's all. It's base."

Jonesy raised one eyebrow and regarded him curiously for a few seconds. "In your line of work, you'd best get used to it. Some of the best intelligence starts off as gossip."

"This isn't a cloak-and-dagger dime novel," Doug said.

"Then I guess you don't want to hear the rest," Jonesy said with a shrug, turned back to face the bar, and began eating his dumplings.

Doug waited as long as he could, taking a couple bites of his shrimp, but finally sighed and asked, "Is it relevant to Tim's death?"

Jonesy shrugged. "Maybe."

"Then perhaps I should help you decide if it is."

Jonesy laughed, almost spitting out a bite of dumpling. "If you say so, partner." He wiped his mouth, still chuckling. "One of Ming Lin-wen's older brothers, Ming Zhonghu, was one of the first graduates of the Whampoa Military Academy. He's a colonel now in the Nationalist

Army, and a prominent member of what's called the 'Whampoa clique' in the Nationalist Party—a bunch of right-wing kooks who are fanatical supporters of Chiang Kai-shek. Think Generalisimo Franco and the Spanish Nationalists, only Chinese."

He glanced around before leaning close and whispering, "He's also widely rumored to be a member of the Blue Shirts Society—a secret fascist organization within the Nationalist Party, and a sort of unofficial military secret police, far more fanatical and secretive than the *Juntong*. He took part in the 1927 purges that decimated the communists, and is said to have personally strangled more than a dozen men."

Doug frowned. "I don't see any relevance to Tim's death."

"I'm getting to that part," Jonesy said, letting his irritation show. "He's said to be in frequent communication with his brother-in-law, Wu Shan. He comes to Shanghai often, and always meets with Wu Shan, but doesn't always see his sister. On at least two occasions, Colonel Ming Zhonghu has dined at the residence of one Du Yuesheng."

Jonesy delivered that last line in dramatic fashion, elongating the words while still staying quiet, and after dropping that bomb he leaned back and folded his arms across his chest, a satisfied smile creeping across his lips.

Doug felt a chill run up his spine. He became conscious that his breath was coming shallow and fast, and he took a deep breath to calm himself.

He glanced around to be sure no one was nearby. "But there's no reason to believe this Colonel Ming Zhonghu knew anything about Tim," he said, keeping his voice low.

Jonesy shrugged. "Word of Tim's inquiries could have gotten up to Du Yuesheng himself, and Du could have asked his friend Colonel Ming to do something about it. The colonel would have probably assigned the task to his brother-in-law and the local *Juntong*."

Doug shook his head. "It's overkill. Du wouldn't need to go that high up, not for a local reporter who was getting nosy. He could easily have his own men take care of it for him, or any of his minions on the Shanghai Police—"

Doug stopped, a cold dread sinking into his belly.

Jonesy's green eyes narrowed, and he stared hard at Doug. "What? You're thinking something. What do you know that you're not telling me?"

Doug looked away, his mind racing. It couldn't be Geoffries—he just didn't seem like a cold-blooded killer. *No*, he told himself, *it wasn't Geoffries*.

So why did he suddenly feel so apprehensive about the party tonight?

He looked back at Jonesy, and was startled to see genuine concern on his face. "Are you alright, pal? You look like you've seen a ghost."

Doug straightened. "What are you doing tonight? Want to go with me to a party?"

21

Doug chose to wear his good summer suit that evening, and as it grew dark the temperature dropped just enough that he didn't regret not staying in his linen suit. He hired a rickshaw on Honan Road to avoid getting too sweaty on a crowded streetcar, or by walking, and fanned himself with his hat as he rode downtown.

The runner dropped him off in front of the Cathay Hotel just after the bells of the Anglican Church a few blocks away chimed nine o'clock, and he waited there for Jonesy.

Almost as soon as he'd taken a place near the door to wait, he saw Dai Chi get out of a rickshaw a half-block away, and they locked eyes. The young communist leaned against the wall about twenty feet away, and lit a cigarette, pretending to watch the crowds go by.

It was almost ten minutes before Jonesy arrived, hopping off the streetcar at the corner of the Bund.

"You're late," Doug said.

Jonesy waved a dismissive hand in the air. "Parties in Shanghai don't really get going for at least a half-hour after they start, if not an hour."

"It's not that kind of party," Doug said. "It's just a small gathering."

The Sassoon House—technically a residential annex of the Cathay Hotel—had its own entrance and elevator, and an Indian doorman held the door for them and bowed. "Good evening, sirs. How may I assist you?"

The brisk air conditioning almost gave Doug a chill as they stepped inside. "We're guests of Mr. Geoffries."

"Welcome. Take the elevator to the seventh floor, number 710."

The Chinese elevator man took them to the seventh floor. "Number 710 is half-way down the hall, on the left."

Geoffries himself answered their knock, dressed in a navy blue silk suit, a half-full high-ball glass in his hand. A look of surprise crossed his eyes for a second, but vanished almost right away.

"Mr. Bainbridge, how good of you to come," he said, shaking Doug's hand. "And I see you brought a guest. How are you, Mr. Jones? It's been a while."

It was Doug's turn to give them a surprised look. "You know each other?"

"We're acquainted," Jonesy said, his expression unreadable.

"Do come in," Geoffries said. "Can I offer you a cocktail?"

"I'll have a martini," Jonesy said.

Geoffries smile was fixed. "Of course, how could I forget? And Mr. Bainbridge, a Black Thorn?"

"No, gin and tonic, please," Doug said, glancing at Jonesy out of the side of his eye.

"Coming right up. Do make yourselves at home. Mingle and enjoy yourselves."

As Geoffries walked toward the small bar in the corner, Doug looked at Jonesy, who was looking around.

"Swell place, huh?" Jonesy said.

Doug had hardly noticed. It was a sizeable suite, and about a dozen people clustered in small groups around the couches, drinks in hand, engaging in animated conversations.

"How do you know Mr. Geoffries?" Doug asked.

"Oh, Captain Geoffries?" Jonesy said with a hint of a smile. "We've known each other a while. He arrested me once, about five years ago, not long after I got to Shanghai. He wasn't a captain yet, though. He was a detective inspector—and technically his men arrested me, but back at the station he offered to let me go for a 'donation,' no charges filed."

Doug decided he didn't want to know what Jonesy had been arrested for, so he just said, "I didn't know you had a criminal record."

"Oh, sure," Jonesy said with a big grin. "I spent some time in prison during the Great War. Draft evasion and sedition—meaning I had the gall to exercise my first amendment rights and criticize the war. Then I got arrested a couple of times for, um, personal things."

Doug looked away, and pretended to watch Geoffries finishing their drinks.

"That's what brought me to the captain's acquaintance," Jonesy said, apparently unashamed. "I was with this fellow in his room at the Palace Hotel, just across the street, and the folks in the next room called the cops on us. We weren't hurting anybody, but that's how it goes. Geoffries offered me a deal—I make a small 'donation' every month, and I don't have to worry about getting arrested. I took him up on it. It's made things a lot easier."

Jonesy took another look around as Geoffries turned away from the bar with their drinks. "Never been here, though. Nice to see what my money helps pay for."

"Here you are, gentlemen," Geoffries said, handing them their cocktails. "Allow me to introduce you around the room."

As soon as Geoffries finished the introductions, there was a knock at the door, and he departed to greet more guests.

"Told you," Jonesy said, nodding toward the four people who came in.

Doug ignored that. "You could have mentioned you already knew the host when I invited you. Especially since I shared my apprehensions."

Jonesy gave him an enigmatic smile, took a sip of his martini, and walked away to mingle.

Doug was engaged in small talk with a Canadian couple a while later, when he saw Ming Lin-wen enter on the arm of the large man who had escorted her at the Jade Dragon on Friday. Her husband. Wu Shan.

There were probably twenty-five or thirty people here now, and yet her eyes found his within seconds of walking through the door. Her gaze lingered for several seconds, and he saw a faint smile raise the corners of her mouth, before she looked back at their host and gave him a charming smile.

A few minutes later, screams from outside, accompanied by a screech of metallic brakes, stopped all conversation, and everyone rushed to the windows. As they opened windows, people stuck their heads out and looked down at Nanking Road.

Doug squeezed his way through the crowd, and looked down. A large collection of people stood in the middle of the road, around a stopped streetcar, looking at the body of a young man lying in a pool of blood on the street. Cars, bicycles and rickshaws stood idle on either side of the crowd.

Doug looked hard at the body's face. Nanking Road was well-lit, and even from the seventh floor Doug recognized the face of Dai Chi.

Police constables arrived from both nearby intersections, blowing whistles and shoving their way through the crowd.

"Everyone, the police have things under control," Geoffries said from behind them. "Don't let's be morbid about it. Come, have another cocktail, relax, try to enjoy the evening."

Most of the guests stepped away from the windows, shutting two of the three. But Doug stayed at his window, leaning out and watching the activity on the street.

"He ran right into me!" the streetcar driver shouted in Shanghainese at the police constables, almost hysterical. "There was no time. I couldn't stop. It was almost like he did it on purpose."

Doug jumped when a hand clasped his shoulder, and his breath caught.

"Coming, Mr. Bainbridge?" Geoffries said with a smile that definitely did not extend to his eyes.

Doug tried to return the smile, but only managed a weak one. "Yes, of course. I apologize."

Geoffries' hand released his shoulder, and then patted it in a show of joviality. "Come, let me refresh your gin and tonic."

As he pulled down the window, Doug heard a woman telling a police constable in Shanghainese, "There were two men who were trying to rob him, just over there. They're gone now, I don't see them anywhere."

As the window closed, Doug marveled at how well sound travelled up from the street. Must have something to do with the acoustics of the tall buildings, he concluded.

When he turned around, he noticed the large *Juntong* man— Wu Shan—standing off to the side, not participating in any conversation.

And staring at Doug.

He had not come running to the windows like everyone else. He had not acted surprised or disturbed in the least.

Doug felt a chill run up his spine, and he shivered in spite of himself. Wu Shan's men had tried to arrest Dai Chi, he surmised; and rather than be taken and tortured, the young man committed suicide by running into the path of a streetcar.

Doug began to feel a little queasy.

The crowded room was suffocating, and he squeezed through to the hall, finding the bathroom and closing himself inside.

It was a spacious bathroom, with double sinks under a lit vanity, and across from the sinks and the commode was a bathtub large enough for three people. Doug turned on the cold water at one of the sinks, and splashed it on his face.

The door opened, and Wu Shan marched in, closing the door behind him.

"Excuse me," Doug said, trying to sound offended. "I was just about to use the facilities."

"You kill Tim McIntyre?" the big *Juntong* officer asked in English, his narrow eyes seeming to bore into Doug.

"No!" Doug replied, and then switched to Mandarin. "I've been trying to find out who killed him."

The large man grunted, and said in Mandarin, "Why should I believe you?"

This took Doug aback. "Why would I have killed Tim? I had no motive."

Wu Shan stared at him, and Doug could easily imagine a political prisoner squirming under that intense gaze. He stared back.

"You are not an innocent man," Wu said after a while. "The communists watch you. The Japanese have Korean spies watching you. You tell people you are in Shanghai for business, but you do not work. I do not have any reason to believe you."

Doug wondered how much Wu Shan knew about him, and a sense of dread sank into the pit of his stomach. Did they know about his connection to ONI? Or, of more immediate concern, did Wu know what happened Tuesday afternoon?

"I have been trying to find out who did kill Tim," he explained. "But I don't know who did." He decided to say no more.

Wu Shan continued to stare at him for a moment. "You are a suspicious person, Bainbridge Douglas." He reached into his jacket and removed Tim's 1935 date book.

It took Doug a second to grasp the implication.

"It was you," he said. "You ransacked my apartment yesterday. I blamed Kawakami, but it was you."

No wonder Mr. Hwang had been so strange about the break-in. He supposed he would be the same way if the secret police came to his building and demanded entry to a tenant's apartment.

"Why did you take these from Mr. McIntyre's apartment?" Wu Shan asked, suspicious. "Why did you keep secret that you had these? Why did you not go to the police?"

Because I don't trust the police, Doug thought, but he just shrugged. "I thought I could figure it out myself. The police weren't investigating."

Then a new thought crossed Doug's mind—why hadn't Wu given the date book and files to the police himself, if he'd had them for more than twenty-four hours? Why question Doug about his reason for keeping them to himself, when Wu was doing the same now?

And why would Wu even be concerned with the murder of an American civilian in the International Settlement?

"You're trying to frame me."

22

Wu's expression gave nothing away.

"You know who killed Tim," Doug said. "But you want to pin it on me."

Still, Wu said nothing.

"But if your men killed Tim, why blame it on me?" Doug asked. "Surely there are better people to frame for murder. Why not the communists? And what does it matter, now that your men are dead?"

"My men did not kill Mr. McIntyre."

"But they were seen arguing with Tim outside of the Jade Dragon, and he left with them right before he was killed."

"My men did not kill him."

Realization dawned on Doug. They hadn't killed Tim themselves—but they had taken him to his killer.

Kawakami? No, that didn't make sense. He was their enemy, and he killed both of them the next night.

Then whom? Tim didn't seem to have enough information to be a real threat to any crooked cops. So that left the Green Gang, but their hierarchy and workings were still unclear—and again, there wasn't enough information in Tim's file to expose that group.

Then a piece of the puzzle seemed to fall from the sky. *Geoffries*.

Doug realized with a start that their host had offered him a Black Thorn when they arrived—that was Tim's drink.

His mind raced. Wu and Geoffries were connected enough to socialize on a Wednesday night. Geoffries was obviously crooked, and his name did appear in Tim's notes. It wasn't such a stretch to imagine Wu's men bringing Tim to him that night.

Or eliminate Doug's threat tonight.

"Are you taking me now?"

The shake of Wu's head was so slight, it was barely noticeable. He opened the door and stepped out.

Doug searched the room for Jonesy. They had to get out of here.

It had gotten crowded. Will Geoffries was working the room, an attractive Chinese girl on his arm who couldn't have been more than eighteen, and he approached Doug.

"Having a good time, Mr. Bainbridge?"

"Yes, thank you," Doug said, forcing a smile.

"I have to tell you, I was more than a little surprised to see you arrive with Mr. Jones earlier," Geoffries said. "I hadn't taken you for that type."

"What? Oh! No, I'm not," Doug said. "Mr. Jones and I have a mutual friend—*had* a mutual friend, that is."

"Oh, I see. I apologize for making assumptions."

"It's fine, don't worry. But I'm definitely not one of Mr. Jones's, um, friends."

Geoffries looked amused. "Well, then perhaps you would be interested in spending time with one of Madam Tsang's girls? Madam Tsang runs a very high-end establishment, offering the best female companionship to men of means, such as you and I. Shung Lai here is a perfect example."

Doug was startled, having not expected that kind of offer. "Oh, thank you, but no. I—I don't think so."

Geoffries shrugged. He spun Shung Lai around to face him, leaned down to kiss her on the lips, and moved his hand down to squeeze her buttocks.

Doug looked away, embarrassed. The way they were positioned at the entrance to the hall, he was the only one who could see.

Geoffries let go of Shung Lai, whispered something in her ear, and she walked away.

"Perhaps you might be interested at some point. You are, after all, a man of means, are you not? You are well-dressed, well-spoken, well-mannered—and you haven't worked a day since you've been in Shanghai."

He stared Doug directly in the eye.

Doug felt the hair rise on the back of his neck. Wu had said the same thing only a few moments before.

"I also know you're all alone in Shanghai," Geoffries said. "And while Miss Ming might invite you back for a repeat engagement at some point, I would not count on it being often. She has many options, you see."

Doug felt his heart drop into the pit of his stomach.

"What do you want from me?"

"I want you to tell me everything you know."

"About what?"

A cruel smile crept across Geoffries' mouth. "Don't let's play games, Mr. Bainbridge. You know what I want to know. Come with me, we'll go where we won't be disturbed."

"I know you couldn't afford all this on a police captain's salary," Doug said as Geoffries took his shoulder and guided him down the hall.

"Family money," Geoffries said.

Doug shook his head. "No wealthy English family would leave money to a son who went into police work. English society is too hierarchical for that."

"I supposed Mr. Jones told you about our little arrangement," Geoffries said, opening a door and ushering Doug into a large bedroom.

"It would take an awful lot of those 'arrangements' to pay for all this," Doug said, motioning around the stylishly decorated room.

Geoffries' smile was cold, fixed. "Are you making spurious accusations, Mr. Bainbridge? Or do you have some knowledge you'd care to disclose to me?"

"I know there are a lot of gangsters in this city—but the members of the biggest organized crime syndicate in China seem to rarely get arrested, and never charged. At your precinct alone, several have been released without charge."

"It is not always easy to build a case against organized crime, Mr. Bainbridge."

"You and I both know that's not true for the smaller organizations," Doug said, defiant. "But for the Green Gang, there seems to be a free pass. Only, we both know that pass isn't free."

Geoffries expression turned to ice. "The commissioner is an idealistic bastard, always prattling on about weeding out corruption in the SMP. I thought at first your friend Mr. McIntyre was from his staff. I offered him to name his price. When he wouldn't, I had my men look into him. Once I found out who he was—a meddling reporter—I knew I had little time. If he wouldn't be bribed into silence, he would have to be silenced another way."

"So you killed him," Doug said, less forcefully than he'd intended. He felt more sadness than anger. He had wanted it to be Kawakami all along. And Geoffries had been friendly to him.

Geoffries just chuckled. "So now I'm going to ask you the same question I asked Mr. McIntyre the day before he died—what is your price, Mr. Bainbridge?"

A door flew open to Doug's right, and Jonesy burst from a closet with a pistol aimed at Will Geoffries.

"As soon as I read in Tim's file that he met with you last Thursday, I knew you were the one," Jonesy said, his voice dripping with venom. "You had too much to lose. I just needed to hear it from your mouth."

Doug stared at Jonesy with open mouth. "You never said anything about Tim meeting Captain Geoffries."

"Not now!" Jonesy said, not looking away from Geoffries.

"Are you going to shoot me, Mr. Jones?" Geoffries asked, amused. "You'll never make it past the elevator. There is a room full of witnesses out there who will identify you for the police."

"I don't care," Jonesy said. He cocked his pistol.

Geoffries' hand flew to his side and emerged with his own gun, just as Jonesy fired. Geoffries' own gun fired a split-second later, but then a spray of red emerged from the back of his suit, and he crumpled to the ground.

Jonesy dropped his gun, clutched his left shoulder, and dropped to his knees.

Doug saw blood soaking through Jonesy's jacket.

"Make sure the son-of-a-bitch is dead!" Jonesy said through gritted teeth.

Doug knelt beside Geoffries' body, and placed his hands at the side of his neck. Even before he did, he knew from the giant gaping hole in the captain's back that there would be no pulse.

The door to the room flew open, and several men stood in the doorway, staring down at Doug next to the body.

"Call an ambulance!" Doug said. "My friend has been shot."

The men in the doorway looked from Geoffries's body to Jonesy, now slumped back against the closet door, still clutching at his bloody shoulder. They dashed off a second later, shouting for someone to call an ambulance.

Doug went over to Jonesy, whose eyes were half-closed. His breathing came fast and shallow.

"Help is on the way, Jonesy," he said, putting his hands on either side of Jonesy's shoulder and pressing hard.

The magnitude of what had just happened sank in, and he shook his head and chuckled. "You dumb bastard," he said. "Why didn't you tell me what you had in mind?"

"I wanted to kill the son-of-a-bitch myself," Jonesy said. "And I did, God damn it. I did. You would've tried to talk me out of it."

"What now?" Doug asked.

"If the doctors get me fixed up, let's just hope the judge doesn't send me to hang." He smiled, but Doug didn't.

"What are you going to do?"

"I'm gonna tell the cops that Geoffries confessed—and that he fired first." He looked Doug in the eye. "And you're my witness, understand. Geoffries fired first."

Doug chuckled. "Whatever you say, Jonesy."

He'd earned that much.

23

Thursday, June 6

Doug slept poorly after he was finally allowed to leave the police station downtown around one-thirty in the morning. He wondered how Jonesy was doing, and thought about going to St. Luke's Hospital instead of going home, but decided against it. The police were probably there, and he'd had enough interaction with them for a while.

He wasn't as exhausted as he expected, however, as he got dressed in the morning and walked to the Cantonese tea house for breakfast. He hadn't slept well, and yet he felt lighter than he had since before Tim's death.

He lingered most of the morning, drinking tea and contemplating the last six days. Li Baosheng arrived mid-morning, smiled when he saw Doug sitting in the corner, and waved. Doug returned both.

"How are you today, Mr. Bainbridge?" he asked in English.

"I'm just fine, thanks, Bao."

Bao grinned, turned to the man behind the counter, and spoke to him in Fujian.

Doug left a few coins on the table, waved to Bao as he left, and walked to Tianjian Road.

Rev. and Mrs. Allen were both at the church, and he found them in the kitchen preparing a giant pot of Congee for the one-penny lunches they served daily.

"Good morning, Douglas," the minister said, stirring the pot while his wife chopped vegetables.

"Good morning, Reverend. Mrs. Allen," Doug said, nodding to them each in turn. "I came to share some news."

"Oh? Good news, I hope. It seems you've had a fair run of bad news lately."

"Yes, it's good news. We identified the man who killed Tim. Unfortunately, he won't stand trial, but he's dead, which I suppose is the next best thing."

The minister nodded. "Yes, that is good news, mostly. It will bring some closure to Tim's loved ones. We will also pray for the family of the man who killed poor Tim—they will be grieving the loss of their loved one, too."

Doug felt ashamed that in all the hours since he'd seen Jonesy shoot Captain Geoffries , he hadn't once thought about Geoffries' family back in England.

"I got a call this morning from the Hung Wei Sanitarium," the minister said. "Dr. Wong there said he's releasing Li Sung on Saturday, and he asked if we would escort her. I told him we'd be happy to. Would you like to join us, Douglas?"

Doug shook his head. "No, thank you, Reverend. I didn't know her, and I think it would be awkward for her to have a stranger there."

"I'm sure you're right. What about that nice woman at Tim's office who called the day of his funeral? Miss Sherman, I believe. Did she know Li Sung?"

"I don't know. I'm sure they met, at least, but I don't know how well they knew each other."

"I'll give her a call this afternoon, and extend the offer. The more support we can give Sung when she leaves the safety of the sanitarium, the better off she'll be. We owe that to Tim."

Doug nodded, feeling a lump form in his throat. "I agree. Thank you, Reverend."

**

St. Luke's Hospital stood at the intersection of Seward and Boone Road, a couple of blocks east of Broadway. It was a large three-story brown brick building that occupied the entire block, all the way to Nanzing Road, near the river.

Doug entered off of Seward Street, beside a plaque that announced St. Luke's to be a mission of the American Episcopal Church. He found himself in a long corridor with a ceiling nearly twenty feet high. Glass windows lined the corridor, with etched lettering announcing the offices of this or that doctor—most with English surnames, though Doug saw a few Chinese ones.

A young nurse with light brown hair sat at a desk beside the large open staircase. "May I help you, sir?" she asked in English, with a southern drawl.

"I'm here to visit Mr. Arthur Jones, who was brought in late last night," Doug said.

The nurse consulted an open book in front of her, flipping the page and running down the list with her finger. "Yes, Mr. Jones came out of surgery this morning. He's recovering on the third floor." She pointed at the stairs behind her.

Doug found an American doctor walking past on the third floor, and asked for directions. The doctor asked a Chinese orderly to escort him.

Doug followed the orderly down the center of a long ward, rows of metal beds on either side, most occupied by convalescent men.

"You look like hell," Doug said with a smile when he reached Jonesy's bed. A massive bandage covered his entire shoulder, while strips of gauze bandage wrapped around him diagonally. He was paler than usual, but his gruff demeanor returned when he heard Doug.

"You would too, if you got shot, smart-aleck."

"I assume the cops have spoken with you?"

313

"Only about a dozen times," Jonesy said with a smirk. "I ain't changing my story, though."

"Me neither," Doug said with a grin. "I think I was interviewed by five different detectives last night, but I told them all the same thing."

"And?"

Doug chuckled. "They said they'd 'look into' Geoffries' bank accounts, to find the source of his income. We'll see. Either way, I think you'll get off Scot free."

"Your mouth to God's ear."

Doug played shocked. "Why Jonesy! I didn't know you *believed* in God."

"Just an expression, smart-aleck," Jonesy said with a rueful half-grin. Then he straightened his shoulders and turned defiant. "And what if I do? I've got nothing against the Almighty. He ain't never done anything to me—only his followers."

"Amen," Doug mumbled.

"What's that?"

"Nothing. I see someone brought you flowers."

"Yeah, Gladys came by earlier and brought those. She was all teary and sad—afraid she was going to lose me like she lost Tim. I told her it would take more than a dirty cop's bullet to do me in."

"How long before you can go home?"

Jonesy made a face. "A week, they say. I don't know if I can stand a week's worth of the bland broth they've been feeding me. If I were a different sort of man, I suppose I'd enjoy the nurses feeding it to me, but..." he trailed off and shrugged.

Doug ignored that. "You need your rest. The doctors know best. You should listen to them."

"Yeah, yeah."

"Anyone else come to visit you?" Doug asked.

Jonesy shook his head. "Gladys sent well-wishes from Chuck Wainwright and some of the others, but she was the only one who came."

Doug saw the disappointment in Jonesy's green eyes, even though his expression remained gruff.

"Maybe I'll come by and see you again," he offered.

"Sure, that would be swell," Jonesy said, and quickly added, "If you want to."

Doug found Sean Nolan in a booth at the Black Horse Pub that evening. He was sitting beside the black-haired girl Doug had seen him kissing on Sunday. She was talking non-stop, and he appeared to be half-listening while staring at his mug of beer.

"Mr. Nolan?"

Nolan's eyes grew wide when he saw Doug standing beside the table. "Yes, what do you want?"

"I wonder if we could have a word?"

"Sure thing, mate," Nolan said, too quickly. He jumped from his seat, belatedly excusing himself to the girl, and followed Doug to a corner of the pub.

"I wanted to tell you that a mutual friend of ours, Mr. Jones— Jonesy—"

"Yes, what about him?" Nolan interrupted, suspicious.

"I was about to tell you that he was shot in the shoulder last night."

"Oh, God!" Sean Nolan looked genuinely distressed.

"They operated on him overnight, at St. Luke's Hospital in Hongkou, and he's recuperating in the men's ward," Doug said. He watched a look of relief pass across Nolan's face, and he felt his heart soften a bit.

"He could use some visitors, to keep his spirits up. I—I'm sure he'd be very happy to see you."

A look of surprise crossed Nolan's pale blue eyes, and a hint of smile turned up the corners of his mouth.

"Thank you," he said, quiet, voice cracking.

Doug nodded, patted Nolan on the shoulder, and left.

He knocked on his neighbors' door when he got home.

"Oh, Douglas! Nice to see you," Charlie said, with a surprised smile.

"I thought you and Bao would be interested to know, we found out who killed my friend Tim McIntyre," Doug said.

"That's wonderful news. Well done!"

"It was a police captain," Doug said. "Tim was about to expose him for taking bribes from the Green Gang."

"How dreadful," Charlie said. "They've arrested him, then?"

Doug shook his head. "He's dead."

"Oh, I see. Well, it's still justice, isn't it?"

"It is indeed."

Doug hesitated.

"Douglas?"

He forced a smile. "I wanted to thank you both for your assistance, and your gracious offers of friendship and support. It hasn't been unnoticed." He hesitated again. "I apologize for my reluctance to embrace your offers. I hope you'll forgive me."

Charlie nodded. "Of course. Thank you."

"Now if you'll excuse me, I need to apologize to someone else, in a letter. I wasn't very forthcoming with her, and she didn't deserve that."

He wasn't sure why he confessed that to his neighbor, but perhaps that was what he'd needed to do.

"Someone you care about?" Charlie asked, one eyebrow raised.

Doug looked at the ground, but smiled to himself as he thought about Lucy. "Yes."

He saw the knowing look on Charlie's face, and felt the urge to disabuse him of false assumptions. "No, it's not what you think—I'm not looking for attachments. Besides, I enjoy being alone."

"Oh, I understand—Bao is the same way. Likes his alone time. Wanders all over the city by himself, lost in his own head." Charlie's expression grew serious, and he pointed a finger. "But remember, there's a difference between spending time alone, and *being* alone. Bao doesn't have to *be* alone, because he has me. We have each other. Who do you have, Douglas?"

Doug didn't answer, and looked away.

"If you want to change your life, you must take a chance on something, or someone. I did, and now I'm here, and I'm happy. Take a chance, Douglas."

Charlie had a twinkle in his eye as he closed his door.

Doug sat at his kitchen table, a blank piece of paper in front of him. He wrote the date, and the words, "Dear Lucy," and stopped.

He stared at the paper for a long time. Darkness fell, and still he sat at the table.

After a while he got up, got undressed, and lay on his bed. He stared at the ceiling, unable to sleep.

The next thing he knew, he was swimming in a pool. It was indoor, with floating lane dividers, but there was no one else around. The air was humid and smelled of chlorine. The water was clear and warm, and the only ripples were from his own movement as he swam down a lane.

He wore a pair of dark swim trunks. *That's strange*, he thought. *I don't remember ever wearing swim trunks before.* He tried to remember when he'd bought them, but couldn't recall.

Then he saw Lucy sitting at the edge of the pool, dangling her feet in the water, languidly kicking them forward and back. She wore a light blue bathing suit, in the daring modern style that showed full legs and cleavage, and she was leaning back, watching him.

He swam toward her, but it took longer than he expected. He swam harder, but his progress was slow. Finally he reached her.

"It took you long enough," she said, though she didn't look angry. Her beautiful blue eyes seemed to be smiling at him.

"But I'm here now."

"Are you here to splash me?" she asked, pulling her legs up and wrapping her arms around her knees.

He shook his head, stung. "No, I would never splash you. Come on, get in and swim with me." He held out his hand.

She relaxed, but stared at his hand for several seconds before she grinned, took it, and slipped into the water.

He felt the warmth of her body pressing against his, her arms around his shoulders. He opened his eyes.

The first faint pre-dawn light rose outside his window. He jumped up from the bed, threw on fresh clothes, and stuffed a few things into his valise.

He bolted from his apartment, ran down the stairs, and hurried to Honan Road as dawn broke across the city. He hailed a rickshaw, and clambered into the back.

"Railway station, please," he told the runner in Shanghainese.

Doug slept for much of the sixteen-hour train ride from Shanghai to Chongqing. As it travelled west up the Yangtze River Valley, the train stopped at Nanjing, Hankou, and Yichang before a long journey through the Wu Mountains to the plains of Sichuan Province.

As they passed through Nanjing, Doug wondered if they were close to the American Embassy. He wondered what Commander Hilliard would say if he knew what had happened over the last week. He might kick Doug out of the program; they might even discharge him. Doug decided to worry about that later.

318

It was late Friday night when he walked through the front door of the Imperial Hotel in Chongqing. After getting a room, he asked the attendant in Mandarin if the Kinzlers were expected soon.

The attendant checked the registry. "Yes, Mrs. Herbert Kinzler and her daughter are expected on Sunday morning. Shall I leave a message for them?"

"No, thank you." Doug scolded himself for arriving a day early, but decided to spend Saturday sightseeing around Chongqing.

Sunday, June 9

Doug enjoyed the look of shock on her face when Lucy turned around from the front desk and saw him standing in the lobby.

"Doug? What are you doing here?"

Mrs. Kinzler beamed. "Why, Mr. Bainbridge! How lovely to see you again. Are you staying here, too?"

He smiled at the older woman and nodded. "Yes, I am. May I speak with Lucy alone for a moment?"

Mrs. Kinzler's eyes gleamed, and she touched Doug's arm as she turned away. "Of course you may." Then she told the Chinese bell-boy in a loud and slow voice to take her to the fifth floor.

"I must say, you were the last person I expected to see here," Lucy said after the elevator door closed and her mother disappeared.

Doug thought she didn't sound displeased.

"I had to see you," he said, and took her hand.

She didn't pull away, but she didn't hold it back, either. "Why is that?" She looked at him with an intensity that made him want to look away, but he held her gaze.

"I owe you an apology," he said. "I should have told you everything from the beginning, and I'm afraid I may have ruined everything by keeping secrets. I'm sorry."

Her fingers wrapped around his hand.

"Thank you, Doug. I accept your apology. Was that all?"

319

His heart pounded, and sweat broke out across his forehead in spite of the coolness of the lobby. "No," he began, and his voice cracked. He cleared his throat, ignoring the amused half-smile on Lucy's lips, and stared down at her hand in his. "I want you to come back to Shanghai. I want you to be with me. I really like you, Lucy. I may even love you. I know that's crazy, since we haven't known each other long— but I don't want to be without you."

A giant grin spread across Lucy's mouth, and she threw her arms around him and squeezed. He hugged her back.

"I know I'm being awfully bold and forward, but I don't care."

He held her tighter. "I like you bold and forward."

She let go and took a step back, but took both of his hands in hers as she looked at him, wearing a serious expression.

"I want to finish my education," she said. "That's very important to me. I don't care what Mother says, or anyone else. I have a year left at Vassar, and I'm going back to get my degree. I need you to say you'll wait."

"I'll wait."

She smiled, and exhaled in relief. "Then I'll come back to Shanghai after I graduate. I'm not saying I'll marry you, though," she added, though Doug thought there was a touch of hope in her tone. "I'll want my own place, and a job."

He squeezed her hands. "Anything you want. Just come back to Shanghai. Come back to me."

She beamed, and threw her arms around him again. He kissed her for a long moment, and didn't care how untoward it was to do that in public.

After they broke the kiss, he led her by the hand to a pair of plush lobby chairs.

"I'll find you an apartment near mine," he said, and they began making plans for the future. After several minutes, when their excited planning lulled and they sat back in contented silence, he added one more thing.

"I want to warn you, just so you are aware—my next-door neighbors, the only neighbors on my floor, are a pair of homosexual men. They're not bad fellows, though—they are actually very nice, if you get to know them."

Lucy leaned forward, her elbow on her knee and her chin in her hand, with a funny smile. "How fascinating!"

That wasn't the reaction Doug expected. "I wouldn't exactly call them 'fascinating'—they *are* deviant."

Lucy waved a dismissive hand in the air. "Don't be such a fuddy-duddy. It *is* fascinating. There are some homosexual couples in New York, you know, in Greenwich Village. I've been to coffeehouses down there with friends from Vassar, and I've seen them. You don't find them everywhere, you know."

"That's because it's deviant."

"Oh, pish-posh. It's not as deviant as you might think—I attend an all-girls college, you know. I've met my share of girls—and professors—who are of the Sapphic persuasion. And plenty of other girls experiment from time-to-time. It's not so unusual."

Doug wondered if Lucy had 'experimented,' but decided not to ask.

He didn't care, anyway. She'd said she was coming back. She'd said she'd be with him.

He kissed her again, then leaned back in his chair, her hand in his, and stared into her eyes with a big, goofy grin.

He was happy at last.

Thank you for reading The Jade Dragon. If you enjoyed this book, please tell a friend, update your social media, and/or write a review on Amazon, Goodreads, or other forum.

Questions or comments? Feel free to contact me at
www.garretthutson.com
You can also sign up for my monthly newsletter and receive a free short story featuring the adventures of Jonesy, our favorite reporter about town in Shanghai.

If you enjoyed The Jade Dragon, be sure to check out the next adventures of Doug, Lucy and Jonesy in **Assassin's Hood**.

Also by Garrett Hutson:

In A Safe Town

Hidden Among Us (Martin Schuller Spy Catcher, book 1)

Spy Tango (Martin Schuller Spy Catcher, book 2)

About the Author

Garrett Hutson writes upmarket mysteries and historical spy fiction. He lives in Indianapolis with his husband and their dogs, cats, and a turquoise green-cheeked conure. He has one grown daughter. You may contact him at his website, www.garretthutson.com.

Acknowledgments

I first began playing with this story in the summer of 2013, in love with the setting of Shanghai during the 1930s, and thought it would be an excellent setting for a murder mystery. But the story really came to life as my project for National Novel Writing Month (NaNoWriMo) in November 2014.

Many people contributed to the development of this book. Many thanks to my awesome partners in the IndyScribes critique group—Laura VanArendonk Baugh, Stephanie Cain, Stephanie Ferguson, Marcia Kelly, Peggy Larkin, Jim Meeks-Johnson, and Jim Thompson—who patiently read and critiqued many sections of the first draft, and provided excellent feedback. Thanks to Brenda Havens and Michael Kiesow Moore, who provided valuable feedback on the opening chapters.

I owe a debt of gratitude to the wonderful people at Midwest Writers Workshop for making me the writer that I am today. There is no better writers conference than MWW.

My deepest thanks to Jessi Rauh, Stephanie Cain, and Elizabeth SanMiguel, who read the entire manuscript and provided valuable insights and feedback. They helped bring out the best in this story.

Thanks to Steven Novak for the amazing cover, and to Julie Bickel for designing the maps.

And lastly, my deepest gratitude and devotion to my husband David Lee, for letting me live the crazy life of a writer, and always being supportive through all of its myriad ups and downs. I love you.

-Garrett B. Hutson, June 2017